MEAN BAYOU

KAREN YOCHIM

ISBN: 1475057598

ISBN 13: 9781475057591

Library of Congress Control Number: 2012905871
CreateSpace, North Charleston, SC

Dedicated to the late Shelley "Pappy" Yochim, and Buddy Yochim, who first introduced me to the Atchafalaya Swamp, "…the baddest swamp there is."

Thank you to all friends and family who read the manuscript and offered valuable feedback. Special thanks to Jeff Davis Taylor, whose loyalty and expertise made it possible for me to complete this novel.

Much gratitude also goes out to Paul David, Dr. Neal Tishman, Roland Rivette, Chief Richard Mizzi, Lt. Moore of Louisiana Department of Wildlife & Fisheries, St. Landry Parish Sheriff's Office, St. Martin Parish Sheriff's Office, Lt. Allen Venable of the Metro Crime Unit, Lafayette Parish Sheriff's Office. All these people graciously helped with questions. Any mistakes are my own.

...Ehh maudit Bayou Teche
T'apris la vie du un pauve malheureur...
(...Oh mean Bayou Teche
You took the life of a poor unfortunate man.)

Hadley Castille, world-renowned Cajun fiddle player and songwriter wrote, *Maudit Bayou Teche. Maudit Bayou Teche* can be heard on Amazon.com.

Note: The Atchafalaya Swamp stretches over 750,000 square miles. It is the largest river basin swamp in North America.
For readers not familiar with Cajun names:
Detective Lanclos' name is pronounced: Lahn-clo
Moise Angelle's name is pronounced: Mo-eese Ahn-gelle

MONDAY

1

LANCLOS IN THE FIELDS

Down along the western levee of the great Atchafalaya Swamp in St. Beatrice Parish, on a farm six miles from the town of St. Beatrice, Detective Mitch Lanclos was working in his fields on a weekday, having taken a few days off to take care of some farm business. Sheriff Quebedeaux was glad to give him the time off, as Lanclos had been able to clear up two murder investigations within the past week. The first case involved an abusive husband who had shot his estranged wife in the head. He believed a friend of hers had talked her into leaving him, so after killing his wife, he'd driven to the friend's house and shot her as well.

The second case involved young thugs from New Orleans who had been dealing crack out of a house on the south side of the Parish. A neighbor who complained about their activities to the Sheriff's Department had turned up dead. Lanclos tracked down a terrified witness to the beating death, convinced the reluctant man to talk, and was able to arrest three men for the murder.

His part in the investigations completed, Lanclos needed the time off because a windstorm had blown over two pecan trees in his fields, and he hadn't had the time to take a chainsaw to them. Free to do the work, he'd driven his farm truck along the muddy headland to the back tree line of his hundred acres with two heavy-duty chain saws. After sawing the trees into firewood, he would then haul the foot long pieces back to the smokehouse, load by load. If he was lucky he'd have both trees reduced to a neat wood-pile stacked by the smokehouse within two days.

The trees had been stripped of nuts by trespassing pecan thieves who had sneaked into his fields from the back tree line, despite an abundance of Posted signs. The fallen trees lay angled across the recently mowed hay fields. Lanclos, a dark-haired stocky man in his forties, mud boots firmly planted three feet apart, worked steadily on one of the old trees, the chain saw screaming. The sweet smell of sawdust swirling in the humid air mingled with the musky smell of the rich bottomland mud that covered his boots.

Lanclos stopped momentarily to rest, arching his back, the cloud of sawdust making him sneeze. He hoped if there was lethal tension building among any residents of the Parish, that they could keep a lid on it until he finished with the trees. He hoped he'd also have a chance to screw down a few metal roofing sheets that had blown loose on the barn before being called back to the office. Gazing across the fields toward the barn, out-buildings, and farmhouse for a moment, he pulled a handkerchief from the back pocket of his jeans and wiped sawdust from his face.

A chicken hawk dive-bombed a field mouse, snatching it up out of high native field grass, and something scuttled behind Lanclos as it ran for cover. He watched the hawk as it flew to the treeline to enjoy its tiny meal, then he fired up the chainsaw once more and got back to work.

2

GERALD DELIVERS
DEVASTATING NEWS

Two miles from the town of St. Beatrice, on a back country road, a small cypress house, set up on cement blocks, stood high on a bank forty feet from the edge of the gumbo-colored Bayou Perdue. The vintage house was built in the Acadiana manner, with rusty tin roof, a front porch with four wooden posts, and two front doors.

Philomena, a petite Creole woman, in the habit of sitting in one of the two rockers on her front porch, sipped morning coffee. It was seven-thirty and already the thin red line on the plastic thermometer nailed to one of the porch posts read eighty-two degrees. Within an hour or two, she expected the temperature would climb to ninety, despite it being mid-September.

The spider lilies she had planted so long ago to line the front brick walk had multiplied like the loaves and fishes and were blooming in clusters. They bordered the uneven bricks from the row of white iron bedsteads that formed her front fence all the way to the warped porch steps. The lacy red of the blooms cheered her as she drank from a mug that advertised Emile's, a now burnt-out restaurant where Philomena had cooked in her younger days.

She admired the vigorous red of the lilies, wishing she had more vigor of her own in her old age. But at ninety-two, she knew she was lucky to be alive and sitting on her own porch, drinking coffee she'd brewed herself. "Thank you, Jesus, for all our blessings!" she said aloud, then repeated her words just in case He didn't hear her the first time.

A marmalade tomcat ventured out from under the sagging porch and complained to her. "All right, all right." Philomena rose from the rocker, joints creaking, and tossed the last of the coffee off the porch. While steadying herself, she looked down at her shaggy pink slippers to make sure her feet were planted safely and took up the cane hooked over the arm of the rocker. "I'm going to fetch some food," she assured the hungry cat advancing toward her, tail waving like a snake.

There were two front doors in the old Acadian style, and Philomena chose the kitchen door, letting the door slam behind her. "Be patient. I can't no way move as fast as you can, you," she chided as she poured food into a bowl. "You such a pain. Trouble's a good name for you," She set the bowl onto the porch as the big tom pounced upon the food, gobbling greedily. "You must weigh twenty pounds, Trouble. You big as a dog, you,"

A mosquito landed on her arm. "I don't have enough blood in my body to be feeding you. You got to go." She slapped it and wiped the black squished bug and some blood off her thin forearm. "It's all that high grass down by the bayou just breeding mosquitoes." She'd ask her nephew, Alfred, to see about knocking that high grass down next time he came to visit.

She crossed to the refrigerator where St. Jude gazed from a calendar page. "St. Jude, protect all us lost causes," she whispered as she opened the door for a pitcher of sweet tea between a dented aluminum pan of field peas and ham and a covered plastic bowl of macaroni and cheese.

A knock on the door startled her. She turned quickly and peered toward the door surprised to see Gerald Theriot. She'd known him since he was born, although he was far from being a baby now. He was somewhere in his thirties and solid as a rock. She suspected he'd been lifting weights for his arms were almost as thick as his neck.

"*Comment ça va*, Miss Philomena?" Gerald asked.

"Gerald Theriot!" Philomena smiled, grabbing her cane where it leaned against the table and stepping carefully toward the door.

The sunlight at his back cast him in darkness so that she had to blink to make out his features: the black brows, the square face, the Saints visor cap slanted low on his forehead. "I'm doing good, and you?" She opened the door for him. "Come in and have some sweet tea with me."

"No, no, Miss Philomena. I have a cold drink in the truck, me. I just wanted to tell you something on my way to the levee."

"And what is that? Let me close the door then. I don't want mosquitoes getting in." She passed over the threshold as he backed up. "We can sit out on the porch." She settled herself in the rocker and hooked her cane on the arm. "If I'd known I was getting company, I'd have fixed up better."

"Oh, that's nothing, Miss Philomena. You look fine," Gerald looked around, then leaned against a white four-by-four post. He rubbed his palms together as though brushing off dirt, then jammed them into his jeans pockets. "See...well, how it is, is..." He looked toward the beaded ceiling of the porch then down at his scarred work boots. "See..." he raised his right hand and pushing up the visor, wiped his forehead with the back of his hand. "Man... it's hot today."

"Yes, it is." Philomena picked up the Benoit Funeral Parlor fan she had stuck under her cushion and began slowly fanning herself.

Gerald sighed. "I better get that beer out of the truck. Can you wait a minute?"

"I have more time than money," she laughed.

She watched Gerald march to the pickup parked at the end of her brick walk and frowned. Gerald seemed nervous, and she wondered if he was in some kind of trouble. She hoped he didn't want to borrow money from her like her nephew often did. She had barely enough for herself. Yet that was unlikely. Gerald's father had plenty of money. He wouldn't turn to a poor old Creole lady such as herself for money.

Gerald leaned over the side of his double-cab black truck into a red cooler he kept there and retrieved a dripping can of beer from the ice. He quickly snapped off the fliptop and took a few swallows while standing by the truck. Then swiping his mouth with a beefy forearm, he turned back toward the house.

He didn't meet her eyes until he had repositioned himself against the porch post. "You know what, Miss Philomena? I'm just going to have to come out with it, that's all. See, Celeste and me… well, Celeste, you've met my wife, haven't you? She wants to live along the bayou now. She's decided she doesn't want to live in town anymore, and she wants me to build her a house along the bayou." He bit his bottom lip, then took another drink and waved a mosquito away. "Damn mosquitoes. It's a good way to get West Nile fever."

Philomena felt a slow icy trail creep along her spine, despite the heat. "Now this house you got here, Miss Philomena. This is the house granddaddy built and said you could live in for the rest of your life. all those years ago he said that. How long ago was that anyway?"

The icy trail spread up her neck and the back of her head. She had the *frissons* or goose bumps, all up and down her skinny arms. Her voice rasped when she spoke. "I've lived here since I was in my late twenties."

"And how old are you now, if you don't mind me asking," Gerald tried to smile, but it was one of those stiff awkward smiles that stick to the upper teeth.

"No, I don't mind you asking. But I'm not sure. As near as I can figure, I'm somewhere between ninety-two and ninety-five. I was born at home and the family Bible burnt up with mama's house when I was a girl, so I don't know for sure."

"Okay, but you've lived here most of your life…right?" Gerald, hopeful that he could make his point, finally met her gaze.

"Oh, yes. That's a fact. This is my home for so long I can hardly remember what any other place I ever lived in looked like."

"But see, Miss Philomena. You're getting old now and it's not good for you to be out here away from town by yourself. There's all kinds of psychos running around in the swamp. You could get yourself killed by some crackhead. Or what if a moccasin bit you. What then? You're out here all alone on the bayou."

"Oh, I have a phone. I know to call 911."

"Yeah, and how you going to do that if you're lying down by the bayou snakebit?"

"Oh, I don't go down by the bayou. The bayou bank is too steep for me. I stay right here by the house."

"Okay, but what if you have fell down and can't get to the phone? You need somebody close by so you can yell. Look around here. There's nothing over there but pasture." He pointed south down the road and then swung the arm holding the beer can toward the north, "and all's that's down that way is woods."

"There's the Bergeron house right through those trees." Philomena adjusted her head rag, nodding towards her neighbors' farm beyond the bottomland woods to the north. "They could hear me over there."

"I doubt it. I don't think a little bit of a woman like you could yell loud enough for them to hear." They both gazed at the thick hardwoods and pines between Philomena's place and the Bergerons. A rooster crowed and dogs barked from beyond the trees.

"Hear that? They've got three pits, two Catahoulas, a couple of deer hounds, and a bunch of fighting roosters over there. Like I said, they'd never hear you." Gerald paused and waited for a mosquito to settle on his arm, then swatted it.

"Gerald, save your breath. I'll never leave my house to live in town. I didn't like it when I was young, and I sure don't want it now. I'm happy out here on the bayou. I have all I need."

"Well, the thing is…" Gerald hunkered down, leaning his elbow on one knee.

"Celeste is hell-bent on me building her a house out here…. and daddy says it would be okay. He'd give me the land….but," he hurried to add, "you can take as much time as you want to find you another place. And I'll help you. There's a retirement home in town. It's nice. I went there with Celeste once to see her uncle."

"I don't need a retirement home. Alfred brings my groceries once a week. Junius brings my box of commodities. The church ladies check on me and bring me clothes and all such. I don't do without. I have more than I need or want. See there?" She pointed to a garden plot to the south of the house. "I raise my own okra and tomatoes and purple hull peas. Alfred digs my garden every spring. There're ten or more chickens running around here, so I have plenty of eggs."

There was a long silence. Trouble finished eating and slunk off into the high grass and weeds at the edge of the woods. A chicken hawk screamed overhead, and Gerald tilted his head back to watch it. Two hens scuttled under the house for safety. The air was thick with humidity. Gerald pressed the sweating beer can to his face then drained it and squeezed the can until it collapsed.

"Look, Miss Philomena. I want you to be safe and happy. But I got to do this for my wife. I'm sorry if Paw Paw Merlin said you could stay here the rest of your days and now I have to go and say otherwise, but I have to. You don't know my wife." Gerald looked sadly at the squashed beer can, shaking his head.

Philomena stared at him, then began rocking back and forth, as she carefully laid the fan beside the cushion. "You're telling me to get out of my house," she whispered. "I'm ninety-two or some such, and you're saying I have to go away from here?" Her mouth gaped and her head tilted a few inches to one side as she stared at him in shock. Her face was incredibly smooth for her age, the flesh a burnished cocoa, but as his words sunk in, a deep furrow appeared between her eyebrows, and her dark eyes glittered as though she had a fever.

"But look at it from my side. Daddy let you stay on all these years since Paw Paw died. Never charged you rent. All's you have to pay is your utilities for all those years cause he knew that's what Paw Paw wanted. But here's the thing. My wife wants me to build out here and she's determined. But don't worry, I'm going to help you find something." Gerald looked toward the truck. "Look. I have to go meet a man on the levee about some crawfish traps. I'll give you lots of time. Two, three months even."

"But, Merlin said this was for me. That I never have to move out. That I can live here til I die." Philomena squeezed her hands together until the swollen knuckles made her wince.

"But, Paw Paw never put it down on paper. There's nothing at the courthouse or anything like that. And you're too old now to stay out here by yourself. Like I said, you don't know my wife, Miss Philomena." Gerald pleaded with his eyes. "She makes up her mind for me to do something, then I won't have any peace til I do it. And I have to live with her, you don't." He tried again to smile, but the smile didn't work. It hung on his face in a lopsided way until he gave up and turned to go. "I'll see you later. I'm real sorry about all this, believe me." He raised his hands in frustration, then dropped them in defeat.

Philomena watched him as he walked back to the truck and tossed the crumpled beer can into the back. She sat there, numb, as he ground the truck into gear, managed a half-hearted wave without looking back at the porch, and slowly drove off.

She remained sitting in her chair without moving for over an hour. She didn't notice the hens venturing back out from under the house. She didn't notice a hummingbird busy at the Seven Sisters' rose bush which she'd started from a cutting years before. She didn't notice the swallowtail butterfly making graceful circles around her red four o'clocks. She didn't see the brown egg lying between the roots of one of the two ancient, stunted cedar trees in her front yard. She didn't notice the cardinal perched on the muscadine trellis or the moon vine curling around the makeshift bedpost fence. She just stared straight ahead, still as a statue, as a mosquito whined near her ear and crows cawed from the woods.

It wasn't until she remembered she hadn't yet eaten breakfast and that she needed to keep her blood sugar level, or she'd likely faint or grow dizzy that she rose from her chair and taking up her cane, stepped slowly toward the kitchen door. As though sleepwalking, for nothing seemed real since Gerald's visit, she slowly spoke. "St. Jude. They say you the Saint of Lost Causes. Please help me. I can't believe what this man says. It can't be true! I can't be having to leave on out of here. I been here way too long for that. I been here seventy years and then some. I don't know _how_ to go. Please help me with this. Make this stop happening."

She felt wobbly so she sat on one of the wooden chairs by the kitchen table, and lowered her face to her open palms. She felt too numb to cry, but wished she could, because the pressure of wanting to cry felt heavy and oppressive, weighing her slight body down. She stayed like that, face cradled in her hands, thoughts whirling, overwhelmed with fears and anxiety so that her fingers trembled.

"I can't move out," she pleaded aloud. "I wouldn't even know how to move somewhere. All my plants, the chickens, my things, the garden, my cat. I no way can do it." She felt as vulnerable and fragile as one of the baby chicks her hen had hatched in June. Something had gotten to them in the coop the second night. Something had squeezed in between the boards of the coop and taken those chicks right out from under the mother hen while she was sleeping. She'd guessed it was a chicken snake flattening itself to slide through the cracks. Making itself small...just like Gerald was making himself small to do her this way. She shook her head from side to side. "No," she moaned. "He just can't do me like this."

She knew she should eat something. It had been too long and her sugar would be dropping so fast, she'd get dizzy and light-headed. She'd have to eat something, but the very thought of eating turned her stomach. Maybe she could keep down a few bites of mac and cheese. That always settled her down. She raised her face from her hands and took a deep breath. She had to be strong and get up and eat. If she got sick they'd carry her off somewhere for sure.

WEDNESDAY

3

ALFRED'S BAD SIGN

Alfred Narcisse, Philomena's nephew, was having a bad day. He'd awakened at dawn to see an owl standing on the ground in his backyard, always a bad sign, so he wasn't surprised at the angry encounters he'd had so far that day. He'd already been ordered off two farms for stealing pecans, and it was only nine-thirty in the morning. Louis Arcenaux had even fired a warning shot toward the ground to get Alfred's attention. It wasn't the first time he'd been threatened with a gun for trespassing, but it had rattled him. Making things worse, Alfred Meche had demanded he dump all the pecans he'd already picked onto the ground.

He pedaled slowly towards Philomena's house, feeling guilty as he hadn't visited her all week, an almost empty burlap sack folded in the basket. Still feeling angry that he'd been caught on the Arcenaux and the Meche farms, he kept an eye out for pecan trees along the road. He passed a few trees noting with a quick glance along the ground that they'd been picked recently. He wasn't willing to stop just for a few scattered pecans that passing by pickers and squirrels had left.

After a quarter of a mile he stopped to check one of his favorite trees. It was on the corner of Herman Delcambre's property and fenced in by barbed wire. However, there was a payload of pecans lying outside the fence along the road in the high grass. He leaned his bicycle against an eight-foot railroad tie, black with creosote,

serving as a corner-post for the Delcambre fence. He grabbed the
empty sack and hunkered down to start picking. This was what he
liked to call two-fisted picking. So many had fallen from the wind
and rain the night before that he could grab three or four with
one hand and be tossing them into the sack, while the other hand
was busy grabbing three or four more. Most of them were free of
their black husks, so he could pick faster than if he'd had to peel
away their wet spongy jackets.

He'd been there about fifteen minutes when a green and white
pickup pulled up alongside the road. "What the hell do you think
you're doing?" asked Delcambre, leaning his head out the window
where his elbow rested.

"What's it look like? I'm picking," said Alfred, looking up only
to see who it was, then resuming his work at top speed.

"And whose tree is that you're picking?" Delcambre cleared his
throat.

"I'm pretty sure it's yours."

"So why you picking it then?"

"Because," Alfred spoke toward the ground, not breaking
his speed. "Anybody can pick alongside the road. Them's God's
pecans."

"Oh, is that right?" Delcambre ran a tongue over his teeth.
"Who says?"

"You know it's all right, Mr. Herman. We been over this before...
for years now."

"I know what the law says. Right-of-way by the road and all that
shit. But what I say is....it's my tree and get the hell out of here!
Next thing I know you'll be sneaking under the fence and getting
the rest of them. If I have to keep kicking your good-for-nothing
ass off my place, I'd just as soon cut that tree down. Then we'd be
finished with all of *dat*!"

"Now, Mr. Herman. You know I wouldn't go through that
barbed wire. Just let me get through with these here and I'll be
out of here." Alfred scooped a handful into his sack, wet leaves
and all.

"You deaf? Get the hell out of here!" Delcambre pulled a cell
phone from his shirt pocket. "I'll call the Sheriff and say you're on

the wrong side of the fence, you little bastard. Where you need to be is over at Philomena's."

"That's where I'm going soon as I finish picking."

"You're finished picking!" Delcambre started punching in numbers. "You'll be in jail for trespass inside a hour. How many times does that make now? Sheriff's sick of feeding your sorry ass."

"Wait up! Wait up! I'm going!"

"I don't know how a little lady like Philomena deserves a worthless screw up like yourself. All the trouble she's got now, and you're out stealing pecans."

"Auntie doesn't have no trouble." Alfred hurriedly swooped up his sack and balanced it on the bicycle. "She's got nothing to trouble her about."

"You ain't heard? Gerald Theriot kicked her off that place. He's fixing to build a bayou house there so's his wife will get off his back. Where you been? Holed up with a bottle?"

Alfred stood still as the fence post, then slowly turned toward the pickup. "True as I'm sitting in this Ford, son. I heard it two days ago. I'm way ahead of you and you better be catching up with your bidness instead of aggravating everybody in St. Beatrice Parish."

Alfred shook his head. "It's not true. I was just there Sunday."

"It's true. Believe it. It only just happened. So you'd best be getting out of here and taking care of your family."

Alfred slowly turned the bicycle back out onto the road and getting it rolling, threw a leg over and deftly mounted.

Delcambre turned off onto a dirt lane that followed the fence line back to his house, beeping at three of his chickens that were pecking in the ditch. They scrambled into the high grass under the barbed wire, squawking and fluttering their gray and white speckled wings.

Alfred picked up speed as his anxiety grew and his energy rose. Delcambre must be wrong, he thought. He's trying to get at me. It can't be true cause Auntie lived there as long as Alfred could remember. Gerald Theriot would never throw her out of there. He couldn't anyhow. She was supposed to be there all her life. That's what she'd always told him, and what his mama had always told him before she'd died. "When Philomena gets too old, promise you'll go by there and see to her...or live with her...take care of her. She's all you got now. You're all she's got."

He could see the rusty roof of her house now just past the pasture where Gerald's father kept his mare, the brown and white paint, Melody. He was breathing hard from pedaling so fast. As he got closer, he saw Melody, neck stretched as she drank out of a chipped bathtub parked next to the fence, a twenty-foot pole barn in the background. Then he saw his aunt in her cypress rocker. There she was. Just like always. Nothing was wrong. Old man Delcambre was just lying to him to get even. Alfred smiled broadly, teeth gleaming against his dark skin as he slowed the bicycle at the iron bedpost fence.

"Hello, Auntie. I'm coming to see you."

"Good morning, nephew. How you doing? You doing okay?" Philomena smiled as Alfred walked the bicycle to the front porch and leaned it against the warped steps.

"Not so good, Auntie. I got kicked off three places already just trying to pick pecans is all."

"I keep telling you. Ask the people first."

"I'm not doing all that work just to give them half of what I make."

"That's the way it is though," Philomena said gently. "You can pick mine all you want." She indicated the native pecan trees on the north side of the yard.

"Those are for you. You need yours to bake with."

"I don't need all of them. You're going to end up in jail again if you don't stop stealing."

Alfred sat on the top step and wiped his face with the hem of his tee shirt. "I'm done with going to jail. I'm sick of waxing all those patrol cars."

"Then quit giving them a chance to lock you up." Philomena sighed and stared off down the road.

"You know what that old s.o.b. Delcambre told me?" Alfred pushed out his bottom lip in indignation.

"What'd he say now?"

"He said Gerald Theriot told you to leave out of here. Leave your house! It's not enough to be stingy and mean; he's a liar too."

Philomena took a deep breath. "You want some sweet tea?"

"Quit changing the subject, Auntie. Tell me he's crazy, why don't you?"

Melody whinnied in the pasture, then lay down on the grass and rolled back and forth on her back, hooves pawing the air. "Well, tell me something, auntie," Alfred pressed on.

"It's true," her voice cracked.

"What you mean it's true?" Alfred felt the ice run up his spine again. "What you saying?"

She pressed her lips together, then crossed her arms, looking down at him. "Gerald came by and said he's going to build a house here. His wife wants to live on the bayou."

Alfred stood abruptly. "What? What is he? Crazy? He can't throw you out. This is your place! Always has been."

"Alfred! Don't get all worked up now. I don't need that."

"He can't do that. You're staying right here. I'll get a lawyer!"

"With what? You got no money. A lawyer can't do anything. Merlin never signed a paper about it. He just said I could stay here for the rest of my life. Merlin cared a lot for me, but he's not around to protect me anymore."

"Why didn't you send for me? Why'd I have to hear this from that rotten old man?"

"Because I knew you'd start acting crazy, just like you're doing right now. And next thing, you'd do something to get yourself put back in jail."

"That's right! I'm going to get crazy. Meantime you stay right here. Don't do nothing! You're not going nowhere!" Alfred shook a finger at her.

"I don't have anywhere to go no how. Where you going now?" Philomena grasped the arms of the rocker and pulled herself halfway out of it. "Please don't go getting yourself into trouble. I can't take much more. I'm already done in."

"Don't worry yourself, Auntie. I'll take care of this. You just sit there and relax." Alfred walked the bicycle down the path to the road, then swung a leg over and rode off north toward St. Beatrice.

4

ALFRED PUTS A CURSE

Alfred followed the road along the Bayou for five miles until he approached the village of St. Beatrice. He passed Eric, a St. Beatrice Parish deputy, in his white patrol car, and nodded in greeting. The deputy nodded back and kept driving south. Probably making his rounds, Alfred thought. He didn't pay any mind to Alfred, which was a good thing. Alfred had enough on his mind without worrying about the law.

There were three places he planned to check to look for Gerald Theriot. There was one of the town's two gas stations where he knew Gerald liked to go for meat pies that the owner imported from Natchitoches for his small grocery business. There was one of the two bars in town where Gerald could be found occasionally playing bourrée in the house game on Wednesdays and Fridays. There was the restaurant where Gerald could be found occasionally playing one of the poker machines in the back. That is if Gerald wasn't on a construction job somewhere. Gerald was a carpenter. Alfred knew he was between jobs as the contractor he worked for was waiting on the financing to start a new house an hour away on the far side of the parish.

He slowed the bicycle on Bergeron Street, but did not see Gerald's Chevy pickup at the Turn-Around Texaco, so he picked up speed again and continued on to the main highway headed east toward Guidry Street and the Idle Hour Saloon. The Idle Hour was an old frame house converted into a bar. The tin roof was rusted, the cypress boards of the house were painted forest green, the door lipstick red. Red neon flashed in a window and as Alfred surveyed the parking lot, he thought to ride toward the back to check for Gerald's truck. In the back lot, a few pickups were parked by a dark green, open-lidded dumpster. A black cat investigated something in the back of one of the pickups. Gerald's Chevy was not in the back either, so Alfred rode around the building back toward the front.

As he rounded the corner, Wayne Toup's *Two Step Mamou* blasted from the jukebox as the front door opened. Johnny Melancon stepped out of the dark interior of the bar. "Hey, Alfred. You want to make some money? I got a job for you."

Alfred braked the bicycle. "What you got?"

"I need somebody to help me with a load of firewood. I got to split a truckload of it and deliver it to some dude in Lafayette."

"When?"

"Tomorrow is good. Early. About seven-thirty. Meet me at my place. Out back in that metal building by the barn."

"I'll meet you." Alfred nodded and pedaled out of the gravel parking lot toward Highway 27. This time he turned off toward the Cajun Delights Restaurant which was another quarter mile going east. He didn't even have to go all the way there as he could plainly see all the cars and trucks in the parking lot. Gerald's black Chevy was not among them. Turning around, Alfred headed back west on Highway 27, hating to give up when he was so fired up to have it out with Gerald. On the off chance Gerald was home, he thought of bicycling all the way to his house on the other side of town, but just then he caught a glimpse of a black pickup in his peripheral vision and whipped his head around. There was a black pickup far down a side street he'd just passed. Alfred braked and, as traffic was light, made a U-turn, then crossed Highway 27 easily and headed down the side street.

It was Gerald's pickup all right, parked in front of Red's Barber Shop. There were two other trucks parked in front of the tiny barbershop. It was more like a shed: twenty feet wide and thirty feet deep. Alfred leaned the bicycle against the metal rails of the cement steps leading to the doorway, beside the red and white striped barber pole. He narrowed his eyes and climbed the steps, taking a deep breath as he opened the door.

Gerald was waiting his turn in a metal folding chair, boots planted about three feet apart, his eyes on a magazine, *Louisiana Duck Hunter*. Ulysses Champagne, wearing coveralls and western boots sat in the chrome and black-cushioned barber chair. Red, a short, stocky middle-aged man whose hair had gone to gray, was trimming the white hair at the nape of Ulysses' neck. Red looked up from his work and greeted Alfred. "Hello, Alfred. Have a seat." A radio playing a Cajun fiddle tune was jammed up beside a glass jar of sterilized combs on the counter under the mirrors.

Gerald jerked up his head, then slowly closed the magazine. Alfred advanced toward him, stopping about two feet from Gerald's chair. Neither man spoke for a moment. They stared at one another, then Alfred raised a shaking finger.

"Now, Alfred," was all Gerald said.

"You can't do it," Alfred waggled his finger back and forth.

"Now, Alfred. You gotta listen to me."

"You can't do it."

Gerald looked toward the front door as though for help or an escape route. He held his hands out as though measuring a catfish, then sighed and spoke softly. "I-got-to-do-this. My wife." He tilted his gold and black Saints visor cap back from his forehead.

"She's ninety-two years old. You can't kick her out of her own house!" Alfred's voice rose and Red stepped forward, tilting his head to hear better, scissors held midway between his body and the back of Ulysses's neck.

Gerald scrunched his forehead, looking miserable. He carefully returned the magazine to the side table on top of the stack of other hunting and fishing magazines. "I gotta do it, Alfred. I'm sorry. We're going to find her something. Don't worry. Something in town where she'll be safe."

"Safe! That's bullcrap! What you think she is now? She's safe out there where she's at." Alfred's eyes bulged.

"Alfred! Watch yourself," Red warned in a low voice.

Gerald stood, adjusting his cap back over his eyes. "I'm going to build on the bayou, Alfred, and there's nothing you can do about it. I'm sorry."

Alfred stood his ground, his skinny chest visibly rising and falling as he breathed harder. "Then I got to put a curse," he said softly. "That's what you got coming to you." He tightened his lips. "A curse on you and your wife. I got no choice."

Gerald looked at the floor. "Take it easy, Alfred. We're going to work something out."

Alfred raised his voice. "A curse on you and your whole family. That's how it is!" He stretched out the forefinger and the little finger of his left hand and pointed them both at Gerald.

"Alfred, get on out of my shop!" ordered Red, stepping forward, scissors glinting.

Gerald stepped around Alfred and started walking toward the door. "It's all right, Red. I'm going. I'll come back another time." He turned as he reached the door. "Go on home, Alfred, before you get yourself into more trouble. This is all going to work out." He opened the door and stepped out onto the cement steps. Alfred turned and followed after him, fingers still pointed at Gerald's back as *Maudit Bayou* played from the radio.

"What was that all about?" asked Ulysses as Alfred went out the door, and stood on the top step arcing his arm so the fingers were still pointed at Gerald, even as he backed the Chevy out of the parking lot.

"It's a long story," said Red.

"I'm listening," said Ulysses, as the door slowly closed behind Alfred.

5

LEON

Leon LeDoux stood at the six-foot sill windows of his law office gazing out at the gardener in the rear rose garden, who was deadheading and pruning the bushes and the climbers. One part of Leon's brain attended to the gardener's careful work, while another part of his mind anticipated the pending entrance of his new secretary, Elaine.

Leon suppressed an urge to raise the window and question the wisdom of any pruning on a particular rose tree that Henry was eyeing as his next project. Henry, one hand holding the pruning shears, the other firmly on his hip, tilted his head as he studied the shape of the rose tree.

The Lafayette law office was in an 1880 three-story, metal-roofed cypress house with fourteen-foot ceilings, wood floors with a matte wax finish, and crown moldings throughout. The stately house was within four blocks of the University of Louisiana, commonly known as UL. Leon's office on the first floor was spacious and sunny. It had a fireplace as did six other rooms in the building. Over the mantel of his fireplace was an oil portrait of his grandfather wearing a tan linen suit and striped shirt, sitting at his rolltop desk, black doctor's bag resting at his feet, alongside a sleeping spotted Catahoula hound.

Leon bore a strong resemblance to his grandfather. They both had a cleft chin and aquiline nose, eerie green eyes and light brown hair. His grandfather had been dubbed Dr. Fever because of his practice of tending to patients in remote communities of south Louisiana back during the yellow fever quarantines of the early 1900s. He had lived near Houma, where that side of the family had begun their life in the United States.

It was Leon's father who had moved his family to Lafayette when he married, so his mother could be closer to her people. Consequently, Leon had been born in Lafayette and had only moved to St. Beatrice when he married Georgette. He had moved there for the same reason his father had moved to Lafayette, so Georgette could be closer to her family. There was another reason as well. Leon enjoyed putting the half hour distance between his father and himself. It gave him more room to live his own life without the hawk eyes and penetrating gaze of his father, Dwight LeDoux.

In addition, the office had eight tall sill windows, positioned in pairs, on the south and west walls. Heavily lined hunter green draperies were tied back with dull gold braids. Leon's former secretary, Mona, who was Elaine's predecessor, had had a great deal to say about the look of the office. This had never caused conflict with Leon's wife, because Georgette showed little or no interest in his office, either the one in Lafayette or the one at home in St. Beatrice.

Elaine knocked softly. Leon turned from the window, eager to see her. "Come on in," he called, voice rusty. He cleared his throat and straightened his silk tie, then quickly ran fingers through his thick hair.

She entered slowly, somewhat timidly, looking toward the broad desk covered with files, letters, and gleaming accessories. He stepped forward from his place by the rear windows, and she saw him then, and stopped near the door. "Oh," was all she said.

"Don't worry. You're not interrupting anything. I was just…"

"I have a message." She looked at a pink slip of paper cupped in her hand and bit her lip. He crossed to the desk and sat slowly on the brown leather chair, then rolled it close to the desk so he could rest his elbows on the gleaming surface. She stepped cautiously to the front of the desk and handed the paper to him. He took it without touching her delicate hand with his chunky one, and held it by one corner as he read it.

"What is this?" he asked, annoyed.

"Oh! Mrs. Brasseaux wants to know why she was charged for calling and questioning some items on her statement. She is... well..." Elaine dropped her voice, "...angry."

Leon laughed. "Angry? For taking up staff time in a busy law office to question items on a bill?" He crumbled the paper and tossed it over-hand into a leather wastebasket to his left.

"But..." Elaine squinted, visibly worried.

"But what?" Leon ran a tongue over his teeth, then smiled, raising an eyebrow in his best imitation of a movie rogue.

"The phone call...when she called last week to question her bill? It only took a few minutes to answer her...and she was charged fifty dollars."

"Yes, yes." Leon sighed. "Is there anything else?"

"Else what?" Elaine took a deep breath, thereby raising the gold locket she wore a few inches, so that it glinted in the afternoon light streaming in from the window in back of him.

He made a circle with his hand motioning that he wanted to speed this conversation along. "Is there anything else you want to tell me?"

"No. I'll go back to my work."

"Elaine. Talking to me *is* your work. Thank you. And don't worry about Mrs. Brasseaux. She can afford it." He laughed. "If you have anything for me to sign, you better bring it soon. I'm taking off early today. I have some business in Baton Rouge." He looked at his watch.

"Yes, sir. I'll be finished with these letters within the next half hour."

Leon picked up a manila file and opened it as Elaine turned away, but raised his eyes as soon as she turned and watched her walk toward the door, her hair tied back with a black velvet ribbon, the short burgundy skirt not tight, but almost, her high slingback heels clicking on the floorboards. He felt a lunge in his groin, but lowered his eyes back to the file, knowing it was too soon to move in on her. She'd only been on staff three weeks. And getting Mona out of there hadn't been easy. It had taken the patience of Job, and Leon was not a patient man.

He grimaced as he remembered the outlandish lies he'd had
to tell Mona to get her out of Lafayette. That Georgette was getting suspicious. That he'd found a private detective's card on her
bureau. That he was worried about her sanity anyway. Anything to
scare Mona off and out of town.

He picked up the Waterman pen she'd given him and toyed
with it, missing her for half a minute. They'd had a great arrangement, and he'd been so happy with their sex life. The passion had
never dimmed during their two year affair. However, he sighed,
she'd begun to ask questions about the phony billings to Arthur,
and that arrangement most definitely took precedence over any
steamy liaisons with Mona.

Mona, Mona, Mona. He felt a tingling on the back of his neck
just thinking about her. He shook his head as though to shake off
his desire, but kept thinking about her anyway. So much for mind
control. He'd better run up to Shreveport and visit her one of
these days as soon as he could think up an excuse to get away.

She was working in the office of one of his classmates from
Tulane. Something he'd been able to arrange for her. Rick was an
old friend and loyal, so he hoped Rick was keeping it all business
and not getting any ideas about her. She had such a body that it
would be hard for any man not to get ideas about her. He wasn't
ready to give her up altogether. Seeing her from time to time was
fairly safe as long as she wasn't in the Lafayette office, growing suspicious of Art's phony billings, and anything else she might turn
up if she nosed around. And she had been getting too proprietory.
He'd never led her on; always said from the beginning that he'd
never leave Georgette and his son. But it doesn't matter what they
say in the beginning, he admitted to himself. They always think
they're going to be the one to unseat the wife.

Within twenty minutes, Elaine was back with a folder of letters for him to sign. He opened the folder slowly and read the
letters carefully, glancing up now and then as she waited, staring
out the window, eyes half-closed like a cat. He took the opportunity to observe her neckline, low enough to show a few inches of
cleavage. He saw just a hint of lavender lace behind the beige silk

blouse, then returned his gaze to the letters and shielded his eyes with a hand to avoid temptation.

When he'd determined they were ready to send out, he signed them rapidly with the Waterman, and leaned back in the high leather chair. He rolled the pen away from him and handed back the letters to Elaine.

"That's it then? I can go now?" His voice was deep and he spoke slowly, as though she were a child.

"Yes, sir." She slid the folder under her arm and turned.

"Elaine," he stopped her, speaking to her back. "You can leave early today as well and let the receptionist take my calls. You deserve a break. You're doing a good job and learning fast. I'm sure you have errands to catch up on."

She looked over her shoulder. "Really?" She smiled, the widest smile he'd seen on her yet. The teeth were so white, too white. He wondered if she had had professional treatment at her dentist's. That smile lasted a few seconds too long, and then Leon realized that it wasn't going to be too soon to put a move on her the first month on the job. The woman was ready now. Leon felt the reaction in his body as he watched her graceful walk toward the door, and he knew, against his better judgment, that he was going to be making his life even more complicated than it already was. And that he was going to have to fight with himself to hold back as long as he could from reaching out and pulling that one in, just as surely as his last marlin at Pensacola Beach.

His logical self chided him: *When are you going to learn, LeDoux? You're jumping from the frying pan into the fire again. What in hell is the matter with you? Get some therapy, for God's sake!*

Leon muttered back to himself as he prepared to leave the office. "There's only one kind of therapy I have in mind, and it's sitting about twenty feet from me right this minute." He adjusted his tie, grabbed his brown leather briefcase, and headed for the door, already thinking ahead to his afternoon meeting with Arthur at Boutin's in Baton Rouge.

6

GERALD AND CELESTE FIGHT

Gerald's family sat at the kitchen table set with plates, red mats, matching napkins, and china bowls of food. French music played from a radio on one of the formica counters. A black and white rat terrier sat by Gerald's chair, watching expectantly for handouts. The large kitchen shone with cleanliness, each appliance polished to a gleam. There were no magnets, messages, or children's art on the stainless steel refrigerator. The stove was spotless, despite a family dinner having just been cooked there. A ceiling fan with four tulip shaped lights cast a soft glow over the table in the center of the room.

Gerald's wife, Celeste, passed him a bowl of rice and served herself a chicken breast, dark with seasoning, from the platter in front of her. She pursed her lips as she carefully removed the skin from the meat, setting it to the side of her plate. A shank of dark hair fell across her face, casting a shadow. She pushed it back behind her ear.

"Alfred. You know Alfred...Miss Philomena's nephew? He came into the barber shop today," Gerald's voice trailed off as he scooped a generous helping of rice onto his plate.

"I've seen him bicycling around. What about him?" Celeste picked up a bowl of green beans and sausage and spooned a small amount onto a small plate she was fixing for their five-year-old.

"I don't want that," said Cedric, the son, whose face barely cleared the table despite his sitting on a telephone book.

"Well, you're going to have it," said Celeste. "You have to eat that before you get any chicken and rice."

"I want rice and gravy," the boy persisted.

"Yes. After you eat the beans," Celeste passed him the plate and sat up straighter, throwing her shoulders back and sighing. Still not looking at her husband, she sipped from an outsized glass of iced tea and watched the boy intently.

Cedric glumly looked at the beans, the corners of his mouth turned down. "I want rice and gravy."

"Boy, eat before I have to come over there," Gerald said, pointing his fork across the table at the child.

Cedric picked up his fork and pushed a bean around the plate. A tear formed in his eye and ran slowly down his cheek.

"Hardhead," Gerald pronounced.

"I wonder where he gets it from," Celeste said.

Gerald shot her a look that she ignored. He slid his fork through the chicken. "It's tender."

"Oh, yes. When I smother chicken, it simmers for two hours. So what did Alfred want?" She cast a sideways glance at Cedric who still pushed beans around his plate.

"He put a curse on me!" Gerald said, nonchalantly chewing. His brow furrowed as he swallowed.

"A curse!" Celeste laughed. "What do you mean a curse?"

"You know how those people are. They do that." Gerald held up a green bean. "See this, Cedric. I'm eating my beans. They're good. Watch." He smiled as he chewed. "Ummm. They're good. Momma's a good cook."

"I want rice and gravy." More tears fell, dribbling onto his purple and gold LSU tee shirt.

"Why the curse?"

"Why? You know why. It's about me taking Miss Philomena's place back."

Celeste shrugged. "He better get used to it."

"It was kind of spooky. He followed me out of the barber shop and did one of these." Gerald mimicked the gesture Alfred had made, holding out his hand with the index and little finger extended. He took a sip from a can of beer by his plate.

"I wish you'd quit drinking out of a can," Celeste chided.

"Yeah, well." Gerald drank again and set the can down.

"So what did he say...when he did the curse?"

"He just stood in front of me and announced as how he was going to put a curse on me. Joe kicked him out of the barbershop and I left too. Never got my haircut."

"I can see that," Celeste squinted at her son's plate. "Looks like somebody's going to bed hungry tonight."

"Noooo. I want rice and gravy."

"Take two bites of beans, then you can have some."

Cedric took a bite, wrinkling his nose and pushing his lips out.

"And don't be making a *boudee* about your mother's cooking. That don't go over around here," Gerald said.

"Maybe we should push things along a little faster. Maybe find Philomena a place in town. She can live in the projects. They're nice enough. They're brick."

"If there's a vacancy."

"Look into it. I'll go out there and take her a cake or something. I need to step off some measurements anyhow and decide exactly where the placement of the house should be."

"Just wait a while. Don't go out there yet. It's too soon."

"Too soon? It's already been three days. That's long enough for it to sink in."

Gerald gave his wife a warning look. "Wait."

She took a deep breath, put down her fork, and slid her chair back.

"Where you going?"

"Outside...I'm going to smoke a cigarette."

"You haven't finished your dinner. How're we going to get him to eat?"

"You work on it. I'm going to smoke."

"What the hell did I do?"

"You're always so nice to everybody. That's why." Celeste's mouth was a firm line as she grabbed a pack of cigarettes from the counter and fished a lighter from her jeans. "And don't forget, I'm sick to death of living in town in this cramped house." Her face darkened, brown eyes glinting black.

"Maybe if I imported coke like your brother-in-law does... then you could get to live in a huge house like your sister," Gerald blurted out in frustration. "Then you wouldn't have to be so jealous of her and have to try to keep up with her like you want to now. Then maybe you'd get off my back once in a while."

"What did you say?" Celeste's face turned deadly.

"You heard me." Gerald turned his attention to his son.

"You lying, pathetic...Don't you ever say those lies about Leon again! And who's jealous? You're the one who's jealous. Leon's such a successful attorney, and you can't stand it! And don't even try to tell me not to go over to Philomena's and look the property over."

"Do what you have to do," Gerald sighed. "It's heartless. It's cruel to hassle that old woman, but I know you well enough to know you're going to do it anyway."

"Oh, so now I'm not only jealous of my sister, but heartless and cruel to old ladies. Anything else you got to tell me?"

"Just remember what the priest said Sunday. Be kind to your neighbor."

"Why should I? You're always kind enough for both of us." Gerald watched her slam the door so hard, a visor cap fell off the iron hat rack next to it. He turned his attention back to Cedric, still chewing the first bite of beans, his nose even more wrinkled.

Gerald laughed as his son dramatically struggled to swallow the offending beans.

"Here, son," he smiled as he stretched his arm across the table. Pass me your plate so I can give you some rice and gravy."

THURSDAY

7

SLANDER

Celeste Theriot and her sister, Georgette LeDoux, slowly walked toward Philomena's front porch where Philomena sat stone still, her face impassive. Celeste carried a small white box from a French bakery in Lafayette.

"Miss Philomena, do you remember me? I'm Gerald Theriot's wife," Celeste called brightly, flashing an exaggerated smile.

"Oh, yes, I remember you," assured Philomena.

"I brought you something." She held out the white box. Philomena did not comment. After a pause, Celeste forged ahead, the hard-working smile still dominating her face. "Do you mind if my sister, Georgette, and I walk around the property? I'm trying to get some ideas about where I want my house, for whenever we do start building. We won't hurt anything. We just want to get some ideas." Celeste halted halfway up the walk and stretched her right arm out horizontally like a tollgate to signal her sister to stop. She raised her eyebrows and stuck out her chin as she waited, the smile stiffening.

Philomena watched the two women for a moment before answering. She felt that icy dread up her spine once more and felt frozen in place, except for one errant finger that kept tapping on the arm of her chair. Chickens clucked and crows called while she was trying to formulate a response. A boat engine strained far down the bayou and a battered pickup passed on the road, its muffler missing, which drew everyone's attention toward the road.

After the truck had passed, Georgette glanced at Celeste and back at Philomena. She placed her hands lightly on the narrow belt of her tailored slacks and tapped the pointed toe of her red snakeskin boots on the brick walk. "This isn't going well," she muttered so only Celeste could hear her.

"Sssh," warned Celeste, taking a step closer to the porch. "Miss Philomena?"

"Go ahead," Philomena finally said. "But watch your step. It gets slippery down there by the bayou. Watch out for snakes." She closed her eyes and began silently mouthing a prayer of protection to St. Jude.

"Thank you, Miss Philomena. We'll be careful." Celeste walked the baker's box to the front porch. "Here. This is for you. An assortment of croissants and beignets. You're going to love them, I know." She watched Philomena carefully, but as she saw no sign of receptiveness, she gently placed the box on the top porch step, giving it a last fond look as though she might change her mind and take it back.

"You don't have to bring me presents. I just want to stay on my own place," Philomena's voice rasped.

"Oh, but I want to. And I know you want to stay here. But we're going to find you the nicest place you've ever seen. You wait." Celeste spoke hurriedly, white teeth glinting in the sunlight.

"This right here is the nicest place I've ever seen."

"This old house that's falling down? You just wait til we find you a place with all new bathroom fixtures and appliances. You'll have a new washer and dryer and TV." Celeste looked over her shoulder at Georgette. "Isn't that right, Georgette?"

"My TV works fine and my washer does too. I still hang out my clothes on that line by the back porch."

"Hang out your clothes? At your age? What do you do when it rains?" Celeste tilted her head.

"I don't do a wash when it rains."

"Well, we're going to bring you up-to-date. And you're going to see what you've been missing all these years." Celeste turned toward her sister and made a motion with her head toward the back of the house. "Come on, Celeste. Let's do what we came for and leave Miss Philomena in peace."

Georgette slowly joined her and they walked toward the south side of the house looking all around them as they passed by the winter garden of new cabbages, broccoli, and Brussels sprouts. They paused at the back of the house and gazed toward the slow-moving gumbo-brown bayou. Georgette slapped a bug on her fore-arm, then flicked it away, gold bracelets jangling. "You're going to have swarms of mosquitoes here. I don't know why you want to go through all this just to live out here. You're going to go stir crazy and want to move back to town inside of a month. That's if you don't die first of West Nile Fever."

Celeste took a deep breath. "You just wait til you see the brick house I've got in mind. You'll change your tune in a hurry."

"I doubt it," Georgette said, looking around at the rusty wheel-barrows, tires, and tin cans full of flowers that crowded the area around the back stoop. "You'll have to spend a month just clearing all this out and getting it hauled away." She gave an impatient wave of her hand,

"Oh, come on. You're just being negative. You have to have vision," Celeste said, rubbing her hands together. "Let's see. I think they should start somewhere around here." Celeste walked to the back stoop. "That will set the house back more from the road."

"You're going to flood wherever you are."

"Georgette! This is going to be a raised Acadian cottage. It'll be five feet up on brick pillars."

"You're nuts. Leave the old lady where she is and forget about this project. I can smell dead fish right this minute." Georgette wrinkled her nose and frowned. "And look over there." She pointed a long manicured finger toward the woods to the north. "Those *Bergerons* live over there. He still keeps fighting roosters even though they outlawed cockfighting. He keeps hunting dogs in kennels! You want to listen to dogs howling and roosters crow-ing at four o'clock in the morning?" Georgette pulled a cigarette pack out of her shoulder bag and shaking out a cigarette, lighted it. "You want one?" She offered the pack to Celeste.

Celeste shook her head. "I can walk over there and get treatments from Claudine."

"Treatments! How often do you need a treatment? You can
drive over here in ten minutes from town if you have a headache
or something. And besides, Claudine Bergeron is kind of spooky
anyhow. You don't need neighbors like that. Besides, you don't
know what all kinds of people will be stopping by over there for
treatments from her. You can be so naïve."

"You know something, Georgette? You're turning into kind of
a snob lately," Celeste laughed. "This is Louisiana. You have to be
ready for anything. You know that." She bent to smell a rose on a
handmade trellis by the corner of the house.

"Me, I'm ready to move to Lafayette. I'm tired of this whole
area. Maybe in Lafayette I can hear about something besides the
price of soybeans, ammo, or 4-wheel drives....or how the church
needs a new roof!" Georgette smoked her cigarette and gazed off
toward the mare quietly munching grass in the field to their right.

Celeste straightened abruptly. "Lafayette! What does Leon
think of that?"

"As long as we can turn a large profit on the house, he doesn't
care. He breathes, eats, and sleeps dollar signs. You should know
that by now," Georgette sighed. "Lafayette is starting to attract a
lot of notice. If we don't buy there now, it'll be too late. Everything
will be already overpriced."

"I wish Gerald thought about money once in a while. I can't
get his mind off hunting, fishing, and trapping. By the way, please
don't mention we came out here today. He'd kill me. We had a
fight last night."

"I probably won't even see him."

"Just don't forget to keep quiet if you do."

"What were you fighting about?"

"I was trying to get him to hurry up with moving this whole
thing along," Celeste indicated the property with a sweep of her
arm. "Then he started in on Leon."

"What about Leon?" Georgette ground out her cigarette with
the heel of her boot.

"Oh, he started trying to say Leon fooled around sometimes with smuggling coke or some such. I really tore into him for saying anything like that. He's so jealous of Leon's success."

"Smuggling?" Georgette tucked in her chin and jerked her back straight. "That's dangerous talk! Doesn't he know Leon's planning on running for State Representative one day? He can't go around badmouthing Leon like that. You know Leon. He'll sue him. He loves to sue people anyhow. I think he does it in his dreams. Sometimes when he's sleeping I can see that nasty smirk on his face and I always say to myself....There you go, suing somebody again. He's such a bastard. But I'm stuck with him forever. He'd never let me divorce him. It would ruin his chances to claim he's a family man. Sometimes I think I just hate him, plain and simple." Georgette smiled sideways. "But I get even. I spend as much of his money as I possibly can...and then some. And I throw plenty of it into my safety deposit box at the bank. If the bastard ever knew how much I'd socked away he'd have me shot."

"Georgette, for God's sake. Take it easy. Leon's not that bad. I think you have PMS or something today. Maybe you better stop by Claudine's and get a treatment yourself on the way home."

"Well, you're the one who started it all with this slander talk about Leon smuggling drugs. That'd put anybody in a bad mood." Georgette pursed her lips and pushed her sleeves up.

"Don't worry about Gerald's saying that. He was just trying to get at me any way he could. I as much as told him he was walked over by everybody cause he's so nice all the time and that made him mad. And he's mad at me for hating his aunt's house in town. He loves that moldy old house. He kind of grew up there; he spent so much time with her and his uncle. Come on, let's walk down to the water." Celeste took off down the lawn toward the weedy, muddy bank.

"I'm not going down there. I'll wait right here," Georgette poked in her purse for another cigarette. "And hurry up. I've got a list of errands to do for Leon as long as...never mind."

8

LEON SEES RED

Leon blinked as he was hit with a blast of cold air entering Anatole's and adjusted his eyes to the dim interior. The hostess nodded and smiled. "Good afternoon, Mr. LeDoux. Your father is right this way."

He followed the hostess through two sections of the dining room loud with conversation, to a quieter section off to the side where his father waited at a corner table.

His father, an older version of Leon, still handsome, yet with a fleshy jaw and neck and deep creases at his forehead, smiled and waved Leon into the seat across from him.

"Hello, son. Right on time."

"I try to be. Doesn't always happen though," Leon said amiably. He wondered as he settled into his chair why he felt tension from the moment he'd seen his father. Dwight LeDoux appeared to be in a good mood. He was dressed well, as usual, in a tan cotton suit, blue and white striped shirt, and French blue tie. It looked as though he'd just seen a barber for his silver hair was impeccably shaped and combed straight back as always.

"Being on time is still one of the best indicators of good breeding, even though our country is growing coarser by the day."

"With a fifty-percent school dropout rate, it'll only get more so," Leon nodded at the waiter who took their drink orders. "We're being overrun by barbarians from within," he said when the waiter had left the table.

"For now anyway. You have to stay open to all the possibilities. Anything can happen. And I do mean anything." Dwight pushed out his chin as though to loosen his shirt collar, then smiled again giving no indication that anything was amiss. Leon, however, remained on alert.

Dwight inquired about Leon's family and sipped from a stemmed water glass as he listened attentively to Leon's account of the week's family anecdotes, smiling and nodding at the appropriate moments. Leon began to relax.

"That's my grandson for you," he laughed as Leon spoke of his son Beau's passion for boiled shrimp and how he'd devoured an entire bowl of the family dinner the night before with a little help from Jack Rat, the family Jack Russell/Rat Terrier mix.

By the time the filets and baked potatoes and salads had arrived, Leon had almost completely relaxed. "How come Mother didn't join us today?" he asked.

"Oh, she's gone on a field trip to New Iberia. She and her friends are attending some event at the Shadows this afternoon. She sends her love of course."

"Sounds like a nice outing for her."

"Oh, yes. She and her friends stay busy most of the week."

When the two had almost finished their filet mignons, Dwight laid his fork down at a perfect angle on the plate and ran a tongue over his teeth. He took a sip of his daquiri and cleared his throat.

Leon's stomach clenched, but he kept a poker face, nonchalantly raising an eyebrow as he chewed, watching his father.

"I've been hearing some things that are quite disturbing to me, son."

Leon sniffed. "And what would that be?" He sawed off another piece of steak.

"Let's just say there're some nasty rumors going around Lafayette and Baton Rouge."

"And?" Leon lowered his head like a bull. "What? Let's have it."

Dwight sighed as though he'd already tired of the subject. "Son, when you decided on law school, do you remember what I told you?"

"Probably. Refresh my memory." Leon took a healthy swig of rum and soda.

"I told you what I feel strongly about…that there are too many lousy lawyers in our country…and I wasn't willing to pay for law school unless you intended to rise above the herd and be the best you could be. Remember?"

"Of course."

"And that if you weren't going to contribute to the profession and truly help people that I'd rather pay for you to study business administration or anything rather than law. Do you remember all that, son?" Dwight regarded Leon gravely, pursing his lips as he waited for a reaction.

"Yes, I do. I remember the whole conversation. And where is this going?"

Dwight took a long breath, exhaling slowly before answering. He glanced around him. The table on their left was empty and hadn't yet been cleared. The man and woman on their right were just finishing, paying the check, and getting to their feet.

Dwight leaned in slowly and lowered his voice. "Look, Leon. I've long had my suspicions that you've got something going with the realtors you recommend to your estate families. But I quieted my thoughts because I couldn't bring myself to believe that you would lower yourself to taking kickbacks. Then when the Duprees passed on, and that marvelous house of theirs, a jewel of Lafayette history, sold almost immediately and way too cheap…and then changed hands within the month for two hundred fifty thousand more than the survivors received…I was no longer able to deny the writing on the wall."

Dwight bared even teeth as he enunciated each word. "My son…kickbacks from a realtor for recommending him or her to the heirs of estate properties? Duping trusting out-of-town relatives when they take you at your word and don't know the market here? What's the difference between that and the gangbangers who are carjacking and holding up citizens in broad daylight all over Lafayette, demanding money at gunpoint? Can you tell me? What's the difference?"

Leon frowned. "Dwight. How could you think such a thing of me?" He coughed into his napkin. "I mean really. Who's been filling your head with such horseshit?"

"Oh, I could go on and on all afternoon, son. Just because I'm retired doesn't mean I don't still see my friends. Lafayette's still a small city. And many of us older attorneys are still practicing and keeping up with what's going on around here. Oh, and now that I think about it, there is a difference between you and the gang-bangers. They don't have the breeding and education that you do. Which makes what you're doing ten times worse."

"Dwight, whoever's spreading vicious rumors about me.... they're jealous of my success. I've made a lot of money and done it all the right way."

"And no one could ever prove otherwise, right, son?" Dwight frowned, swirling his water glass so the ice cubes clinked.

"Certainly not. No way. I'm clean as a whistle." Leon speared the last bite of steak and popped it into his mouth.

"Yes, clean as a whistle. I'm positive you make sure of that." Dwight ran a finger around the rim of his glass making a humming sound. "Did you ever play with different levels of water in the glass? To get different frequencies? It's interesting." Dwight stopped making the sound and cleared his throat. "There's more to this lecture, son. I was just taking a break. All this rotten business is very stressful for me, because it involves my only son."

"Lay it on me, then. I can't stay away from the office too much longer," Leon said, tugging momentarily on his shirt collar. "Might as well get it all out and off your chest."

"I intend to do just that," Dwight said, lowering his voice. "I keep hearing about you meeting with Arthur Rainey here and there around Baton Rouge. Arthur Rainey whose reputation stinks to high heaven, as a flim-flam man, a con, and an expert at sucking people into his bogus real estate deals."

"What are you doing, hiring detectives to follow me now?" Leon tore off a piece of roll and popped it into his mouth.

"Oh, I don't have to hire detectives, son. There are plenty of people in Baton Rouge who know all about Arthur, and, unfortunately for our family name, know you as well."

"What exactly has he done wrong?"

"How much time do we have here?" Dwight looked at his watch, then leaned in, narrowing his eyes. "Let's see, there's selling lots for two developments that got stalled and somehow never got their roads built and sewer lines laid. There's that scam he pulled with the bald eagle on the hundred acres of forest he had a contract on to develop…and then held up the owner for much less than it was worth because he couldn't develop it with an eagle's nest on it. Then there's the warehouse fire and the office building fire, both of which he was fully compensated for….and the Devereaux estate and the slick way he had Mr. Devereaux committed so his son, Arthur's friend, could take over the estate." Dwight smiled. "Should I go on? I can you know for another twenty minutes at least, about your Mr. Arthur Rainey."

"If all that's true, how come he's not in prison?" Leon looked bored and fingered a spoon, tilting it back and forth.

"I'm sure he will be. There are plenty of people trying to put him there. But my concern is why my son would have a drink or a meal with a man so shoddy as that."

"First I've heard any of this. I think you're making it up."

"You can't expect me to believe that a smart lawyer such as yourself, hasn't heard all of this. With associations such as Arthur Rainey, next thing I know you're going to be mailing out those rubberized refrigerator magnets with your picture and legal advertising on them. You're already advertising in the newspaper. You're turning into a sleaze, son, which is your business, but it reflects on our family name."

"Dwight, you're talking crazy stuff. You may have too much time on your hands since you retired. Why don't you take up golf? Or go over to Red's and work out?"

"You know, son. You're right about that. I've taken up piano lessons. I always wanted to get back to the piano. I had such a busy practice that I foolishly let it go for many years. I may be able to buy Judge Reinhardt's Steinway. His widow is first making sure her grandson doesn't want it."

Dwight made the humming sound again with his finger on the rim of the glass. "But getting back to the unpleasant aspect of our visit. I'm afraid there's still more to all this." He gazed across the table with eyes gone sad, lids drooping.

"I've heard much, much worse than what I just mentioned. Something I can't discuss here in a public place. But something that would put a man in Angola for a long, long time." He had dropped his voice so low that Leon looked puzzled and cupped his left ear.

"Dwight. I can hardly hear you. Did you just say what I think you did?"

"You heard me."

Leon laughed. "Dad! Please!" His jaw dropped and he shook his head, looking around as though seeking a way out of the restaurant.

Dwight leaned back in his chair, crossing his arms, eyelids half closed as he watched his son shift back and forth in his chair.

"I'm in shock. You're talking crazy. How many daquiris did you have before I got over here? Are you all right? I mean, really?" Color rose in Leon's cheeks.

"Oh, yes, son. I'm all right," Dwight said slowly. "Just a touch sick to my stomach is all. I can't help but think of what your great grandfather would say if he knew about your dealings. A man who would risk his life to go into backwater quarantined villages to help those suffering with yellow fever. What would he think about your shady associations and all these nasty rumors? I've always tried to live up to his standards, but I don't know what happened to you."

Leon glanced at his watch. "Yes, yes. Grandfather was a saint, and you are a saint, but I've got an early afternoon appointment. I'm not retired like you, so I'd better be getting back to the office. Do you want me to get this?" He patted his mouth with the cloth napkin and dropped it to the right of his plate.

"No coffee? Dessert?"

Leon raised a corner of his upper lip in a subtle snarl. "Coffee? Dessert? Are you kidding? First chance I get I'm going to have a talk with Mother about you."

"Go ahead back to the office if you have to. I'm sorry all this had to be said...but it did. Be careful, son. I'm afraid the word is out on you. If kickbacks were ever proved, you'd be disbarred of course. You know that, son. But Angola? Now that's as bad as it gets. I can't picture you surviving such a fate. A man as used to luxury as you are locked up for years in that hellhole?" He dismissed Leon with a bored half salute and looked around for the waiter.

Leon slid his chair back, stood and turned to leave. He looked back over his shoulder. "You haven't been discussing any of this insanity with Mother?"

"God, no! You think I want to put her in her grave?" Dwight said, neck still twisted as he scanned the room for the waiter.

Leon abruptly walked away from the table, shoulders squared, face red and pinched. He quickly corrected his angry expression as he passed through the dining room, shoulders back and head held high. He waved to a couple on the way out, nodding and smiling to another table. As he entered the reception area, he circled around a family of tourists that was being ushered into the dining room,

He muttered as he approached the swinging entrance doors, pushing on the brass plate. "Damn you, Dwight," his upper lip curled again as he passed into the bright afternoon light. "You always did find a way to look down your nose at me. Just never good enough for you, huh, old man? And then to accuse him of kickbacks! How cheesy! He'd never resort to nickel and dime bullshit such as that. He had a real estate investment partner who always split fifty-fifty with him on the deals he turned him on to through his estate cases, through a straw man, of course. But kickbacks! Dwight should know his only son better than that. His only son was smart as a fox and nothing so mundane as kickbacks would ever cast a shadow over his career. He was in the big leagues, nothing penny ante for Leon LeDoux. He didn't have time for smalltime larceny.

As he walked by the bright landscaping that bordered the parking lot, brakes screeching and horns blaring from the nearby intersection, he looked around to make sure he wasn't seen, and spat into a bed of orange marigolds.

9

LEON OUTRAGED AGAIN

Leon slowed as he reached his home, passing the two-hundred foot paved circular driveway, hardly noticing the bright colors of the autumn flowers the landscaper had recently planted, then turned into a side drive toward the four door garage angled beside the house. His forehead was furrowed into deep creases, his frown severe, and his stomach clenched. Unused to this mix of uncomfortable emotions, he jutted out his chin and raised his top lip into a sneer as he used the remote to open one of the overhead doors.

The two-story brick house with its wide and deep front porch, its four varnished, thick columns, its French doors and side and back terraces, looked overblown and boring to him. His usual pride in its prestige and statement that he was such a success did nothing for his inner turmoil. It might as well have been a sharecropper's shack for all the good it did him that afternoon. Something had to give, he decided as he slammed the door of the car and strode from the garage. He would not tolerate such disrespect as he'd suffered in the last three hours. He had to do something to alleviate his discomfort and unease. Between his father's dire warnings and Mona's subtle threats, he knew he was pushed to make moves and take some kind of action.

"Damnit it all to hell!" he muttered as he crossed the terrace to the side door.

He rang the doorbell because he knew Georgette would have deadbolted the door as he insisted she do whenever she was home. He fumed as he waited for her to answer, then jammed his finger on the buzzer a second time, looking around at the twin four-foot high terra cotta urns planted with ferns flanking the red door. "Place looks like a goddamn Greek temple," he stewed.

He jabbed at the buzzer once again, wondering again why he ever married Georgette in the first place. He felt the bonds of marriage and domesticity tightening like a noose around his neck. He rubbed the back of his neck as he waited. "What are you doing in there?" he muttered. "Answer the damn door, would you?" If he'd never gotten so weighed down with all the demands of marriage and family, he could be sitting on the deck of a Costa Rica beach house by now watching the Pacific roll in and roll out. He had enough trouble with the women outside of marriage, let alone having to deal with his venal wife and her irritating, low-rent family.

He was too smart to be in this position. He would not be held back by Georgette, their spoiled son, Mona's treachery, his father's interference in his dealings, and all the rest of the endless demands on him. If there was any action he should take, it was to extricate himself from all the family frustrations in his life. Nobody appreciated his hard, grinding work. Nobody appreciated how he got up, dressed well, and went in to the office everyday while they goofed off. Nobody cared that he'd accumulated millions of dollars through brain power and expertise. No one in his family appreciated his entrepreneurial abilities; his instincts for accumulating the fortune that they loved to spend. They were all too limited to see the kind of man he was. None of them could see beyond their nose. Unlike him, they all suffered from mediocrity.

America was built on his kind of guts and his kind of risk-taking vision. Rum running, Prohibition, Moonshine. Cocaine was just the latest illegal commodity. If people were stupid enough to use it knowing how addictive it is, then it might as well be him who makes the money instead of the next guy. Yes, Leon LeDoux had vision, and he liked that word. The only vision Georgette had was what allowed her to keep all the names and plots straight on her daily soap operas.

He swatted at a mosquito, then pulled out a white handkerchief and wiped the squashed bug and blood smear from the back
of his hand. With a growl, he reached out to the buzzer to mash
it again, when the door opened. Georgette wore a red terry robe,
her hair wrapped in a towel turban, her face wet and shiny.

"What have you been doing? I've been standing out here getting eaten up by mosquitos and punching the doorbell."

"Sorry. I was in the Jacuzzi."

He followed her into a dayroom, the skylight illuminating
them.

"Aren't you going to give me a hug at least?"

"You're all wet."

He put his arm around her lightly, patting her back. "Okay,
okay. I'm sorry. I had a bad day at the office, and a really lousy
lunch with my father."

"What's wrong between you and Dwight now?"

"Same old shit, different day."

"You'll feel better after you eat. Delores made a roast."

"Come on in the den with me first. I need and deserve a drink."
He led her by the arm through the high-ceilinged, lightly furnished recently remodeled dayroom, still smelling of fresh paint,
then down a hall, past the arched entry to the living room and on
to the open door of the den.

That room, lighted by track lights on the wooden beams, was
furnished with two brown leather couches and two red leather
armchairs. An outsized six foot tall black Rutledge safe towered
in a far corner. A collection of six Oriental rugs overlapped the
glazed Mexican tiles. The room smelled of gardenia spray.

"Delores has been spraying that damn air freshener crap in
here again. What's the matter with her? Slow learner or what?"
Leon growled.

Georgette sniffed. "I tell her but she forgets."

"Either she needs to learn English better, or you need to learn
Spanish," Leon barked.

She sank onto one of the couches and Leon crossed to a short
bar set up against one paneled wall. A rough cypress framed paint-
ing of a Cajun standing and poling a dug-out pirogue along a

heavily wooded bayou hung over two shelves of assorted stemware and highball glasses.

He set about filling a stainless ice bucket from the small refrigerator behind the bar, rattled ice cubes into lowball glasses and liberally poured the vodka. He carried the drinks to where she had settled back on the couch, arms crossed in front of her.

"You have that look. Something's on your mind," he said, sitting at the other end of the couch. He shifted position so he could lean back against the cushions and kicking off tasseled loafers, stretched his legs out on to the marble and wrought iron coffee table.

"You can tell?"

"Of course I can tell."

She smoothed the terry cloth over her knees, then played with the ends of the belt.

"Is it that bad? What? Did you get in a fender bender?"

"No, no, nothing like that. But there's something you need to know," she blurted.

He leaned back and took a deep breath, then a long drink. "Okay. I'm ready." He made a come-on gesture with his fingers.

"I don't know what's going on in Gerald's mind, but Celeste told me he was saying things about you the other night."

"Me? What things?" He gave her a stiff smile.

"Wait. Let me get some vodka down first." She reached for the glass and took a sip, making a face as she swallowed.

"Georgette. Go on and tell me. You're not going to hurt my feelings. Gerald and I never liked each other from the get go."

She avoided his eyes and took another drink.

"Georgette. Let's have it, damnit!" He slapped his knee.

"You're not going to like it," she squeezed her eyes shut.

"So what? Out with it."

"Okay. But don't take it out on me, promise? You know how you get. I'm just the messenger."

"Damnit, Georgette. Just spill it, will you? I'm not going to take out on you whatever some swamp-dwelling coonass said about me."

"Celeste and I went out together today. She wanted to prowl around that old Creole lady's property they're going to take back to build on. You know, Miss, what's her name, Philomena?"

"I know what you're talking about. Celeste's big dream house on the bayou. The old lady Celeste has decided to kick out now that she's feeble and in her nineties. Says a lot about your sister who is as big a bitch as your mother. That's where she learned it; at your mother's knee."

"For the last time, Leon. Mama's not a bitch. Just because you all can't ever say a decent word to each other."

"Yeah, yeah, yeah. Okay. Your mother's a sainted goddess. Get on with it. What does all this have to do with me?"

"We were out down on the bayou bank there and Celeste starts telling me about a fight they'd had the night before. And how Gerald was running off at the mouth about how you've been smuggling cocaine in through Texas all these years, and that's why we have so much money. And if he was only a drug smuggler, why then they'd be rich too, and she'd be happy." She looked down. "Or words to that effect," she murmured, biting her lip.

"Would you please repeat what you just said?" he said in a dangerously low voice.

Georgette whispered, "Gerald told her he knew you'd been smuggling coke... for a long time."

"What in the hell?" Leon stood, splashing some of the vodka on his jacket sleeve.

She pressed her back against the couch and flinching, turned her head away. "I said you wouldn't like it."

"Jesus God! Your family! I've been telling you for years. They're all nuts!"

She looked up at him wide eyed, talking fast. "I told her that was slander. That you'd never do anything like that. You were too smart to fool with drugs. And that she'd better make sure he never repeated anything like that to anyone ever again or he'd end up in court cause you'd sue him."

"Why that bastard. He's even stupider than I thought. What the hell. Sue him? And get what exactly? He makes just enough to get by. Was he drunk?" Leon sputtered, and a drop of saliva flew from his mouth.

"I don't think so." She shook her head and took another drink, then placed the glass gently back on the coffee table. "You've got to tell me, Leon. Is there anything to this? Where would he get this idea?"

"He's a crazy coonass! How the hell would I know where he gets these bonehead ideas. Of course there's nothing to it. Do you honestly think I'd jeopardize everything I've built all these years to haul cocaine into Louisiana? Every week you read about troopers finding another big haul coming in on I-10." He leaned over her, eyes narrowed, face pinched. "Who the hell do you think you're married to, woman? Look around you. Everything you see is because of my hard work as an attorney." He jabbed a thumb at his chest. "And I'm going to throw it all away, get disbarred, and go to Angola? Are you out of your mind? Quit watching all that shit on daytime TV. You're getting brain damage from it!"

"Has it ever been true? Did you ever...you can tell me," Georgette pressed on.

"Now you're calling me a liar?" His face was getting red. She flinched, and he swilled the last of the vodka and headed back to the bar.

"I'm not calling you a liar...I'm sorry. I had to ask."

"Good God, Georgette!" He splashed more vodka into the glass.

"I said I'm sorry!"

"Forget it! We're not going to have this insane conversation again."

"I'm going to go get dressed now." She rose from the couch tugging the collar of the robe tight around her throat.

"You do that. I'm going to catch up with Gerald, have a talk with him and set him straight. And you can count on that happening."

"Please don't lose your temper with him. Please talk calmly to him."

"Calmly? I ought to put his lights out for saying something like that behind my back."

"I don't want you to talk to him when you're angry. Things could get out of control."

"What things? I would never lay a hand on him. I'm a lawyer, remember? We let them take a swing at us, and then we throw them in jail. That's the way to handle a lunatic such as your brother-in-law."

She turned her head, watching him at the bar and felt a headache coming on. It started at the back and was slowly working its way around to her temples. She had pushed the possibilities from her mind, but she knew now that Gerald's accusations were true. Leon's blustering had told her all she needed to know. She eyed the black safe in the corner, wondering just what could be locked up in there alongside her jewelry and the ready cash he kept there. She clutched her stomach, feeling as though she'd been punched as she turned toward the door.

"Dinner will be ready soon," she called as she left the room, tightening the belt of the robe as she headed down the hall toward their bedroom.

FRIDAY

10

ROY CHECKS HIS TRAPS

Roy Bergeron stepped out onto his back porch and surveyed the overcast sky. It was going to rain later in the morning, so he wanted to get out on the bayou and check his traps before it started coming down. He turned back into the spacious country kitchen and looked over his wife Claudine's shoulder. "Can you hurry that along?" he asked, as she poured bacon grease off into a tin can for mixing with the dogs' food.

"What's your hurry?" Claudine, a slight woman, with shiny black hair hanging down her back past her waist, set the cast iron skillet back onto the burner and adjusted the gas flame.

"It's fixing to rain and I want to check all my traps before dinner."

"Okay, okay. Give me a second. It's almost ready. How many eggs you want?"

"Two's good." Roy looked out the window over the double sink and watched the current. The wind was changing, and the brown bayou was rippled with the effects of the air disturbance. The water glinted in the fast moving current where occasional breakthroughs of sunlight filtered through overhanging willow, cypress and water oak branches. Three yellow-belly turtles rested on a dead log flush against the opposite bank. Someone's lost red plastic gas can bobbed along with the current, contrasting sharply with the surrounding coffee-colored waters.

Claudine carefully set Roy's plate down on a woven mat on the cypress plank table, the wood a weathered silver gray. "Here you go. I'll bring your coffee in a minute."

He looked her up and down as she walked back to the stove, admiring her easy movements and slim figure in the black jeans and pink LSU tee shirt. "I'll take it to go. Put it in the thermal cup."

"Say please," Claudine chided, glancing back at him over her shoulder. "Caught you looking," she laughed. "You want me to put some biscuits in a sack?"

"No, please. This is good. I ought to be back by ten." Roy bolted down the fried potatoes, eggs and bacon. He ate two biscuits with Claudine's homemade blackberry jam and pushed his chair back. "Okay. I'm out of here. Don't forget to feed the roosters and the dogs." He grabbed her by the shoulders, leaned over and kissed her slowly and fully on the mouth, then abruptly smacked her rear.

Claudine laughed again, "I'm not a horse." She stretched on tiptoe to reach down a canister from a vintage glass-front kitchen cabinet.

"Later, darlin," Roy said as he grabbed his coffee and banged out the backdoor. Crossing the wide back porch, and starting down the well-worn path to the boat, he spoke soothingly to his hounds, clamoring and yipping in their kennels. "I'll be back. Take it easy. She's going to feed you. Hang on."

Setting his mug in a holder in the boat and kneeling, he pushed the ten-foot skiff down the slick muddy bank into the brown waters of the bayou. Jumping into the boat, and seating himself, he cranked up the Merc 15, yanking on the rope two times to kick it into action. As the motor complained, growled, and then burst into life, he watched two fox squirrels chase one another up and down an oak on the opposite bank, their reddish tails swishing back and forth like plumes. He lowered the visor of his cap over his dark eyes as he let the engine idle for a few minutes, then steered his way out into the middle of the bayou and headed downstream toward his first slat trap.

The first marker, a plastic milk jug, bobbed in front of the nine hundred feet of woods that had been in Claudine's family for generations, and that bordered the south side of their farm. He pulled next to it, hauling up the homemade catfish trap that was empty except for some waterlogged plants covered with slimy, khaki-colored moss. Dropping it back into the water, he steered toward his next trap that lay close to the far edge of the woods and about two hundred feet from Miss Philomena's house. As he slowly raised it from the water, he noted something out of place on the bank out of the corner of his eye. When he saw there was nothing in his second trap, he let it drop back into the water and eased the boat closer to the shore.

Something pale was sticking out of the mud two yards from the edge of the water, smeared and blurred by the shadow of thick weeds. Roy drew closer, leaning out of the boat to peer at it, frowning as he strained to see better in the gloom of overhanging branches. Foliage caught at his hair and scratched his face as though to warn him away, but he persisted despite the overhanging branches. After staring for several minutes, he pushed his cap back, wiped his eyes with the palm of his hand and swore: "Jesus, God Almighty." Then, engine idling, he shut off the motor, slowly and reverently made the sign of the cross, and whispered, "Sweet Jesus, have mercy on us all." He stared at the bank for a few long moments as though in a trance, then pulled the cell phone out of the case attached to his belt and punched in 911.

11

ROY REPORTS

Roy Bergeron called from outside the bathroom door where Claudine was taking a shower, "Hey! Hurry up! Got an emergency to tell you about!"

"I can't hear you," she yelled over the rush of the shower spray.

Roy opened the door and hot steam smacked him in the face. "Man! You got a sauna going in here."

"Somebody's coming for an eleven-thirty treatment," Claudine said, tucking her face around the lavender shower curtain.

"*Chère*. Hold on to something before I tell you this. I don't want you to fall down."

"What? Are you kidding? What are you talking about?" Claudine poked her face out around the curtain again, eyes wide.

"You holding on?"

She retreated in back of the curtain again. "Okay! Okay! I'm holding on to the towel bar. What you got?"

Roy stepped closer to the shower and this time he pulled the curtain aside an inch or two so he could see her. "When I was out checking my traps? I found a dead body. Over there," he gestured toward Philomena's house.

"A dead body?" Claudine turned off the shower and yanked back the curtain. "What the hell?" Roy grabbed an oversized lavender towel from a brass towel rack and held it out to her.

"Yeah! I'm not lying. A dead body!" He winced. "A sure enough dead body. I saw it in the muddy grass by the bayou and called 911.

They're over there now going over everything. Mitch Lanclos was out on his tractor when they called him. He's over there now with a whole crew. They taped off Miss Philomena's whole place."

"Who is it?" Claudine vigorously dried her arms.

"They don't know yet. I have to go down to the Sheriff's Department later on and give a statement because I found the body."

"You!" Claudine stopped toweling herself and stared at him. "Why do you have to go down there? Are you a suspect?"

"No, no. It's just routine." Roy took the towel from her and tapped her shoulder. "Turn around. I'll get your back."

"Maybe it's that nephew of Miss Philomena's. Alfred." Claudine obediently turned, lowering her chin and pulled the dark, wet hair up off her neck, twisting it into a coil.

"Naw. What I saw was a white man. Except he wasn't so white, cause he was covered with mud."

"This is scary. Did you hear anything strange last night?"

Roy rubbed her back so hard she had to support herself with one arm against the pale green tile wall. "I didn't hear a thing. But we both fell asleep watching that boring movie, remember? And the TV stayed on half the night until I woke up around three and turned it off."

"Maybe that's why you woke up. A noise out there."

"Could be." He started toweling the lower part of her back.

"Thank God, Antoinette is already gone to school."

"When she comes home, don't let her out of your sight."

"Believe me, I won't," she said. "No matter what, I've got to get ready now. Paulette needs a treatment for fever and she'll be here in ten minutes. That's what you get for being married to a *traiteur.*"

"Okay. I better get back anyhow and see what's going on over there. Keep your gun handy. There's no telling what kind of psycho we got running around out here." He wrapped the towel around her shoulders and kissed her quickly on the mouth.

"I'll come over soon as I'm through with Paulette." She wrapped the towel tightly around her torso, then tilted her head to look in the steamed mirror over the sink. She rubbed her hand in circles over the cloudy mirror, trying to clear it.

"I'm taking the boat again. They won't let you past the tape between our woods and Philomena's. Just come through the woods to the bayou bank where I am. And keep the doors locked until Paulette gets here. Then make sure the front and back doors are locked before you leave."

"All right, but I'm not worried. If there is somebody on the run, they're far away from here by now."

"You never know these days what people are going to do. You just have to figure everybody's crazy and act accordingly." Roy passed through the hallway and on into the kitchen, stopping by the stove to lift the lid from a cast iron pan for two more of the biscuits. He bit off half of one and stowed the other in the pocket of his flannel shirt. By the time he reached the door, he'd finished the first one and was fishing in his pocket for the second.

12

A TREATMENT

Paulette Fruge knocked on the Bergeron's front door while peering off towards the woods that lay between their property and Philomena's. When Claudine answered the door, Paulette tilted her head in that direction.

"Claudine! What on earth is going on over there?" She frowned, still focused on the south end of the property.

"Come on in, Paulette. I don't know what all is going on over there. Roy just went to see about it." Claudine held the door open, while Paulette reluctantly stepped over the threshold.

"But Mitch Lanclos' truck is over there. And two Sheriff patrol cars. And an ambulance! Did something happen to Miss Philomena? Was she murdered or what?" Paulette's eyes were wide with alarm. "I mean should we go over there and see about it? See if we can help the poor old lady?"

"Don't worry yourself, Paulette. Roy will let us know if they want any help over there. Just let Roy tend to it."

Paulette clutched her purse closely to her chest and tried to see out the living room windows. "Are you sure we shouldn't go see about it?"

"Yes, I'm sure. You know if Mitch Lanclos is over there, why everything will get taken care of."

"Yes, I guess you're right," Paulette sighed. "Okay. I'll let the men handle whatever it is. But I sure hope nothing's happened to Miss Philomena. Now there's a sweet little lady if there ever was one. And doing on her own like she's always done. Poor thing! Nobody to look after her except that worthless nephew of hers. You know the one I mean. That Alfred. Now what possible good can he be for her ever? I ask you."

"He comes around once in a while to help her, I'm pretty sure. I know we look in on her when we think of it. She always seems to be doing just fine on her own though. I hope I'm doing as well when I'm her age. If I ever get to be her age, that is. Would you like a glass of sweet tea before we get started?" Claudine asked as she led the middle-aged woman into the small living room and motioned for her to sit in one of the midnight blue upholstered armchairs.

"No, thank you. I've got to get back. I'm in the middle of something at the house. But this headache is killing me, and I just had to hurry by for a treatment." Paulette placed a palm on her forehead and stood before the indicated chair without seating herself. Accustomed to Claudine's treatments, she knew the procedure well, and closed her eyes as she waited for Claudine to begin.

Claudine placed her hand on the crown of the woman's head and held it there for several minutes as she prayed quietly in French. It was so quiet in the house they could hear the murmur of the refrigerator in the next room. A sweet herbal concoction was simmering on the stove and Paulette sniffed the soothing aroma which somewhat lessened her distress. She felt the warmth of Claudine's hand penetrating her scalp, and the welcome beginnings of relief.

Claudine lifted her hand from Paulette's head and, still repeating French prayers, began making signs of the cross all down the front of the woman's body without touching her. When she had worked her way down to her feet, she straightened and walking around behind her, repeated the procedure all down her back, still without touching her.

When the treatment was finished, Paulette opened her eyes, smiled and nodded, knowing not to ever thank a *traiteur*, for that was believed to negate the treatment. She slipped a folded bill from her pocket and pressed it into Claudine's hand.

"I've got to be getting back. We're putting new tile in the bathroom today and I want to make sure the tileman isn't giving Walter fits. You know how he gets. He works himself up and then there's no calming him down. Before you know it, he'll be coming over here for a treatment for his nerves." Paulette walked toward the front door again. "I want a raincheck on that tea though. And I want to find out what's going on over there." She opened the door and stepped through to the front porch.

Claudine watched her go to her sedan, parked in the circular limestone driveway, then locked the front door, and hurried back to the kitchen to stir the herbal concoction. She tasted the tea with a small spoon, was satisfied that the flavor had developed enough, and turned off the gas burner. Then she covered the pan, quickly looked around to see if she'd left any lights on, and let herself out the back door headed for Philomena's property.

13

THE PATH THROUGH THE WOODS

C laudine left the house as soon as her client was out of sight. She let the kitchen screen door bang behind her as she stepped onto the wide cluttered back porch. The porch had six vertical wooden posts, a forest green deck, a tongue-in-groove ceiling painted sky blue to keep mud-daubers away, two outdoor ceiling fans, a few traditional slatted rocking chairs, and a variety of wire traps piled all around the perimeter.

There were crab traps, crawfish traps, and turtle traps stacked relatively neatly by threes, leaving room only for the back porch steps. A white hen stood on one of the stacks, clucking wildly. "Did you just lay an egg, Lulu?" Claudine smiled at her favorite hen and stepped down from the porch, eyeing the woods that lay between her house and her neighbor's property.

She could make out some movement through the thick hard-woods and pines out toward the bayou, and set out across the wide lawn towards a narrow dirt path that cut through the trees to the water. A man yelled something that sounded like "underneath." She recognized Detective Mitch Lanclos' voice. She always felt uncomfortable around him as he was the first man she'd ever gone out with in high school. Even though more than twenty-five years had passed, she knew Mitch had never forgiven her for marrying Roy. He had turned out to be one of those men who falls hard for someone at an early age and never gets over it, giving credence to the old expression: *Old loves die hard.*

Stepping carefully along the pine needles and leaves of the path, she flashed on a scene from a long ago dance during senior year. Roy had come back to town from a pipeline job in Texas and dropped by the auditorium to pick up his younger brother, Virgil. Rabbit season had opened, and they were going to the family camp in the Atchafalaya Basin to hunt with their father and his friends.

Roy had seen her standing on the sidelines talking to one of her girl friends while Mitch had gone outside with some of his friends to sneak a beer. Roy asked her to dance one slow dance to one of Johnny Allen's swamp pop ballads. She looked at him in surprise. She knew who he was, of course. St. Beatrice was a small bayou French town where everyone knew everyone, but they'd never spoken before that evening.

He was wearing muddy blue jeans and a grubby tee shirt, stretched out at the neck. His workboots were worn and mud caked. "I'm sorry to look like this," he'd said. "But I just got back in town and I'm on my way home to clean up...but then I saw you...."

During the slow dance, he held her loosely, somewhat formally, then brought her back to where he'd found her on the sidelines. He left before Mitch returned a few minutes later, but not before telling her he'd call the next day. She watched him leave with his brother, the words of *Angel Love*, the Johnny Allen song, still playing in her mind. Roy had graduated two years before, and older boys tended to have star quality. Her excited girl friends, circling around her, asked a multitude of questions about that dance. "What did he say? Did he ask you out? Is he still dating Regina?" and so on, until Mitch returned from outside with his cronies which instantly put an end to the girls' interrogation. There had been such silence among the girls when he returned to her side, that he looked around at all of them quizzically.

That night was the last time she ever went out with anyone but Roy. They were married as soon as she graduated that spring. Mitch was invited to the big Cajun wedding at St. Joseph's, as were all the rest of her school friends, but he didn't attend the ceremony nor did he attend the pig roast and huge feast held afterwards in a public park a quarter mile from the western levee of the great Atchafalaya Swamp. Furthermore, he didn't speak to either one of them for several years after the marriage, and still would barely speak at all to the present day.

The fact that he'd never pressured her for sex the many months they'd dated must have rankled him, because after they broke up, he began a series of affairs and became well-known for being distant, cold and heartless as soon as women fell in love with him. That was the way it was at least, until four years later, when he got one of Claudine's friends, Lanette, pregnant and subsequently married her.

Claudine stepped along the path carefully, knowing she must not disturb any terrain near a dead body until the law had a chance to do their work. She eyed the ground, watching as always, for snakes. Any bayou resident knew to tread carefully when walking outside, and knew too that wearing boots and carrying a big stick was always wise. Even better was keeping a pistol handy, but Claudine had brought neither stick nor pistol, and she was wearing sandals, so she proceeded with a good deal of caution, stopping only to pick up an owl pellet, grayish fur and a tiny tooth visible in its dense round shape. Delighted, she cupped it carefully in her hand to take back to the house to show her daughter when she came home from school.

After she'd passed the first few hundred feet of woods, she was surprised to see drag marks disturbing the lay of the leaves and the pine needles. She'd accompanied Roy enough times on hunting expeditions to learn a few things about tracks. So at that point she stopped, certain that they wouldn't want her to walk any further with a dead body up ahead and the Sheriff's Department investigating a possible homicide. She didn't know whether to return to the house and go around by the road, or call out.

She decided to yell for Lanclos: "Detective! I think I've found something! Over here in the woods! It's Claudine."

"Stay right there! Don't move! Don't touch anything!" Mitch barked, and she wondered if he still held a grudge after all these years, as she waited frozen in her tracks, serenaded by birdsong, and sniffing the fresh bayou air.

He cursed under his breath as he approached her a few minutes later, casting his eyes around the path and the woods as he slowly walked nearer. "Damnit, Claudine. This is all a crime scene! You shouldn't be out here. You might disturb something we need to see."

"Hello to you too," she said, crossing her arms in annoyance.

"Hello, Claudine. Now, are you happy?" Still not looking at her, he hunkered down three feet away to study the drag tracks. Wiping a hand over his mouth and chin as he squinted at the marks, he looked up, still unsmiling. "Now, slowly turn and walk back exactly how you came. Do not disturb anything further on your way out."

"Is that sort of like 'Don't let the door hit you in the ass on the way out?'" she laughed.

"There's nothing funny about anything out here today, Claudine. Now go home." He eyed her, a sour expression on his face until she obediently turned and stepped away.

"I'm sorry," she said. "I didn't mean to mess up anything, but I did spot the drag marks. Can't I get a little credit for that?"

She couldn't help but notice that Mitch had put on some weight since the last time she'd seen him. Not much, but some. His neck and lower jaw had filled out. His dark eyes were more lined over the wide cheekbones, and his mouth was set into a downward curve, as though life had left a bad impression upon him. His waist was thicker and his voice deeper than she remembered. She wondered if he'd bothered to notice any changes in her looks, so determined was he not to meet her gaze. She had never let her figure go, was only five pounds over her high school weight; but nevertheless, she knew she had also changed during all those years. But then, she was quite sure he didn't give a damn what she looked like anymore.

"We already knew the body was moved. We were getting ready to inspect every inch of this woods today. I need you to stay away from here." His voice, still gruff, angered Claudine, as she turned and started back toward her house. She looked over her shoulder, wanting to say something sarcastic, but his head was bent over as he continued to examine the trail, and she thought better of it.

It wouldn't kill him to thank her and give her a little recognition for her detective work, she huffed to herself. She wondered uncomfortably if his dismissal and apparent lack of interest in her bruised her ego. She had to admit that it did.

"The hell with it," she said aloud as she banged the kitchen screen door open. See if she'd give Detective Lanclos any more help in his investigation. A hardhead like him could just find out his own facts without further assistance from her. *Tête dure fait cul mou.* She turned on the gas burner under the enamel coffee pot and stretching for a shelf, yanked a mug down from the cabinet.

After a few sips of steaming coffee, she settled down, and forgave Lanclos. He'd always been good to her that year they'd spent so much time together. She was the one who'd hurt him. She could cut him some slack. He was on duty, and it was true that she might have messed up something out there in the woods. In the future, she'd try to stay out of his way. It was apparent that, no matter how many years went by, they weren't going to be friends ever again. But there was nothing she could do about it, so she'd just put it out of her mind. First man who'd ever kissed her, and now he acted like an enemy.

"Men!" she said aloud. "You can't live with them. You can't live without them, and they sure won't let you shoot them!"

14

PHILOMENA RECALLS

It was almost eleven when Lanclos approached Philomena's front porch once more. An enamel dishpan sat on her lap. She was shelling field peas and tossing the empty pods off the porch for the chickens.

"What you got there, Miss Philomena? Getting ready for dinner?"

"If I don't pick these before they turn yellow, the chickens will pick them for me. They'll snatch them right off the vines."

"You got to stay on top of things around here, huh?" He smiled, and she returned his smile. Her eyes crinkled, then she dropped her eyes back to her task.

Lanclos removed his cap and fanned himself, then looking hot and uncomfortable, sat on the top step and sighed. He looked around from side to side, then turned back toward Philomena.

"What did you find out down there?" she asked softly.

A hysterical cackling hen raced across the yard chased by a brilliant orange and rust rooster twice her size. Lanclos watched them until they'd run out of sight into the woods at the edge of the yard.

"Don't mind T'Rouge. He chases my hens all day long. Don't know when he takes time to eat."

"I'm used to it. My rooster acts up at my place too." He fanned himself again. "To answer your question, Miss Philomena. We don't know yet what happened down there by the bayou. There's a dead man lying down there on the bank. Are you sure you didn't hear anything unusual last night? Anything at all out of the ordinary?"

She stopped shelling the field peas and squinted to her left. After a pause, she took a breath, "I think maybe I woke up because dogs were barking. Maybe over at their place." She nodded towards the Bergeron's farm. "But I'm not sure. I might have been dreaming it. Whatever it was, it was late and I was half asleep. I dropped right back off, I can tell you that. I sleep good, each and every night, thanks be to the Lord. I know some can't say that, but I can. I've always been a good sleeper."

"Does that happen often? The dogs barking in the middle of the night?"

"Sometimes. Yes, I guess you could say it happens a lot. Possums, coons, skunks, coyotes, fox. They all pass through here. Stray dogs."

"You don't recall any car engines starting up? Voices?"

She thought a minute, then shook her head. "No. I surely don't."

"When's the last time you saw Gerald Theriot?" He spoke casually and slowly with the ease of a question about the weather.

"Gerald? Why, he was here not too long ago. Let's see…" she pursed her lips in thought, her hands holding an eight inch pea pod. "The days run together for me. But it was sometime in the last week or two."

"Where did you see him?"

"Why, he came by here to see me." Her voice dropped. "He had some bad news to bring me."

"What news?"

She swallowed, closing her eyes. "He told me I had to leave here. He was going to take this whole place back." The horse in the pasture whinnied as though to corroborate. "See, he was fixing to build a house here. His wife…." She raised a hand, fluttering her fingers, but didn't finish her sentence.

"His wife?"

"Yes. His wife. Celeste. You know her?"

"I know her."

"Gerald said she wanted him to build her a house on the bayou. And he had to do it. He was sorry about it. About me having to leave." She sighed, scooping up some of the pale green field peas in one hand, then letting them fall through her fingers back into the pan.

"So he said you had to leave here?"

"He sure did." Her voice was resigned and tired.

"And when was this supposed to happen? How long did he give you?"

"I don't know. He said something about finding me a nice place in town. I told him I didn't want a nice place in town. I wanted to stay here for the rest of my life. Then he said I was too old to be out here by myself. It was too dangerous. I told him I was fine out here by myself."

"How long have you lived here?"

"Since I was in my thirties. That's a long, long time cause I'm ninety something now."

"So what did you tell Gerald?"

"I didn't say too much. I was kind of in shock, I guess. After he left, I just sat here rocking til it was almost dark."

"He hasn't been back since?"

"No, but his wife was out here. Celeste. She came out with her sister one afternoon. She said they wanted to measure something out there." Philomena gestured toward the bayou.

"What did she have to say for herself?"

"Not a whole lot. She brought me some éclairs in a fancy box from a bakery in Lafayette. Then they walked on back down there toward the bayou."

"How long did they stay?"

"About half an hour maybe."

"You didn't go with them?"

"No. I don't go down there hardly ever. Snakes. But I did keep an eye on them."

"How did you do that?"

"I went to the back of the house. My bedroom. I didn't want them stepping on any of my flowerbeds. The chickens do enough damage the way they scratch around everywhere."

"I know they do. They always made my wife angry cause they ate her roses. They love to eat red flowers. What did those two women do back there?"

"Not much. Celeste walked around. Looked like she was counting her steps off. Planning where her house would go. It gives me a stomachache just thinking about it." Philomena placed a hand on her stomach and paused, shutting her eyes. Lanclos waited quietly until she resumed. Philomena sighed, opening her eyes. "Then they talked for a while. Then they left." She shrugged. "That was it."

"You hear anything they talked about?"

"Some. The windows were open."

"What did you hear?"

"They were mostly talking about their husbands. How the sister's husband might get her to move to Lafayette. How she held onto his money in secret."

"In secret?"

"She hides his money from him or something like that."

"Anything else you remember? Anything at all?"

"Something about how he maybe has a girl friend. But she doesn't much care. Can you imagine that? I mean not caring about something like that?" Philomena frowned, shaking her head. "People these days. I just don't know what gets into them. It's the devil, I guess. What else could it be?" She shuddered. "Me, I don't even like to say his name. It scares me." She made a sign of the cross and muttered something.

"What else?"

"The sister got mad about something Celeste said about Gerald. He had told her something about the husband. I didn't get what. But she was mad about it all right. Something bad about her husband. She was sticking up for him."

"You sure you didn't hear what it was? Think back." Lanclos pressed on, leaning forward, intent.

"No, I wasn't that interested in any of it. I was worried about my bulbs. My spider lilies were just starting to come up back there. I didn't want them stepping on the new shoots with their fancy boots."

"And you're sure you can't remember anything else those women talked about?"

"Nooo," Philomena said thoughtfully. "I sure can't think of anything else they said than what I already told you. If I was to guess what I heard, I guess it was something about smothering. Somebody smothering cause of drugs maybe. I just don't know. I don't go around trying to listen to what other people are saying when it's not for me to hear. I have enough trouble without getting into other people's trouble."

A black hen made her way around the side of the house with nine black chicks chirping loudly as they followed, racing to keep up with her. The hen stopped at the edge of the garden and the chicks darted in and out and around her, scratching right along beside her, chirping loudly all the while.

"Why are you asking me all these questions about Gerald?" Her voice was timid. A 1960 Chevy pickup drove slowly by, the white-haired driver craning his neck to see why the squad cars and the ambulance were parked along the road. "That's just my neighbor from down thataway," Philomena said, pointing south.

Lanclos watched him drive on, then turned back towards her. Lanclos twisted his mouth. "Now, about that body down there." He paused, hesitant to tell her. "I'm sorry to have to tell you - it's Gerald Theriot."

"Gerald?" Her eyes got wide and she pressed the back of her hand to her mouth.

"We don't know what happened to him. But he's dead."

"Drowned?" Her voice rasped. "That bayou's taken thirty people since I can remember. Thirty people drowned over the years, three of them related to me, and about ten trucks and cars gone in that bayou. That's a mean bayou. Don't let anybody tell you different."

"We don't know yet what killed him."

"Moccasins?" she whispered. "Alfred hacked one in half with a hoe last month." She winced. "I lost a little brother to a whole nest of moccasins when I was somewhere around nine or ten. That's how come I stay away from the bayou. Like I say, that's a mean bayou."

"We just don't know yet," Lanclos repeated.

"Alligators, maybe." It wasn't a question. "There were ducks living out there. They disappear one by one. Unless it's a human alligator shooting them for supper."

"If it was an alligator, he'd be gone. They drag off their prey."

Philomena shuddered. "I know. I know. Why you think I stay away from down there."

"I'm going back down there. They'll be taking the body before too long. If you think of anything...I don't care what it is...something you forgot to tell me...please call me." He fingered a business card out of his shirt pocket and handed it to her.

She held it with care, holding it with forefinger and thumb about two feet from her face. "There're a lot of numbers on here. Which one should I call?"

"Try the cell phone first. I always keep it with me." He slapped a mosquito on his arm. "Please don't be afraid to call me any time. I want to hear from you."

"I'll call you if I find out something. Don't you worry about it. I'll call you," she assured him, eyes bright. "The sooner you find out what happened to Gerald, the sooner I can rest."

"That's fine," he said, "And now with Gerald gone, maybe you'll get to stay here after all. I sure hope so, Miss Philomena."

"I prayed to St. Jude about it," she said matter-of-factly. "I put it in his hands. He's the Saint of Lost Causes, you know. Anytime things look black, well, that's when a person needs to talk to St. Jude about it."

"Well, then, you see?" He smiled and raised a hand in farewell, as he turned and walked back down the steps.

His name was called from down by the bayou. He stepped up his pace and rounded the corner of the house, casting one last glance back at Philomena before she was out of sight. She had returned to her task of shelling the field peas. It pleased him to see her at her work, and he wondered if he'd ever make ninety. He doubted it, even though both his grandparents had worked their farm until they were in their nineties. His life was immersed in death and violence, and he experienced few tranquil days. Furthermore, he liked it that way.

He certainly wasn't glad Gerald Theriot was dead. However, he liked having still another case to obsess about. If it turned out that Gerald was murdered, he'd think of little else until the case was solved. He would hardly notice what he ate. He would drink non-stop cups of coffee. He would dream about the case when he slept. If he slept. More often than not, he was awake by three-thirty in the morning, ready to go again. And he was always on a case.

The murder rate in Louisiana stayed high compared to the rest of the country, and there was never a shortage of victims in St. Beatrice Parish. Men in fights over drugs, gambling, and women. Women at the hands of boyfriends, husbands, transients, psychos. Louisiana stayed in the top three states for homicides against women year after year. Why so many in Louisiana? He'd decided long ago that people in Louisiana tended to be more intense than most other places he'd visited.

As he reached the bottom of the rise from the house, the medical examiner motioned him over, and he joined him at the mud-hole where Gerald's body lay, the men swatting at mosquitoes as they worked around him; Roy Bergeron watching from the edge of the bank.

"What you got, Rusty?" Lanclos asked.

15

RUSTY MEAUX

"**S**omething was gnawing on him during the night. Chewed a third of his face off. Could be there was already blood there that attracted some wild animal." Rusty Meaux, the medical examiner, gazed at the body. Two of his assistants kneeled, one on each side of the dead man, their heads bowed so low as they scrupulously searched the ground around the makeshift grave that they might have been praying.

"And it looks like black powder on his hands…and in his pockets. I still don't know what killed him. It was no robbery though. He's still got his watch and his wallet. I have some ideas though. I'll know more when I get him on my examining table and can run some tests." Meaux was stocky, medium height, and with a craggy face that looked as though he'd spent most of his life outdoors. "From his liver temp, I'd say he was killed somewhere between midnight and three in the morning. He's a muddy mess now, but I'll know more later once I have a chance to clean him up and really examine him. For now I think we can set about moving him."

"I've got two men combing those woods. If there's anything there, they'll find it. We'll be out here another hour or two. If you need to talk to me, call my cell." Lanclos said as they both stared down at the muck on Gerald's body. The hands were encased in plastic bags, the clothes caked in black mud. The staring eyes were sunken in greenish shadow, and the mouth was a bloody gaping hole.

He shook his head. "We don't know what happened to him, but that was a good man."

"Isn't that always the way?" asked Meaux. "Just like the song says, 'Only the good die young.'" He held his gloved hands away from his body, and motioned to one of his assistants. "You find out anything from the old lady?"

"She doesn't know anything. She's in her nineties. Goes to bed with the chickens."

"Never heard anything?"

"She might have heard dogs barking, but she said they bark at everything anyhow."

"That'd be about right." Meaux twisted his mouth back and forth. When the assistant stepped up next to him, he held his hands out, fingers splayed, as though to accentuate his orders. "Put him in the bag. DO NOT change his position. I want him supine....just like he is. Try not to change anything you see there. Make sure you keep an eye on that new tech. Do as much as you can by yourself. Don't let him do much. And tell him why you're doing everything you do. He's got to learn fast on this job."

Lanclos squinted over at the woods as though he might see something important to the investigation before his men did. Dogs barked and a rooster crowed from the Bergeron farm. Philomena's rooster answered from his position perched on the wooden handle of a wheelbarrow full of marigolds tilted next to a sweet gum tree close to her house. Lanclos could see portions of the Bergeron house through the trees, mostly just the back porch and a sliver of cypress siding of the south wall.

"Gerald, Gerald, where is your truck?" Lanclos asked, swinging his gaze back toward the body. "Where the hell did you leave your truck? And how come he's out here in the dark with no headlight or flashlight? And it's raining and black out last night?"

"Watch it, damnit, you're turning the head!" Meaux barked. The two young men frowned with concentration as they tried to obey orders and avoid criticism. As they bent over their task, the experienced man holding the head and shoulders; the new man handling the legs, they inched towards the open body bag lying on a stretcher.

"Slowly. He's not a slab of beef. Jesus, God! Watch it." Meaux growled deep in his throat.

Lanclos brought his attention back to the body and observed the assistants as they worked. Roy Bergeron waited at the edge of the bayou, his boat tied to a cypress stump. He watched the work detail as well, while he scratched a mosquito bite on his forearm.

When the men had successfully zipped the bag, they stood, nodding to Meaux who gave the okay for them to carry the stretcher up the hill to the van.

"Son of a bitch, but this isn't the right day to be training a new assistant," Meaux complained.

"What happened to Jake? He was with you for how many years?"

"Jake moved to Texas. He's all in love with some woman in Beaumont. He always did let his dick run his brain." Meaux peeled off his gloves. "Come by my cousin's funeral home later. Maybe I'll know more by then. Maybe five, six o'clock."

"I'll be there in person if I can or else I'll call." Lanclos nodded and the men turned away from each other. As Meaux started up the hill toward the van, Lanclos called to Roy. "Go home and eat dinner. I'll call you when I'm ready for you to sign a statement down at the Sheriff's Office."

Roy moved his hand toward his face in a salute and turned to his boat, hungry and trying to remember if Claudine was cooking crawfish fettucini or froglegs for dinner. Whatever it was, he was ready for it. They usually ate at eleven, and it was already noon. His stomach complained as he unhitched the line.

"Don't talk about this with anyone, Roy," Lanclos added, his voice rough.

"I wasn't planning on it, me," Roy said as he tossed the line into the boat and jumped aboard.

"And tell Claudine not to talk about this with anyone."

"I'll tell her," Roy called as he moved to the stern to start the engine.

"And keep the dogs in their kennels. I don't want them trampling and tearing up those woods…not until we've searched every square inch. It may take two days before I'm satisfied. I'll let you know." Lanclos called through cupped hands around his mouth.

"You got it," Roy called as he yanked the cord.

Lanclos watched him as the engine caught, and Roy turned the boat toward the farm causing the brown bayou waters to lap the muddy grasses of the bank. He watched the water swooshing over the mud castles the crawfish had made for a few minutes, his face pensive, then he turned his attention back towards the woods and began walking towards the treeline to catch up with his men.

16

TÊTE DE CABRI

Claudine and Roy ate froglegs and crawfish fettucini at their long cypress kitchen table. Roy was so hungry he ate twice as fast as Claudine. She watched him in silence as she sipped iced tea and thought about the events of the day.

"You better eat yours before it gets cold," chided Roy.

"Oh, I'm eating, I'm eating." She picked up her fork and took a bite of the fettucini, chewing slowly as she mused.

"Lanclos wants us to not let any dogs out for a while. He's got to inspect the woods for clues or whatever."

"I'll be careful. He kicked me out of there. I had even found something for him. He's always so down on me."

"What did you find?"

"It looked like something was dragged through there. The grass and weeds were mashed down."

"Like how? What do you think happened?"

"I guess maybe somebody dragged Gerald through the woods... while we were sleeping a couple of hundred feet away. It gives me the creeps." She rubbed her arms vigorously. "And Antoinette's bedroom is closer to the woods than ours. It's all so frightening."

"So you really think Gerald was murdered? Sweet Jesus! Nobody would murder Gerald. Everybody liked him."

"What do you think happened to him then?"

"I don't know. Maybe he had a heart attack or something."

"He's too young to have a heart attack."

"Tell that to Dennis. He keeled over last year, and only thirty-eight years old."

"Dennis was a bad alcoholic though. He had serious liver damage. Gerald has always taken pretty good care of himself."

"Maybe he fell and hit his head. There was a big chunk of cement near there, from where they were trying to keep the bayou bank from eroding with salvage from that bridge they replaced on the north side of town. And it's been there for years. Covered with mud and slime. He could have slipped on it."

"But what would he be doing there at Philomena's in the middle of a rainy night?"

"He was thinking about building there. At least that's what I heard in town the other day."

"You never told me anything about it."

"I forgot. Have too much on my mind all the time."

"What about Philomena?"

"What about her?"

"What was she supposed to do if he built there?"

"Oh, Gerald would find her something in town. He was a good man. Wife's a bitch, but he's always been okay."

"I haven't seen him to talk to for a long time."

"Sorry, sweetheart. But you've missed your chance."

"See? It's like I keep telling you. If you have something to say to somebody, don't wait around and put it off. Cause we never know."

"Especially if you live in Louisiana," Roy smiled. "I've already lost three of my best friends from school, and I'm not even forty yet."

"That's because all your friends drink too much, drive too fast, and stay up all night playing Lowball and bourrée, not to mention the racetrack and......"

"All right, all right. I get it." Roy held up his right hand as he put a heaping forkful of fettuccine into his mouth.

"I'm glad we have the woods between us and Philomena's. Otherwise every time I looked over there after this, I'd get the *frissons*. I have to go into town now though."

"What for?"

"I have to take some *Tête de Cabri* in to Marlene. She's on day shift at The Roadhouse."

"What's the matter with her?"

"She thinks she's coming down with something and she has to keep working because Brenda is in Corpus Christi on vacation. I'm going to teach her how to make a tea that'll knock it out."

"You sure that stuff works?"

"It worked on you last winter if you recall." Claudine picked up a frogleg with two fingers and nibbled at it.

"Yeah, I remember." Roy scraped up the last bite of fettucini and finished his beer. "Don't stay any longer in there than you have to. That place gets rough."

"I'm not worried about it. It doesn't bother Marlene to work there in the daytime. It's only at night it gets crazy."

"You never know what kind of assholes are going to show up in there. Remember when Cowboy got knifed in there a couple months ago? The cops get called out there three or four times a week."

"Yeah, but that's always at night. I'm just running in and out."

"I have to go in to the Sheriff's Office and make a statement sometime today." Roy wiped his mouth with a paper napkin, crumpled it, and tossed it onto his plate next to the slender frogleg bones.

"Make a statement? Does that mean Mitch thinks you had something to do with it?"

"No, no. Whoever discovers a body like that…well, they have to sign a paper that says how they found it…something along those lines." Roy stood. "Thank you for dinner. Delicious like always, chère." He smiled. "And now I'm off to the barn for some hay to mulch the garden. I've got my cell on me, so call me when you're on the way back from The Roadhouse so I know you're all right. Oh, and I almost forgot. Mitch says don't tell anybody about Gerald. He hasn't told his wife yet."

Claudine made a zip gesture with forefinger and thumb across her mouth. "Don't worry. I know how to keep my mouth shut. You need anything in town?"

"You could bring me a six-pack and some potato chips. You don't find a body every day. It kind of gets to you." Roy picked up his plate and carried it to the sink. "Poor old Gerald. It's always the good ones get killed. Never the sons-a-bitches."

"Oh, I can think of a few sons-a-bitches around here got themselves killed."

"Yeah, me too. Still, Gerald was a good man and we could use more like him in this parish. Too bad it wasn't that snooty wife of his instead."

"Hush up. She comes for treatments sometimes."

"Yeah, well try treating her for her attitude problem sometime."

"Oh, I think to be suddenly a single parent with a little boy to take care of...she's going to go through an attitude change all on her own."

"*Le Bon Dieu ne punit pas avec un baton,*" Roy pronounced, face somber.

"God doesn't punish with a stick is right." Claudine finished her food and stood, scooting the chair back with her legs.

17

T'BRO'S AUTO SHOP

Claudine drove slowly towards town along Delcambre Road, conscious of the bayou's brown waters, flecked with bright glimmers of sunlight flashing through the overhanging willows and water oaks. The water view was similar to what her great, great grandmother saw on a daily basis. Her grandparent, for whom she was named, grew up along this same bayou and farmed the same property and looked out at the same live oaks and cypresses that Claudine did each day.

She was on an errand her grandparent might also have run - delivering herbs to a client. She passed the first scattered frame houses and trailers on the outskirts of St. Beatrice, and a modest family owned gas station and grocery where old-timers in coveralls and visor caps advertising the local feed store, sat visiting on metal folding chairs, holding red Community Coffee Styrofoam cups and speaking in Cajun French as they did each morning.

She beeped at them in greeting and they waved in return. She passed T'Bro's Auto Shop and slowed, wondering if she should stop and check the air in her tires as long as she was right there. With gas going sky high she knew she had to keep up with that. She decided to wait. There was too much going on right now. She'd ask Roy to check them at home.

T'Bro was rolling a tire into the garage, shaggy black hair contrasting sharply with the faded blue of his mechanic's coveralls. He was moving toward a black pickup on the hydraulic lift. It reminded her of Gerald's truck so she braked and backed up a few feet to see better. There was a telltale sign on the rear window: *Keep Working. Millions of Welfare Recipients are Counting on You!* Claudine frowned and backed up a few more feet, so she could turn into the parking lot. She got out of the truck, hauling her big purse after her, and walked over to the double garage entrance, stopping at the bay where T'Bro was under the truck, neck cranked, peering up at the underside. "Hey, T'Bro. *Comment ça va?*"

"*Pas mauvais.*" T'Bro turned his head to see her and smiled. "Hey, Claudine. Where's Roy?"

"He's at the house. I'm just running an errand. What you doing?"

"I got to fix old Gerald's ball joint. It broke on our wonderful road last night." He placed a greasy hand firmly on the problem by the rear left wheel.

"Went into one too many potholes, huh?" Claudine spoke with what she hoped was a casual tone.

"*C'est vrai.* You hit enough of 'em, this is what happens to you." He stuck his bottom lip out, pondering the job ahead of him.

"All those casino billions were supposed to fix these roads," she said, turning away, eager to phone Mitch.

"Yeah, and your Ma ain't Catholic," he smiled at her. "You got something wrong with your pickup today?"

"No. I just stopped to check the air in my tires."

"Help yourself," he nodded toward the air pump.

"Thanks, T'Bro. I'll see you."

She walked back to the truck, pulling her cell out of an inside pocket of her purse, and retrieved the card Mitch had given her from a jeans pocket. She called the number and leaned against the front of the truck as she waited.

"Detective Lanclos."

"Hey, this is Claudine."

"What you got?"

"I'm at T'Bro's Shop." Her voice was high and excited. She lowered it and took a deep breath to slow herself down.

"And?"

"He's got Gerald's pickup on the lift. It's got a broken ball joint - from last night."

"What did you say to him?"

"Nothing. I didn't say anything."

"Tell him I said to stay right there. Tell him, don't let anybody near that truck," Lanclos barked. "And tell him not to do anything to it. Don't touch anything more than what he has already."

"Well, you don't have to yell at me. I'm the one found it. You could at least say thank you."

"We'd have found it. But thank you, if that's what you want. And keep your mouth shut about Gerald...to anybody. I mean anybody." He ended the call abruptly.

"Bastard," Claudine fumed, narrowing her eyes. "There's a limit," she said as she walked back toward the garage.

"What's the matter? You got trouble with the air hose?" T'Bro turned again from inspecting the pickup's damage.

"I got a message for you. Detective Lanclos says to stay right there and don't let anybody near Gerald's truck." Claudine pressed her lips together and slipped the cell back into her purse.

"Huh?" T'Bro tilted his head, forehead set into four deep creases. He took a red rag from his pocket and wiped his hands, twisting each finger into the cloth one at a time.

"What for?"

"He said he'd be right over." She shrugged and looked away, setting her lips into a firm line. "And he said don't do anything to it."

"Well, I'll be damned. Now how in the hell?" T'Bro stuffed the rag back into his pocket, walked back out from under the truck, stopping beneath the hitch and stared at her. "You working for the Sheriff's Office now, Claudine?"

"No, no. Just wait. He'll be right along." She took a few steps away. "I'm going to get on with my errands now. See you." She gave him a reassuring smile and crossed back toward her own truck, deciding to just go and not fool with the air pump. She didn't want to give Mitch another opportunity that day to irritate her. He'd already done it twice. She had the *Tête de Cabri* to deliver and when troubled, she knew the best remedy was to get on with her own business and shut everything and everybody out of her mind. She'd learned that philosophy the hard way, and she planned to stick with it for the rest of her life. It worked out much better than getting involved with other people's messes. Besides, she'd learned everybody was going to do whatever they wanted anyway, so why waste time interfering in their affairs?

18

MICHOT'S FEED STORE

Herman Delcambre marched into the fifty-foot wide metal building holding an antique black powder Kentucky rifle in the crook of his arm. He crossed past the piles of fifty-pound sacks of cracked corn and horse feed and dog feed that lined the path to the rear of the store. The smell of the various grains was heavy in the air and the warped floorboards creaked as he stomped his way to a small gathering of farmers who were sitting on tin chairs talking in Cajun French.

"What's wrong, Herman?" asked his cousin, Jean, who stood behind the counter at the cash register. He leaned over the counter, prepared for a story, as the other men halted their conversation about the encroaching soybean rust, and watched Delcambre attentively.

"I'll tell you what's wrong!" Delcambre held up the rifle, his hands covered with grey work gloves. "See this? Some son-bitches were in my woods last night outlaw hunting deer. I woke up in the middle of the night hearing a shot. I go out on the porch and see their damn lights. I run into the house for my shotgun. I pull on my pants and boots and run for the truck. But by the time I get all the way down the drive and across the road and into the woods, they're gone. I was so damn mad I couldn't get back to sleep all night." Delcambre's chest heaved as he took a few deep breaths, his face pinched with anger. He shook the rifle. "Then soon as it's light, I go back out there and walk around the woods, trying to figure out what went on last night."

The men slowly shook their heads in sympathy for the poaching, their lips firm with judgment. Jean came out from behind the counter and stood next to him in support.

"Then I see this! Lying on the ground by a fallen tree. They must have seen my porch lights come on and beat it on out of there so fast they dropped it. I got those bastards now. I'm taking it to the Sheriff's Department, and once they find out whose it is… they're going to jail. I'm so damned sick of these thieving outlaw hunters coming on my property. But before I drive over there, I wanted to come by here and calm down some. I don't want to go over there yelling and carrying on or they might throw me in jail."

"Hold it out for us to see. Maybe we've seen it before somewhere. It's a treasure," said Robert.

"Take it by the gunsmith first. Maybe he's worked on it before."

"Call Moise Angelle over at Fish & Wildlife," said Jean.

"I called him already. He's going to keep an eye out. He's the one told me to take it to the Sheriff's Department. Hell, I was going to keep it. It's got to be worth a few thousand."

"If they find out whose it is, it's confiscated anyhow. Make sure you get it back in that case. It was your property they were poaching."

"You're going to play hell getting it back. Something that valuable might just disappear from the property room. You better keep it. Chances are they'll never find the owner. And I doubt they'll spend too much time on it anyhow."

Claudine Bergeron entered the feed store then and walked to the counter, nodding at the men. Jean left Delcambre's side and rounded the corner of the counter to wait on her.

"Yes, ma'am. What'll it be today?" he smiled at her.

Claudine hooked thumbs into the back pockets of her jeans. "How you doing, Jean? It'll be fifty pounds of chopped corn. Two fifty-pound bags of that house dog feed you got. And a bottle of dog wormer."

Jean called to a young man who was stacking sacks of goat feed at the far side of the building. "Jo-Jo! Load Miss Claudine up with a fifty chopped corn and two fifty Redbone dog feed, you. The black Silverado out front."

Claudine paid her bill and took the brown paper bag of wormer and her receipt and change. She tucked the receipt and cash into her wallet and turned away from the counter, nodding to the men again. "How you all doing today?"

They smiled at her, nodding, and asking after her family. She spoke the niceties with them and eyed the rifle. "That's a beautiful antique you got there, Mister Herman. Looks almost like my great, great-granddaddy's."

"Is that right?" Delcambre said. "Come over here and have a look at it then."

He held it out toward her with both hands. "But don't touch it, please."

"Why, you afraid I'll snatch and grab it? I'd like to," she laughed, stepping forward. She kneeled before him where he sat and looked the gun over. "It's a beautiful gun. Your great, great-granddaddy's too? Civil War?"

"No, *Chère*. I'm sorry to say. It's some dirtbag trespasser at the farm. Probably stole it."

"That design on the silver is so handsome. It's a real beauty. Mine was made in Pennsylvania. And it's plainer than yours."

"This isn't mine."

"It is now," laughed Jean.

"Damn right it is," said Robert. "If he wouldn't be so hardheaded."

"Whose is it?" asked Claudine.

"That's what I'd like to find out. Some outlaw poachers left it in my woods last night. Night deer hunting with head lamps. I must have scared them off cause they left it."

"Mr. Herman! You better keep it. If they're poaching, they don't deserve to get it back."

"That's what we're trying to tell him." said Robert. "He wants to turn it over to the Sheriff's Department."

"Oh. I see. Well, that's a tough one. But I doubt they'd be able to find whose it is. And you might never get it back."

"See, Herman. This woman's smart. That's just what we're trying to tell him.

"Hang on to it. Lock it up in your gun cabinet, Herman."

Herman sighed, settling back in his chair. "You know, maybe I will. I'd hate to part with it." He gazed at it admiringly. "What the hell. I deserve it for the aggravation last night."

"Do it," said Claudine. "One of these days stop by the house and I'll show you the antique rifle I've got."

"I will. And I'll get a treatment for my bum knee while I'm at it. I haven't been over there for a long time."

"I know it. And we're neighbors after all."

"He owns so much land around here, he's neighbors to about fifty people," laughed Robert.

"I'll be by, Miss Claudine." Delcambre nodded, and she said her goodbyes and made her way down the aisle toward the double barn doors. Jo-Jo was coming back inside from loading her truck as she exited and tipped him a dollar. "Thanks, Jo-Jo. See you next time."

He tipped his Michot Feed Store visor cap and passed on back inside the building.

19

LANCLOS AT T'BRO'S AUTO REPAIR

L anclos could barely restrain himself and keep somewhere close to the speed limit on his way to town and T'Bro's Auto Shop. He squealed his tires as he rounded a curve hard by the bayou, narrowly missing a danger sign that marked a ten foot wide and six foot deep drainage ditch that drained from soybean fields into the bayou.

He couldn't wait to take custody of Gerald's pickup. Who knew how much it had been tampered with already? Soon he'd be able to dust it for prints, and he'd be able to interview T'Bro about the circumstances leading to the truck being in his garage.

Lanclos felt the blood singing through his veins, and his energy level was the highest it had been all week. He loved nothing better than a new case and a puzzle to be solved. He was sad for St. Beatrice to lose Gerald Theriot, who had never done anything to anyone. However, the possibility of a new murder case to work on invigorated him. He'd been obsessing over his cases for years. Lanette never had him at home. She'd always been alone, even when he was physically in the house. His mind was usually elsewhere, on whatever case he was working at the time.

Lanette had never understood his love of the undercurrent of tension and unrest that thrived in Louisiana. She was a nester, a nurturer, and loved nothing more than to stay home on the farm and garden. She was totally reliable, and he had never had the slightest complaint about living with her. She showed consideration for what he did and stayed out of his way. She never complained about how he was absent in so many ways for their whole married life. He secretly believed his detachment was the main reason for her wasting away, finally dying of pancreatic cancer.

He had never confessed this to anyone. Certainly not to their son who still lived on the farm and commuted to U.L. in Lafayette each day. Paul had bonded so strongly with his mother that Lanclos didn't want to give him a reason to resent his father more than he already did. And he certainly didn't want to cause him any more grief than he was still experiencing now, only a year and a half after her death.

As Lanclos arrived at T'Bro's, he immediately spotted the black pickup and slowly pulled in to the garage door, just four feet from where the truck sat, elevated by the lift. T'Bro was working under the hood of a Trans Am in the next bay, only coming out from under when Lanclos slammed his own truck door.

Ajax, T'Bro's younger brother, slid from beneath the Trans Am on a crawler, and still supine, raised his head and regarded Lanclos. He wore greasy blue coveralls and scuffed black motorcycle boots. His black hair hung straight below his ears; his face was a narrower version of T'Bro's. Even though younger, Ajax looked older than his brother, owing to a heavily creased face and tired, sunken eyes. "Hey, Detective," he said, waving with the wrench he held in his left hand, then slid back underneath the Trans Am.

"Hey, T'Bro. Hey, Ajax. How you all doing?" Lanclos spoke easily, not wanting to put T'Bro on his guard. If he made him nervous, he might forget some important detail during their interview.

"Hey, Detective. I'll be right with you. Just give me a few seconds."

Lanclos ducked and stepped under Gerald's truck, looking for any damage that had occurred. He peered up at the broken ball joint, studying it, until T'Bro joined him and assured him he hadn't begun working on it yet. "I got your message to stay away from it," he said.

"Let's go into your office and talk. Can we do that?" Lanclos asked.

"Sure we can. Come on. You want some coffee? I always keep a fresh pot around when I'm working. They say caffeine helps you think, did you know that?"

"I live on it. Let's go." Lanclos walked with him toward the back of the garage and to a narrow office with an open door. Another door led out the back of the building and Lanclos saw T'Bro's yellow vinyl-sided house at the back of the lot against a background of pine trees. T'Bro's red tow truck was parked there next to a Toyota Avalon.

"You're doing good, T'Bro. I see you bought an Avalon. That for your wife? Everytime I see you, it's in a truck."

"Nah. That's not mine. It's for a customer." T'Bro walked around the side of a black metal desk and sat heavily on a cushioned office chair, motioning for Lanclos to sit on one of the two gray metal chairs in front of the desk. "Have a seat, Detective. Wait. I forgot the coffee." He got back up and crossed the room to a shelf where a coffeemaker kept a glass pot full of dark brew steaming hot. He poured them each a cup in purple and gold Mardi Gras mugs and handed one to Lanclos.

"You take anything in it?"

"I drink it black. Thanks."

T'Bro carried a few sugar packets to his desk and tearing off the corners of each, busied himself sweetening his mug. He stirred it slowly with a white plastic fork and when he finished, pushed out his lips and took a tentative taste. "Whew, that's hot. Watch it!"

"Ajax doing okay?" he asked. He knew Ajax still had brain damage from a fearful wreck that T'Bro had caused fifteen years before when he was still drinking and drugging. He also knew that T'Bro had felt so guilty about Ajax being thrown from the smashed truck and his subsequent two month coma and injuries, that he'd taken Ajax in and looked after him ever since. There had been small improvements over the years as new pathways had developed in Ajax's brain, but he was still a slow learner and his moods were unpredictable. Everybody in St. Beatrice was pleased to know that T'Bro had sought redemption for what he'd done by taking good care of Ajax over the years, and no one had ever seen him take another drink since the accident.

"He's doing good. He's a big help to me. You know I have a lot of business."

Lanclos nodded. "You've done a good job with him." He paused as T'Bro's wife, Cecilia, came into the office with a handful of papers. Short and petite with long, shiny black hair falling half-way down her back, she wore denim cutoffs and a striped low-cut knit top showing more cleavage than was proportional for such a small woman.

"And what's the Sheriff's Office want with us today?" she smiled as she laid the papers into a wire tray on the corner of the desk.

"Just want to ask T'Bro a few questions," Lanclos said, smiling back at her.

"Okay, I know when I'm not wanted." She pointed to the papers. "Those need attention today, please," she said and turned back toward the door leading to the house.

Lanclos waited until she was gone, then settled back in his chair, hands folded in his lap. "So, tell me all about how you came by Gerald's pickup. Everything you can remember."

T'Bro took a deep breath and blew out air as he thought. His eyes flicked up and to the side as he recollected the events of the night before. "Okay. He calls me in the middle of the night and tells me he's in a ditch and could I come pull him out. I look at the clock. It's somewheres around three-thirty, I think. The bedside clock is illuminated, but I'm groggy and half asleep. But I think it's about that time. Cecilia slept through the whole thing. I whisper to him that I'll get it first thing in the morning, and would that be all right, cause I'm exhausted, and felt half sick. See, I picked up something somewhere. I was just getting over it, but I'd taken some nighttime cold medicine, and you know how that shit knocks you out. I could tell he didn't like hearing it, but Gerald's the kind of guy who doesn't get angry easy, so he said all right. He'd just have to sleep in the truck. He told me he was wore out anyway, and he had a pillow and blanket in the back of the double cab. I told him I'd get there first thing when I woke up and I'd bring him some hot coffee and doughnuts."

T'Bro looked at Lanclos as though to check on how his ver-sion of the story was going over. Lanclos nodded, not wanting to interrupt his train of thought. His eyes flicked up and to the right again. "So then, I go right back to sleep. And then the phone rings. And it's Gerald again. Only this time he tells me he's changed his mind and he's going to take off cause every time he dozes off, a truck or a car goes by and he wakes up. He tells me he's got a key in one of those magnetic metal cases stuck inside the front left fender. He tells me to tow it back to my shop, figure out what the damage was, and fix it. He'd call me in the morning. He says he's near his property at Miss Philomena's and he'll just walk over there and sleep on the porch or something. I say okay, that's fine. And then I go right back to sleep again. No more phone calls the rest of the night." T'Bro shrugged and held his palms out in a gesture of finality. He picked up his mug and slurped coffee, holding up a finger to signal he was taking a break.

Lanclos waited patiently, glancing briefly at a framed photo of T'Bro posing by a stock car at a dirt track. "Okay. So next morning I go where he said. There's the truck. There's the key where he said it was. I hitch it up, yank it out of the ditch, and haul it back here. I put it on the lift. I see the broken ball joint. Then here comes Claudine. She recognizes the truck, calls you, and then marches back to relay your orders not to touch it. So what is it, Detective? Gerald hit somebody or something?"

"Hang on. Do you remember anything unusual about where it was stuck? Anything at all."

T'Bro shook his head slowly from side to side. "Naw. Just a ditch. A few beer cans. Bottles. Fast food bags. The usual dumbass litter you see along the roads around here."

"Okay. I'm going to dust it for prints. Nobody but you has touched the truck, is that right?"

"No. I mean that's right. Nobody but me. Unless somebody messed with it after he took off last night. Now that I can't vouch for."

"Did Gerald sound all right when you talked to him? Sober?"

"I can't say nothing about nobody drinking and driving, me." T'Bro looked down at his coffee.

"So what you're saying is, he sounded like he was drinking," pressed Lanclos.

T'Bro shook his head. "Like I said, Detective, I can't say nothing about nobody's drinking and driving, me." He still didn't meet Lanclos' eyes.

"All right. I'll take that to mean he sounded like he was drinking. So...I think we're done here. For now." Lanclos stood, leaving his half empty coffee mug on the desk. "I'll get back with you if I need to. In the meantime, let me know if you think of anything at all. Any little detail you might have forgotten." He placed his card on the desk. "You can always get me on the cell phone."

T'Bro picked up the card and leaning back, opened the center drawer of his desk and dropped it inside. "I'll do that. But you still didn't tell me what's so important about the truck."

"Later maybe." Lanclos turned and headed for the door. As he passed through, he glanced through the backdoor window toward T'Bro's house. "How come you got customers bringing new Avalons here to you instead of to the dealers? That car's gotta still be on warranty." He nodded toward the gleaming white sedan.

T'Bro laughed. "You know what kind of reputation I have as a mechanic, Detective."

"I know you're good at what you do, T'Bro." Lanclos headed toward Gerald's pickup. "How about lowering the truck so I can go over it. I'll be here a while."

20

CLAUDINE TIPS LANCLOS

Main Street changed names on the outskirts of St. Beatrice, becoming Delcambre Road. Claudine noted Detective Lanclos' pickup as she passed T'Bro's, and took her foot off the gas for a few seconds, as it occurred to her that she should report Herman Delcambre's newly found rifle. Even though it was a poaching situation, it was only a quarter mile from her house, and could have implications for his investigation.

But then, she remembered how surly and ungrateful he had sounded that morning already, and put her foot back on the gas once more. She'd helped him twice already and received no appreciation, so the hell with it. In the event the poaching incident had any connection with Gerald's death, let Mitch find out about it on his own. He'd already told her he'd have found out anything she'd already reported in his own time. So let him. He was on his own. If he still wanted to hold a grudge twenty-five years later, that was on him. She had no control over other people's thoughts, grudges, resentments, etc.

When she'd driven a quarter of a mile, however, her conscience started bothering her. What if the black powder rifle did have something to do with Gerald's death? If Delcambre held onto it, and didn't take it down to the Sheriff's Office as he initially planned, Mitch might never hear about it. And all the men at the feed store had pretty much talked him out of turning the gun in.

She sighed, checked her rear view mirror and turned around in a rutted grassy entrance that tractors used to enter a field.

"Here we go again," she said, heading back to T'Bro's.

Mitch's pickup was parked next to a Sheriff's Office patrol car, and both were parked in front of the bay where Gerald's truck was now back down off the lift.

Lanclos was kneeling by the driver's door examining the floor. Farrell LeBlanc, a deputy in black uniform, was standing beside him. Mitch turned away from his work to nod at her as she closed her truck door and slowly walked toward him.

"I need to talk to you," she said, her voice sounding tense, and not like she'd intended. She resolved to modify her tone. She didn't want him to think he'd gotten to her.

He stepped away from the truck and came toward her, a questioning look on his face. He indicated she should move away from the garage with a brief jerk of his head. They both walked to the rear of her pickup. Mitch leaned an arm on her tailgate and waited. "What you got?"

"I thought you might like to know something I found out at the feed store just now," she said, her tone still revealing irritation, despite the attempt to sound detached.

"All right, let's have it," he said.

The sun was in her eyes, so she pulled her visor lower. "Herman Delcambre says he had poachers last night in his woods. He heard a shot and so he got out of bed, went outside and scared them off. When he got down there at daylight, he found a black powder rifle lying by a fallen tree. I didn't know if that might have some connection to....Gerald's death," she finished, lowering her eyes from Lanclos' bold stare, and crossing her arms.

Lanclos watched her for a moment without speaking as he thought about the information. He finally turned his head and followed a sugar cane truck with his eyes as it rolled slowly toward town, cane husks flying out and littering the road. "Anything else? You see the rifle?"

"Yes, he had it with him. It looks like my heirloom. Except it's got fancy scroll work on the plate."

"You just left there?" He glanced back at her.

"Yes. Not five minutes ago."

"Farrell," he called. "I got to go! Stay by the truck. I'll be right back."

"I got it," called LeBlanc, raising a hand to acknowledge the order, as Lanclos turned away from her pickup and hurried to his own truck.

He slid into his pickup, started the engine, backed up, and took off without another look at Claudine. She was speechless as she watched him gun the motor and head back towards town.

"You're welcome," she finally called as he sped down the road.

T'Bro came up behind her. "Like I said, Claudine. You sure you're not working for the Sheriff's Office?"

"Yeah, T'Bro," she whirled and barked at him. "I'm undercover! What you think?" She brushed by him, got in her truck, slammed the door, and backed up as he scrambled to get out of her way. She was so angry, she peeled off out of his parking lot like she was sixteen years old and headed south, pounding the steering wheel with one hand and yelling, "Mitch, you sonofabitch! Mitch, you sonofabitch!" all the way home.

21

LANCLOS CHASES THE RIFLE

L anclos headed off from the feed store down the Old St. Regis
Highway. He was headed for the auction barn ten miles out
of town toward the small French town of St. Regis. He had
learned at Michot's Feed Store that Delcambre had taken himself
and his new black powder rifle away from the socializing circle of
farmers to attend the weekly livestock auction at Perrodin's.

He drove fast past miles of harvested cane fields, the brown,
broken stalks all that was left of the once brilliant green of the
graceful, waving sugar cane. He only hoped, fast as he was going
that he didn't slam into a slow-moving cane wagon or tractor. He
felt he had to hurry in case Delcambre got around to letting someone touch that rifle. He'd already asked the old men at the feed
store if anybody had touched it, and they all chorused, "*Mais, non!*"

Lanclos still hadn't had a chance to change out of his farm
clothes, so he would blend right in with the farmers who fre-
quented the auction barn. He slowed a mile before the barn as he
passed through an assortment of warehouses and businesses such
as a fence company, a cement company, a gravel and shell yard,
and still another feed store.

The tomato red auction barn stood in the middle of an expanse
of grass and a packed dirt parking lot. Several dozen trucks were
parked on both sides of the building. Some were new, sleek double-cab models, some older beat-up pickups. There were about a
dozen thirty-foot trailers attached to some of the heavier trucks.

They were empty from either having transported cattle, hogs, or horses to the auction, or empty because the owner was inside buying livestock to take back to the farm.

As Lanclos drove around the parking lot, he looked for Delcambre's truck. Toward the rear of the red metal building where the five hundred foot stockyard began, he spotted the older gray three-quarter ton Ford that Delcambre had been driving for years. Lanclos found a parking space nearby and after locking his own gray pickup, walked along the row of trucks until he was abreast of Delcambre's.

He peered into the locked side window. There in the gun rack above the seat was the rifle. He stared at it with a sigh of relief. It was safely in the rack where no one, for the moment at least, could touch it. He turned to begin his search for Delcambre, so he could get his own hands on that weapon as quickly as possible. Walking fast to the huge metal building, he entered by a side door and worked his way through the high-ceilinged vast front office, past yards of bulletin boards advertising hay, hunting dogs, quarter horses, and acreage, and through a dark metal door into the auction arena.

The arena was packed with farmers in overalls, coveralls, plain jeans, and khakis. They wore an assortment of visor caps advertising feed stores, pipelines, oil field supply outfits, and other area businesses. Some of the men wore camouflage as if they were stopping off on their way out of town for a hunting trip. There were close to a hundred men sprawled on the semicircle of ten tiers of wooden built-in benches, most of them conversing in Cajun French.

Lanclos scanned the crowd, as a worker opened the wooden door to the stockyard and zapped a half dozen pigs with his Hot Shot stick as they hurtled into the bullpen, positioned to the left of the entry door. The auctioneer, high in his open window, and in full voice, began the auctioneer spiel as the pigs squealed in protest at the electric shock from the two-pronged Hot Shot.

Some of the men held up hands in recognition as they saw Lanclos, then returned their attention to the bidding on the pigs. Lanclos, satisfied that Delcambre was elsewhere, stepped carefully along the third tier of benches, as men shuffled their boots to let him pass. He headed for the elevated door to the catwalk that led out into the stockyard, hoping he'd find Delcambre there, inspecting the cattle in the holding pens.

Sure enough, Delcambre was at the end of the two hundred foot wooden catwalk, leaning on the railing and watching a cowboy checking out a cutting horse fifteen feet below in a wide aisle between rows of pens. As he walked along the catwalk, the cattle below in the pens, lowed and bellowed by turns, crowded into their new and unfamiliar surroundings. Calves huddled beside their mothers, and all the animals had numbers attached to their backs.

Ordinarily, Lanclos would have taken the time to look the animals over. But he didn't want to waste a moment getting to Delcambre and finding out whatever there was to know about the black powder rifle.

"Herman!" he called.

Delcambre's broad back was curved as he watched the cowboy below. He straightened at the sound of his name and turned to see. "Hey, Mitch. *Comment ça va?*"

"*Bien, et tu?*" Lanclos bellied up to the railing as the cowboy backed up the cutting horse with a gentle tug of the reins. "Herman, that black powder rifle you found in your woods?"

"Uh-oh. I had a feeling about that rifle." Delcambre twisted his mouth into an expression of displeasure, as both men leaned on the railing watching the cowboy who now worked the horse sideways a few steps, first to the left, and then to the right.

"Anybody touch it but you?"

"No. Like I said, I had a feeling about it. I didn't let anybody touch it."

"Mind if I take it for a while? I can't tell you why just yet, but I'll give you a property receipt of course, and if it's not what I think it is, I'll bring it back to you out at the farm immediately. Maybe as soon as tonight."

Delcambre shrugged. "You're the boss. It's locked out there in my truck right now."

"Let's go." Lanclos jerked his head in the direction of the parking lot, and the two men started back across the stockyard, the cattle complaining loudly of their fate in the holding pens below.

22

LANCLOS BREAKS THE NEWS

L anclos, the rifle safely stowed in the gunrack of his truck, headed down the St. Regis Highway back toward St. Beatrice. While in conversation with Delcambre, he had learned of the circumstances at the man's farm the night before. He had listened to Herman's version of the events of the night for about fifteen minutes before sending him back to the auction barn, and had full cooperation from the farmer regarding the gun. Without telling him about Gerald's death, he told him he was investigating a situation, and that the gun might have significance in the matter, and he promised him he'd return the gun to him if he couldn't find the rightful owner. Now he had the unpleasant task ahead of him of informing Celeste of the death of her husband, which made his stomach tighten.

He hadn't eaten anything since breakfast and was feeling hungry, but he had to talk with Celeste first, before she found out from someone else. He wished he'd had time to change out of his farm clothes since that morning, but his farm was not on the way to Gerald and Celeste's house in town, and he didn't want to take the time to drive out to the farm and change because he wanted to be the one to tell her of the death. He had to observe her reaction and ask her some questions. If it weren't for following up on Claudine's discovery of Gerald's truck and wanting to chase down the rifle before anyone else touched it, he'd have been at Celeste's house over an hour ago.

As he followed the highway, passing pickups and the occasional sedan, he focused on what Delcambre had reported to him. Reviewing the events of the night before in the woods on the bayou across the road from Herman's farmhouse, he played several possibilities in his mind. Much as if he were watching a movie, he allowed several scenarios to play out in his mind's eye.

When Mitch concentrated on the possibilities relevant to an investigation, he could not only see in his mind's eye, but touch, taste, and smell as well. He had the ability to enter into these imaginary scenes as thoroughly as if he were actually there. Lanclos had a natural ability to imagine scenes so real he could lose himself in them and be lost for hours. It was a peculiar strategy, but it had always worked for him. If an imagined possible scene appeared to fit with the facts as he knew them at the time, he would play with it until the emerging facts no longer worked with that particular scene in his imagination.

His ability to do this, he was sure, had a lot to do with his tendency in childhood and teenage years to stare out the windows of his classrooms and transport himself elsewhere. He had been so adept at these reveries that classroom teachers could call out his name and he wouldn't respond. They thought he was being obstinate; he knew he just hadn't heard them.

By the time he reached the city limits of St. Beatrice, he snapped out of his trance and started watching for Evangeline St. where he needed to turn for the Theriot house. Halfway down the street, he saw the white frame house with the wide porch and two front doors. He pulled in the shell drive and saw Celeste's sedan parked in front of the wooden garage set toward the rear of the property, surrounded by pink and red ten foot high camellia bushes.

He parked halfway into the shell driveway. Blue hydrangea bushes lined that side of the house. An aggressive wisteria twined its way into the siding of the house, its trailing branches even working their way into the cypress hurricane shutters and toward the soffits of the gleaming new red metal roof. A blue jay in one of two ancient cedar trees in the front yard scolded a tiger cat sharpening claws on the bark.

He sighed as he walked toward the house, part of him dreading telling the wife what had transpired; part of him eager to learn all he could from her about the rifle and the events of the night before. A dozen hanging baskets of flowering houseplants decorated the wide front porch. White wicker chairs, plant stands and a ceiling fan provided an inviting atmosphere to the area. While he waited for Celeste to answer the door, he distracted himself from his unpleasant mission by studying the design of the outdoor fan and debated installing one on his own front porch.

Celeste opened the door a few inches, then seeing who it was, she opened it wide, and smiled. "Mitch Lanclos! I haven't seen you for…." Seeing his serious expression, her face fell, mouth open in mid-sentence. "Oh, no. What? What is it, Mitch?" She stepped back, clapping a hand to her mouth as he opened the screen door and entered.

"Hello, Celeste," he said softly. He bit his tongue, trying to pace himself. "May we sit down?"

"Oh, please, yes. Come on over here." Forehead lined with worry, she led him to a seating arrangement in a far corner of the front room. She motioned for him to sit in a wingback chair. "What happened?" she asked dully, her hand now at her throat as she stood in front of him, managing to keep her voice steady.

"Why don't you sit down first?" He settled himself into the comfortable chair, and waited for her to sit on the couch opposite him. Over the tapestry covered couch hung a framed print of a duck hunter, chocolate Lab by his side, against an autumn wetlands landscape.

Between them lay a highly waxed coffee table with an assortment of magazines. *American Rifleman* and *Southern Living* were neatly arranged next to a crystal candy dish. A silver container of potpourri threatened to make him sneeze. He could feel the warning tickling in his nose. This was no time for sneezing, so he picked up a magazine and laid it on top of the mixture.

Celeste sat primly, knees together and legs angled to the side. She folded her hands, quietly waiting for whatever was to come, her face a mask. Despite gauze draperies, light streamed in from tall sill windows on the south side of the room lending her face a golden glow and making her wide eyes sparkle.

Lanclos sat forward and placed one hand flat on each knee. He cleared his throat. "I'm very sorry to have to tell you, Celeste, that we found Gerald dead today."

"What do you mean dead? He can't be dead." She stared at him, uncomprehending. He moved closer to the edge of his seat, prepared for anything she might say or do.

"We don't know what happened to him," he spoke slowly and softly, watching her carefully. "That's what I'm trying to find out."

Her face tightened as the news began to sink in. She squinted, peering at him as though she couldn't see clearly, and tilting her head. "That isn't possible. Not Gerald! You're mixing him up with somebody else. He's fine! There's nothing wrong with Gerald," she babbled, voice rasping.

"Roy Bergeron was checking his traps on the bayou. He found Gerald lying on the bayou bank by Miss Philomena's property and called us this morning."

"Miss Philomena's?" she said, voice rising. Her face grew pale as she began breathing rapidly. "Miss Philomena's did you say?" She tugged at the fingers of her left hand with her right, voice shrill. "She killed my Gerald? That old lady?"

"No, no, no." Lanclos made a calming gesture with his hand. "She has no idea what happened. Are you all right? Can I fetch you a glass of water?" He half rose from the chair.

She waved a hand back and forth. "I'm okay!" she protested, voice louder. "Why can't they tell what happened to him? What was he doing over there?" Her neck was red and the color quickly rising to her face, almost matching the red of her lipstick.

"I was hoping you could tell us something about that. Do you have any idea why he'd be over at Miss Philomena's?"

She shook her head slowly, lips slightly open, eyes glazing.

"Are you certain of that? Think back," Lanclos narrowed his eyes as he watched her.

"I can't think why," her voice trailed off as she began to cry. Hot tears ran down her face, and she wiped them with the back of her hands. She made choking sounds as she cried.

Lanclos waited patiently, remaining very still, not taking his eyes off her.

When she became visibly calmer, he threw out another question. "Did Gerald have any health problems?"

"No, never," she answered quickly, sitting up straighter.

"The medical examiner will have some answers for us later today, I'm sure. In the meantime, I want you to tell me anything you can about last night. Are you sure you're all right though? Why don't you let me get you a drink at least?" he offered.

She closed her eyes for a moment, then slowly opened them and met his gaze. "Really, I'm okay." She took a deep breath, and looked out the windows to her left, swallowing hard. Her voice broke, but she gamely began to speak of the night before. "He had been out by the levee at Maurice Saison's camp. He's an old friend. But I'm sure you know that. He came back late. They'd cooked out there so he wasn't home for supper. I'm not sure of the time, but I was already getting ready for bed. He was going back out there to spend the night. He said they'd done a little hunting, and he wanted to shoot some more squirrels. He loved squirrel in brown gravy." At this, she started to cry again, bowing her head and placing her face in her hands. "I'm sorry," she fluttered a hand toward him. "I can't help it."

Lanclos looked around the room for a tissue. Seeing none, he pulled a clean, folded blue bandana from his jeans pocket and crossed the room with it. He sat beside her and offered it to her. "Here, wipe your eyes with this."

Celeste raised her face, now streaked and blotched, took the pressed and folded bandana and pressed it to her eyes.

"Look, may I go into the kitchen and get you a drink, please?"

She nodded without speaking, silently crying and blotting her eyes.

He passed from the living room to the kitchen beyond and went straight to the refrigerator. Opening it, he quickly found a can of Dr. Pepper and then opened a cabinet looking for a glass. He selected a glass and hurried back to her with the drink.

Celeste touched the sides of her eyes with the now unfolded bandana. "Thank you," she said, as he popped open the soda and slowly poured it into the tilted glass.

"Keep sipping this. It'll help."

She obediently took a few sips and then leaned back against some throw pillows, closing her eyes, and holding the glass with both hands as though she might drop it.

Lanclos returned to his seat. "Can you go on now?"

She nodded. "Yes. Thank God our son is at my sister's. I don't know how to tell him. He worships his father."

Lanclos waited.

"That's about all I know. He told me he'd be back sometime today, and later on maybe we'd drive to Lafayette and take in a movie."

"So what time do you think he left?"

"It must have been around eleven-thirty. Maybe a little later. I'm not sure. To tell you the truth, I wasn't interested in the time because I was reading a really good crime book about a lawyer who's accused of killing his wife." Her eyes widened, and she swallowed when she realized what she'd said. "Oh, Mitch. I would never do anything to hurt Gerald."

Lanclos nodded. "I'm not here because I think you had anything to do with this, Celeste. But I have to figure out what happened to him."

She closed her eyes and took a deep breath.

"Did he go off hunting often?"

There was a pause. Her eyelids fluttered. "More so at the beginning of each hunting season than towards the close. I'm used to it." She looked visibly better, and despite some puffiness under the eyes, she appeared to be collecting herself.

"Do you know of any trouble he's had with anyone recently?"

"Everybody liked Gerald. I don't have to tell you that. You already know it's true. He did say someone put a curse on him though." She took another sip of the soda.

"A curse?"

"Yes. Alfred, I don't know his last name. That nephew of Miss Philomena. You know who I mean?" She looked at him for confirmation.

He gave a quick nod. "I know Alfred. His last name is Narcisse."

"That's right. That's him. He put some weird curse on Gerald at the barber shop a few days ago. He was angry with Gerald because we had to ask his aunt to move into town so we could build out there. The property belongs to Gerald's family, and his father said we could build on it if we wanted." She pressed her lips together as if to silence herself.

"A curse, huh? Well, well, in this day and age." Lanclos withdrew his pocket notebook and flipping it open, began writing. "And what day was this?"

"Okay. Today is Friday. The night he told me was chicken night. That would be Wednesday."

"Chicken night?"

"I have set menus for each day of the week. I guess that makes me kind of a control freak, huh?"

"Not necessarily. Can you think of anything else?"

"You mean about anybody giving Gerald trouble?"

"Anything at all."

She sat in silence for a moment, then shook her head. "Not really. I can't think of any problems he had with anybody."

"How about you? Did you and Gerald have any problems?"

"Not more than any married couple, I guess. We argued once in a while. Not that often."

"When's the last time?" He watched her expectantly.

"You mean the last time we argued?"

"Yes."

"I'd have to think about that for a minute." She closed her eyes again and leaned her head back against the cushions. Her jaw worked back and forth as she thought it over. She opened her eyes and kept her head back, resting on the back of the couch, as though she were too weary to raise it again. "The other night we argued a little bit about when Miss Philomena should have to leave to move into town. I wanted her to be moved sooner than Gerald did. He wanted to give her more time, as much as she needed."

"You wanted to speed things up?"

"Yes. I said it would drag on forever if we did it his way." She looked out the window. "I told him he was too nice to everybody." Celeste started crying again and pressed the back of one hand against her forehead. She grabbed one of the throw pillows with

Happiness is Homemade embroidered on it and clutched it to her abdomen.

Lanclos waited her out, alternately watching her and taking notes. When she stopped crying, he gently asked her if that was all they argued about. She nodded.

"That's all I can remember."

"Can you think of any family member who may have been angry with Gerald?"

"Oh, no. Like I said, he got along with everybody."

"Everybody in the family?"

"Everybody." She pushed out her chin for emphasis.

"All right then." He closed his notebook. "I just have to ask you one more thing and I'll leave you in peace."

"Yes?"

"Would you please come out to my truck and look at a black powder rifle I have in the gun rack? I want to see if you recognize it as Gerald's. I didn't want to bring it in with me. I don't want to handle it more than I have to in case it is his."

"You found it with his body?"

"No. Down the road from the scene, as a matter of fact. I just have a hunch it might be his."

"He did take a gun with him to Maurice's. I haven't looked in the gun cabinet to see what he took."

"Come on then and see for yourself." Lanclos stood and turned toward the door, opening it for her. Celeste slowly crossed the room and passed through the screen door as he followed her outside.

As they walked toward his truck, she raised the wet balled up bandana. "I'll wash this and get it back to you."

"Keep it. I have a dozen of those things." He led her to the passenger side of the truck, opened the door, and pointed to the racked gun.

"Please don't touch it, but tell me if you recognize it."

It took only a glance. "Oh, yes. That's Gerald's for sure. See that long scratch on the stock? He would never allow the gunsmith to smooth that out. He kept that gun exactly like it was when his father gave it to him five years ago. He said that scratch was part of

American history. It was his great grandfather's in the Confederate Army."

"I can just imagine the history of that gun. Look where the forearm is bowed with wear. But the thing is, Gerald wouldn't use a rifle to shoot squirrels. There wouldn't be anything left of the squirrel! So that doesn't make sense. Think back. Are you sure he said he was squirrel hunting with Maurice Saison?"

Celeste frowned, looked again at the gun, then her eyes flicked first to the left and then to the right as she recollected. After a moment, she brought her gaze back to his. "I'm sure he said that he and Maurice had been squirrel hunting out at the camp."

"Okay. There must be some other explanation. Thank you, Celeste. I'm sorry I had to ask you all these questions on such a sad day as this."

"That's all right, Mitch. I know you're trying to do your job. Please call me as soon as you know anything more," she sniffed, then dabbed at her nose with the blue handkerchief.

"You can count on it." He closed the truck door. "Are you going to call someone to be with you? Can I take you to your sister's?"

She shook her head. "I'm going to go in and call her pretty soon, but first I need to be alone for a little while. My head is splitting. I need to lie down."

"All right. Here's my card. Call me if you think of anything you may have forgotten."

"I will. I promise." She took the card and slipped it into a skirt pocket. "Goodbye, Mitch." She turned and walked back toward the house. He watched her walk slowly away, at first with spine erect, then slowly her shoulders rounded and her back curved as the weight of her loss bore down upon her.

23

AT CASTILLE'S CAFE

After inspecting Gerald's truck and towing it to the Impound
Yard, Lanclos decided to drive over to Castille's for a quick
meal. He was hungry and uncomfortable conducting all
this business in his work clothes. Yet he still didn't want to take
the time to drive out to the farm and change clothes or eat, so
he turned left on Main St. and headed up toward the café at the
corner of Main and Bridge Streets.

The café was a faded brick building left over from the twenties.
The apartments upstairs were rented out to Jeff, the cook, and
Annie, the waitress, a newcomer in town from Arkansas.

Lanclos found a dark varnished booth toward the back and settled himself in it facing toward the front of the restaurant. When
Annie approached him with a menu, a mug, and a pot of coffee,
he smiled for the first time that day. "Hello, Annie. Yes to the coffee, but don't go yet. I'll take a quick look at the menu and tell you
what I want right now. I'm in a hurry."

"That's fine, Detective. I'll wait. Our dinner rush is over." She
poured his coffee slowly and with care, as she did everything, no
matter how busy the café was. Then she stood with one hand on
her hip waiting for his order.

"That special any good today?"

"It was so good we're out of it." She nodded at the clock over
the front door. "We ran out about 12:30. You just missed it. You

know better than to come in here this late." She tilted her head and tightened the back of a pearl earring.

He sighed. "I can't catch up today. Okay, how about just bringing me a bowl of the chicken gumbo? Remember, it's got to be steaming hot."

She nodded. "I know," she recited. "So hot it'll burn your mouth."

"That's how I like it." He paused, deciding. "And a side of potato salad and a side of red beans. Okay? Oh, and you better throw in some cornbread. Please." He handed her back the menu and pulled out his notebook while he waited for the food.

As he flipped through the notes, one part of his mind was planning his next move. He decided to drive by Alfred's trailer and try to catch him at home before he drove out to the levee to interview Maurice Saison. The chances that he'd find Alfred home were slim to none, but at least he could leave his card. Alfred spent half his life driving around the area on his bicycle. The man must have the best cardiovascular system in St. Beatrice Parish. Not only did he not have a license any more after three D.U.I.s, but he couldn't have afforded a car anyway as he had never held a job as long as Lanclos had known him.

It was difficult for him to focus on his notes. Distracting thoughts bounced around in his mind, and being hungry didn't help his concentration. Various items on his agenda competed for attention. He hadn't brought up the information Philomena had given him about the conversation between Celeste and her sister, Georgette, regarding Leon LeDoux. He would though. He had to feel the time was right. If he got lucky maybe he could ask about their conversation when both the women were together. And after he interviewed Alfred and Maurice, maybe he'd be able to learn some solid information from Rusty Meaux, the medical examiner. And he had to call Moise Angelle to ask him to accompany him to Delcambre's woods so the farmer could show them where he found Gerald's rifle. Going there with Moise, an expert tracker, tripled his chances of finding something helpful in those woods. As long as Delcambre was sure someone was poaching in his woods the night before, Moise was going to be interested in helping him explore those woods. Moise was hell on outlaw hunters. Always had been, always would be.

He hadn't been at all satisfied with Celeste's blowing off his questions about the time Gerald left the night before. She was into some page-turner of a crime book and didn't notice the time. How many wives wouldn't notice what time a husband took off late at night? And she also minimized the argument they'd had about Philomena and the time it would take to relocate her. And he bet that argument was a shouting match, especially if Gerald was spitting out accusations against her brother-in-law.

Nothing that Lanclos hadn't heard before, but apparently Celeste had never heard those rumors about LeDoux. Lanclos knew from years in the Sheriff's Office that where there was smoke, there was fire, but evidence was required to put out the fire, and so far the Sheriff's Office had no evidence on Leon. It didn't mean they would never get any evidence on him, but to this date there was none.

However, Lanclos was a patient man. He was certain that one day, somehow, some dirt bagger would give them what they needed to save his own skin. It never failed. It was only a question of time.

"Here you go," said Annie, approaching the booth with a tray loaded with dishes. She placed a wide, deep gumbo bowl on a plate in front of him. She placed a small side dish of white rice to the left of that. Then she unloaded a dish of yellow potato salad and a dish of red beans, lining them up with his water and coffee. After these, came a silver mesh dish with a napkin lining. In it were four squares of jalopeno cornbread. Next, came a small plate of butter patties on white paper squares. "And here is a surprise for you," she announced, lowering a plate with a generous slice of yellow cake. "Jeff sent you out his famous pecan pineapple cake, which he said you've got to try."

Annie stepped back and admired all the food she'd brought. She rapped on the now empty tray with her fingers as though it were a drum. "Ta-da! Go for it, Detective!"

He smiled up at her. "You know if I eat all this, I'll never get my work done today. I'll have to go home and take a nap."

"Oh, no. That's what we have coffee for! I'm coming back in a minute to fill up your mug." She flashed him a smile and took off for the front booth where another customer was beckoning.

Lanclos watched her move away, and even though mired in a new investigation, he couldn't help but notice her walk. She moved like a dancer, leading with her hips, shoulders back, chin up. She was wearing an emerald green dress of a silky material that clung to her figure, and her blonde hair hung in curls down her back. Most Cajun women had dark hair, and Annie's blonde hair stood out in Cajun country. He supposed she was somewhere around thirty-five, and he knew she'd been through a lot based on prior conversations, yet she maintained a cheerful optimism which never failed to improve his mood whenever he saw her.

He talked roughly to himself: *Cut the crap, Lanclos, and get back to work. She doesn't want some old shit-kicker like you. She's probably still in love with that asshole she fled from up in the Ozarks.* Annie had told him she'd left an alcoholic, womanizing ridge runner when she moved to Louisiana. He had to admit he desired Annie. He knew he stayed to himself too much out at the farm when he wasn't working, but it didn't seem respectful to start seeing someone just a year and a half after his wife died. He knew his son wouldn't like it for starters. But then, his son, being a mamma's boy, would never like it, no matter how much time had passed. Maybe when this investigation was over, he'd ask her out. They could drive to Lafayette for dinner and a movie.

In contrast, seeing Claudine that day had irritated him. He didn't know why he invariably had feelings of resentment and discomfort whenever he ran into her, quite unlike the feelings he had when he saw Annie. He supposed he should be grateful to Claudine for helping him find Gerald's pickup and rifle, but he couldn't bring himself to feel any gratitude. *You're a regular old S.O.B., Lanclos,* he told himself.

Bringing his attention back to the gumbo, he spooned white rice into the steaming bowl, picked up the spoon, and had at it.

24

ALFRED HAS A VISITOR

Alfred answered the knock at his trailer door reluctantly. He had been just about to sit down to rice and gravy, red beans, and two fried pork chops, along with two biscuits and a beer to wash it all down. He groaned as he opened the door, fully expecting it to be one of his friends which meant he'd not have enough to offer another plate, so would have to offer half of his. Not to mention the fact that he had only two beers left in the refrigerator - almost certain to be discovered if the visitor was either Icky or Felix. Either of them would open the refrigerator and start hunting the first minute they were inside the trailer.

It was almost a relief to see his visitor was Detective Lanclos. Alfred took a quick step back in surprise and as he retreated, Lanclos stepped up to the threshold. "Hello, Alfred. You going to let me come in?"

"What's wrong? What'd I do now? I didn't do it whatever it is." Alfred stepped back another few steps and beckoned the detective inside. "Come on in, Detective. I was just going to eat. Let me put it up first before the cat gets to it." Alfred picked up the full plate from the breakfast bar that separated the tiny kitchen from the living room and placed it in the oven. The smell of fried pork was still heavy in the air as he turned down the zydeco coming from a plastic clock radio and motioned for Lanclos to sit on one of the high stools at the counter.

"Sit down if you want. I don't guess you want a beer."

"No, thanks. I just want to ask you a few questions. That be all right?" Lanclos sat on one of the two stools and hooked his heels on the bottom rung, then leaned an elbow on the counter and made himself comfortable.

Alfred sat on the other stool, crossed his arms and leaned back against the edge of the bar. "That's all right. Ask me."

"When's the last time you saw Gerald Theriot?" Lanclos kept his voice low and serene, as though the question was of mild importance.

"That's easy. I saw him in town about three, four days ago. I forget which day." Alfred waited expectantly, tightening the muscles of his crossed arms.

"Where in town?"

"It was in the barber shop."

"You getting a haircut?"

"No. I just went by there to tell him something."

"And what was that?"

Alfred licked his lips. "It was about my auntie."

"About what?" Lanclos remained very still.

Alfred looked around the room, then down. "Gerald, he had told my auntie to get out of her place. I asked him about that."

"And....what happened? What did Gerald say?"

"He said he had to do it, and it would work out all right."

"And then what? What'd you say?"

"Nothing much. There wasn't much I could say."

"Did you threaten Gerald?"

"No." Alfred raised his gaze and met Lanclos' eyes. "I didn't no way threaten him."

"You sure about that?"

"Now how I'm gonna threaten Gerald? All they'd do is come after me. The police, the sheriff...somebody would."

"So what'd you do?"

"I just said something about how it wasn't right and he got up and left. He knows it ain't right, him."

"The way I heard it, you threatened him. Put a curse on him."

"Yeah, okay. I put a curse...but that's not a threat. Like I'm gonna kill you...or watch out, I'm gonna get you!"

"So how'd you put the curse on him?"

Alfred unfolded his crossed arms and held up his right hand, forefinger and little finger extended. "Just like that. That's all I did. Pointed those two fingers at him. If that's against the law then I don't know nothing about it."

"Okay, Alfred. Anything else happen? You never saw him after that?"

"Never saw him again since then. I been nervous about it cause I didn't want him taking it out on Auntie Phil." Alfred crossed his arms again, both hands tucked under his armpits.

"What do you mean, taking it out on Philomena. Taking what out?"

"I mean like getting even with me for putting the curse on him."

"When's the last time you went by your auntie's?"

"Lessee," Alfred rolled his eyes up as he recollected. "It would have to be day before yesterday. I took her by some cayenne peppers I grow out back." Alfred jerked his head toward the kitchen door at the back of the trailer.

"You got a garden, Alfred?" Lanclos raised his eyebrows.

"Oh, yes. Always. Auntie raised me to garden. We don't like to buy stuff at the store. All that poison they spray on everything. That don't wash off, no. She has a garden and I have a garden. Twice a year I dig hers and I dig mine."

"Now that's a fine thing. You keep that up. And I'm not even going to take a look in case it's true you grow pot back there." Lanclos took a small spiral notebook and ballpoint from his shirt pocket. He flipped open the notebook and wrote for a moment in it, as zydeco continued on the radio. Alfred tried to read what he was writing upside down, but couldn't make it out. Lanclos raised his eyes and saw Alfred straining to see. "Don't worry. I'm just putting what you told me. Nothing more, nothing less." Alfred nodded, pushing out his bottom lip and visibly relaxing.

"If you think of anything else to tell me. Something you may have forgotten that has to do with Gerald, let me know. Here's my card." He placed the business card on the counter next to a bottle of hot sauce.

"How come you so interested in me and Gerald and Auntie?"

Lanclos narrowed his eyes, inhaled deeply and leaned back against the counter once more as he slipped the notebook and pen back into his shirt pocket. "Gerald's dead, Alfred."

"Dead? What happened? He get in a wreck?"

Lanclos shook his head. "We don't know yet what killed him."

Alfred looked puzzled. "Wait. You don't think my curse killed him, no?"

Lanclos' mouth turned up at one corner in a world-weary smile. "No, Alfred. We won't send you to Angola for cursing somebody if that's what you're worried about. As long as that's all you did." He exhaled a lungful of air. "Now, is that all you want to tell me? Sure there's nothing else?" He quietly watched Alfred, looking as though he had all the patience and time in the world.

Alfred lowered his gaze and sat quietly, wishing Lanclos would leave so he could eat his dinner before it got cold. The two men sat in silence for a few minutes; the only sounds the hum of the refrigerator and the announcer on the radio talking about an upcoming catfish festival.

"I'm waiting," Lanclos finally said.

Alfred snapped his head up. "I was waiting for you," he said, wetting his lips.

"I'm waiting to see if you've told me everything you have to say. Or if you thought of something else to tell me." Lanclos spoke slowly and ended by tilting his head back and gazing at the white snap-out panels of the ceiling.

"Oh, no, I can't think of anything else there is to tell you." Alfred shook his head emphatically from side to side and pursed his lips.

"You sure about that?"

"Yessir. I'm sure as I can be." This time Alfred jutted his chin for emphasis. "That's it! That's all there is."

"If I find out otherwise, you're going to be in the shit, Alfred," Lanclos warned, curling his lip.

"No sirree. That's all I got to say. For real, Detective." Alfred looked at him with wide earnest eyes, trying to convince him to leave him alone.

Lanclos held up a finger in caution. "Save it, Alfred. That would most likely be a yes. Whenever you do that wide-eyed innocent act, I know you're guilty as sin. Go on back to your dinner. See you later." Lanclos slid off the stool and headed slowly for the door.

Alfred kept shaking his head with a woeful softly spoken, "no, no, no." Then as soon as Lanclos closed the door after him, Alfred rounded the counter to the kitchen so he could retrieve his dinner plate from the oven. Since it was now cold, he slid it into the microwave to heat.

As he waited for the "ping" that meant the food was hot, a slow smile spread over his face. "Auntie, I think you're going to get to stay at your place now, after all," he said aloud. "And next time, don't be telling me not to curse somebody cause this time it looks like it went and did the job!"

25

THE CAMP

Lanclos drove along the Western levee of the Atchafalaya Basin on a macadem two-lane, then cut up across the fifty-foot high levee on a diagonal dirt trail until he reached the flat grassy and rutted top. Here he turned left onto the grassy crown of the levee where four-wheelers and pickups had created a makeshift road. Tire tracks had worn the grass flat and ground it into the mud, even though driving on the levee was discouraged. It made for stress on the levee and led to deterioration of the formation, yet hunters, fishermen, and camp residents continued to drive on top and up and down on it anyway.

Lanclos drove less than a thousand feet before he found a small wooden sign at the beginning of the dirt drive that led to the camp he was seeking. The hand-painted sign read: *Coonass Heaven – If you don't have any business here, then stay the HELL out of here!*

Lanclos laughed as he turned into the drive, ruts still filled with rainwater from the thunderstorm of two nights before. The road was lined with thick elderberry, privet, blackberry, blood-weed, native grasses gone to seed, and swamp mallow. Swamp maples, cypress, and water oaks formed an arch overhead keeping the road in deep shadow.

At the beginning of the drive to the cabin was a sign nailed to an oak tree. It was a poster from Louisiana Wildlife & Fisheries offering a cash reward for information about any violations of hunting or fishing laws. It went on to give the number for Operation Game Thief, and promised anonymity.

Lanclos wasn't fooled by the sign. He knew Maurice Saison was one of the more active poachers in the whole parish. He's been caught at it a few times through the years, but he wasn't one of the big offenders. One of these days, however, one of the officers would catch up with him again. And he'd have a *bec-croche*, or heron, or a deer he'd shot headlighting at night and Lanclos' friend, Moise Angelle, would nail his ass to the wall over it.

Moise was notorious for going after outlaw hunters. His father had been shot by one of them because he, in his career with Fish & Wildlife, had been famous for obsessively hunting down the outlaws. It was nothing for Lucky, the father, to go without sleep for three or four nights patiently waiting for one of them to take out a boat or truck in the middle of the night. Moise's fury at his father's murder had motivated his career to outdo his father in dogged persistence and relentless pursuit of outlaw hunters.

Lanclos was obsessive in his chosen detective work once he got his nose into a case, but Moise made him feel slow and ponderous by comparison. Moise's habit of haunting the Atchafalaya Basin and other area habitats at all hours of the night had caused his wife to leave him. Lanclos had never seen evidence that Moise had even noticed.

At the end of the drive he turned into a limestone circle drive in front of a board and batten tin-roofed cabin. He parked in back of a green-and-white Ford truck, so mud-splattered that the license plate was partially obscured with a fine, orange clay spray. The tailgate had been replaced with nylon netting to improve gas mileage; one taillight had red tape over the cracked lens to make it street legal. A bumper sticker advertised KOUI, the local French radio station.

Lanclos slid out of the truck and made his way to the front stoop, calling out: "Maurice! You in there?" The stoop was only six feet wide with an overhang from the metal roof. Nailed to the exterior of the cabin were the bleached skulls of an alligator, a cow, a wild hog, and a collapsed and torn hoop net. The steps creaked as he climbed them. "Hey, Maurice. You around somewhere?" He banged on the front screen door with the side of his fist.

He waited, listening to the shrill, high-volume swamp cicadas and the screams of hawks overhead as they flew in unison, swooped to investigate something, then soared back to scouting position in a cypress tree to Lanclos' left. A chartreuse lizard darted across the screen door. Lanclos took a deep breath of fresh air, wondering all over again why he had still not bought a camp after all these years.

"Hey Detective. What you got?" Maurice peered around the side of the cabin. "I'm in the back cooking. Come on." He waved for Lanclos to follow and retreated back around the side of the building. Lanclos left the stoop and hurried to catch up. As he rounded the cabin, he saw an outhouse left over from the twenties or thirties set to the side of the mowed yard. Twenty feet to the rear of the cabin was a rusty-roofed cement block outdoor kitchen. The blocks met wraparound screen halfway up, so that there was ventilation on all four sides. Lanclos knew Maurice was cooking shrimp stew long before they entered the outdoor kitchen.

Maurice held the screen door open for him, and he stepped over the threshold onto the cement floor, eyes almost immediately finding the Coleman stove at the rear of the room where a pot of the stew simmered. A wooden table and four metal folding chairs were placed against the screened wall to his left, set with a bottle of habanera sauce, a jar of pickled *merliton*, a restaurant style salt shaker, and a roll of paper towels. There was a strong smell of gun oil in the room, mixed with the aroma of the shrimp stew and fresh coffee.

"Sit down, Mitch. I'll bring you a cup of coffee. I just made some. Or would you rather a beer?"

"No, I just had lunch, thanks. I'm good. I saw your *Coonass Heaven* sign. There's a couple of ladies in St. Beatrice you better hope don't see it. They'll probably spray paint it," he laughed.

"Yeah, right. Like it's a dirty word or something. And I'll tell them, *Coonass* means a hardworking Cajun who don't ask nothing from nobody. No handouts needed." Maurice turned off the flame under the stewpot. "There. I turned my stew off. It's done anyhow."

Lanclos sat at the table and looked around the room. A deep stainless-steel laundry sink sat at the back wall. A varnished pine chest of drawers was placed diagonally at the far corner of that wall and a radio with a duct taped antenna played softly on top of it. At that moment, a fiddler played *Tit Galope Pour Mamou.*

"There. Now I'm with you." Maurice crossed to the table and sat heavily onto the chair, fumbling a cigarette from the pack in his shirt pocket. "You smoke?"

Lanclos shook his head as Maurice fired up his red plastic lighter, then adjusted the flame. "I got a flame thrower here," he laughed, sliding a metal ashtray from a motel chain closer.

"Do you have any idea why I'm here?" Lanclos studied Maurice's face.

"I'm pretty sure you didn't come all the way out here to talk about my *Coonass Heaven* sign, but I'd like to think you come all the way out here on a social call, not a business one." He blew smoke out of the side of his mouth away from Lanclos.

"I wish it wasn't business, but..." he hesitated. "A friend of yours is dead. Gerald Theriot."

Maurice's eyes bulged, and he jerked his head forward, choking on smoke. He wiped his mouth with the back of his hand and blinked rapidly. "That can't be!" he sputtered.

"It's true. I'm sorry."

"But...I just saw him. He was over here yesterday." Maurice rubbed his forehead, stunned. "He was fine...doing good. What happened to him?" He screwed up his face as he tried to process the information.

"We don't know what happened. A trapper found him yesterday by Bayou Perdue. He was lying on a bank in a mud hole. I know he was a close friend of yours so I thought you might be able to help with the investigation."

"*Mais, oui.* God, anything." He took a deep drag from the cigarette, causing the end to burn hot and bright. "I can't believe..." His voice trailed off with the smoke he exhaled.

"Can't believe what?"

"I can't believe Gerald's dead. You sure? I mean are you positive it's Gerald?" His voice cracked.

"Oh, most definitely. The body we have is Gerald Theriot." Lanclos sat very still, waiting for the initial shock to pass. After a few moments, he asked, "What did you all do yesterday?"

"Let me think. My head's spinning." Maurice rubbed the back of his neck. "Sometimes I can't even remember for sure what I did this morning." He blew out air in a thin stream and sniffed, as his eyes flicked to the left and then to the right. "It was late afternoon. He came out here and we drank a couple beers. We do that a couple of times a week."

"That's it? A couple beers?"

"Yeah, I cooked. Some garfish *boulettes*. I'd just finished grinding when he showed up at the door." He jerked his head toward the vintage grinder bolted on top of a narrow cabinet against the opposite wall next to the Coleman stove.

"Did he say anything that led you to believe he was troubled? Worried? Worried about anything...anybody?" Lanclos slipped a small spiral notebook and ballpoint from his shirt pocket.

Maurice gazed at the ceiling and took another drag from his cigarette. He frowned. "Not really."

"What did you all talk about?"

Maurice shrugged. "Just the usual. Price of crawfish. Price of gas. He was thinking about replacing his tailgate with netting like I did mine. Wanted to know where I got the gar." He fidgeted with his goatee. "You know. The usual bullshit."

"Did he talk about anything else? Anything at all you can think of."

"Yeah." Maurice paused to think a moment. He spoke slower than previously. "He was saying how his wife wanted to build a big ass house on the bayou and how he would rather just stay in town where they are. He said he felt real bad about having to kick Miss Philomena out of her place, but that he had to do it to keep his wife happy."

"What else did he say about it?"

"Just what everybody knows anyhow...that if his wife wasn't always trying to live like her sister and Leon do, then maybe she'd leave him alone about it, and they could live in peace at his aunt's house like they been doing." Maurice's face darkened with righteous anger. "Biggest mistake Gerald ever made was to marry that bitch. But I guess everybody in town knows that by now. Including you?" He met Lanclos' eyes looking for confirmation.

"Nobody can figure what goes on between married people," Lanclos replied. "You know that as well as I do. Doesn't pay to try either."

"Maybe that's true...except in this case." Maurice stood his ground, his fingers smoothing the goatee all along his chin.

"You have a personal reason to be so angry with her?"

"Not really. But Gerald's been a close friend for so many years, that it's almost like it's personal with me." Maurice made an expression of disgust and looked out the screen.

"After all this, I'm badly in need of a beer. You sure you don't want one?"

Lanclos waved his hand no. He flipped open the notebook and wrote in it while Maurice retrieved a beer from an olive green refrigerator about three feet from the stove on the opposite wall.

He tore off the tab, then took a long drink, wiping his mouth with the back of his hand as he returned to the table. He sat down shaking his head. "This can't be. It no way can't be." He opened his mouth again, then closed it.

"You thought of something else." Lanclos made a statement.

"Not really. Just something dumb."

"Nothing's dumb here. What is it?"

"Well, I guess we had more than a couple by then. And you gotta remember, Gerald and me go back a long ways. Even elementary school. Our fathers used to race horses at the old bush tracks. We'd hang out Sundays at the races, me and him."

"I know you did. I spent plenty of weekends at the old tracks too. So what did you just remember?"

"He was sitting right there where you are....and he leaned on the table with both elbows and looked me straight in the eye. He asked me, just like this here, 'Dammit, Maurice, tell me the truth. Do you think I'm a pussy-whipped, sorry son-of-a-bitch for what I'm doing? Kicking Miss Philomena out and building Celeste her goddamned, bullshit brick house over there?'"

He took another long drink, eyes closed. "He said his daddy always warned him about how women will always try to control you. They'll cry, they'll give you the silent treatment, cut you off and all like that, just so they can run your life. And little by little, some men will give in just to keep the peace, then one day the poor bastard will wake up and everybody's laughing at him cause his wife has nailed his balls to the wall, and she's the HNIC. Now that's a shameful thing for any man, but most especially shameful for a Cajun man!"

"And you said?"

"I looked him back straight in the eye and said, brother, don't haul me into that mess. I ain't getting into the middle of that with you and your old lady."

"And that was it?"

"No. He kept pushing me for an answer. 'Come on, Maurice. I need you to tell me the truth.' I felt sorry for him. He looked so.... like worried about it. His eyes even changed color. They almost looked bloodshot...or...red-rimmed...whatever. So I gave him his answer." Maurice set his lips in a firm line.

"And? What did you say?" Lanclos leaned closer.

"I finally told him what he needed to hear. I told him what everybody knows anyhow. That if Celeste wanted to live in a big, fancy house like her sister...she should of married a lawyer too... and left Gerald out of her plans. And I guess I'd had enough beers that day to tell him that he'd never be able to afford to make the kind of money that son of a bitch Leon LeDoux makes, and he shouldn't have to make himself miserable the rest of his life trying to play catch up, and he never would be able to catch up with LeDoux anyhow...unless he'd win the lottery maybe, or enter a poker tournament in Vegas maybe."

Maurice having worked himself up, made a fist and brought it down onto his knee. "That s.o.b. Leon. That stupid Celeste. Here she had one of the best men for miles around and she was on his back all the time to make more money. Buy this! Buy that! It's no wonder he's dead at age thirty-six. He was married to a money-grubbing bitch." Maurice tightened his lips and a vein at his temple throbbed as his face reddened with anger.

Lanclos watched him in silence as Maurice worked his neck, twisting it from side to side, trying to loosen it. His patience paid off when after a long pause, Maurice finally spoke again. "Yeah, and he talked about something else too. I just thought of it." He sniffed, staring at the floor remembering. "He said somebody had thrown a plastic bag full of animal guts into his front yard the night before. He couldn't figure out what that was all about."

"What kind of animal?"

"He said it looked like squirrel or rabbit."

"He had no ideas what that was all about?"

"No, sir. Nothing. He figured some hunter was too drunk or lazy to take the guts home and bury them."

"He didn't have any enemies?"

"Gerald?" Maurice raised dark eyebrows. "Everybody liked Gerald. He never did nobody nothing."

"You can't think of anybody who had it in for him?"

Maurice studied the rafters. "Like I said, I been knowing Gerald since third grade. That's when they put us in the same class at St. Beatrice Elementary. We took up together that year, and we been tight ever since. Except after he married Celeste, he'd come out here to visit. Celeste always acts like I'm tracking dogshit into her house or something when I go by there. So I pretty much stay away from there. He'd come out here at least once a week, sometimes more. He could relax out here, get away from her. Be himself."

Maurice screwed up his face and lowered it into the palm of his hand. Then he raised his head, pulled up the bottom few inches of his tee shirt and wiped his nose. "Sorry. I can't believe he's dead."

"Don't apologize. I'm sorry I'm the one who had to tell you."

"Look, Detective." Maurice's hand shook as he pointed a finger at Lanclos. "You need any help. Anything at all. Just let me know. I know everybody in this town. I know every square inch of everywhere around this town. Me and Gerald both. We've hunted and fished all over this parish. I'll do anything I can to help you find his killer."

"We don't know that this is a murder."

Maurice swallowed. "But you asked if he had enemies."

Lanclos just looked at him.

"Well then. I guess I just misunderstood. I'm jumping the gun already. Look. There is something else. I think he was working himself up to backing out of the deal with Miss Philomena."

"Oh, yeah, and how's that?" Lanclos leaned forward.

Maurice jutted out his chin and worked his mouth back and forth, while remembering. "He said something like, 'What if you knew something you were doing was dead-ass wrong, but you thought you had to do it anyhow? what would you do?'"

"And you said?"

"I said no way. If I knew something was fucking wrong, and I didn't want to do it, nobody could make me. But then I'm not pussy-whipped cause I ain't never going to get married. I don't care if she looks like Angelina, I will not have a woman telling me what to do!"

"And he said?"

"He didn't say much. But if looks could kill, I'd be the dead one. He just stared at me for a long while, and I could hear the gears turning in that hard head of his." Maurice rolled his eyes heavenward. "Sorry, Gerald. Not to bad-mouth the dead, but you know what I mean." Maurice lighted another cigarette, pulling hard on it and blowing smoke out the screen.

"And that was it?"

"He finally got around to saying something. He said maybe I was right, even though I was an asshole, and maybe he should just go home and tell Celeste how things were going to be. That he wasn't going to kick an old lady out of her house just so Celeste could show off to her sister." Maurice twisted a smile onto his face. "I guess I got him all fired up, cause he stuck out his chin about a foot."

"You think you got to him then?"

"I know I got to him. Whether he kept up the head of steam, I can't say."

"I will tell you one thing."

"What's that?"

"It looks like some animal was gnawing on his face."

Maurice looked like he'd been punched, and his jaw dropped. He leaped out of his chair so fast, it toppled backward. "He was out hunting?"

"Maybe. There was black powder on his hand. Any thoughts on that?"

"He owned a black powder rifle. It was his great grandfather's from the Civil War. He belongs to the Sons of the Confederacy, and some weekends he travels to those Confederate reenactments and camps out in a tent with some of his buddies from there."

"He say anything about going hunting when you last saw him?"

"I don't remember anything like that," Maurice mumbled, shaking his head back and forth. "An animal gnawing on Gerald?" He looked at Lanclos, eyes wide in disbelief.

"Do you own a black powder firearm?" Lanclos asked.

"No. My guns are in the house locked in a gun cabinet." Maurice jerked his head in the direction of the house. "But no black powder. Just a .22, two shotguns, and a couple of pistols. A .38 and a .22. Oh, and a .50 caliber."

"Just the usual hunter's collection," Lanclos nodded. "So you wouldn't know why Gerald had the rifle with him last night. Is that right?"

"Yeah, that's right."

"See, the way I heard it was, you were hunting with him last night. Out here," Lanclos said casually.

"Celeste tell you that?"

Lanclos just looked at him.

"Maybe he just wanted to make an excuse for being out here. I told you she keeps a tight rein on him. Did keep a tight rein."

Lanclos sighed. "That's not all. She says he left the house late last night to come back out here. That you were going hunting again."

"That's the first I heard about that." Maurice shook out another cigarette and lighted it.

"Why don't you just tell me the truth, Maurice. Does it have anything to do with the two of you trespassing over at the hunting club back there?" He jerked his head to the east. "And going after a deer? And it's not deer season yet? Anything to do with that?"

Maurice bent over, cupping his cigarette with his fingers and took a long drag without answering.

"Tell you what. Go get that deer rifle of yours and let me smell it. I can tell if you fired it recently."

"What would that prove? It's not against the law to shoot. Why do you think I live out here in the Basin?"

"Maurice! Wake up! I'm not looking to turn you in to Fish & Wildlife, but I have to find out what happened to Gerald. That's what you want, isn't it? He was a good friend. But you have to help me out here."

"All right, all right. It's true. Everything you said is true. We sneaked over the line into the hunt club woods late in the afternoon. We messed around over there for about an hour, but didn't see anything. He shot at a beer can a few times, just to use the gun. You know it's not good to leave guns sitting around without using them once in a while. After that, we gave up, quit, and came back here."

"What time did he leave?"

"I can't be exact...I don't wear a watch. You don't need a watch when you live in the swamp. But it was dark already. I know that much. But it hadn't been dark more than an hour or two."

"So maybe around eight or nine?"

"Maybe so. I'm sorry. I really can't be sure. When you're drinking beers, it throws you off. Time gets lost somewhere."

"And what about this story of his to Celeste? That he was coming back out here to hunt some more?"

"Like I said. That's the first I heard about that."

"That better be the way it was. I better not find out you're bullshitting me again."

"I only left out the hunt club part because of my record. I'm still on probation." Maurice tightened his lips, shoved out his chin and stared outside through the screen. He sniffed. "Did you ever stop to think that maybe Celeste is the one who's lying? That maybe he never did say he was coming back out here? That maybe she's leaving something out that she doesn't want you to know? Like maybe that part about Miss Philomena?" Maurice's face flushed with righteousness. "Maybe he finally stuck up for himself and they had a fight. And she just conveniently left that part out of it."

Lanclos looked out the screen, running a tongue over his teeth, distractedly drumming his fingers on the table, momentarily lost in one of his reveries. The two men sat for a few moments, cicadas and swamp birds providing a loud chorus all around them. A small brown spider swung by a gossamer thread from a branch, and a chartreuse lizard scuttled diagonally up the screen. Lanclos watched the lizard as he thought about what had been said, while Maurice waited, keeping very still. Finally, Lanclos turned his head, bringing his attention back to the room.

"Okay. We'll leave it at that. But if I have to come out here again, don't bother blowing smoke at me. I know you know all about what the law says about interfering with an investigation. That would be a real good way to violate your probation."

Maurice crossed his arms over his stomach and nodded curtly. "I'm a lot of things, but I'm not stupid."

"All right then, I'm going to leave you to your shrimp stew. Thank you for your help," he said in a softer tone. "And that <u>was</u> all very helpful." He scraped the metal chair back and stood, closing the notebook, returning it and the pen to his shirt pocket. Outside, the drone of the cicadas rose higher, reaching full volume. Bullfrogs croaked along the bank of the bayou to the east of them. The radio announcer began a newsbreak in Cajun French, and Maurice stood too, shoulders slumped in dejection as he bit at the inside of his mouth.

"Enjoy your stew," Lanclos said as he headed for the door.

"I got no appetite now." Maurice clamped a hand on his stomach. "In fact....."

"Take it easy. If you think of anything else, give me a call." Lanclos slipped a card from his wallet and laid it on an upright crab trap that served as a catchall table by the door.

"I will, I will," Maurice rasped as he brushed by Lanclos and bolted out the front door, headed for the woods at the edge of the yard. The sounds of Maurice throwing up and the harsh cawing of crows followed him all the way back to the truck.

26

THE CURSE REVISITED

Claudine slid oatmeal cookies out of the oven and set the cookie sheets on the kitchen table to cool. She had made time in her afternoon to bake them, hoping the gesture would help her elderly neighbor assimilate the dreadful events of the day. At Philomena's advanced age, such excitement as a dead man so close to her house would surely upset her far more than it would someone of a younger and more resilient age.

While they cooled, she cut circles of wax paper so she could line a round tin container and put the papers between layers of the cookies. She needed to hurry because she had to start supper for the family. Antoinette would be returning from school shortly and she wanted to be home when her daughter got off the bus, especially since she hadn't seen her since the day before.

Nibbling a few irregular cookies, she finished packing the gift tin with the most perfect of the batch, and closed the lid on the project. Then she crossed to the walk-in pantry closet and selected a pint jar of homemade blackberry jam from one of the wooden shelves. Closing the pantry door with a backward kick, she gathered the gifts, placing them into a paper shopping bag and left the kitchen by the back door.

As she crossed the porch, an orange and red rooster tore across the back yard chasing a black hen who squawked as though she were going to be killed. The dogs, observing the drama from their kennels, began to howl and trot back and forth, crisscrossing their twenty by thirty space, yelping and running into one another.

"Quiet out there!" Claudine yelled, her ears hurting.

She rounded the house toward the front yard, minding Lanclos' orders to stay out of the woods. She'd have to use the road to go over to Philomena's. Hurrying along so she could be back when Toni got home from school, she glanced to her left toward the woods marked off with yellow Crime Scene tape and said a prayer for the soul of Gerald Theriot. As she finished her prayer with a melodic *Amen,* she felt uneasy even walking by those woods, knowing his body had been dragged through there only the night before.

As she approached Philomena's house, she saw Alfred bicycling up the road. She regretted this as she was in a hurry and didn't have time to get involved in a social situation and a lengthy explanation of the dramatic events of the day. Resolving to keep her visit under ten minutes, she held the paper bag close to her body so the glass jam jar didn't break and watched where she was putting her feet so she wouldn't trip as she followed the brick path to the house.

Climbing the steps, she knocked on the door and called, "Miss Philomena? It's Claudine from next door."

Alfred swung into the yard then and braked suddenly so that the bike skidded, gouging a four foot rut into the grass. Claudine suspected he did it to show off. "A grown man showing off on a bike," she muttered.

"I'm out here in the chicken coop," Philomena answered.

Claudine crossed to the side of the porch and peered around the corner of the house toward the leaning cypress coop. Philomena came to the narrow doorway of the structure, holding a galvanized pail. "Hello, Claudine. Is that you? I'm just scooping out some manure for the garden."

"I brought you some cookies fresh from the oven. And some of last summer's blackberry jam."

"I love blackberry jam. I ate my last jar last month. And I love cookies!" Philomena made her way up the dirt path toward the house. "This is so nice of you. Maybe you'll have some sweet tea with me?"

"Oh, no, thank you. My daughter's due home from school any time now, and I want to be at the house when she gets there. I'll just set these down for you."

"Don't go just yet. Come on inside for just a minute, can't you?" The old woman rounded the porch and joined Alfred at the steps, setting down the pail of straw and chicken manure. "Alfred, put this around the edge of the garden for me, will you please. I mean later on, before you leave. But be careful not to put it too close... it'll burn."

"I know all about that, Auntie." Alfred cupped her elbow in a large hand guiding her up the steps. "How you doing anyhow?"

"As well as can be expected with them finding a dead body in my back yard this morning." She reached the deck of the porch and paused, catching her breath. "But I guess that would be news to you, huh, nephew? Now, you all come into the house and we'll have some sweet tea." She wiped her brow with the back of her hand. "And it's hot today."

Alfred held the screen door for the two women and after they'd entered, he slipped inside and remained standing by the door. Claudine smiled and nodded at him in greeting, then turned to Philomena.

"I'm very sorry about what happened on your property. Whatever it was that happened. I don't guess they know anything as yet, but I wanted you to know we're thinking of you, and I was hoping all the excitement wasn't too awfully upsetting."

"I did have my share of nerves this morning, yes I did. It's scary enough to have a dead body turn up at my place, but wondering too if there's a murderer running around loose out there...well, it's hard for an old lady to go through. Let's just say that."

"If you get scared or nervous...you know you can call us. Roy will come right over and get you. We've got a spare bedroom, you know."

"Oh, thank you. I'll be all right. I've lived alone here for so long, I probably couldn't sleep in any other bed but my own. If I get nervous, I just lock my bedroom door. And I keep a hammer in there just in case."

"A hammer?"

"I expect I could do a lot of damage to somebody's face with a hammer if I had to...even if I am very, very old."

Claudine laughed. "I expect you could. And I hope you never have to find out if you can or not."

"Auntie. I can stay with you for a few nights if you want," Alfred offered, his voice raspy.

"No, no, Alfred. I'll be all right. You better just stay on at your place like you been doing."

"That detective was by my trailer. He axed me a bunch of questions." Half of Alfred's face was in shadow as he remained pressed against the wall by the screen door.

"Well, what did you tell him?" asked Philomena.

"Nothing. I didn't know nothing to tell him."

Philomena started to say something, then thought better of it, and closed her mouth.

Claudine looked back and forth at the two of them, then began her exit. "Well, I'd better be going now. So I can be home for Toni. You enjoy those cookies, you hear? Next time I'll bake some peanut butter cookies. And please, Miss Philomena, take a nap every day for a while. Get your rest. This was a lot for you to have to go through. It's a lot for anyone at any age."

"I'll take it easy. I really will. And here, let me give you a little something in return." The old lady turned, opened the refrigerator, and picked two foil wrapped peppermint patties from one of the shelves in the door. "Eat one of these on your way home. And here's one for your daughter too."

"Thank you, and remember to call us if you need us. That's what neighbors are for."

Claudine left with a nod at Alfred and stepped carefully by Trouble who was sitting serenely by the door licking a paw,waiting for his next meal.

As she started down the brick walk, she heard Philomena hiss to Alfred, "Did that detective ask you anything about why you go around putting curses on people?"

"Naw, naw, Auntie. Now how would he know anything about all of that? You didn't tell him?"

"I'd be too ashamed to tell it."

"It worked though, didn't it?"

"*Alfred!*"

Claudine scratched her head as she started down the road. "Curses?" she asked aloud. "Dead bodies! Curses!" She shook her head and unwrapped a peppermint, wondering if this wasn't the wildest day she'd ever experienced. She'd be glad to see her daughter get home safe and sound. The events of the day had put her on edge, and she felt nervous for her family's safety.

As she began to cross her front lawn, the school bus arrived, its bright yellow color providing a safe, comfortable break to her edgy mood. Antoinette stepped off the metal steps, stopping to turn and wave goodbye to her friends. She was Claudine's height and build and had her facial features, combined with the dark complexion of her father. She leaned her head over and when her long black hair cascaded down, she flicked her head upright, tossing the thick hair back over her shoulders.

"Mom! My algebra test! I passed!" She trotted over to her mother, the bookbag slung over her shoulder bouncing against her side.

"That's great, honey! I never did catch on to algebra when I was in high school."

She hugged her daughter, holding her close for a few beats longer than usual. "Come on in the house. I baked cookies, and just wait til you hear what happened. You're not going to believe it!"

27

LEON THREATENED

Leon LeDoux had finished with his last client for the day and was preparing to leave the office for home when still another call was put through to him.

"So I hear you took your new secretary out to lunch already," said Mona, calling from her new job in Shreveport.

"Is that any way to start a phone call, Mona? Come on. It was her birthday. That's not okay?" said Leon, pushing back in his office chair and rolling his eyes. "And how did you hear about that so soon anyhow? You got spies?" He spoke in his usual slow, measured manner.

"I wouldn't go so far as to call them spies, but word gets out."

"Look, the woman does a good job so far and I thought it was a thoughtful thing to do. I'm a nice guy, remember? As I recall, I did the same thing for you when you started on this job."

"That's exactly what I'm talking about, Mr. Nice Guy. Is she going to get the same special treatment?"

Leon frowned. "Mona, am I under interrogation here?"

"Just remember who you're talking to. This is me! Mona! And I know you so well."

"Elaine's just a nice, hard-working woman. There's nothing going on more than a simple gesture on my part for her birthday."

"Keep it that way, Leon. I don't want to get any more reports from down there that something's brewing between you and her. I won't tolerate it."

"Mona, if you know me as well as you say you do, you know I don't take orders from anyone."

"I'm not giving orders, Leon. I'm telling you to stay away from her or I'm going to hear about it."

"Jesus, Mona! Did you burn the toast this morning or something? What the hell is the matter with you? That new job stressing you out?"

"You will regret it if I hear anything suspicious about the two of you," her voice lowered. "You will really, really regret it. That's all I'm saying."

"So now you're threatening me?" Leon's voice turned cold.

"Call it whatever the hell you want." The line went dead.

He stared at the phone, forehead furrows deepening, and pushed his lips out into a rigid line.

Elaine buzzed him. "It's your wife. There's an emergency."

Leon whipped forward, the back of the leather chair flipping vertically to support him. He punched a button on the phone. "What's the matter, baby?"

"Oh, God, Leon. Are you sitting down?"

"Yes. What is it?"

"It's Gerald. Oh, Leon," she gasped. "Gerald's dead!"

"What? What? Where?" He gripped the arm of the chair.

"Celeste just called me. She's coming over with Mama. Little Cedric's still here with us. Mitch Lanclos came by her house to break the news. He asked her all kinds of questions. She thinks he suspects her! They don't know what happened to him. They found him on the bayou bank in front of Miss Philomena's. Please come home."

"I'll get over there as soon as I can…within the hour. Jesus!" His mouth gaped as he struggled to compute the news.

"I'll keep everybody right here with me until you get home. Hurry!"

"Wait a minute! What the hell happened to him?"

"Like I said they don't know yet. God, Leon! My thoughts are spinning. I can't think straight. It's like there's a switch gone off in my head!"

"Go fix something for the kids to eat. That'll give you something to do until I get there. Be careful, baby. I'm on the way!" He hung up and buzzed for Elaine, then started cramming papers into his briefcase. When she opened the door, he waved her in.

"Elaine. A family emergency. My brother-in-law is dead. They don't know what happened to him. I've got to get home right away." He spoke uncharacteristically fast.

"Oh, Mr. LeDoux. I'm so sorry." Elaine clasped a notebook tightly to her abdomen.

"Elaine, when no one's around, you can call me Leon," he said as he swung the briefcase up and stood. "Is there anything you need me to sign before I go?"

"I've got three letters almost ready, but they can wait." Her expression was earnest as she continued to clutch the notebook. A worried expression brought her carefully shaped eyebrows closer together.

"Please call Wilson and tell him what happened. We were meeting for a quick drink at Rodrigue's at five." He licked his lips, his mouth gone dry.

"I'll take care of everything. Don't you worry."

He sighed before rounding the desk, shaking his head slowly. "Damned if there isn't always something," he said irritably. "Does it ever end?"

He followed her out of his office, this time oblivious to her figure, passed her desk, and posture erect, crossed the lobby and exited the building. Blinking rapidly in the bright sunlight, he trudged to the parking lot on the south side of the building.

"Son of a bitch!" he called out as he saw the bird droppings on the windshield of his Lincoln. "And I just had this car washed today!"

28

BUCKSHOT

Lanclos easily found a parking space in the paved lot of the Chaisson Funeral Home. The building resembled a plantation house with four columns in front, each as thick as a fat man. Lanclos guessed the front porch to be at least fifty feet wide and twenty feet deep. The sparkling white porch had no furnishings, no potted plants. The business obviously didn't want mourners hanging around in the front smoking cigarettes, for there were none of the usual institutional, sand-filled cement urns in place to discard cigarette butts.

Lanclos had met Rusty at Chaisson's frequently over the years because whenever an autopsy was required, Rusty chose to perform it at Chaisson's. Arnold Chaisson was his first cousin, for one thing. For another, Rusty had never bothered to install the equipment required for performing autopsies in an autopsy room of his own. As Rusty put it: "Arnold's got everything I need right there. Why not? It's all in the family. Anyhow, I always pay him for the use of his equipment, and you know how funeral directors love money."

Lanclos entered the funeral home by a grand carved wooden door with an elaborate brass doorknob. He passed on through the foyer with a few dark varnished side tables underscoring oval gilt framed mirrors on opposite walls. Each table held an assortment of silk flowers. There was a cloying smell of artificial lavender that immediately irritated his nose, and increased his annoyance at having to meet Rusty at Chaisson's.

The subdued lighting came from retro wall sconces as he made his way down the long hallway toward the rear of the building. He passed the office and spoke briefly with Florence, the secretary, about his appointment with Rusty in the embalming room. Then he passed by two dark viewing rooms and a kitchen where families could drink coffee and eat when gathering for their sad, funeral home occasions.

The red light was on in a stainless coffee urn so he slipped into the room and grabbed a Styrofoam cup, gratefully filling it with steaming brew. He had been running on adrenaline all day, but he felt an energy drain upon entering Chaisson's and needed some caffeine before meeting with Rusty.

He quickly drank half the cup and thought of taking Rusty coffee, so he filled another, topping his off before continuing on down the hallway to the double doors at the rear of the building. A sign warned: Staff Only. Do Not Enter. He rang the buzzer and finished off the coffee while he waited.

A young man with a short haircut, wearing a white dress shirt, gray tie, and black trousers presently answered the door, and seeing who it was, beckoned Lanclos inside.

"He's expecting you, Detective," he said with the grave politeness of a mortuary employee. He held the door opened wide, and once Lanclos had crossed the threshold, the young man walked back through it toward the office.

Lanclos passed into another hallway, but this one was well lighted with long fluorescent panels. The lighting was so different in these two halves of the business establishment, that he had to blink a few times as his eyes adjusted to the glare.

He quickly made his way to the swinging doors of the embalming room. Without knocking, he pushed them open, and there was Rusty in the center of the huge, white-tiled room, standing by one of the four stainless worktables. Gerald's naked body lay supine on the table, covered discreetly at the hips by a folded white sheet. The harsh smell of antiseptic filled the room.

On the far wall under a row of high windows were four stainless laundry style sinks. Various hoses lay coiled beneath them. The sinks were necessary for many operations, not the least of which was for draining blood from corpses for the embalming process. The floor was also tiled, and two plate-sized brass fittings covered the drainage holes for hosing down the room. The pallor of Gerald's corpse was startling in contrast with Rusty's dark complexion. "Damn, it's hard to see Gerald like this," said Lanclos.

"Unfortunately, we're all going to look like that one day. This job gives you perspective." Rusty wore reading glasses pushed up onto the top of his head, and a rumpled white cotton buttoned coat. "And just wait'll you see what I've discovered."

"Here, I brought you some coffee."

"No, I'm good. You drink it. You're going to need it." Lanclos set it down.

"What you got?"

"See there?" Rusty pointed his gloved hand at the ragged and chewed side of Gerald's face.

Lanclos bent to see. "What? It's all torn up."

"Those dark holes? See over there?" He pointed to a calibrated glass jar resting on a square worktable beside the autopsy table that held five black beads.

"Looks like double-ought buckshot."

"So what does that tell you?" Rusty gave Lanclos a satisfied smile.

"12 gauge shotgun."

"Yep. 12 gauge shotgun. And they were deep. Deep inside his head. There's not much muscle in the face, so they went deep. I had to do some tedious digging with the tweezers all right. But I'm good, and I got every one of those babies out."

"Sonofabitch. So Gerald was murdered after all." Lanclos slapped a hand onto his face and slowly rubbed mouth and chin, already feeling stubble even after shaving early that morning.

"Either that or a hunting accident." Rusty, still smiling with satisfaction, crossed his arms and stared at the corpse.

Lanclos filled his mouth with air, blew his cheeks out, then released the air with a whooshing sound. "And the black powder on his hands?"

"He must have been shooting somewhere. Too bad we don't know where yet."

"He was shooting earlier yesterday with a friend out by the levee. He had a black powder rifle. But you told me he was killed somewhere between midnight and three in the morning. Right?"

"Yeah, and when he was shot, he rolled onto his side. See there?" Rusty pointed to the darker skin on the right side of Gerald's body. "You can see the lividity better now that I've cleaned him up. But when whoever it was moved him, laid him on his back on the bayou bank...whoever it was, must not watch crime stories on TV, or he'd have known better."

"Maybe the murderer is just dumb. You ever think of that?"

"That would make a lot of sense when you consider what else I found." Rusty reached to the side table again and picked up a clear plastic bag. "Some of this was stuck to his clothes."

Lanclos took it gingerly with his left hand and held it a foot from his face, examining the contents: a fishhook attached to a spindle. "Looks like a number two. Somebody planning to bait catfish lines. Could have gotten stuck to him in a vehicle when he was being transported. Or maybe it caught on him when he was laid out on the bayou bank." He handed the little bag back to Rusty.

"There's more." Rusty picked up another clear plastic bag and handed it over.

"Looks like deer scat to me. What you think?"

Lanclos held the evidence toward the light and narrowed his eyes. "That's deer shit all right." He handed back the evidence bag to Rusty. "Maybe whoever moved Gerald carried him in the back of a pickup. Maybe there was a dead deer or two in the bed of the truck." He frowned and pressed his lips together as he considered this theory.

"So, like I said before...could be a hunting accident?" Rusty raised his eyebrows in question.

"Wouldn't make sense to go to all that trouble. All you'd have to do is call the Sheriff and report a hunting accident. Nobody's going to convict you for a hunting accident in the state of Louisiana. Unless you have a real good motive for wanting the person dead."

"Yeah, I guess you're right." Rusty carefully lined up his collection of discoveries, then reached for the coffee on the steel worktable. "I changed my mind. Let me try some of that." He took a sip and made a face. "Eww! Stuff got cold. Tastes like kerosene." He walked over to one of the sinks and dumped the coffee, tossing the cup into a barrel-sized waste container.

"So where are we with all this?"

"Did I mention Herman Delcambre found Gerald's black powder rifle in his woods down there by the bayou in front of his farm? Somebody was outlaw hunting over there last night. He heard a shotgun, but by the time he got in his truck and drove over there, whoever it was had hauled ass."

"That would explain the deer."

Lanclos nodded. "Sure would. And I'm headed home. I've been running around interviewing people all day. And I'm pretty sure just about every one of them was lying to me about one thing or another. With Alfred you can pretty well tell he's lying if his lips are moving. The rest of them it's not so easy, but I have a nose for lies. It comes with the job." He smiled at Rusty. "But then you know all that. You've been in the business long enough, you too." He raised his eyes to the high windows. "I got to go. It's getting dark fast, and I want to have supper with my son. Moise Angelle and I are going over to Delcambre's woods at daybreak with Herman to show us where he found Gerald's rifle. If there's anything there, you know Moise will find it."

"You got that right. Man has a nose like a bloodhound and the eye of a hawk."

"And you know who he got it from."

Rusty smiled. "Sure do. Lucky Angelle. Best tracker in the state of Louisiana. Probably in the whole, entire South."

"*C'est vrai.* Look. When you get the report finished, fax it to me. Okay, buddy?" Lanclos clapped a hand on his friend's shoulder.

"You got it. There'll be a wait for the tox report though. I sure hope you wrap this up fast. There's some bastard out there doesn't need to be running around loose in the parish."

"Don't worry, we'll get him." Lanclos spoke in a softer tone in Gerald's direction. "We'll get him for you, Gerald."

He took a moment to scan the high ceiling covered with white acoustic tiles and banks of fluorescent lights. "Meantime, Rusty, will you please put an addition onto your office and build your own autopsy room? I hate this place. It gives me the creeps, and I have to meet you here a couple dozen times a year."

Rusty gave him a wry smile. "I'll get right on it, Mitch."

Lanclos headed for the swinging doors. "See! That's what I mean. You've been saying that for the last ten years!"

29

LANCLOS SURPRISED

His son's red pickup was in the forty-foot wide cypress pole barn that had served as the family garage for twenty years. Every time Lanclos eyed its rusted roof and weathered uprights, he thought once again of building an enclosed garage, but more pressing affairs in his professional life always demanded his attention.

Two wet chocolate Labs, their muzzles sprinkled with silver hairs, bounded toward him from where they'd been swimming in a pond a hundred feet from the rear of the pole barn. They leaped and danced around him as though they were still young. Water flicked from them as Lanclos sparred with them for a few minutes, until he finally called, "Enough!"

They calmed themselves and trotted beside him toward two wide flower beds and an arched trellis forming a boundary between the front yard and the gravel turn-around driveway. Leggy rose bushes, not pruned since his wife died, were in bloom. The brilliant red roses made sharp contrast with the white trellis. A smaller, climber rose covered part of the lattice of the trellis. Lanclos felt sad each time he saw the roses because he knew how hard his wife had worked at her flowers, and how she loved them. But the flowers were all on their own now, and he was pleased they continued to do so well, as he had neither the inclination nor the time to work with them.

As he walked up the overgrown brick path to the two-story farmhouse, he wondered if Paul had eaten dinner, or had started cooking dinner for the two of them. Events of the day and early evening had kept him so focused on Gerald's death that he had not noticed how hungry he'd gotten since eating at Castille's. If Paul had gone beyond heating a pizza and actually cooked a dinner, he'd be most gratified, but he doubted it.

"Go on back and jump in the pond again," he said to the dogs as they tried to follow him inside. They looked forlorn as he blocked their path and waved them away from the door. He watched them run back toward the fields, recently cut for hay by the same farmer who worked Delcambre's fields. Lanclos had little time to farm his own hundred acres, and had used the same farmer for the past twenty-five years. In the past, the farmer had raised soybeans, but after Lanette had been diagnosed with cancer, Lanclos had told the farmer to stop hiring the crop duster and using pesticides, fungicides, and herbicides, and go to native grasses for hay only with no chemicals allowed. His family had been gratified by the return of lightning bugs and an increase in hummingbirds and butterflies since the crop duster had quit spraying.

He passed on through the spacious, seldom-used living room. The lined draperies were closed and the bulky, upholstered blue furniture looked charcoal gray in the dim light of the room. "Yo, Paul!" he called as he quickly moved through an archway into an equally dim dining room where a long oak dining table and formal high back covered dining chairs sat neglected and useless. A lace doily under a bowl of painted wooden fruit sat in the middle of the table, but there was no other evidence of family use in the narrow room.

He pushed on the swinging door that led to the well-lighted, large country kitchen. "Paul, you around?" The smell of chili simmering on the oversized range increased his hunger. A round pine table and matching chairs took up a good portion of the middle of the room. On it were a stack of mail in a straw basket, a china bowl with bananas and red and green apples, two purple placemats, and an assortment of condiments in glass jars: Chow-chow, Tabasco sauce, and pickled Merliton.

The door to the laundry room at the back corner of the kitchen opened. "Hey, Dad. I was just throwing some clothes in the dryer."

Paul raked fingers through his dark hair, smoothing it back on both sides. He looked much more like his mother than his father, although he had inherited Lanclos' strong chin and thin lips. His deeply set eyes were very much like his mother's. They gave the impression of sensitivity and loneliness, although Paul was seldom lonely as he had always had a solid set of friends throughout his young life. His face was leaner than his father's; his build thinner and less muscular. He was taller than his father, putting him at slightly over six feet.

Lanette had obsessed about Paul for years. She had lived through him and made him her life. She seldom saw friends, and refused requests over the years to volunteer at the Altar Society, or Mardi Gras committees, or the annual church Catfish Festival. She had even refused to help with Sheriff Quebedeaux's reelections.

He had also thought her doting on Paul was over the top, but wondered if his own emotional detachment had caused the enmeshment with their son. In hindsight, he wondered if she'd turned to Paul for the endless, lengthy conversations she craved and that he'd always resisted over the years. We are what we are, he told himself, and there was nothing he could do about it now for she was long in her grave.

"You eat yet, son?"

"I grabbed a couple of hamburgers in Lafayette, but I'm making chili. I didn't know if you'd be home for dinner." Paul nodded toward the stove where a lid rattled on a steaming pan. "I thawed some deer meat chili out in the microwave. It was some you made with those deer steaks you got from Uncle Stanley."

"Oh, yeah. I forgot that was still in the freezer. Is it ready yet? I've had a really long day, and I'm very hungry."

"I'll serve it up right now if you want." Paul turned to the stove.

"Give me just a minute, son. I'm going to get out of these clothes. I'll be right back." Lanclos thumbed through the mail, dropped it all back in the basket, and passed on into a long hallway that led to the bathrooms and bedrooms on the south side of the house. Once in his bedroom, he yanked off his clothes, threw

them into a tall woven hamper and selected a pair of folded jeans
from a stack in the cedar-lined closet. He took a folded tee shirt
from an assortment on a shelf over the jeans and pulled it on without looking at it. With barely a glance at the rest of the bedroom,
he returned to the hallway and reentered the kitchen, just as Paul
was placing a plate holding a large bowl of steaming chili on one
of the tablemats.

"There you go, Dad. Dig in."

"I'll wait for you." Lanclos pulled out a chair and sat, watching
Paul as he served himself and brought his own bowl to the table.

"I love deer meat chili," said Paul, as he sat and immediately
lowered a soup spoon into the bowl.

"Hold up, son. We haven't said grace. What would your mother
say?"

Paul bowed his head and Lanclos waited until his son recited
hurriedly, "Bless this food that we are about to receive from thy
bounty. Amen." The two men picked up their spoons and began
to eat. After eating half their food in silence, Paul paused, holding his spoon midway between his mouth and the chili. "Dad? You
working on something important right now?"

"That's a funny question. Why do you ask?"

"I don't know." Paul lowered his spoon into the bowl and
scooped up more chili.

He looked up again, without raising the spoon. "You look a
little worn out is all."

"Oh, yeah? Do I?" Lanclos laughed. "I'm not surprised. I've
been going at top speed all day. And yes, I'm working on something important all right."

"Somebody went and got murdered around here?"

Lanclos was raising his spoon to his mouth, but paused, then
lowered it back into the bowl. He nodded briefly and pushed his
chair back a few inches.

Paul raised a hand and tilted his head. "Never mind. I know
the drill. You'll tell me more when you know more and not until."

"That's it. You got it." Lanclos once again raised the spoon
toward his mouth.

"Just tell me if it's anybody I know. You don't have to say anything. You can just nod."

"Paul," Lanclos lowered his head and looked at his son like a bull about to charge.

"I know. I know. I'll shut up."

"Don't shut up. Tell me about school. You have all your work caught up? Any papers due? What's going on over there?"

"School's great. I've got it all under control. There's only one class I'm not sure about. But maybe I'll be able to pull it off and keep my B average this semester."

"That's good news. But then, I expected it." Lanclos scraped the bowl with his spoon. "You took care of Sky already?"

"Yeah, he's good. He's in the back pasture. I gave him some molasses with his oats tonight."

"Well then. Let's wash these up, so we can catch the news." They carried their dishes to the sink and Paul leaned against the counter to do the washing up.

"You're in a good mood tonight. What's going on?" asked Lanclos, as Paul began running the hot water to rinse the dishes for the dishwasher.

"I have a hot date this weekend."

"Oh, yeah? Who with?"'

"Remember last week when Shooter and I went four-wheeling over at Dwayne's farm with some friends from UL?"

"I remember."

"Well, this girl I knew from high school…but she's a couple of years behind us so I never really talked to her. She was there."

"And I take it you liked her?"

"Like her? That's an understatement. You should see her!"

"What's her name?"

"Antoinette Bergeron." Paul swiped a plate under the running water with a long brush. "Long, long black hair. Big ones…out to here. Man!"

"Which Bergeron family is she?"

"Her dad works offshore. Her mother's a *traiteur.* You know them, don't you?"

"Roy and Claudine Bergeron. Sure I know them. I went to school with both of them."

"Yeah, well I thought I'd take her to the movies in Lafayette. Maybe get a bite to eat at Ceci's. You think maybe you could let me have fifty bucks? Don't forget I'm going to be cleaning out the gutters this weekend."

Lanclos crossed his arms. "I'll front you more than that. Enough for Ceci's, the movies, and a tank of gas. I wouldn't want you getting caught short." Lanclos stared at his son's profile, the first twinge of surprise at hearing about Claudine's daughter giving way to a warm glow of unexpected pleasure all along his shoulders and the back of his neck. He didn't understand this pleasant reaction to his son's interest in the girl, but then he didn't understand a lot of things about himself lately.

Paul looked up from placing a plate in the dishwasher. "What're you laughing at, Pop? What's so funny?"

"Nothing. I was just remembering my first real date." Lanclos turned away from the sink.

"Your first real date? That must have been a hundred years ago, huh, Dad?" Paul put the last dish into the dishwasher. "What'd you take her out in? You hitch up the team to the buckboard?"

"Come on, smartass. Let's go watch the news."

SATURDAY

30

MOISE ANGELLE ARRIVES

Moise Angelle knocked on Lanclos' farmhouse door a half hour before they had planned to meet. It was still dark, however, the eastern sky was beginning to lighten enough so the ground fog in the fields was a layer of silver smoke. The chocolate Labs came hurtling out of the mist from the fields barking joyously and skidding around the corner of the garage.

As they galloped toward the porch to greet Moise, Lanclos flicked on the porch light and welcomed his friend. "Come on in and drink some coffee with me. I'm filling a thermos for us to take along. Hurry and get inside here before those dogs jump all over you."

Moise crossed the threshold just in time to avoid the shower as the Labs shook themselves, spraying the porch furniture. He was a sturdy, barrel-chested man with slim hips, and wore a gray gabardine windbreaker and boot-cut jeans over scuffed, tan calf-skin boots. "I've been up since four o'clock, and about coffeed out already, thanks. The coyotes were howling and barking all night. They woke me up and I never got back to sleep." He followed Lanclos into the kitchen.

"I know I'm early." Moise glanced at a black iron skillet on the stove that held the remainder of a fried potato and egg breakfast.

"I'll be right with you. Let me just grab my jacket and cap. We going in your truck or mine?"

"Let's go in mine. Then you can fill me in on what's been going on while I'm driving."

"That'll work. And there's plenty going on." Lanclos finished pouring coffee into the thermos, tightly screwed on the cap, and crossed the room toward a pegged rack loaded with visor caps in a variety of colors and insignias next to the back kitchen door. He selected a faded green cap, slapped it on his head, and with a practiced downward yank, positioned it firmly. Then he picked up a pistol in its pocket holster and pointed toward the living room. "Let's go. My jacket's on the coat rack yonder."

"You've been busy lately. Haven't talked to you for a while," said Moise as he followed Lanclos through the living room. "Doesn't look like you ever use the living room anymore, huh?"

"Yeah, I stay busy as hell. Paul and I live mostly back there in the kitchen when we're home. The living room was for Lanette. I never spent much time in it even when she was still with us." Lanclos pulled a lightweight denim jacket from one of the S-shaped wooden hooks of the coat tree. He slipped it on and slid the holstered pistol into a side pocket, then opened the front door for Moise.

"Got us a good fog this morning," he said as they followed the brick path to Moise's beat-up and faded red truck.

"Yep. It's thick enough that a big rig and some cars piled up on I-10 this morning. But it's lifting. By the time we get there, we'll be able to see well enough." Moise hiked himself up onto the split upholstery of the driver's seat and slammed the door.

"I see you chose one of your undercover trucks today," Lanclos laughed.

"How many of these old beaters you got now?"

"Four or five. In my business I have to keep a low profile." Moise flipped up the truck's worn sun visor that immediately flopped down again. "Damnit!" He punched it back up.

"We meeting Delcambre at his woods or his house?" he asked as he turned down the volume of the Cajun fiddle music on the radio.

"He said for us to go to the woods and he'd spot us from the house and ride on over there."

"Old Herman Delcambre. I haven't see him in a while."

"He pretty much stays to himself. I'm glad he went to the feed store and told the farmers over there about the black powder rifle, or else I'd never of known about it."

"And were you there at the time?"

"No. I was following up a lead on Gerald's truck. I was over at T'Bro's Auto Body. You know Claudine Bergeron? Roy Bergeron's wife? The *traiteur*?"

"Oh, yeah. I know some people get treatments from her. They say she's good. What's she got to do with it?"

"She went by the feed store yesterday and heard old Herman talking about some outlaw hunters the night before in his woods. Heard him talking about the rifle he'd found lying over there. She thought she'd better tell me about it in case it had something to do with our investigation."

"Smart lady."

"Smart enough."

"How'd you find the truck at T'Bro's?"

Lanclos cleared his throat. "Claudine again. She knew Gerald's truck and spotted it at the garage."

"Damn, Mitch. You better hire the woman."

Lanclos gazed out the window without answering.

"Uh-oh. Look here." Moise slowly pulled onto the shoulder of the blacktop and braked. "Did you see that?" He opened the door and got out.

Lanclos craned his head to see, then got out and joined Moise at the side of a dead yellowish bobcat lying off the road in a clump of milk thistle and fragile pink mallow.

"That's the second bobcat I've see hit alongside the road in the past two weeks," Moise said, sadly looking down at the dead animal, its mouth open in a silent yowl. "I see one or two dead coyotes a week alongside the roads, but hardly ever a bobcat. Too many houses going up around the parish. Not enough habitat left."

A red-and-white milk delivery truck passed on the way toward St. Beatrice. A yellow school bus passed after that and children pressed their faces to the window, pointing at the bobcat as the men walked back to the truck.

* * *

"You can turn in there," directed Lanclos as Moise slowed at the beginning of Delcambre's woods. Moise turned off the black-top onto a narrow dirt lane that followed the edge of the farmer's ten acres of bottomland bayou woods.

"Park anywhere along here. He'll see us and come over from the house." Lanclos picked up his thermos, unscrewing the stain-less cup and the cap. "You want some coffee now?"

"Naw, I'm good. Go ahead."

Lanclos poured half a cup of the steaming coffee and twisted the lid back on.

Moise sat quietly, eyes narrowed, as he surveyed the woods, sniffing the light breeze that drifted through the cab. Lanclos sipped the coffee, a small smile at the corner of his mouth, as he realized that whenever he went out into the country with Moise, it was very much like being with a bird dog.

"You know," Moise broke the silence. "If the outlaw hunting here the other night had anything to do with the Guillory broth-ers, I'll likely be able to tell." He shook his head slowly back and forth. "Those two sons-a-bitches. I can almost smell those two if they've been anywhere around here."

"And it's no wonder what with their grandfather and your father being enemies for so long." Lanclos clamped his mouth shut, immediately regretting his words.

"I know that goddamn Eli Guillory shot my father." Moise pounded his palm on the steering wheel, lips tightening. "I just can't prove it. I hope he's doing a slow turn in hell."

"I'm sorry I brought it up. I didn't think."

"You don't have to bring it up for me to remember it. I think about it a hundred times a day." Moise worked his jaw, tense mus-cles visible in his face. "My father...lying there in the woods... ants crawling all over him...maggots...and him unable to move. Paralyzed from a bullet in his spine." Moise shook his shoulders as if to throw off the image. "Thank God they think he must have passed out toward the end."

Lanclos watched his friend, biting his tongue before he could offer some lame sympathetic statement. Instead, he waited.

"And as for those two brothers, Elrick and Toy, let me tell you. They continue to sell fresh deer meat to restaurants when the season's been over for two months... all over the state of Louisiana, and even into Texas and Arkansas. They think nothing of selling loggerheads and out of season ducks, *sac-a-lait,* and alligator to crooked restaurants. Damn outlaws! They don't care. I've put them in jail three times. They hate me. They send me messages through the pipeline, bragging about what they've gotten away with. Psycho bastards. Just like their grandfather Eli. Rotten bloodline. It's only a matter of time, and I'll have those skinny bastards back in jail."

"Or worse," said Lanclos, finishing the coffee and tossing the last drops out of the window before replacing the cup on the thermos.

"Yeah, or worse is right." Moise set his jaw.

"I think Elrick, Rick's the worst one," said Lanclos. "He's the oldest and leads Toy around by the nose."

"They're both worse," said Moise, "but how can they help it with those rotten genes?"

"At least you have the satisfaction of knowing that old man Eli is dead."

"Yeah, but pneumonia was much too easy a way for him to go," snarled Moise.

"Look at it this way. He died less than three months after your father. Consider the timing of it... *Le Bon Dieu ne punit pas avec un baton!*"

"Maybe so." Moise's tone was softer, as he continued to stare through the windshield at the woods.

"You gotta ease up, Moise. It's no good for you to keep that anger stoked."

Moise didn't answer him right away, his hands clenched on the steering wheel.

"Eli's in jail for drunk and disorderly. And he's so notorious for outlaw hunting that the governor has the deputies escort him out of jail in the middle of the night to shoot enough deer for one of his political banquets in Baton Rouge. And the old s.o.b. gets swamp fever which turns into pneumonia and kills him."

"What'd I tell you? Justice was done!"

The men watched as a brown swamp rabbit bounded through a clump of ferns in the midst of a group of saplings and young cedars. A light breeze drifted through the cab and Moise sniffed the air. "I love the smell of the bayou. I should have built on the bayou instead of two hundred feet back from the road." His hands relaxed on the wheel and he dropped them onto his lap.

Lanclos congratulated himself on defusing his friend. "Old Herman's smart to keep his woods intact. He's kept his land from eroding. You remember Eric LeFleur? He chopped all his trees down, keeps the bayou frontage mowed, and he tells me the other day he's losing a foot a year to erosion. Every time an outboard passes fast, the waves chew away at his shoreline."

"Eric should of known better."

"He did know better. His wife got after him. She's scared of snakes."

"That's what he gets for marrying a Yankee," Moise laughed. "Serves him right."

Another breeze strong enough to lift some of the dark hair on the back of Moise's neck passed through the cab.

"Aaaah," said Lanclos. "I love a breeze. Clears the air, and I think Herman's arrived."

Delcambre rode up on a black four-wheeler, parking behind them. "Morning, you all. *Comment ça va?*" he asked, sauntering over to Lanclos' side of the cab.

"*Bien. Bien.*" The two men got out, slamming doors, and positioning themselves by the pickup, shook hands all around. Moise crossed his arms and leaned against the bed of the truck. Lanclos laid an arm along the rim of the bed as they looked expectantly toward the farmer, who was dressed in blue coveralls.

Delcambre pushed a straw western-style hat back on his forehead and pointed toward the south. "We're going to be walking toward that group of water oaks over there. That's where I found the rifle. Just throwed up against that log it was."

"Go ahead, Herman. Lead us the way you went into the woods the other night,"

Lanclos directed. "Then we're going to let Moise tell us what to do. He's the expert tracker,"

Delcambre nodded, and the men slowly began to file into the woods.

They passed a foot-wide beaten trail leading to the bayou. "That's a nutria or coon path to the water," said Delcambre, his voice deep and husky.

A few more yards and Moise stopped and pointed toward some fresh tracks that looked like a dog had passed. "You heard coyotes lately?" he asked Delcambre.

"Last night I did. Woke me up."

"They were on the move last night over at my place too. That's about five miles from here."

"They get around."

"Have to. Not much habitat left for them around here."

A chicken hawk perched on the power lines by the road watched the men as they moved further into the woods. Another hawk screamed as he wheeled high above.

"Over there by that log. That's where I found it," said Delcambre, pointing to a rotting log ten feet ahead of them, covered with drab-colored, curled resurrection fern.

"Okay. Then let me go ahead. Stay here for a few minutes until I tell you." Moise slowed his pace, treading so carefully that he stopped short with each step. When he reached the log, he hunkered down to examine the ground and waved the other two over.

"There's nothing I can see anywhere around here," he said when they'd caught up with him.

"Don't forget, it rained the night Gerald died."

"Washed any blood away."

The men stayed still, carefully observing every detail around them: the grasses, mosses, tiny white star-like flowers, ferns and lichen all silent witnesses to the events of two nights before.

As they waited and watched, Lanclos and Delcambre standing, Moise still kneeling, a cane truck passed slowly on the blacktop, a few sedans and a pickup unable to pass on the deep-ditched and narrow road, and forced to drive at ten miles an hour.

Delcambre looked up and laughed. "Look at that. There go some mad Frenchmen, them!"

"Look here," said Moise. "I think this may have been where Gerald fell. See that?" He pointed to an area five feet from the log where some of the ground cover was broken. "It's hard to know for sure, but some of those clover stems and flowers are broken for a few feet there. He could've landed hard there as his rifle flew off, hitting the log."

The two men kneeled by the area, heavily shaded by the thick canopy of swamp maple, sweet gum, and water oak. They quietly studied the ground for a few minutes.

"I believe you're right," said Lanclos. "There're no animal trails anywhere around here that would have done that."

"All right then. Now you say Rusty found five buckshot in his face. So the scatter was small," Moise said, standing and looking around at the woods. "So here's what we're going to do. Let's fan out and go forty paces to the north. We'll guess the shooter was somewhere between forty and fifty feet over there somewhere." He swept his arm in an arc to indicate the search area. "So walk slowly and keep your eyes open. Do a sweep of the ground at every step. We may get lucky and find a shell."

"Let's do it," Lanclos nodded at Delcambre and the three men began their exploration of the terrain.

A three-foot, fat, black moccasin slithered across Moise's path so he stopped, waiting for it to continue its way toward the bayou. "Watch for moccasins. One just passed. You see one, there's another one around somewhere."

"And I come out with no pistol today, me," said Delcambre.

"And now I lost count of my steps," said Lanclos.

"We're about twenty-five feet from the log," said Moise.

The men continued their paces until they reached forty feet. Moise stopped, holding up a hand. "Let's stop here and survey first to the left and then to the right of where we're standing."

The three, bent over, stepped carefully to the left, turning their heads slowly as they examined every inch of the ground under the trees and interlacing vines and briars. That accomplished, they repeated the search to their right. When they finished, Moise stood straight, arched his back and directed them on. "Now, we're going to step ten more paces north and do it all over again."

The men counted off the added steps and began their search once more. It was on this second try that Lanclos spotted the bright red of an empty shotgun shell.

"Uh-oh," he said, fishing a crumpled latex glove from his jacket pocket. "Got something here." He kneeled down, peering at the shell half hidden by a clump of grass.

Moise hurried over, a thorny vine scratching his cheek. Putting up a warning hand to Delcambre, he stopped a few feet from the spot, studying the ground before stepping further.

"Son of a bitch, Lanclos. You did good!"

"*You* did good, Moise. You're running this show!" Lanclos smiled widely, white teeth gleaming. He carefully retrieved the shell, picking it up by the rim with forefinger and thumb, avoiding the brass base, which could possibly hold a print. He held it up to the light so Moise could see clearly.

"That's the baby we were hoping for. That's a fresh shell! I'd bet my bottom dollar, that's it!"

Lanclos circled halfway around and held it up so Delcambre could see the prize.

Delcambre nodded, smiling, as Lanclos slipped the shell into a small brown envelope he had stashed in another pocket.

"And now we keep looking, right?" asked Delcambre.

"Oh, yeah, we have to keep looking," said Moise. "We got lucky, but that doesn't mean we can't find something else out here. Back to work!"

"We have a lot of ground to cover. I'm going to call my house-keeper and tell her to put on a few more steaks. She's cooking steak in brown gravy. You all will have dinner with me? I eat at eleven." He pulled a cell phone from its belt case.

Lanclos looked at Moise who flashed a wide smile and touched a handkerchief to his scratched cheek. "*Mais, oui.* We wouldn't miss out on that invite, now would we, Mitch?"

"Thank you, Herman. You can count on us!" Lanclos said as he bent under a wide cobweb stretched between two saplings.

31

RUSTY PHONES LANCLOS

L anclos was looking out the window of Moise's truck as they drove toward his farm after eating the steak dinner at Delcambre's, when his cell phone rang. He answered as they passed a farmhouse where a woman was setting up a wagon full of hay and pumpkins in her front yard for an autumn display.

"Yeah, Rusty, what you got?"

"After we talked, I kept working on the autopsy, and once I'd sawed the skull open and gotten in there to see what the hell, I found a subdural hematoma. On Gerald's right side. The meningeal artery ruptured from a blow to the head. That's what led to the hematoma."

"Yeah, okay. So it was from when he fell? After being shot?"

"No, it wasn't like that. There's a bruise under his thick hair. Looks like he was hit with a metal object. And hit hard."

"Hard?"

"Yeah, hard enough to kill him. It wasn't the shotgun killed him. It was the blow to the head."

"How do you know it wasn't the shotgun did it?"

"Because the hematoma came first. I can tell from the bleed pattern and the clotting factor. He died right before he was shot. He must have been staggering around and falling down seconds before he was shot. I give a blow-by-blow description in my report... no pun intended." Rusty chuckled. "Sorry. I couldn't resist that."

"Are you positive, Rusty? That it was the blow to the head that killed him?" Lanclos looked over at Moise who raised his eyebrows in surprise.

"I'd swear to it in court. Is that positive enough for you?"

"Son-of-a-bitch. Now how the hell am I going to make sense of this news?"

"Hey, don't ask me. I'm just the medical examiner. You're the detective."

"Yeah, yeah. Look, thanks a lot for calling and keeping me up to date. I thought we were getting somewhere in this investigation, but now, we're back to square one. How big do you figure the metal object was?"

"The contusion and dent in the skull, there where the skull is thin...the pterion, corresponds with a striking area of about sixteen centimeters. A rectangular shape about four by four centimeters. That's what it was all right. It'll all be in my report so you can understand better what I'm talking about." Rusty cleared his throat.

"What the hell? Something like a square-faced hammer?"

"Could be. I can't narrow it down that close."

"All right, Rusty. Thank you."

"You know where I am if you have any more questions."

Lanclos returned the phone to its holder and looked over at Moise. Moise kept his eyes on the road while stretching out an arm and turning down the volume on the radio.

"So what'd he say?"

"Gerald wasn't killed by shotgun blast. Somebody slammed him in the head with a metal object."

"So how does that get him into the woods getting shot at night before last?"

Lanclos shook his head. "Damned if I know."

"Yeah, but you know how it goes. First you find this out. Then you find that out. Pretty soon it all hangs together."

"It better start making sense soon before the trail goes cold. It's already day number three."

"Not really. It's really more like day number two because he was killed after midnight yesterday."

"All right, I'll give you that. It's day number two. But the trail's getting cold anyhow. And it's making me restless...like I don't want to waste any time sleeping until I find out what happened."

"You'll find out what happened. This is a small town. Everything comes out sooner or later."

Lanclos ran a hand over his face and closed his eyes. "First he's hit, then he's shot." He repeated, "First he's hit, then he's shot."

"Quit driving yourself crazy. Leave it alone for a minute. Your brain's in overdrive right now, and that's not how you're going to figure this thing out. You'll do your usual careful field work. Interview a bunch of people, take your notes, let it all simmer in there for a while...and blam! The answer will come to you when you least expect it."

"I hope you're right, buddy," Lanclos said, staring out the window at a man on a tractor mowing two acres of rolling lawn.

"I know I'm right. I been knowing you too long. And you just keep getting better at the murder business."

32

MOISE BREAKS A DATE

D
ixie Patin lived in a 1925 Acadian-style cypress house, raised two feet above the ground on cement blocks. The house sat on a sparsely built rural road leading out of Levee Town, a village hard by the western levee of the Atchafalaya and twenty miles south of St. Beatrice.

A homemade sign close to her black mailbox advertised nursery plants for sale. There were over a hundred black two gallon and three gallon pots arranged around the yard holding a great variety of young flowering bushes, herbs, and an assortment of annuals and perennials in flats beneath the twin ancient cedar trees. After knocking on the door to the living room side of the house, he turned and studied the thriving collection of blooms as he waited for Dixie to answer.

Spiky monkey grass and pink dianthus bordered the cracked cement walk to the front porch. Grass and tiny weeds were beginning to fill the cracks and as his eye traveled up the path to the porch steps, he spotted a turquoise earring tucked beneath a golden dandelion growing from a crack near the bottom step.

"Hey, you," Dixie called from the door. "What you doing so early? I didn't expect you til later on."

"Hang on," Moise said, going back down the steps to retrieve the earring. He bent, picked it up, and wordlessly held it aloft.

"You are wonderful! You never miss a thing. That's one of my favorite earrings. I've been looking for it everywhere."

"Everywhere but where it was."

She pushed open the screen door and held it open for him, kissing his cheek as he passed, then throwing her arms around him and hugging him hard.

"Thank you, darlin," she said, fitting the earring into her ear. "Now this sucker isn't going anywhere!"

"How about fixing me a cup of coffee while I tell you something I want you to do for me. That be all right?"

"Come on in," Dixie said, leading him through the front room into a narrow kitchen. He sank onto a bench beside a small round table tucked into the corner.

"I just made some coffee, and was ready to jump into the shower and start getting ready for our date tonight."

"Sorry. No date tonight. I have to do something...and so do you."

"Damn! I was looking forward to going out for dinner and seeing that new thriller that just opened in Lafayette." She brought him a cup of steaming coffee. "It's all right. I'll heat up some of those crawfish and crab *pistolettes* instead. You want one?"

"Save me one or two. But not right now." Moise slapped a hand on his stomach. "I just grabbed a *boudin* on the way over here."

Dixie arched a dark eyebrow and placed her hands lightly on her hips.

"I'll bet you a hundred bucks that breaking our date is all about work. You taking a boat out in the swamp again tonight? Somebody snitch on another misfit?"

"Could be. Sit down and I'll tell you what I need you to do for me."

Dixie took a deep breath, pushed her rolled denim sleeves up and sat in a chair opposite him, crossing her legs and smoothing out the front of her khaki shorts. "Go ahead. Let's have it." She rested elbows on the table and propped her chin with one fist.

"You know Collette Viator about a half mile down the road toward town?"

"I've seen her a few times. The one who lives in that rent house around the bend...next to that mildewed doublewide?"

"That's her. If you drive by and see a man over there. Let me know. Toy Guillory. That's his woman."

"I just saw her at Dupuy's Grocery today. She looked half asleep or drunk."

"Pain pills. She loves pain pills. Toy gets them for her."

"Well, I don't mind doing your snooping for you. Maybe I'll start walking a mile a day and pass by there. I need the exercise to keep my figure."

Moise leaned back and surveyed her body with one eye closed. He nodded slowly. "So far, so good. But don't get complacent."

"You!" She threw a salt shaker at him that he caught with an instant reflex.

"What about if I have to make a Hotshot delivery down to Morgan City? Or Texas?"

"I've got other people watching out for him. But, let me know if you're leaving."

"Don't I always let you know when I'm loading up to make a run?"

"Yeah, you do." Moise set the silver-capped salt shaker back next to its mate.

"I'll keep an eye out. What's he look like?"

"You don't know Toy? He's in and out of Levee Town all the time."

"I know of him. He's the one with the brother who's always in some kind of trouble."

"That's the one. They both stay in trouble. Elrick...Ricky... is the brother. Belton is the father. They live on a houseboat in the Basin. Toy has long black hair. Mustache. He looks a lot like Ricky. But Ricky's got six inches on him. They're both skinny. Both have brown eyes, sunken, dark circles underneath. Neither one of them looks like they ever change their clothes. Always the same. Greasy jeans, black or brown tee shirts, visor caps. They spray paint their shrimp boots black so the white doesn't show at night when they're outlawing. Both wear their hair pulled back with an elastic. Toy sleeps over at Collette's on average once or twice a week."

Dixie nodded. "Okay. I'll let you know right away if I see either one of them. And I know better than to ask you what it's about, don't I?" she smiled.

"It's very important, is all I can tell you. And I know I don't have to tell you to keep it to yourself."

"Who am I going to tell anyhow? That old couple next door? They don't even speak English and my French stinks."

He slid the empty cup toward her. "I could use another cup of this."

"Sure, darlin." She picked it up and crossed to the stove.

"And if you do see either of those two anywhere, either at Collette's or in the village, call my cell right away. Leave a message where you saw them and what time it was if I don't answer. And don't get close to Collette's property if you do see him over there. Just let me know."

"Don't worry. I can be just as sneaky as you."

"Be even sneakier than me with those two. I mean that. They don't play."

"Sure. I get it! I get it! And just what are you going to do to make up to me for breaking our date tonight?" She returned with the full cup.

"I'll make it up to you just as soon as I can. How about Pat's in Henderson? Will that do it?"

"Pat's is always a good way to make it up with me. You must be rich. And besides taking me to Pat's? What else are you going to do?" She narrowed her eyes at him, a small smile at the side of her mouth.

Moise leaned back, pulling her down onto his lap and lifting her hair, kissed the back of her neck. "Dixie, Dixie. *Mon coeur*," he crooned.

"You smell my perfume?"

"Yes, *chère.*"

"You like?"

"Yes."

"You better like it. It's some you gave me for Christmas last year."

"I forgot."

"How much you like it?" she laughed.

"This much," he said, lifting her as he stood, holding her in his arms and heading with her toward the other side of the house.

"I thought you had work to do in the swamp," she said as he pushed open her bedroom door with his shoulder.

"Not til it gets dark," he said, lowering her onto the double bed and gently positioning her against the double row of pillows arranged in front of the brass bedstead.

"Uh-oh. Sounds like I'm in for it."

"Yep. You sure are." He started unbuttoning his shirt.

She fingered the turquoise earring. "And don't mess with my earring," she said with mock seriousness.

"I wasn't planning on it." He stretched an arm to pull the cord of the ceiling fan over the bed.

"It's not that hot today," she said.

"Not yet it isn't," he said.

33

THE SAVOY ROADHOUSE

T here were over fifty pickups and sedans at the Savoy Roadhouse by nine-thirty in the evening when Lanclos pulled into the well-lighted parking lot. He took a moment to drive around the lot and survey the cars and trucks before selecting a spot under a large oak and parking his truck.

The long established Savoy's was known throughout Acadiana for music and dancing. People drove for miles on the weekends for the rock and roll and Cajun music. The sixty-year-old frame building had been added onto several times over the years. It sported a new red metal roof and an orange flickering neon sign in the shape of a giant "S." There was also a wraparound porch heavily decorated with metal signs advertising various brands of beer, soda, and tobacco. Some forest green wooden benches lined the porch with a few dented and tarnished brass spittoons separating them.

Deep vibrations from the drums and bass within thundered outside and Lanclos wished he'd brought his son with him knowing he'd appreciate the music, but he never took Paul along on an investigation. Just then, two young men came hurtling out of the front door, racing across the porch and down the steps, eager to fight. They ran to an open space along the tree line, one shoving the other as they moved quickly along to a wide enough area for a fistfight. Then, the one who'd been shoved along, whirled and landed a punch smack on the aggressor's chin.

The man staggered back, wiped his chin with a palm, then spit on his hands, and laughed. "You sorry bastard! A lucky punch is all you're going to get off of me." He swung at his opponent and landed a punch on his abdomen that knocked the wind out of him as he bent over, blowing out a great stream of air. The punch made him sick, so he waved the other man away and, still bent over, trudged to the bushes underlying the trees and threw up noisily into them.

Lanclos walked over to the two men. "All right. That's enough. You two get out of here before I arrest you both for disturbing the peace and fighting. And don't let me see either one of you driving home, or you're going to have DUIs besides. So start walking."

"Aww, Detective. It ain't nothin. We was just messing around. This dickhead here was looking funny at my girl friend."

"I don't care what you idiots are fighting about. I'm here on business and you're getting in my way. Now get out of here!"

The man who'd been sick, still halfway bent over, looked sideways at Lanclos. "I don't feel so good." He held his stomach with one hand and with the other wiped his mouth.

"You're going to feel a lot worse in a minute if you don't get out of here."

"Will you tell my girl friend we're walking home? Her name is Regina," the aggressor said.

"I'll tell the guy at the door for you."

"She's wearing a silver dress. You can't miss her. She's a babe!"

Lanclos pointed toward the road. "Hit it!"

"Come on, Toot. We gotta go," said the sick one, somewhat recovering. The two headed for the road side by side and Lanclos turned back toward the roadhouse smiling as he remembered his youth and old fighting days.

As he pushed open the double front doors and crossed the threshold, he was hit by a blast of cranked up music from the onstage cover band. He took a moment at the door to pass on the message about Regina to the beefy doorman, then showed his badge when the man tried to collect a three dollar cover. Lanclos did a quick survey of the room, scanning the long bar and the dozen tables where dozens of customers were drinking and laughing and trying to talk over *Born on the Bayou.* He caught a whiff of marijuana laced with overtones of perfume, sweat, beer and whiskey.

A dozen couples were dancing in front of the stage on the narrow floorboards. Two young women customers in tight low-rider jeans with fringed tee shirts performed their own individual dances immediately in front of the band. Eyes closed, they held their heads back so their long hair swished as they twisted and turned gracefully to the beat. A man held a beer bottle aloft as he watched them intently, swaying in time with the music. Knowing the lyrics by heart, half the audience stopped their conversation to sing along with the chorus, most of them waving their arms for dramatic effect.

He pushed through to the bar, signaled to one of the busy bartenders for a Dr. Pepper, paid, and went toward a door to the back room where he knew a *bourrée* game was in progress, as it was every night but Sunday at Savoy's. Once he closed that door behind him, he sighed with relief at the quiet within that back room. It was insulated and cooler. Ceiling fans circulated the air-conditioning and five card players and a dealer sat at a round table in the center of the room. Shaded lights hanging low from chains illuminated the players. There was a stack of bills in the center of the table, and he watched a woman get *bourréed* as he waited at a respectful distance from the group, not wanting to interrupt the game.

The houseman, Val, spoke softly to her. "Sixty-five dollars for the pot, Germaine." The woman was in her sixties with short dyed black hair and a lipstick red dress with a manicure to match. She sighed and counted out the money from the neat stack in front of her and threw it unceremoniously onto the pile of bills. The man next to her laughed and threw his arms over the money, raking it toward him.

Val nodded at Lanclos. "You want us to deal you in, Mitch?"

"No, thanks. Not tonight. I'm here on business." He took three steps toward the table, slowly meeting everyone's eyes. "How you all doing tonight?"

They all smiled and nodded and assured him they were doing all right, except for Germaine. who said, "*C'est pas bon.*"

"If I know you, Germaine, you'll win it back by midnight," said Lanclos. He looked around the table.

"Anybody here see Gerald Theriot Thursday night?"

Val and two other men nodded. "He was here."

"Anybody remember what time that was?"

Val frowned. "Must of been about eleven when he showed up. I'm not sure. Anybody?"

One of the players nodded. "I think so. Something like that."

"How long did he stay?"

"He played for a couple hours. Won a lot of pots, I know that."

"He got about a hundred off of me," laughed a gray-headed man, stroking his unruly beard with spread fingers.

"Me too," said a young man with a neat black goatee seated across from the dealer.

"So he won how much would you say altogether?" asked Lanclos.

Val jutted out his bottom lip and studied the ceiling as he thought. "I'd say he won about three hundred."

"That'd be about right," agreed another.

"How did he seem?"

"He was his usual. Had a few beers. Friendly. Said he had something to do and left earlier than usual. The house fixed a shrimp stew and he didn't even stay for that."

Lanclos nodded. "All right. If any of you think of anything else, give me a call at the Sheriff's Office, will you please?" He placed a few business cards in the center of the table.

"Will do," Val said.

"Sure," said the goateed man, glancing around at the others, who all nodded.

"You ought to stick around," said Val. "Joleen is serving us crawfish *étouffée* tonight."

"Thanks, I'd like to, but I've got to go," Lanclos said, finishing his soda and holding up a hand in farewell. "Thank you all for your help. I'll be seeing you." He turned and walked back out into the loud dancehall where the band was playing *Gimme Two Steps*, wishing as he quickly made his way through the crowd that he had the time to play a few hands in the back room. Nothing like a few hands of cards to clear the mind, but Lanclos knew he'd better head home and get some sleep. It had been a long day, and he'd be back at it again by dawn the next morning.

As he passed a couple in a torrid embrace by the open door of a car, he rubbed his eyes, feeling weary, and made his way to his truck, glad to be headed home.

34

LANCLOS SHOOTS A SNAKE

After leaving the Savoy, Lanclos had a mind to drive by Philomena's and make sure everything was all right. Her house was on the opposite side of St. Beatrice from the roadhouse, so he drove through town, then on past the city limits onto Delcambre Road. As he approached her house, he slowed and looked toward the property checking to see if all appeared to be well. He saw a bobbing light from the chicken coop set to the north of the house on the opposite side from the horse pasture and about twenty feet from the woods that separated Philomena's from the Bergeron farm.

He thought it peculiar that there was a light on in the chicken coop at this late hour when he knew Philomena went to bed early. It was now eleven-thirty and she should be fast asleep unless something was wrong.

He clicked off the headlights, pulled over and braked as quietly as possible. He retrieved his Maglight from the center console and patting the gun in his pocket, eased himself out of the truck, and gently closed the door.

The front light cast a yellow glow over the porch and a few feet beyond, so that the bushes bordering the porch were illuminated. There was a soft light at the rear of the house from Philomena's bedroom. He walked quickly toward the bobbing light in the hen house without using his flashlight. When he reached the outbuilding he heard gentle muffled clucking and eased up to the doorway then pressed his back against the cypress planks of the coop. Slowly he turned his head so he could see within.

Philomena's back was to him with a shotgun braced on her shoulder and clearly aiming at something.

"Philomena," he whispered.

"Oooh!" she startled, swinging the shotgun around.

"Don't shoot, Miss Philomena!" he held up his hands. "It's me. Detective Lanclos."

"Please, Detective. Go shoot that damn snake! My hen has chicks under her wings."

He quickly stepped forward and joined her inside the room-sized coop. He clicked his flashlight on the laying boxes, which formed a neat row along the middle of the back wall. Some of the hens were bedded down in the boxes, other were perched on a five foot wide roost and trying to sleep. A six foot long brown and dull gold chicken snake was slithering into a laying box slowly working his way under a brown hen. Lanclos put out his arm to guide Philomena back toward the door. He stepped forward, raised his pistol, aimed, and shot the snake.

Instantly it writhed, snapping into and out of coils, then snapped its head out from under the hen, raising up a foot from the straw filled box and opening its mouth wide at its aggressor.

Lanclos took another step forward and shot the snake's head off. The raised portion of the snake dropped, but the body kept writhing in a sinuous death dance.

Philomena's hand went to her mouth. She moaned. "If you only knew how I hate snakes, Detective. Thank you so much. I hope he didn't swallow any of the chicks."

Lanclos stepped up to the box and shined his light on the snake. "It's bulging in one spot. He may have eaten one already." He picked up the tail feathers of the hen and looked beneath her at the cuddled yellow and black chicks. "How many did she have?"

"She had ten today when I saw her parading them around the yard."

Lanclos looked again. "Okay. I count nine. He just got one."

"Thank you, Jesus! I woke up when I heard them clucking and knew something was wrong. I grabbed my 12 gauge. I mean my father's 12 gauge."

"Your father had that gun?"

"My grandfather had this gun." She held it out for him to see. "I learned how to shoot by the time I was ten years old."

"Good for you, Miss Philomena. I'm glad you can take care of business when you have to."

"Oh, yes. But I hate to have to come out here and shoot snakes. I can't stand to be anywhere near them. They give me the shivers. Now I won't be able to get back to sleep. I'll have to sit up and drink coffee all night."

"Well, I was just passing by to check on you, and when I saw the light in the coop I wanted to see if everything was all right."

"Oh, I'm so glad you did. Would you like me to fix you a cup of coffee?"

"It's too late for me to drink coffee, thank you. I'll be getting on home as soon as I see you to the house. But let me toss that snake into the bayou first."

"Oh, no, no. I bury any varmints or snakes under my rose bushes. Alfred's coming by in the morning and I'll get him to do it for me. Just toss him outside on the ground if you would please."

Lanclos raised the snake up by the tail and dangled it. "He's six foot easy."

She backed away shuddering. "I can't stand them. I just can't stand a snake."

Lanclos laughed. "We got enough of them in Louisiana, that's for sure." He walked the snake outside and dropped it in loops three feet from the chicken coop.

"Let's get you into the house," he said. "Come on." He beckoned to her and she followed his lead and came out of the hen house, shotgun loosely held under her right arm, and flashlight in the other.

"Looks like you have a Maglight like mine," he said.

"Isn't this pretty? Alfred gave it to me." She trained the beam of light toward the house.

"That's a nice present for you. You need a good light out here."

"Oh, yes. He got tired of me using my kerosene lantern. Said I needed something I could grab quick."

"That's true."

Lanclos followed her toward the front porch and the welcoming yellow light that cut a swath across the front yard. She slowly mounted the front steps as he patiently guided her by the elbow. They crossed the creaking boards toward the kitchen door and she clicked off the torch.

As they stepped into the house, Lanclos watched her place the flashlight on the kitchen counter. He studied it for a moment as she leaned the shotgun into a corner by the doorway to the back of the house.

"How long ago did Alfred give you the flashlight?"

Philomena turned smiling. "Why, I just got it yesterday as a matter of fact. You really like it?"

"I sure do. You don't happen to know where Alfred got it, do you?"

"He found it on his way over here. He bicycles everywhere. He's always finding stuff alongside the road. People lose things, or throw out things. Alfred's always on the lookout for something free."

"Miss Philomena, I'd like to take this flashlight along with me tonight, please. I'll leave you mine in its place, if you don't mind. They're pretty much alike." He laid his on the counter.

"Why, that would be all right...but why?"

"Because we've been looking for one like this. Just like this. I'll have to ask Alfred tomorrow to show me where he found it."

"Oh, he won't mind showing you. If he remembers."

Lanclos pulled a folded handkerchief from his pocket and picked the flashlight up with it. "In the meantime, you stay safe. Lock the door after me."

"I always do. Thank you so much for shooting that snake for me." Philomena wrung her hands. "I'm so glad I didn't have to do it."

Lanclos laughed. "How many snakes have you had to shoot out here over the years?"

She sighed. "All told? In all these years out here? About a hundred, I guess. That's why I have such beautiful roses. They make great rose fertilizer."

"I'm going to remember that," he smiled and carefully holding the wrapped Maglight, he stepped out into the night.

SUNDAY

35

MOISE RETURNS TO DIXIE'S

L ate the next morning, Moise showed up at Dixie's with a stainless pan filled with six cleaned and filleted *sac-a-lait*. "One of the swampers gave these to me last night. You remember Remi? The old-timer who lives on the houseboat in the Basin? I took you out there last year."

"I remember. He boiled some crawfish for us."

"You hungry for some fresh fish, *chère?*"

She took the pan from him and kissed him fully on the mouth. "You have to ask? I'll have these babies ready in no time. I just got back not five minutes ago from a Hot Shot run to Morgan City. I haven't eaten since I grabbed a fast food breakfast on the way down there."

"While you're doing that, I'll go out and pump up that tire on your wheelbarrow. It's low."

"Thank you, and be careful in the tool shed. I think some critter is living in there somewhere. Butch has been doing a lot of excited sniffing around the outside of it. Probably another possum. You want some iced tea first?"

"I'll wait until we eat. I just finished a soda."

He went outside by the kitchen door and down the steps to the yard, taking a moment to survey the vegetable gardens, fig and pear trees, and the whitewashed trellis heavy with Confederate jasmine.

He caught a whiff of something that bothered him, and he searched for the source of the smell, finally focusing his attention on an area to the side of the house where an antique cypress cistern stood a few yards from the house. As he got closer to the high structure, he frowned, stopped, and leaned his head back to survey the rim.

Making a low sound in his throat, he headed toward the tool shed twenty feet from the back porch. A wildly clucking white hen stepped back and forth on the peak of the rusty corrugated metal roof. Moise ignored her and entered the shed, blinking in the shadowy interior. The back wall was lined with wooden shelves crowded with a collection of mason jars, oil cans, garden clippers, paint cans, tins of mineral spirits and turpentine, kerosene and propane lanterns, boxes of nails, screws and bolts, and various boxes of hinges and other assorted hardware.

On the south side of the building were four ladders. Two extension ladders lay on the dirt floor, and a wooden and an aluminum stepladder of different heights leaned against the rough wall. He chose the aluminum stepladder, hoisting it up and away from its position, then tilted it toward the door and maneuvered it out of the shed.

He carried it back to the cistern and without opening it, leaned it against one of the iron bands that circled the vertical cypress planks. Securing the base of it into the ground, he climbed steadily, the hen still maniacally clucking from the tool shed roof.

When he reached the top of the ladder, he peered inside, then squeezed his eyes shut and bowed his head, reaching at the same time into his hip pocket and yanking out a faded red handkerchief.

"Son of a bitch!" he said softly, opening one eye and looking back over the rim again. He mopped his face with the handkerchief, then stuffed it back into his jeans.

Descending the ladder, he crossed back toward the tool shed. This time when he entered, he scanned the four rafters, checking out an assortment of coiled ropes that hung on nails from them. He lifted off a coil of half-inch hemp, toting it back to the ladder.

The hen flew off the shed roof, and finishing with her chorus, went about her daily business of scratching and pecking in the grass, until a large, well-fed black rooster came streaking from behind the tool shed chasing her. She jumped squawking, hit the ground running, and launched another loud tirade as she raced from him across the grass, feathers flying.

Moise paid no attention to the mating chase as he approached the ladder with the rope slung over his shoulder and began to ascend once again. Working the rope into a lasso, he lowered the working end into the shadowy depths of the cistern, and with great care, began his work, as sweat trickled down his face and the back of his neck.

Ten minutes later, Moise entered the house by the kitchen door, stomping his feet on the doormat. "Hey, baby. We got a problem."

Dixie looked up from the black iron griddle she was tending, lightly sautéing the fillets. "What's the matter?"

"Where's Butch?"

"He's right there," she nodded toward the far corner of the kitchen where the Rottweiler dozed beneath the table.

"Great. Let him sleep. We have a lot of work to do."

"What about the fish? It's almost ready."

Moise looked at the griddle. "All right. Let's eat first. But don't turn on the water. We'll eat the fish. I'll get some cans of soda out of the cooler in the truck. Throw out the iced tea. And do-not-turn-on-the-faucet. Got it?"

"I got it. What is going on, Moise?"

"First we eat. Then I'll tell you. Okay?"

She shrugged. "I know better than to argue with you when your mind's made up."

Moise nodded. "I'm going to get the sodas. Serve us up some fish."

They ate in silence as Butch, groaning, moved out of the way of their feet. He flopped on the floor next to Dixie's chair, his breathing giving way to snoring.

"Why's Butch so tired today?"

"It's hot and he's bored. I need to take him for a run."

"Can't. We have too much work to do."

"Will you please tell me what is going on?"

"I sure will. Soon as we finish eating."

"Okay. Okay."

When they'd finished, he carried both plates to the sink and lowered them into it. His hand by habit rose to the faucet, then as he remembered, he pulled it back.

"Okay, now you can tell me. We finished eating." Dixie came up behind him and hugged his waist.

"Remember when I asked you yesterday to keep your eye out for the Guillory brothers?"

"Yes."

"The other people I had looking for them? Ricky and Toy must have gotten the message because they sent me a message back."

"And?"

"There's a bad smell coming from your cistern. I got a ladder out of the tool shed and climbed up so I could see inside."

"Uh-oh. What is it?"

"There's the remains of a deer floating in there. They kept the haunches and backstrap of course. They never toss that out. But the rest of it is rotting away in there. We're going to have to drain the cistern today. And I'll have to drop down inside and scrub it out with bleach. We can drape the hose over the rim and rinse it out when we're done."

"My God, Moise. Why would they do that?"

"Cause they know I'm checking up on them. They don't like that, and they hate me. And they think by coming to my woman's house and doing something in the middle of the night that they're scaring me off. But of course they really know better."

"God, Moise. I knew I should have spent the money to hook up to city water. I made coffee with that water this morning." She made a gagging sound. "I brushed my teeth with that water." She gripped her throat, making a face.

"Then don't kiss me," he smiled.

She made a choking sound in answer.

"Look. You boiled the coffee water. You spit when you brush your teeth. Don't worry. You feel all right, don't you? We're going to fix the cistern up good as new. But it's going to take some hard work. And it's hot today."

"How'd you happen to notice?"

"Baby, how long have you known me?"

"Five years and counting."

"Aren't I always the first one to catch a whiff of something?"

"Yes, you are."

"Well?"

"I'm mighty glad you went out back and discovered what was going on in my water supply. This might have continued for days before I noticed anything wrong."

"Yeah. Let's get to work. And by the way, you better plan on staying at my house for a few nights."

"Okay, but I have to bring Butch."

"Of course."

"How long should I pack for?"

"I don't know yet. Depends."

"When we get done working, I'll start packing for a week."

"That sounds about right."

"Might be kind of fun. Like playing house."

"My place isn't as comfortable as yours now. I'm hardly ever there."

"I'll make it nice."

"Don't make it too nice. I won't know how to act."

"There you go again. You're so afraid I'll want to move in," she chided. "What you don't get is, I like my house. I don't want to move to your house."

"That's good, *chère*. That's why we get along so well. Let's keep it that way."

36

GERALD'S VIEWING

The parking lot was full at Chaisson's Funeral Home. In addition, cars and pickups lined the street in front on both sides, bumper to bumper. Lanclos had to park almost a block away, then quickly walked to the well-lighted building.

Several men sat in a huddle smoking on the wide veranda, and Lanclos nodded at them as he passed through the main entrance. Once inside, he crossed to the guest register resting on a lectern against the wall to his left. He signed his name glancing at the names above his in the book, then turned back a page and read all the names that came before. He knew most, if not all of the people who'd signed the book, except for a few from out of town whose names he didn't recognize.

He took a funeral card from the rack above the guest registry, read it, and placed it carefully into his breast pocket. The card had a color picture of Gerald, gave his dates, and included a sentimental poem about grief and a verse from Corinthians.

He passed along the hallway to the first viewing room where the priest had already begun the Rosary. "Holy Mary, Mother of God, blessed be the fruit of thy womb, Jesus," the assembled mourners recited along with him, as Lanclos slipped into the room to stand behind the last row of chairs. He studied the people, able to identify many of the assembled just by their bearing and the back of their heads. The priest, Father Jules, stood on the far side of the room near to the monitor set on a table displaying family photos which clicked into view one at a time.

Gerald lay in the shiny bronze coffin in a cocoon of white satin. The lined lid glowed from the reflection of overhead lighting. Although Lanclos couldn't see that far, he knew a Rosary would be entwined in Gerald's hands. A woman prayed on a wooden kneeler positioned in front of it, and several dozen lavish floral arrangements were angled on both sides of the coffin.

When Father Jules was finished reciting the Rosary, Lanclos planned to pay his respects at the coffin. He was also curious to see what kind of reconstructive work had been done on Gerald's face. He was positive it wouldn't look like hamburger as it had when Lanclos had last seen him. His throat constricted at the perfumed air of the room, a cloying synthetic smell of roses and lavender.

Abruptly a cell phone began playing a few bars of the theme music from *Bonanza*. Heads jerked around, looking for the source of the interruption. The priest paused, his expression grim, as he had to deal with this at Mass more times than he'd ever thought possible. A man jumped from the second row, patting the pockets of his shirt and then his pants. He looked wildly around, beet red, for his phone. His wife ran to the coffin and peered into it, then snatched up the offending phone and clicked it off. She stomped over to him, shaking her head, and handed it to him.

"I'm so sorry, everybody. It must have dropped out of my pocket when I leaned over and made the sign of the cross over the coffin. I'm so sorry."

Father Jules nodded. "You're forgiven. Please, people, remember this lesson for the future. Turn them off. If we may continue, please."

Lanclos used the interruption as an excuse to step outside the room and walk down to the kitchen to see who was there and to pour a cup of coffee. As he entered the room, he saw a few men standing by the doughnut tray and the cakes that were put out for the visitors.

"It's hard to believe he's gone," said T'Bro. "I still can't get my head around it."

"Jo-Jo, when did you last see Gerald?" a man asked.

"Shee-it. We were out at Lennie's crawfish pond just a week ago trying to get us some *gros-becs.*" T'Bro elbowed him as Lanclos walked in.

Lanclos nodded at them, pretending he hadn't heard and crossed to the coffee urn. He poured a cup and turned around.

"You find out anything yet, Detective? I mean like who killed Gerald?" asked Lloyd.

Lanclos pressed his lips together and shook his head slowly back and forth.

"Damn. Who would do such a fucked-up thing as that?" asked Jo-Jo. "Him of all people? Everybody liked Gerald."

The other men affirmed this with grave nods. T'Bro slid a chocolate-covered doughnut off the tray and placing it primly on a napkin, leaned into it and took a bite.

Lanclos sipped his coffee. "You been here long?" he asked the men.

"Yeah. Our wives are in there," Jo-Jo nodded toward the soft slow sound of the Rosary recitation that drifted into the coffee room. The men looked at each other, then back at Lanclos as if expecting him to reveal something to them.

"Any of you all have any ideas what could have happened to Gerald?"

"No, sir. We just been talking about that. We can't make any sense out of it," Jo-Jo spoke for the group as T'Bro started on the second half of the doughnut. "You have any leads? I guess you can't say anything about it though, huh?"

"We'll find out who did it. Don't worry." Lanclos dumped the rest of the coffee into a stainless sink, then tossed the cup into a swing-top receptacle.

"I'm going back inside. If you think of anything that might help us, give me a call at the Sheriff's Office."

"Oh, yes, sir. We surely will," said Jo-Jo. T'Bro nodded as he slid his hand toward a frosted doughnut with bright blue sprinkles.

As he crossed the threshold back into the carpeted hallway, he turned and looked at the men. "You all know shooting herons is a federal offense, right? And that goes for any other birds that aren't game birds. You got that?" He squinted at them, brow furrowed.

"Yes, Detective," they chorused, all eyes wide and innocent.

"Don't forget it. I catch you shooting the wrong birds, or Fish & Wildlife catches you, and you're going to cough up thousands of dollars in fines *and* do the time."

"Yes, sir," they chorused again.

Lanclos passed back into the hallway and reentered the viewing room, remaining respectfully at the back of the room as the priest began leading the Sorrowful Mysteries. While the collected friends and family intoned the Hail Marys, Lanclos gazed toward the first row.

Gerald's immediate family sat on four velvet covered settees at the front of the ten rows of folding chairs. Leon and Georgette sat together with their two children to the left of the room. Celeste and her mother and father sat on the couch next to theirs without Gerald's son. Gerald's mother and grandmother and sister sat on the third, with his two surviving brothers to the farthest right. Lanclos knew that T.J., the youngest brother, had died with two of his friends in a car wreck before he'd even graduated high school. Death was nothing new to Gerald's family.

Lanclos kept his eyes on the family as the Rosary proceeded. He recited along with the mourners, but his mind was not on the prayers. He kept his gaze fixed on the various members of the family, then shifted his attention back and forth to the friends on both sides of the room.

Loud weeping began, and Lanclos focused on the source of it. A young woman who was sitting in back of Leon and Georgette had burst into tears and was consoled by a friend sitting next to her. Georgette turned around and looked at her impatiently, then whipped her head back around, stiffening her spine. The young woman kept crying loudly and Georgette turned around again and gave her a tissue, putting her finger to her lips to signal her to quiet down. Lanclos recognized her then as one of Gerald's cousins and the friend with her as another cousin.

When the gathered friends and priest had completed the Rosary, the priest made a sign of the cross, stepping to the side a few feet toward Gerald's mother, where he began speaking with her in hushed tones. Lanclos walked down the aisle and rounded the corner to speak to Celeste and her mother.

"I'm very sorry for your loss," he said to them, offering his hand to the mother. The woman had short black hair streaked with silver and wore a dark purple dress. Her hand was damp and limp, and her expression flat. He then turned to Celeste. "Call me if you need me," he said to her.

"Thank you, Detective," she said.

"Your little boy is all right?"

"Oh, yes. Thank you for asking," she said in a monotone. "He's with the neighbors. It's heartbreaking. He keeps asking for his daddy."

The priest had finished talking with Gerald's mother and was making his way through small clusters of people lining the aisles. Lanclos crossed to the mother and told her softly how sorry he was about the tragedy.

Her face was pale and there were dark circles under her eyes. Her hair, also streaked with silver, was tied back with a black velvet ribbon. She wore a black silk dress, and he wondered if it was the same dress she'd worn for her husband's and her son's funerals, all within the past five years. He couldn't conceive of what it would require to get through all those losses in such a short time. She pressed her lips together in a tight line as though she were trying not to cry.

"Thank you, Mitch," she said, her voice breaking.

"Gerald was a fine man," Lanclos said. "We will all miss him very much."

She nodded and swallowed without speaking. Janice, a sister, reached an arm around her mother and lightly stroked her back.

"You signed the guest book?" she asked. He nodded.

He slowly crossed to the coffin, made the sign of the cross, and paused there for a few moments. Besides the Rosary he'd known would be entwined in Gerald's fingers, he saw a small plastic toy and picture of his son tucked in the lining of the coffin lid, and beside it a wedding photo of Gerald and Celeste. He was amazed to see how Gerald looked. Most of the damage had been camouflaged by makeup and the artful way his hair was combed forward.

When he finally turned from the coffin, he moved a few feet away toward the couch where Georgette and Leon were sitting. Leon was waiting for Georgette to finish talking with an older man who hovered over her, holding her hand cupped in both of his.

"Hello, Leon. I'm sorry about Gerald," Lanclos said, meeting his eyes. Leon stood, reaching out his hand to shake, then dropped it when Lanclos didn't respond. Lanclos kept his eyes level as though he didn't notice the gesture.

"Terrible thing," Leon said, looking toward the coffin. "I hope you catch whoever did this before the week's out." He ran a tongue over his teeth, then added, "The son of a bitch!" under his breath.

"Yes," said Lanclos. "Don't worry. We'll get him."

Leon looked away from the coffin and met his gaze. "Either you will, or I will."

"Let us do our work," he said, turning to Georgette who was still talking with the older man. He caught her eye and nodded toward her. She acknowledged him with a quick smile, then returned her attention to the old man who finally released her hand from his bony grip. Lanclos looked back at Leon. "I have to be going. Please tell your wife how sorry I am." Leon gave a quick nod as he looked past Lanclos at the next person waiting in line to speak to him.

Lanclos gave one more look toward the coffin and the banked flowers, then began making his way down the aisle and through the mourners murmuring in clusters. He wondered how many different theories of what happened to Gerald were going through the minds of the friends gathered there. He knew most of the assembled people, and one after the other they nodded to him as he made his way toward one of the doors.

As always when he left a funeral or a viewing, he was glad to be away and outside in the fresh air. The heaviness of the emotions back inside the building had weighed on him, and he headed across the grass toward his pickup, breathing deeply of the cooling late afternoon air.

37

ALFRED POINTS OUT A LOCATION

Passing through town, Lanclos noticed that Alfred was at Sherman's shed, situated in back of a combination quick-stop store and gas station. The tin-roofed metal shed, about the size of a one-car garage was where the locals carried their sacks of pecans to sell. Sherman, a middleman who paid the local pickers by the pound, stored hundreds of pounds in back of the shed until a truck came by once a week to haul the pecans to the processing plants in Atlanta or Houston.

Alfred was picking up both sides of a burlap sack draped over the handlebars of his bicycle, so he could turn it over to Sherman to be weighed. Sherman grappled with the sack, then lowered it onto the scales, as Lanclos approached the entrance and silently watched the process.

"You got forty pounds today," Sherman announced. He picked up the sack, toted it to the back of the shed and dumped it in front of the rest of the sacks. He returned with a clean burlap sack, stamped *Nicaragua Coffee* in big red letters, and handed it over. "I'll just go get your money," he said. "Hello, Mitch. *"Comment ça va?"*

"*Ça va bien, et tu?*"

"*Pas trop mauvais,*" Sherman said, turning to the office desk flush against the wall. He sat in a metal chair, wrote the number of pounds on a memo pad, did the math on a calculator, and wrote down the price. He opened a drawer of the desk, retrieved the cash, and paid off Alfred.

"Here you go, Alfred."

"Thanks," Alfred mumbled, casting a glance at Lanclos as he took the slip of paper, the folded bills and change, stuffed them into his jeans pocket, and turned to leave. He nodded at Lanclos and started to walk past him where he stood in the doorway, back-lit by the bright October sun.

Lanclos followed him out to his bicycle. "You found a flash-light by the road and gave it to Miss Philomena, Alfred?" He spoke softly, not wanting Sherman or a man driving up with a load of pecans in the back of his truck to hear.

Alfred nodded firmly. "That's right. I did."

"Do you want to show me where you found it?"

"Sure, I can do that."

"Do you think you can remember exactly where you found it?"

"Pretty much, yeah. I think I can." Alfred held onto the handle-bars of his bicycle. "Now? You want to go now?" He kicked the stand, preparing to mount.

"Yes. I'd like to go now. Let's just put your bike in the back of my truck. That be okay with you?"

"Sure. Saves me riding a couple miles out of town."

"Let's go then." Alfred picked up the bicycle and followed Lanclos to his pickup. He swung the bike up and over the side of the truck and then circled around to the passenger side.

The two rode in silence out of town, the radio playing *Maudit Bayou Teche* softly in the background.

"You understand French, Alfred?"

"A little."

"You know what that song's about?"

"No," Alfred looked over at Lanclos, waiting for an explanation.

"It's about how the bayou takes lives. Drowning in this case."

"That's the truth. I lost two brothers to the bayou."

"I know that, and I know a lot of other people who died in the bayou. Losing control of their car, their truck. Boat accidents. Murders. A lot of time it's that strong current does it."

"I stay away from the bayou, me."

"Can you swim?"

"No. And that's why my brothers died. They couldn't swim either. Othello, he was fighting and got knocked in. And Sonny, he was fooling around when he was fishing and got caught up in the current. Me, I stay away from it."

"You don't go fishing?"

"Not on the bayou. I go to a lake by the levee sometimes."

"Okay, now watch where we're going so you can warn me when to pull over."

"We got a little ways to go yet."

"What're we looking for?"

"We're gonna see an underground cable sign on the opposite side of the road. It's right after that where I found the flashlight, over on the bayou side."

"Did anybody but you and Miss Philomena touch it?"

"Nope. I gave it to her soon as I found it. All Auntie had was one of those no good little cheap-ass flashlights."

"Okay, there's the cable sign. Now where?"

"It's right over there. I'll show you." Alfred pointed.

Lanclos pulled over and parked his truck in the weeds on the opposite side of the road by the underground cable sign. The men got out of the truck, pausing by a cluster of tall goldenrod as they waited for a truck pulling a cattle trailer to pass. The driver of the truck waved and they waved back, looking at the quarter horse somberly gazing out from inside the grid of steel bars. As soon as the truck passed, the two men hurried across the road. On the opposite side, Alfred began studying the ground, stepping slowly as though looking for something he'd lost.

"Careful how you place your feet, Alfred," Lanclos stood quietly watching. "You don't want to disturb anything."

"Yeah, it was right about here. See?" Alfred pointed at an area of weeds that was trampled and looked like someone had driven over it.

"How do you know it was right there? You sure?"

"I can tell because I noticed that cable sign after I stopped to pick up the flashlight. It was for sure right about here."

"You're positive?" Lanclos moved closer to him.

Alfred hunkered down. "Yep. This is the place where I found it. Look here. You can even see tracks where I braked the bike soon as I saw it. I'm always halfway looking for stuff by the side of the road. You'd be surprised what all I find out here when I'm riding around."

Lanclos looked over his shoulder at a produce truck barreling down on them, on the way to a delivery in town. Some gravel kicked up by the truck flew near the two men, striking Alfred's shoulder. He jumped back, rubbing the spot. Lanclos bent over the area, studying each weed, each blade of grass, each piece of litter, squinting as he went about his investigation. There was a greasy bag that had held cracklings, a round Timber Wolf tobacco container, and a beer can. "You drop that? That your brand?" he asked Alfred, pointing to the Timber Wolf logo.

"Not me. Don't do it."

After long moments of scrutiny, he held a hand over his eyes and looked off toward the woods beyond where they stood. They were at a diagonal point from where Gerald's black powder rifle was found, and a hundred feet from the grassy trail that led beside Delcambre's woods.

"Okay, then, Alfred. You can go on now. That's all I wanted." He dismissed Alfred with a wave of the hand. "Thank you. You going to need me to drive you back to town?"

"That's all right," said Alfred. "I'm headed for home." He hurried back across the road and swung his bike out of the pickup, then mounted it and rode off toward his trailer.

MONDAY

38

SHERIFF QUEBEDEAUX

L anclos, responding to a request for an update from Sheriff "Pep", drove to the Parish seat in Gros Coulee, parked in the Sheriff's Office parking lot, strolled into the squat cement block building, waved at the receptionist, and followed a short paneled hallway lined with framed photos of past sheriffs of St. Beatrice Parish. He entered the office just as Sheriff Quebedeaux was draining a clear plastic cup of soda. He was wearing his customary starched white long-sleeved shirt and grey slacks.

"Hey, Detective. About time you came to see me, you." The Sheriff smiled so hard, his eyes crinkled shut. "How the hell are you, Mitch?" He extended his hand for a strong handshake. "What's the latest on the Theriot case? His boss, Mike, from LeJeune Construction, calls me every day."

He pointed at a chair, and then tossed the cup overhand into a gray metal wastebasket. "Rest your bones a minute. Do you want some coffee? A Dr. Pepper?" He raised thick black eyebrows as Lanclos shook his head.

"No, Sheriff. I'm on my way to Castille's right now to eat."

"Bring me up to date on what you got then."

The Sheriff had been reelected more times than Mitch could remember. A highly popular man, he won each election with ease. Tall and muscular, he had an easy manner about him that appealed to the voters. The fact that he was tough on crime, conducted frequent sweeps of his jail, fired jail personnel with regularity, and met with citizens often throughout St. Beatrice Parish in informal meetings at his sub-stations, all endeared him to the voters. His deputies loved him because he went out of his way to back them up, and because he was so personable, the media loved him and gave his programs careful attention and frequent airtime.

He'd won the nickname "Pep" because of an election strategy he'd used since his first election bid at age thirty-five. His campaign paid a small Louisiana hot pepper sauce company to use his picture on the labels of their hot sauce during the months of the campaign. Many Parish restaurants used the hot sauce, giving it a prominent place on their tables, along with the salt and pepper and napkin holders. The Sheriff's rugged good looks with silver streaked black hair combed straight back, combined with his trademark sardonic smile helped him to a big win at the polls.

"I've been running down every possibility I can think of," said Lanclos as he settled himself in the wooden chair, laying one bent leg sideways so the ankle rested on his knee and lacing his fingers over his stomach.

"Anybody look interesting?" The Sheriff leaned back in his chair, thumped black bullhide boots onto the desk and waited.

"Not really. Not yet."

"Hell, man. Somebody did it! This is a small town. How many possibilities you got?" The Sheriff pulled a white handkerchief out of his pocket and wiped the back of his neck with it. "It feel hot in here to you? Damn A/C's been worked on twice this month."

Lanclos shrugged. "It's a little off. I'm good."

"Aw, the hell with it. Where were we? Oh, yeah, how many people then?"

"That you could make a case for?" Lanclos shrugged, shaking his head. "I don't know. A couple of them maybe."

"Anything you want to run by me?" The Sheriff pursed his lips.

"Herman Delcambre found Gerald's black powder rifle on his land. Gerald's wife had a fight with him the night before he died. He bad mouthed Leon LeDoux to her, and she got angry."

"Leon LeDoux?" The Sheriff's eyes widened. "That sack of shit? He involved in this somehow?"

"I don't know yet."

"One of these days," the Sheriff muttered, smacking a fist into the palm of his hand. "That it? That all you got? I know old man Delcambre all my life. No way he had anything to do with this."

"That black guy you put up in your hotel all the time, Alfred Narcisse. He put a curse on Gerald at Red's Barber Shop two days before he died."

"Alfred?" The Sheriff snorted. "Him? Please!" He made a chopping motion of dismissal with his hand. "What else you got?" He looked at his watch. "My Lucy's fixing stuffed peppers with crabmeat at the house, and I have to get out of here in a few minutes. Keep talking."

"That's about it, unless you consider Miss Philomena who's ninety some. Where we found the body."

"What's wrong with that? Maybe she shot him. I'm still going to be shooting when I'm in my nineties...if I'm still around." He looked heavenward. "Somebody wants to try and kick me out of my house when I'm that age....they're going to be looking down the barrel of whatever I got handy."

"Naw. I can't see her for it."

"Well, hell, man. That's all you got? I'm disappointed. Get out there and get back on the trail. I'm going home to eat crabmeat. Call me if you need anything."

The Sheriff stood and plucked his pearl gray Stetson from a hat rack, then smoothed the brim gently with his fingers and tapped it onto his head with care. "By the way, you can come eat with us at the house if you like. When Lucy stuffs bell peppers, she always makes a couple dozen. And by the way, Theriot's aunt is in the *bourrée* game Lucy goes to every Wednesday. So she's after me about the case too. Just saying."

"Thanks for the invite. Please tell Miss Lucy I hate to miss out."

"Okay, then, Mitch." The Sheriff rounded the desk as Lanclos stood, reached out with a long arm and clapped a large hand on his shoulder. "I'm not really riding you, Mitch. I know you're going to find the bastard. You always do."

The two men exited the office as the Sheriff waved at a deputy coming down the hall. "Call me anytime night or day, Mitch."

"Hang on a minute, Wilson," he called to the deputy as Lanclos pushed the glass entrance doors open and stepped out into the bright light.

39

MOISE STOPS BY LA-LA'S SWAMP BAR

Moise took a side jaunt through Levee Town to swing by Dixie's house and make sure nothing was disturbed. After driving slowly by, he was satisfied that no new vandalism had occurred, and he continued on down toward the road that ran along the western levee of the Atchafalaya.

Preparing to turn off onto the gravel road leading north toward his house, he cast a glance toward La-La's, a small bar set precariously on the bank of the bayou that ran along the opposite side of the road from the levee. This bayou, named Maudit Bayou, was narrower than Bayou Perdue. It had, however, a strong current, and had claimed many a drowning victim over the years. In addition, more than a dozen trucks and sedans had gone off the bank into the water, owing to fog, drunkenness, suicide, or a combination of all three.

La-La's was built of board and batten, with a porch that ran along the front and around the sides to a back deck that hung over the water. It had been used for a movie location years before. Carpenters had built the deck especially for a few scenes from the low-budget horror movie, and La-La and his wife, Gloria, had been grateful for the addition ever since. The porch and deck doubled the size of the bar. However, most of their customers preferred to sit inside the dim interior while they did their drinking.

Occasionally a fight would break out and La-La would make them take it outside. Several fights had gone onto the back deck and ended up in the bayou. A recent fight had splashed down into the water and one of the men had been swept away by the current and drowned, his body never to be found.

Moise wanted to slip inside and check to see if by chance any of the Guillorys were doing their drinking there that day. He parked beside three pickups in the shallow dirt lot in front of the building. One of the pickups had the reddish-brown tail of a fox squirrel attached to the top of the antenna. Four crawfish traps were stacked in the bed of another. Galvanized four foot wide tool chests were bolted in back of all three of the truck cabs.

He stepped up to the porch, where vintage tin signs advertising Redman Tobacco and Dixie Beer were left over from the movie production. A curled and sleeping white bulldog puppy was tied to an iron bench by a leash.

He waited a moment at the door, so his eyes could adjust to the shadowy interior. The swirling neon bars of the jukebox provided sharp contrast to the darkness of the room. Four men hunched over their beers at a bar to his left. La-La was bartending, and his wife, Gloria, was feeding quarters into the jukebox.

The smell of stale beer and fried fish filled the room. La-La provided a midday meal to his local customers seven days a week. He kept food hot in an outsized slow cooker in back of the bar, but Gloria prepared the food at their house a block away from the bar.

All four drinkers turned on their swivel stools to see who had come in, just as Gloria's selection of Johnny Allen singing *Promised Land* began. Belton Guillory, Elrick and Toy's father, sat at the end of the bar, his trademark black fedora slanted over his eyes as though the room wasn't dark enough already. Moise started toward the man, who touched the brim even further down over his eyes, and swiveled back around to hunch back over his drink again.

Moise stopped at the bar, between Belton and a local fisherman named Ira Leger. "La-La, give me a Dr. Pepper, please." He handed over a bill for the soda and took a swig before turning toward Belton.

"You got a problem with me again?" asked Belton.

"Nope."

"What you want then?"

"I was just taking the levee road and got thirsty. That okay with you?"

"They're nowhere around, them. They went over to Texas for some damn thing or other."

"Who you talking about, old man?"

"You know damn well who I'm talking about." Belton pushed his longneck toward La-La and nodded for another one.

"I'm going to drink this outside on the back deck and look at the bayou. Care to join me?" asked Moise.

"Yeah, right. Just what I wanted to do when I woke up this morning. Have a drink with Moise Angelle."

One of the men down the bar laughed so hard, he snorted. Gloria's second selection came on: *Drunkard's Sorrow Waltz.*

Moise sauntered toward the glass doors that led to the back deck. He crossed to the wooden railing and leaned on it, gazing over at the mud brown bayou. Crows called in the distance and squirrels chattered and chased each other in the oak that spread its branches over the tin roof of the bar. He breathed deeply of the fresh, humid air.

Moise took a long drink of the soda and pressed the icy base of the can against his forehead. It wasn't long before he heard the door open behind him. He turned his head to see, but he already knew who it was.

"So you decided to drink with me after all."

Belton, squinting in the sunlight, wearing faded blue coveralls with Liberty stitched on the pocket, stopped two feet from the rail holding his fresh beer. "Why the hell don't you leave us alone? My boys don't do nothing against the law. They're too smart for that. They live off the land. They hunt and fish, and they're good at it. We eat what they kill...or sell it. So what? We're swampers making a living. They should give us a medal. We don't live off government checks like all those fucking deadbeats do. We don't bother nobody, but you're always on our ass. It gets old. If you don't quit harassing us, I'm gonna report you to the law."

"I am the law, Belton, but that's good. That's good! Keep up the good work. I'm real glad to know your boys never hunt out of season or bag more than the legal limit, or sell to restaurants from Houma to Shreveport illegally. I just want to ask your boys a couple of questions. That's all. Nothing serious. Don't catch a stroke, you." Moise smiled, leaning back on the rail, and finishing the soda.

"Moise, one of these days you're going to outsmart yourself. And I hope I'm there to see it."

"Could be. You never know."

"And Elrick gave me a message for you before he left town. Just in case I ran into you."

"Oh, really? And what would that be?" Moise turned around, leaning back on his elbows against the railing.

"He said to kiss his ass all the way to Texas." Belton passed on back into the bar, slamming the door behind him so hard, the glass shivered in its metal frame.

Moise laughed and tossing the empty into a trash barrel at the corner of the deck, followed the walkway around the building back to the parking lot.

40

ANNIE INVITES LANCLOS
TO DINNER

L anclos pulled up in front of Castille's Café feeling hungry and tired. He'd need about three cups of strong coffee to get jump-started. Plus today was the day Castille's always had *ponce* on the menu, and he was in the mood for it.

He looked quickly around the restaurant for Annie as he walked toward his usual booth. Maybe it was her day off, he mused, as he slid onto the high backed wooden bench and leaned against the wall with a sigh. But at that moment, she banged open the double swinging doors to the kitchen and made her entrance, carrying a dinner tray expertly balanced on her right shoulder with an upright open palm.

She passed him by to serve four men toward the front, their table close to the wide picture window. Smiling and chatting with the men, she served their meals and sliding the tray flat under her arm, turned back toward him. She approached his booth slowly, a sly smile on her face.

"Well, hello, Detective. And how's your week going?" She pulled a well thumbed pale green order book from the pocket of a vest she wore over her cotton dress.

"You never miss the *ponce*, do you?"

"Not if I can help it."

"I pass on *ponce.*" She laughed. "Us hillbillies aren't into some of the stuff you Cajuns eat." She pulled a pencil from in back of her ear and held it against the pad, ready to write.

"I can't help it. My grandmother used to make it. It makes me think of her." He smiled out of the side of his mouth. "And just what do you hillbillies eat, anyhow?"

"For starters I have a squirrel marinating in the fridge right now. I hit it driving to the grocery store yesterday after work."

"Roadkill, huh?" Lanclos laughed.

"It's okay if you know it's fresh." She raised an eyebrow. "Now if I didn't know who hit it or when, I wouldn't have jumped out of the car to pick it up out of the road."

"I don't blame you. I like squirrel myself. Haven't had any for a while though. I'm always too busy to go hunting."

"I'm cooking it up tonight. Squirrel in brown gravy. Rice on the side? It'll be ready about six o'clock." She spoke with a sing-song lilt.

Lanclos watched her expectantly for a moment, his mouth half-open as though to speak, but he shook his head. "I'm sorry. I'd love to take you up on that, but I'm in the middle of an investigation, and I barely have time to have dinner with my son as it is."

Annie looked disappointed. "Well, all right then. I understand."

"But Annie." Lanclos held up a hand. "Please put some in the freezer so I can try it when this is over. Will you do that for me?"

She tilted her head and smiled so that her eyes narrowed. "I'd love to do that."

"Thank you. I look forward to it." He nodded toward the order book. "You can bring my dinner and please start pouring the coffee. I 'm going to need about three cups today."

"Long day so far?"

"Been up since four o'clock."

"What you going to have with that? You get two sides. Salad, green beans, corn, or field peas." She quickly looked over her shoulder. "Forget the green beans today. They're soggy," she whispered.

"Field peas and salad then. With Ranch."

"Got it. Be right back with your coffee." She ripped the order out of her book and tore off for the swinging doors to the kitchen.

Lanclos smiled as he watched a mental movie of Annie jumping out of her Honda to retrieve the squirrel from the blacktop. He remembered doing the same thing when he'd bumped a rabbit the year before on the road back to the farm at twilight. He'd quickly jumped out as the swamp rabbit jerked on the road. He'd put it out of its misery with a quick chop to the back of the head and taken it home where he'd immediately stripped off its fur, gutted it, washed it, and put it into a glass bowl with a marinade of vinegar, oil and Cajun seasonings.

He tried to work out in his mind how he could meet with Annie at six and still do all the things he had to do, most importantly attending Gerald's funeral. The Sheriff made sure that someone from the Office attended every funeral in the Parish. In the case of a suspicious death, that person would be the one working the case. He had a lot of commitments, but he regretted having to pass up the chance to be alone with Annie.

"Here's your coffee, Detective." Annie set down a white mug of steaming coffee. "I know you want it black, right?"

"That's right, thank you." He met her eyes and nodded, smiling for the second time that day.

He watched her walk away, realizing just how much he enjoyed watching her, or talking with her, or just being near her. He wanted this woman and wondered just how far he was willing to go with it. Lanclos had never had expectations from life. He looked at it philosophically: what you got, you got; what you didn't get, you didn't get. You just did the next thing there was to do each day, knowing there would always be a full Inbox up to the day you die. So he kept his life simple: do the next thing.

So far, this outlook worked well for him. He had always liked his job. He loved his farm, which had tripled in size when his parents died, and he inherited their adjoining property. He loved his son. Paul had always been healthy and strong for which he was grateful. And when he considered the human misery attached to the cases he'd worked over the years, he considered himself extremely lucky.

41

MOCCASIN BITE

Claudine was drinking her second cup of coffee standing on the back porch and staring out at the back yard. Bayou Perdue smelled fresh that day, and she breathed subtle delicate jasmine and a whisper of perfume from a latticed climbing rose two feet from the south porch pillar.

A light breeze drifted across her skin as she admired the multitude of trees and other plants spreading out in all directions. Some of these were actually still growing from her great, great-grandmother's post Civil War healing gardens. Claudine had replaced any of the original trees and shrubs as they died, working to maintain the garden as it was in the 1800s, but had gradually added some healing plants of her own over the years.

Along with the *plaquemine* or persimmon, were the willow, magnolia, sassafras, mulberry, fig, pecan, pear, and camphor trees. Claudine kept many of her healing plants in pots so she could move them into a greenhouse on the few winter nights when freezes were predicted. She kept *herbe a chien, guimave* or marshmallow, *patte de chat,* or cat's paw, *moutarde,* and *baume* or mint, ginger, horseradish, the glorious *mamou, mauve,* and *tête de cabri* for medicinal teas and other concoctions.

In addition she always cultivated six or seven different kinds of pepper plants, elderberry, *chardron* or thistle, and in season, plenty of comfrey with plantain growing in its shade. Deep into the woods there was an abundance of dewberry and the ever spreading *eronce,* or blackberry.

When she surveyed the multitude of trees, bushes, and plants, she invariably felt a warm feeling spreading over her. Despite never having met her ancestor for whom she was named, she felt protected by her spirit. Because she had such an abiding love for these healing plants and such an interest in giving treatments to hurting people and animals, she was certain she had inherited the right genes for these passions.

Besides the trees and plants there was the house itself. The original house had been added on to over the years. But, the front of the house with its *garçonnière* and walls of *bousillage* retained the integrity of the original 1800s homestead. This pleased Claudine, and although Roy wanted to renovate the house she had talked him out of it.

Knocking on the front door interrupted her reverie. She turned to the kitchen door, put her empty cup on the counter and passed on through the kitchen toward the living room to answer the door.

Looking through the frosted glass she saw Alfred, his eyes frantically wide and face shiny with sweat. "Alfred, what's wrong?" she called, immediately opening the door.

"I got bit. Snake-bit! Can you drive me to the hospital, please, Miss Claudine?" Alfred stumbled on the words and held up his right hand, which was swollen around the thumb and its base. Two nasty holes swelled in the pad of the first joint of his thumb. Alfred stared at the holes in disbelief as he held up the hand to show her the damage. He squeezed the wrist with his left hand. "Big fat moccasin! Them like that have lots of poison."

"When? Where?" Claudine stepped out from the threshold. "Wait. Tell me on the way to the E.R. Let me just run get my keys." She left him standing on the front porch and dashed for the kitchen where her keys hung on a hook by the back door. Snatching the ring of keys off the hook and grabbing her cell phone and wallet, she raced back to the front door. "Go! Get in the truck!"

She slid onto the front seat and barely giving him a chance to get in and slam the passenger door, she backed out of the driveway and screeching on the brakes at the road, took off north, leaning over the steering wheel and pressing 911 on the keypad as she drove.

"Please tell them to get the antivenom ready at Holy Name Hospital," she called into the phone as she accelerated. "Water moccasin. We'll be at the E.R. in about fifteen minutes!"

Alfred leaned against the back of the seat, still holding his hand up.

"The man who's bit is Alfred Narcisse," she said. "My name is Claudine Bergeron. I have to hang up now so I can drive." She clicked off the phone and slipped it into her pocket. "Put your hand down. Just lay it flat on your lap."

"I should have cut the bite with my knife to drain the poison."

"No, no. They don't want you to do that anymore. Just stay quiet and I'll get you to the E.R. as fast as I possibly can. I can usually get to Gros Coulee in fifteen minutes, but sometimes it takes twenty. So relax yourself while I'm driving. Don't think about the snake."

Alfred closed his eyes and rested his head back on the seat. "I can't stop thinking about the snake though. That big white mouth full of fangs came out of nowhere. Zap! You're dead!"

"No! You're not dead! Not even close. Just rest yourself. We'll be there before you know it."

"I was just picking pecans. I reached in a pile of leaves and…"

"Ssssh. Alfred. Don't talk. Just breathe slow breaths." In spite of a solid centerline, she passed a Camry, leaving the car quickly behind as she sped west toward Gros Coulee and Holy Name Hospital.

42

GERALD'S FUNERAL

The Mass was ended, and the pallbearers walked down the aisle to pick up the coffin from its stand. Leon, Maurice, two uncles, Wade and Hercule Theriot, and two brothers slowly marched it down an aisle toward the massive front doors.

Lanclos, standing in one of the rear pews kept his eyes moving in a steady sweep over the crowded church, while at the same time watching the pallbearers slowly and steadily proceeding. The somber men carried out their duty as a musician played and sang at a piano, *You are the Wind Beneath My Wings*. Soft crying was audible throughout the crowd, along with the rustling of more than two hundred people turning to watch the procession file out.

The family then began their slow exit from the front pews. Georgette and Celeste, both dressed in grey, held hands as they walked together beside Gerald's mother dressed in black. Celeste's face was streaked with tears, her eyes red. Georgette stared straight ahead, eyes dry.

Gerald's brothers' wives came next with four teenagers, his sister and her husband following. Next came an assortment of aunts and wives of the uncles who were pallbearers. Then a group of first cousins and their spouses. Lanclos knew them all. He knew everyone in the church, except for some men from out-of-town that he guessed were construction workers Gerald had befriended on the job.

After all the relatives had left the church, the remaining people began to slowly file down the two aisles, the men, generally with a proprietary arm lightly on the waist of their wives or girl friends; the women dressed in a variety of colored dresses, very few in black. Lanclos nodded at many of the mourners as they passed, waiting until most of the pews were empty.

The crowd moved through the grand doors of the main entrance and down the wide cement steps following the sidewalk to the curb where three white limousines waited for the procession to cross the street and file to the five-acre cemetery.

The cemetery, in use from the early part of the nineteenth century, was a sprawling composite of freshly whitewashed above ground tombs. As All Saints' Day was coming up in a few weeks on the first day of November, many people had already freshened their family tombs with a coat or two of white paint. A bright array of fresh and artificial flowers of all descriptions decorated the tombs in sharp contrast to the sparkling white paint, so the effect of the cemetery in the bright sunlight of the day was dazzling.

The bell tolled continuously as the crowd assembled with the priest on the sidewalk and lawn waiting for the limousines to lead them across the street. Two white police sedans blocked traffic for two blocks so the people could walk slowly and safely *en masse.*

Lanclos held back, waiting on the steps until the limousines crept off toward the cemetery, the parade of people coming after, following the priest. He stood alone watching until everyone had crossed the street and turned off toward one of the sidewalks that cut through the tombs. Only then did he start walking toward them, with a nod at Louis Zerangue, the deputy waiting in his patrol car by the curb.

Passing cracked tombs from the early 1800s, side by side with modern ones, he glanced to his left and right at the names and the newly bought flowers and some faded old ones. Mixed in with these were occasional Confederate tombstones with the C.S.A. insignia. His great grandfather's C.S.A. stone was one aisle over. Almost all the tombs bore French names, with an occasional German or Italian name among them.

Way to the rear of the cemetery was the mausoleum and also an area of homemade crosses, metal and wood, from the early 1900s. He turned at the hurried footsteps behind him.

"Wait up!" said Moise. He fell into stride with Lanclos, speaking softly. "I couldn't get here any earlier. I was out in the swamp looking for the Guillory brothers."

"You find em?"

"Just the old man...Belton." Moise spoke softly, although they were out of earshot of anyone. "I thought he was going to shoot me, that old devil." He shook his head. "That family!"

"So where did he say they were?"

"He claims they're over in Texas."

"Probably a bullshit story."

"I know. But I told him I just wanted to ask them a couple of questions. 'You always got questions for my boys. Why don't you leave us alone? We mind our own business. Don't do anything wrong,' he says, 'but you keep harassing us.'"

The procession turned left down a center walkway and proceeded past one hundred feet of still more closely packed tombs toward a grassy area where the funeral attendants, the pallbearers and the family had gathered. The limousines were parked on a driveway at the far borders of the cemetery.

The priest stopped at the Theriot family tombs where a green awning had been set up to shelter the family and as many mourners as could fit beneath it. The family was seated in three rows of folding chairs lined up before the coffin resting on a stand. The grave was covered with a discreet green mat, and a well dressed, carefully coiffed woman from the funeral home directed the event.

Moise and Lanclos stayed back and quietly observed. As the priest began his graveside remarks, the group listened in total silence. Gerald's brothers flanked their mother, and Georgette and Celeste sat holding hands next to their mother and Leon.

The priest kept his talk brief, and then the woman from Chaisson's handed each of the family a red rose and asked them to place it on the coffin. Celeste stepped forward with Gerald's mother first, carefully laying their roses on the burnished metal, slowly followed by all the rest of the family. Two men in work clothes waited under an oak tree, one of them sneaking a cigarette, which he periodically turned around to smoke.

Lanclos jerked his head in the direction of the church parking lot. "Let's go. I've seen everything I needed to see."

They turned to leave just as Gerald's mother began to totter. A funeral attendant in a gray suit pushed forward offering smelling salts. Gerald's brothers rushed to support her.

The two men paused. "It's all right. We can go. They have it under control," Lanclos said. "You mind if I drop by your house tonight. Chew on the case a little bit?"

"Sure. I've got Dixie with me, but she'll leave us alone. She knows the way things have to be."

"I'll come by around seven. I have to have dinner with Paul first."

"All good. I'll see you then."

They walked back the way they'd come. "My granddaddy," said Moise, pointing to a CSA tombstone low on the ground in front of a four foot high freshly painted tomb. "Let me just say something to my parents before we leave." Oval metal frames with hinged covers held photos of his family. A crawfish, a deer, and a bear were etched on his father's tombstone.

Moise stood at the tombs for a moment, while Lanclos stepped away to give him some privacy, gazing toward the crowd still lingering at Gerald's gravesite.

"Okay, that's it. Let's go," Moise said, rubbing his hands together, all business once more.

"Did you tell Lucky you're still keeping after the Guillorys?"

"Oh, yeah. I always have to give him an update. You know I do," said Moise, clapping a hand on his friend's shoulder. "It never hurts to have some expert backup, just in case something goes wrong."

43

AT MOISE'S HOME

Moise and Dixie walked down the pine needle strewn path to the bayou in front of his cedar house on stilts, five miles south of St. Beatrice. The woods around them were made up of bottomland trees: Sweetgum, hackberry, maple, oak, cedar. Vines stretched between the trees, curling and twisting. Several varieties of groundcover with petite lavender and yellow flowers spread over the ground. A narrow, eight foot dock stretched before them over the gumbo brown water. The fading sun still sparkled on the surface of the bayou. A fat black moccasin slid off the mossy bank into the water at their approach.

"Did you see that?" asked Dixie.

"Yup," Moise said, slapping a mosquito on her arm.

"It's so quiet today. I love it here. It's not as quiet at my house. My neighbor likes to play his radio when he's outside. I hate that."

"No neighbors out here for a quarter mile. That's how I like it." He surveyed the scene before them then looked up into the trees. "Mitch is coming by tonight. He wants to discuss the case he's working on. Do you mind leaving us in private while he's here?" Squirrels chattered and a fish jumped, making ripples that caused the water to lap at the bank.

"Of course not. And I promise not to eavesdrop...although I'd love to." She nuzzled up against him. "You can trust me."

"I know it. That's how come I'm still around."

"My boss told me I have to drive to Oklahoma next week on a run. Want to come with me?"

"Always up for Oklahoma, *chère*, but you know I can't right now."

They watched the bayou in silence. A plastic cup bobbed by.

"Damn the litter," she said.

"And most of it piles up on the silt down by the bridge."

He released her hand and put his arm around her shoulder. "Let's go back in the house and fix dinner. I'm getting hungry. I brought some steaks. Do you want to eat outside?"

"Sure. Why not? I baked some jalapeno corn bread and picked the peppers fresh. And that's not all. I baked a syrup cake too."

"Look at that!" He pointed to a brown swamp rabbit poking out from inside a hollow log. The rabbit saw them and ducked back inside.

"What?'

"You missed it."

"You never miss a thing, do you? I can never keep up with you in the woods."

"Wouldn't have my job for long otherwise."

"Later tonight I want you to call up the owls for me. Okay?" Dixie said.

"If you want."

"I want. Now come on. Let's get those steaks on," she said, pulling his arm. The couple started back up the bank through the woods to the house, his arm slung around her shoulders. The rabbit watched them vacate his area and ventured out once more, nose twitching.

* * *

Dixie brought Lanclos and Moise beers where they sat on a futon, on the front screened porch, their feet up on a rough cypress table. "Holler if you need anything, I'll be in the back." She closed the door quietly behind her, giving the men their privacy.

"The crickets are loud tonight," Lanclos commented after a moment of silence.

"They're loud every night out here. But if you think this is loud, you need to come out to my camp." The two men listened to the rise and fall of the crickets' drone. Banks of sound shifted from one part of the woods on the bayou to the other, back and forth, back and forth.

"That sound hypnotizes me."

"Oh, yeah. If I sleep out here on the porch, I'm out in two minutes. Actually, I usually do sleep out here." Moise patted the futon. "But with Dixie here for a few days..." His voice trailed off.

"Don't tell me. You're finally getting married?"

"Oh, no. Nothing like that!" Moise's eyes grew wide. "Please, man! You know I'm never going that route again. I had more than enough of marriage. Marriage is for other people. And the gays are welcome to it in my book."

"Okay. Sorry I brought it up. I never will again."

"That's okay, man. I just get spooked whenever that word comes up." He eased himself down lower on the futon and laid his head back. "What happened though is somebody dropped a deer carcass in Dixie's cistern Saturday night. I have a pretty good idea who it was too."

"The Guillory brothers?"

"Yeah. They know I'm trying to find them. It's some kind of a half-assed warning."

"So you had to drain the cistern. How long did that take?"

"We messed with that...draining it, scrubbing it out most of Sunday. I brought her back here with me just in case they come up with some other idiotic scheme."

"Right. Especially Elrick. You were smart to bring her out here. That's what I would've done."

"She likes it out here anyhow."

"Who wouldn't? We should get that report back from the lab on the shotgun shell by Wednesday."

"If we're lucky. What else we got? Anything?"

"Not a whole hell of a lot. Other than I've already caught everybody I interviewed in a lie."

"You going to do anything about that?"

"Just let them be and watch."

"You got any favorites?"

"Not yet." Lanclos tapped his nose. "But I will. It's just a matter of time. Got hold of a Maglight somebody dropped by Delcambre's woods. That might lead to something. We're running it."

"How'd we miss it when we were over there?"

"A local had already picked it up. Nobody would just drop a Maglight and leave it behind."

"Very promising. Something bad went down over there that night. Those woods are holding onto some secrets."

"But not for long. I have a feeling this case is about to break. I can always tell. And I'm ready for it." Lanclos finished his beer and squeezed the can with one hand, collapsing it.

"It'll be a misstep. Somebody's going to make a mistake. I feel it too."

The men stopped speaking and listened to the rise and fall of the theatre of cricket sound surrounding them until Dixie came back onto the porch a while later with more beers.

"I'm sorry to interrupt, but I thought you all might want another one."

"Thanks," Moise said, stretching a long arm for his. Lanclos shook his head. "No, thanks. I've got to get on down the road." He looked at the luminous dial of his watch. "It's getting late."

"And don't forget, Moise. You promised me you'd call up the owls tonight," said Dixie.

"I didn't forget."

"I've seen him do that. It's unbelievable," said Lanclos. "Why don't you do it while I'm still here?"

Moise stood. "Let's go to the woods down by the bayou then." He led them out the door and down the path to the woods. When they reached a spot near the dock, he sat on his haunches and cupping his hands in front of his mouth began to mimic the hooting of an owl, voice deep and throaty, "Whoonnn, whoonnn."

Almost immediately, an owl answered, and as the three people remained very still, the muffled sound of beating wings came near, high in the surrounding trees.

"Whoonn, whoonn," Moise continued calling them.

Several owls answered from above the three friends, their sounds remarkably similar to Moise's call.

Dixie moved closer to Moise and laid a hand on his back. The three tilted their heads back, trying to see the approaching owls, but they couldn't see them in the shrouding darkness of the trees. After ten minutes, Moise stopped, turning around to lead the way back to the house.

"Wonderful!" said Dixie as she followed him up the path.

"That it is," agreed Lanclos. "Where did you learn to do that anyhow?"

"My old man," said Moise.

"Figures," said Lanclos.

"Yeah, he was something all right," said Moise.

"A legend," said Lanclos.

"Yep. That he was," said Moise.

"You're going to be a legend yourself before it's all over," Lanclos said.

"I don't want to be a legend. Look what happened to my old man."

"Yeah, I see what you mean," Lanclos paused at the front steps. "All right then. I better be getting back to the farm. It's getting late."

The two men shook hands and Lanclos nodded at Dixie. "Thanks, Dixie." He turned toward the truck.

"Moon's getting full," Dixie said, gazing at the sky.

"That's a good thing. Full moon brings all the whackos out of the woodwork," Lanclos said as he walked away.

"They're easier to catch on full moons. You can see better," observed Moise, slipping an arm around Dixie's waist.

"Later," called Lanclos as he slid into the truck.

44

PHILOMENA PROPHESIES

Alfred clumsily let his bicycle fall so that it crushed half of one of Philomena's rose bushes. His thumb was wrapped in a ball of bandage. He slumped along the walk and trod wearily up the steps. She heard the clanking of the bicycle and opened the kitchen door.

"Come in, nephew." In the light from the porch, she could see the bicycle bearing down on the rose bush. "But first, get that bike out of my rose bush, please."

Alfred squeezed his eyes shut and wiped his good hand over his mouth. "Sorry, Auntie. I don't feel so good."

"Hurry up then. Fix the bike and I'll serve you something to eat."

The horse whinnied in the pasture as Alfred trudged back out to the bicycle and pulled it off the rose bush. Letting it drop again with a clatter, he returned to the house.

Philomena was stirring a pot of white beans on the stove. "Sit down. I made white bean soup with fatback. I'll serve you a bowl." She ladled the soup into an outsized gumbo bowl and brought it to him at the table. "Do you want some tea to go with that?"

He nodded and took a spoonful of the steaming soup, then blew on it. Philomena brought his tea and sat opposite him. "Watch it. It'll burn your tongue," she warned as he took a tentative sip. "And I put some of my Tabasco peppers in there too." She indicated a basket full of small red peppers. "There's plenty more if it's not spicy enough for you." He winced at the hot soup, then blew on it some more. "How does your thumb feel?"

"I don't know. They had to take half of it off. It was rotten. It was so bad they kept me overnight."

"You got the gangrene?"

"I don't know what you'd call it. I call it rotten. They just said they had to cut away most of the first joint to save the rest of my thumb cause it was so bad."

"Lord, Lord, Lord," she said looking up. "It's the curse. What did I always tell you about putting a curse? It comes back on you three-fold. Every time."

Alfred tried another sip. "I know, Auntie. I know," he said with his mouth full.

"You better hit the floor on your knees and ask forgiveness for what you did. Tell the good Lord you were ignorant. You didn't believe me. But now you know and you're never going to curse anyone again, so help you, God." She spoke softly as she watched him closely. "You do it, nephew. You hear me?" She looked up for a moment, her lips moving, but no sound coming out. "Let me tell you what's going to happen if you don't get on your knees and ask forgiveness for what you done. More bad luck and calamities will fall upon you. You hear me? You're playing right into the hands of the devil, nephew, when you put curses on people. The devil loves a sinner. He harvests sinners! Listen to me now!" She fixed her eyes hard upon him.

"Yes, Auntie. I hear you."

"Are you going to do what I'm telling you?"

"Yes, Auntie."

"A dead body in my back yard and your thumb half gone. Isn't that enough for you to see what curses can do?"

"Yes, Auntie." He sighed and toyed with the spoon, stirring it back and forth in the bowl of beans. A rooster crowed outside and then more roosters crowed from the Bergeron farm.

"At least you can stay in your house cause Gerald's dead. His wife can't build her fancy house now with him gone."

"Shut your mouth, Alfred!" she said, banging a bony fist on the table so that it shook the bowl, and the spoon rattled against the rim. "Do you think I'd want his death so I could stay on here? You know my faith. I know the good Lord will take care of me no matter what. I would never want someone to die so I could stay anywhere. The good Lord already died for us. The blood of Jesus is enough to save anybody who believes. And now the Holy Ghost is here with us, and you better learn your lesson. The Holy Ghost will take care of us in ways we don't even know about. You better get right with God, boy, and learn a few things about faith." Philomena rapped on the table again for emphasis.

"Okay, Auntie. Okay. Calm down. I'll do what you said. I'll tell the Lord I'm sorry for what I did."

"And be sure to ask for His forgiveness while you're at it," she said. "He's probably already forgiven you, but make sure you let Him know just how sorry you are. And every time you look at what's left of your thumb, thank Him that you didn't lose all of it."

"Yes, Auntie."

Philomena relaxed a bit, settling back into her chair. "Now last night a skunk or a possum ate the head off one of my hens in the coop. I don't know how he got in there because I shut them all up last night, but I need you to bury her for me. Can you do that with that bandage on your hand?"

"I'll do it somehow. Maybe it was a mink come up from the bayou. They can sneak in anywhere."

"I don't know what it was, but it hurts me when critters get my dear hens."

"I'll check it out. Maybe it dug its way in through the dirt floor. They'll do that."

"I don't know. But something has to be done, or whatever it was will be back tonight and kill another one."

"Close the door of the coop today so they can't get in there. They'll go sleep in the trees. They'll be safe in the trees unless an owl gets them. I'll stay over if you want and stay up. Maybe I can shoot whatever it is."

"That would be good. That way I can keep my eye on you. Looks like somebody has to." She reached out a scrawny arm and patted the bandaged hand that was lying on the table. "It'll get better, Alfred. You got to get ahold of your faith, though. And don't forget while you're praying to thank St. Jude. I asked him when this whole mess started to help me. He's the Saint of Impossible Causes, you know. You hearing me?"

"I hear you, Auntie. I'm working on it." He met her eyes for the first time that morning and smiled. "But, I still got to say it's real fine you can stay on in your house now that Gerald's gone." He added hurriedly, "I don't mean it's good he's dead, Auntie. I just mean I'm glad you can stay on here, and I'm going to sleep over here more and more to help you guard your hens. Maybe once a week even. Would you like that?"

"Like I said, nephew, somebody's got to keep an eye on you. And it might as well be me as anybody else. I might be old, but I still have more common sense than you do, it looks like."

"Yes, Auntie. I guess you're right," Alfred said, scooping up another spoonful of beans.

45

TROUBLE AT ANNIE'S

On his way back through town, Lanclos slowed by Castille's Café, wishing once again he'd had the time to take Annie up on her invitation. He took his eyes off the road long enough to glance up at her apartment. The curtains were drawn, the lights were on, but there was a fast shadow moving across the front room that seemed odd to him.

His instincts kicking in immediately that something was wrong, he swung the truck to the right at the corner by the café and turned into the small parking lot in back of the building. The parking lot was almost empty, except for two vehicles and the ever-present green Dumpsters at the back corner.

He noted Annie's Honda and a white Impala parked next to it. The pole light illuminating the parking lot made it possible for him to read the Arkansas license plate. He used the portable radio to run it, finding it was registered to Harlan Hoyt. He didn't know if that was the abusive boy friend from her hometown. He'd only heard Annie refer to the man as Speedy.

Lanclos parked his truck at the curb by the lot, and started walking toward one of the rear metal doors to the building, fully expecting them to be locked at this late hour. The door on his right was to the kitchen of the restaurant. Three empty garbage cans stood beside it. He tried the doorknob on the left and surprisingly, it opened. He stepped into a short, narrow hallway, the stairs to the second floor flush against a wall to his left.

Staying close to the cement block wall as he mounted the stairs, he kept his footsteps as light as possible on the grated iron steps. When he reached the top of the stairs, he looked down the landing toward two doors. Light shone around the edges of one, while the other door was dark and possibly a utility room.

Treading to it cautiously, he paused, listening at the door for a moment, heard a muffled loud male voice, then quiet. He knocked. Silence. He knocked again, louder this time. More silence. Lanclos waited.

Finally, footsteps, then fumbling at the other side of the door. "Who is it?" Annie called.

"It's me, Mitch Lanclos. Got a minute?"

The door opened a crack. "Oh, hi, Mitch. I was just getting ready for bed." She tried to speak in a light tone, but couldn't hide the tension in her voice.

"Just riding by. Thought maybe you'd have a beer with me before I call it a night."

She opened the door another four inches. "It's kind of late. How about a raincheck?" Her eyes shifted slowly to the right. The door was open just enough that he could see her face was bright red and her eyes wet.

He nodded. "Yeah, okay, I get it. Next time, call first," he said amiably. "I should have, but it was a last minute decision as I passed by the restaurant on my way home. I'll see you tomorrow. Get a good night's sleep. Sorry I bothered you."

"Thanks for coming by, Mitch." The door shut, just short of slamming in his face. Mitch stepped back, frowning, then turned toward the stairs, body on alert, blood pounding at his temples.

He took his time descending the stairs, then slammed the back door to announce his departure and crossed to his truck. The truck was parked beneath an oak tree and in full shadow. He slid onto the front seat, leaving the door halfway open and sat with his legs turned to the side, poised for a fast exit. Any earlier tiredness had vanished. He was wide awake and ready for action. He kept his eyes moving from the upstairs windows to the back door, and called Farrell LeBlanc who was on duty that night.

Ten minutes into this quiet surveillance, the back door burst open and a man with a long ponytail wearing a gray tee shirt, jeans and biker boots charged outside, holding a suitcase and dragging Annie along behind him. She pulled back, straining against his tight grip on her slender wrist. He yanked her so hard toward the Impala, she stumbled and fell, scraping her knees on the cement. He jerked her to her feet, then tossed her suitcase into the backseat and pulled her around to the driver's side. He swung open the door, shoved her inside and across the seat, then leaped inside behind the wheel.

Lanclos jumped out of his truck, pulling his pistol, and yelled, "Hey. Let her go!" Advancing toward the car, pistol raised, he called again. "Let the woman go!"

Starting the engine, the man yelled back, "I'm taking her home where she belongs! Stay the hell out of this!"

Lanclos yelled again. "Stop or I'll shoot!"

The man backed up with a lurch and twisting the steering wheel hard, shifted to first with a grinding of gears, and punched the gas. "Back off and fuck you!" he yelled as he spun the tires and leaving rubber on the pavement, shot off.

Lanclos shot at a rear tire as the car reached the parking lot exit. A boom filled the air as the tire exploded and the Impala skidded to the left, jumping the curb and jerking to a stop in the middle of the dark side street.

"Asshole! You got no right! That's a new Michelin!" The man leaped out of the sedan, just as a patrol car rounded the corner and Farrell LaBlanc screeched to a stop three feet from the stalled car in the middle of the road. Hoyt started running as soon as the deputy braked and disappeared down a back alley that ran behind the businesses on the other side of the street. The deputy looked at Lanclos for orders.

"Follow him and I'll see to Annie," called Lanclos. "His name is Harlan Hoyt. He grabbed her and was hauling her back to Arkansas. You get a good look at him?"

LeBlanc nodded with a mock salute, "Don't worry. I got a good enough look at him." He revved his engine, and screeched off down the alley.

"You okay?" Lanclos asked as he opened the passenger door.

She smoothed the hair out of her face and took a deep breath. "God help us. I hope he gets that maniac. Yeah, I'm okay. Thanks to you. I'd be halfway back to Arkansas if you hadn't come along."

"Now that's what they call luck. I just happened to look up when I passed your building. The quick glimpse I got at your front window didn't look right to me."

"That's why they promoted you to detective, I guess, huh?" She gave him a wan smile.

"Let me put in a call and get this Impala impounded and off the road. Why don't you go back upstairs and catch your breath? Maybe make us some coffee. I want to hang around here in case LeBlanc needs me."

"I think a beer would be better...at least that's what I'm going to have."

"Yeah, but it looks like I'm back on duty. So make it coffee for me, please." Lanclos helped her step out and retrieved the suitcase from the backseat. "You sure you're okay. He didn't rough you up?"

"A little. He shoved me. Left some marks on my shoulder, but believe me, I've had worse from him. Why do you think I'm in Louisiana?"

"What's wrong with that guy?"

"How much time you got? He drinks and does pain pills and whatever and gets crazy. His family traces back somewhere to old man Devil Anse so he's a legend in his own mind. He thinks just because he's good looking and his mama loves him, that whatever he says goes."

"I've known a few like that," Lanclos said. "And they're not from Arkansas. Go ahead on back upstairs. I'll bring your suitcase when LeBlanc gets back. If I know LeBlanc, he'll have him back here in cuffs before you're finished drinking that beer. And that'll be for attempted kidnapping and battery charges." He lowered his voice, "and anything else he might have done to you."

"Oh, he didn't rape me if that's what you're thinking. He was saving that for when we got back to Arkansas. He was too worked up and hateful, yelling at me for running away. Accusing me of all kinds of things like I was some kind of whore for leaving him." She shuddered, rubbing her arm. "I thought sure he was going to get away with it, and I'd be locked up somewhere in a cabin back home in the woods where nobody would ever find me."

"Well, he didn't succeed. You're safe now." He opened the back door for her, and she passed on into the building with a weary expression.

By the time Lanclos called in for road service to impound the Impala, LeBlanc's patrol car slowly crawled back down the alley. He pulled up in the street, put his flashers on, and stepped out of the car.

"I lost him, Mitch."

"You actually lost somebody, Farrell?"

"It happens. He must have slipped into somebody's back yard over yonder. If he made it into the woods past city limits, he could be anywhere by now. I called in a BOLO on him."

"They'll pick him up eventually. Meanwhile, we've got his car. That's got to hurt."

"What'd he do?" Farrell two-fingered a tin of tobacco from his pocket and pinched off a piece, tucking it neatly into his bottom lip.

"He was trying to hijack Annie. Old boy friend from Arkansas. Forcing her back to the Ozarks."

"She okay?"

"She got shoved and yanked around, but she's okay. I'm going to take her suitcase upstairs and get the whole story. Then if he's still on the loose, I'll take her by Miss Odile's Bed and Breakfast to spend the night. She sure as hell can't stay here by herself."

"No, no. Go wake Miss Odile up. That dude is probably madder than hell right now you shot out his tire. He's liable to do anything now. I'll wait right here for the tow truck. If I know T'Bro, it won't take him long to drag himself out of bed and get on over here."

"Call me if you need me."

"I'll do that, cousin." LeBlanc nodded and then spit tobacco juice into the gutter.

Lanclos picked up the suitcase and headed for the back door of the building, wondering what time he'd ever get to sleep that night. He thought about calling Paul, but decided not to as he didn't want to wake him up, knowing he had early morning classes. As he mounted the steps to the second floor, Annie opened the apartment door.

"Farrell lost him. He's waiting downstairs for the tow truck to impound the car."

She led him inside the apartment. He set the suitcase down by the door, as he surveyed the room. It was small with only a few pieces of furniture: two blue upholstered armchairs separated by a black steamer trunk, a chrome kitchen table and two chrome chairs. The one room served as living room and kitchen. To his left was a half open door leading to the bedroom and bath.

"You've made this comfortable for only being here two months."

"Thank you. My boss had furniture stacked up in the storeroom next door. He let me use it. His wife, Rose, made the curtains for me." She indicated red and white checked café curtains over the kitchen sink, and white lace curtains on the two windows facing Church Street. "Sit down and have your coffee." She pulled out one of the two red-cushioned chrome chairs.

Lanclos sat heavily, wiping his forehead and eyes with the flat palm of his hand and wearily leaned his elbows on the table.

"Tell me what happened. I'm going to have to write this up in the morning. Start with his name and how he found you all the way down here."

"His name is Harlan Holt, but they call him Speedy. I don't have a clue how he found me. I still can't figure that out. He's a regular Wily Coyote though. He used to run whiskey for his uncle when he was a teenager. I think he learned a lot of his ways from that old, miserable coot, Zeke. Ezekiel Holt." She raised her gaze to the ceiling. "Sorry, Lord, for speaking ill of the dead."

"You been calling back home?"

"Just my one girl friend, Posy, up there. And Momma. They would never give him the time of day, trust me. Posy wouldn't pour water on him if he was on fire cause he got into using more and more pills, cocaine, whatever. It makes him crazy, not that he didn't already have a head start."

"Anybody Posy might have told where you were?"

"I seriously doubt it. She's got brains, and she uses them. Unless she's talking in her sleep these days. Her husband, Big Joe, he doesn't like Harlan either, even if he did find out something from her. And by the way, all Harlan has to do is pull the cell out of his pocket and call his sidekick, Lester, or one of his other derelict friends to come get him. Trust me, somebody's already on the road driving down here from Arkansas to pick him up. I'd put money on it."

"I don't think you better count on his leaving town. He can't outrun a radio, and there's already a BOLO out on him. A Be On the Lookout. I hope you let me take you to Miss Odile's Bed and Breakfast for the night. I'm sure Miss Odile would be happy to put you up. She's got an historic house over there on Moss Street, and I'd be happy to pay for the room."

"No, no. " Annie shook her head. "I've got a .38 in there." She nodded her head toward the bedroom. "He's not getting anywhere near me tonight. He caught me by surprise earlier when I was taking out the garbage, but it won't happen again."

"Listen to me! I don't think it's a good idea for you to stay here by yourself. Not tonight anyhow."

She laughed. "Us mountain people, we know how to take care of our own business. In our own way."

"But, you've been through enough for one night, haven't you? You need to get some rest."

"Not to mention how he shoved me when you showed up." She jerked out her arm with the heel of her hand like a weapon, pantomiming what Hoyt had done to her. "That your new man?" she mimicked, twisting her face into a grimace. "You fucking him now? Nice, huh? See why I moved away?"

"That's why I want to see you safe. A jealous man is an unpredictable man."

"He's unpredictable all right. But, no matter. He kicks at that door, and he's dead meat." She pressed her lips into a firm line.

"Do not shoot through the door, please. Wait until he's visible. And make sure he falls into the apartment. Louisiana law. This isn't Texas...yet. It would be a good idea to come up with a code." He wagged a finger to and fro. "Just between you and me."

"For what?"

"Just in case I'm talking to you, and he's around somewhere close, and you can't tell me straight out."

"Oh, I get it. Okay. So what's the code?"

Lanclos paused to take a drink of coffee. "How about...How are the dogs doing? I have two Labs back at the farm," he explained.

"Okay. How are the dogs doing? That'll work. Just in case he's listening to everything I say on the phone like he did today when my boss called me. The s.o.b. had my arm twisted behind my back the whole time." She rubbed her shoulder and made a face. "Damn, it still hurts."

"Don't worry. We'll get him."

She shook her head slowly. "Uh-uh. I don't mean to be disrespectful, but you'll never get him. Like I said, he's Wily Coyote. If he doesn't want to be found, he can stay hidden in those mountains forever. He could make his way through those woods up home blindfolded."

Lanclos watched her curiously, noting the pride in her voice. "You kind of want him to not be captured?" he asked gently.

"Huh?" She looked startled. "What d'you mean?"

"Sounds like it to me."

"No. It's just a fact that a man like that won't be found if he doesn't want to be. They've got some kind of sixth sense, you know? It's kind of hard to explain to a flatlander. But it's true. Nobody can sneak up on those mountain boys. Plenty have tried." She looked at his empty cup. "You want something else? There's some Danish in there. And some seafood gumbo my boss sent home with me today."

"No, thanks. I'm good. As soon as the tow truck gets here, I'll be getting back to the house. My son's probably wondering what happened to me." Their eyes met and held for a few beats longer than normal conversation called for. Lanclos found himself mesmerized by the way her eyes had shifted from gray to green. He opened his mouth to say something, but nothing came out. He felt awkward and shifted in his seat, looking away.

Lights from T'Bro's tow truck flashed through the front windows. "Uh-oh, there he is now. I've got to go." Lanclos said with relief, getting to his feet. "We'll let you know right away if we find him so you can rest easy."

"Thank you, Mitch, for everything. Like I said, if it wasn't for you, I'd be halfway to Arkansas by now." She rubbed her shoulder again. "I have to be at work at 6:30 in the morning. I better rub lots of Absorbine on this tonight so I can carry a tray. I'll be there until 3:00 if you need to talk to me." She glanced at a clock on the wall. "I hope I can catch a little sleep before then."

He pulled a business card from his shirt pocket and handed it to her. "Call me if you need me for anything. Anything. You got that?"

"I will. I promise." She raised her eyebrows and tilted her head. "And, Mitch? That goes for you too." She sent him a shy smile as he made for the door, his head reeling.

46

ROY TELLS CLAUDINE TO STAY QUIET

R oy and Claudine were enjoying the warm aftermath of a late-night sexual encounter. Claudine's legs were entwined with Roy's, her arm stretched across his chest, head resting on his shoulder. She wore a long faded tee-shirt, but Roy was still naked. A rumpled burgundy colored sheet lay partially over them. Roy punched a pillow and arranged it in back of his head, preparing for sleep.

Their bedroom, painted in midnight blue, was mostly dark except for the night light from a clock radio on the bedside table. This little light cast a soft glow partially illuminating the couple.

"The public library wants me to give a talk about old-time healing plants. The old-timers' remedies. Cajun, Creole. Vanessa Vidrine knows some people who work there, and she was talking about me to them."

"That's good," said Roy, punching the pillow again to reposition it. "When?"

"I don't know yet."

"Take Antoinette with you. She knows all the plants. It'd be a good experience for her."

"She's too busy with school and her new band. You remember they've been asked to play at the church's Catfish Festival, right?"

"Of course I remember. My daughter's first gig. How could I forget?"

"It's coming up this weekend. And by the way, she has a new friend now," said Claudine.

"Oh, yeah? Who would that be?"

"I'm glad you're lying down."

"I can take it. Let's have it."

"Paul Lanclos. He's going to U.L. She met him at a party."

"Mitch's son?"

"That's the one."

"Have you ever met him?"

"Not yet. But we will. I'm sure he'll be at the festival. And he's going to help her paint the family tombs for All Saints'. They're going to scrape and paint each tomb."

"Well, he can't be a bad kid if he's helping get ready for All Saints'."

"No. He's fine, I'm pretty sure. I worry he's maybe too old for her though."

"Maybe they're just friends."

"Yeah, right. She's already gorgeous, and a young man college age just wants to be friends. Ha!"

"You're going to keep a close eye on this, right?"

"Don't worry. I will." Claudine took his hands and laced fingers with him.

"You heard anything about the case?"

"What case?"

"The murder case, of course. Gerald Theriot."

"No. How would I? I've been getting all the fishing and trapping in I can before I have to go back offshore."

"I haven't heard anything either. I'm afraid to call Mitch. He might yell at me again."

"Stay away from him. He's never going to change."

"You'd think he'd be nicer to me since I helped him so much with his investigation."

"Don't help him anymore then."

"It's not him I'm worried about. I always liked Gerald. Everybody did."

"Somebody didn't."

"Yeah, well, I guess you're right. But if I can help find whoever it is, I'm going to. I don't care if Mitch wants to be a shitbird."

"A shitbird, huh? That's a good one." Roy laughed and kissed the top of her head.

"Whoever it was knew he was headed for Miss Philomena's that night."

"Maybe."

"Maybe nothing. Why else would they drag his body there?"

"Maybe they didn't want his body found where he died. Maybe it was even at the killer's place. Maybe they knew that Philomena's place was his property."

"Everybody knew that was his family property."

"So everybody is a suspect. Maybe you did it."

Claudine mock-slapped him. "You better watch your mouth, mister, or I'm gonna have to cut you off."

"You know, come to think of it....."

"What?"

"Never mind."

"What?"

"Go to sleep. It's late."

"Roy! What'd you think of?"

He rubbed his eyes with his knuckles. "It's nothing, really. I was just thinking back to that last *bourrée* game at Savoy's. The night Gerald was killed."

"Yeah, and?"

"I had dropped by there and played a couple of hands with Lonnie after we came back from fishing. It was early. About ten-thirty."

"Yeah, yeah. What?"

"Gerald was already there drinking and playing. Maynard Ducette got on his case for kicking Miss Philomena out. He said something like Gerald should be ashamed for throwing an old lady out on the street."

"And what did Gerald say?"

"He mumbled something about how he was going to go over there that night to tell her she could stay."

"And what happened then?"

"Nothing happened then. Maynard said good, and that was it."

"Well, did you tell Mitch when he questioned you?"

"I forgot."

She raised her head from his shoulder to look at him in the dim light. "How could you forget that? That's important!"

"I guess."

"You guess? You have to call Mitch and tell him."

"No. Let it be."

"Let it be? Are you kidding? It could lead to who did it!"

"It's nobody's business what goes on in card games. It's private."

"Not in a murder case."

"So what if I did tell him? You know Maynard didn't kill him. He's a first cousin."

"I don't know. It sounds important. If you don't tell Mitch, I will."

"No you don't. You don't carry tales about what goes on in card games. It's confidential."

"Bullcrap! This is Gerald's murder we're talking about. Don't you care? What if it was me that was killed? I bet you'd talk then!"

"All right, all right. Go ahead and tell him. Just say I forgot about it. I don't want to mess with it. I have to meet Lonnie at five in the morning. We're going to fish the Atchafalaya River tomorrow. Now let's go to sleep. Good-night, *chère*."

Claudine tucked her head back down on his shoulder. "Okay then. I'll call him. Let's hope he doesn't bite my head off this time."

"If he does, lay some *gris-gris* on him. Put the black cat bone on him."

"I don't do voodoo and curses and crap like that."

"I'm just messing with you. Go to sleep." Roy shifted, turning toward her. He circled his arms around her, and within minutes his breathing slowed and Claudine knew he was asleep.

47

AT THE GUEST COTTAGE

L anclos was showering and getting ready for bed when his cell phone rang. He turned off the hard spray of the shower and stepped out of the stall, grabbing a towel to dry his hands before he answered it.

"Lanclos," he said.

"It's me. Annie. Is this too late?"

"No. I told you to call anytime. What happened?" He scrubbed at his hair with the towel.

"After you left I got so nervous. It's like every sound I hear is him sneaking back up here or something." Her voice was ragged.

"Look. I've got a guest cottage out here at the farm. It's got everything you could need. Completely furnished. A full bathroom and kitchenette. Pack a suitcase and drive on out. You'll be safe here and you can stay as long as you want."

There was a pause. "Are you sure? I mean I won't be in your way?" Her voice was almost a whisper.

"I'm sure. Just take Cemetery Road out to St. Regis Highway and go five miles to LeCompte Road. Turn left there and go three-quarters of a mile to the farm. It'll be on your right. There's a pole light at the front of the property and I'll have the porch light on for you. Pull into the circle drive."

"Okay. I wrote it down."

"Good. I'll be watching for you. It'll only take you about fifteen minutes."

"Thank you. I'm sorry to be such a coward. I thought I was braver."

"It isn't about bravery in this case. It's about common sense and self protection."

"Yeah, I guess." She hung up.

Lanclos went about scrubbing himself down with the bath towel. The bathroom also served as a dressing room. He kept folded farm clothes on shelves in a narrow closet there. He pulled a tee shirt off the shelf and a pair of jeans, which he quickly pulled on, then slipped into fleece-lined buckskin slippers. Peering into the mirror, his hand rasped as he ran it over the day's stubble. He brushed his teeth and combed his damp hair straight back, noticing shadows under his eyes and lines across his forehead that he'd never noticed before.

He had looked in on his son when he'd arrived home. Paul was sleeping soundly in his room with the Labs, one on the bed, one on part of the comforter he'd dragged onto the floor. He hoped Annie's arrival wouldn't wake them up as Paul had to be in Lafayette early for his first class. But the dogs were getting old and one of them was half deaf, so maybe they'd sleep through it. He'd take a beer out on the porch and drink it in the cypress swing he'd made for his wife years before and wait. Then he'd walk Annie quietly out around back to the guest house.

Tired as he was, he felt pleased that she was coming to the farm. He hadn't liked leaving her alone, yet she had seemed so confident and determined to take care of herself. In his job he'd seen so many vulnerable women. Women beaten, held hostage at gunpoint, kidnapped by angry husbands or boy friends, stabbed, shot, drowned, but he'd never felt personally protective of one of the victims until this night. There were various state agencies that handled the different circumstances for survivors, and the coroner and the funeral parlor took care of the rest.

Harlan hijacking Annie was still another drug induced insanity episode. He'd seen enough of them. Once the addiction took them under its dark cloak, they'd lie, rob at gunpoint, sleep in alleys, murder, and yank the wedding ring off their dead mother's hand in the coffin. He'd seen it all. Nothing an addict did could

ever surprise him. He felt gratified every time the street dealers
shot each other in his Parish, Lafayette, Baton Rouge, or New
Orleans. He knew his church didn't see it that way. They were con-
cerned with the loss of life, but he wasn't. He was a Christian and
knew he should care, but there was no use pretending to himself
that he did. He was satisfied that each one's death meant one less
for law enforcement to deal with, and one less spreading misery
around like peanut butter to poor dumb addicts who were blind
to what was happening to them.

And one day he'd get something on Leon LeDoux. Somebody
would talk to save his own ass, or troopers would stop whoever was
running it in for him on I-10. They all got caught or killed eventually. It was only a matter of time.

He spotted her car lights then coming slowly down the road. He
stood and walked off the porch to greet her. The Honda crunched
the gravel in the driveway and then braked in front of the trellis.

She slid a small suitcase off the front seat and stepped out as
he opened the door for her. "We have to be very quiet so we don't
wake the Labs and my son."

"Okay," she whispered.

"Come on, I'll lead you back to the cottage."

He took her suitcase and lightly placed a hand on her back to
guide her along with him as they followed a brick path around the
side of the house.

"Lightning bugs," she whispered as the tiny lights blinked in
the bushes and trees along the path. The guest house stood fifty
feet from the back of the farmhouse illuminated by a pole light
positioned between the buildings. He moved ahead, opening the
front door and flicked on the track lighting by a switch at the door.

The large room was furnished with a double bed and nightstand. At the far end of the room was a kitchenette with microwave
and sink, a refrigerator, and a small round table with two wooden
chairs. The bathroom door was open revealing an antique footed
tub. "There's some wine over there in the cabinet. Would you like
a glass?"

"A night cap?"

"Might help you sleep."

"Will you have one with me?"

"I just had a beer." He opened a cabinet above the sink and took down the bottle of burgundy and a stemmed glass. He poured it half full and handed it to her.

"Thank you. That'll help my nerves." She took a sip.

"Do you have everything you need then?"

"Oh, yes. Don't worry about me. I'll be fine. This place is so comfortable, I'm sure I'll sleep like a rock."

"Do you want me to wake you in the morning?"

"I always wake up at five-thirty, no matter what." Her voice trailed off.

"The rooster will wake you up before that. I'll bring you out some breakfast. You could use a good breakfast after all you've been through tonight."

She smiled over the rim of her glass. "It's been a nightmare, hasn't it? Thank you so much for rescuing me. Not just from him, but now. I don't think I would've slept at all."

They stood there by the cabinet and he put a hand out to lightly touch her shoulder. "I better leave you then so you can get some sleep."

He was surprised at the strong attraction he felt for her. She was no way near as good looking as his wife had been, and Lanette had always taken good care of her looks, exercising and eating carefully. She'd never let her figure go, and she had been studiously careful of her appearance always. And yet, he had never felt compelled to just grab Lanette and pull her to him as he did that moment with Annie.

This passion he felt caught him off guard. He responded to Annie's presence as if she were a magnet, pulling him toward her. He didn't understand the power of the attraction. Her eyes were almost too close together. She had a faded look about her because of the ash blonde hair and the light skin. Her skin wasn't smooth and fine-pored like most Cajun women, and could even be described as borderline rough.

He gave up trying to analyze his feelings and realized he must have been staring at her in an odd way because she looked at him quizzically, then leaned her face toward his and brushed his lips with her own. "Thank you again for saving me...again."

But that lightest of brief kisses was all it took. He took the wine glass from her and set it on the counter in back of him. Then he put his arms around her, pulling her to him, and kissed her softly, as she pressed against him and sighed her way into his embrace. Lanclos was lost in the kiss and her floral scent and the heat of her and the taste of wine in her mouth.

After long moments, he pulled his head back and looked at her fully as he stroked her hair. The crickets' drone was loud outside and his blood sang in his ears. She took his hand and led him to the bed, sitting on the edge of it, looking up at him, eyes heavy lidded. "Come here with me," she whispered. "Just hold me for a while."

Like a sleepwalker, he sat beside her and then shaking his head as though to bring himself back to reality, he placed one hand on her thigh and slipped his other arm around her shoulders, holding her tightly to his side. They sat like that in silence, listening to the night sounds. A south wind was picking up, and an owl hooted from a nearby pine tree.

He knew if he kissed her again, it was all over for him. He would not be able to leave her side until morning. And then she turned her face to him and waited.

TUESDAY

48

LANCLOS AT THE IMPOUND YARD

L anclos took a break at Castille's Cafe after a morning of partially catching up on paperwork and updating Sheriff Pep about the funeral and the Harlan Hoyt situation. He sat toward the back in a booth and looked around for Annie. She shoved open the swinging doors to the kitchen and emerged, holding a tray over the opposite shoulder from the one that had been hurt.

She caught his eye and smiled as she passed by his booth. "Hey, Detective," she said softly. The tone of her voice felt like velvet to his ears. Her slow smile and the way she tilted her head when she saw him was balm to him. Part of the good feeling was relief that she was all right and had made it through the day with no further trouble.

He watched her walk to the front of the restaurant to serve two men in the front booth who were beaming at her in admiration. As she smiled and laughed with them, he realized he already felt territorial, and chided himself for that. He made himself look up at the menu written on a chalkboard above the mirror in back of the counter. He decided on the pork roast, and when she came by his booth, empty tray in hand, and giving him a private smile, he started to order, but she cut him off.

"See this," she pulled a scarf away and showed him a blue bruise on her neck. "It's much darker today. You should see my shoulder." She tenderly tapped the sleeve of her blouse. "Looks wicked under there."

"We need to get a picture of that bruise. Maybe later today when you're done here? I'm glad to see you safe though...and even working today."

"Yeah, well, us mountain women are tough. We have to be." She laughed. "I guess you could say we're survivors, huh?"

"Definitely."

"You done with that investigation yet?"

"Not yet."

"Don't forget, I owe you a dinner."

"Oh, yeah, the roadkill squirrel."

"Oh, making fun of me now?"

"Absolutely not. If I hit an animal on the road, it goes in the pot too. No point in wasting it, is there?"

"Hell no! But mountain people and Cajuns, they're practical. You know what I mean?"

"Sure do."

"You seem to be in a good mood today," she said, taking the order pad out of her pocket, the shy smile back.

"You could say that." He fought an urge to reach out and touch her arm, her hand, anywhere. "How about the pork roast today? How is it?"

"They're saying it's good. What do you want with it?"

"Sweet potatoes and peas."

"Okay. I got it." She slipped the order book into her pocket and turned to go.

"Wait," he said before he had even thought about it.

She arched an eyebrow in question. "Yes?"

"How about tonight?"

"How about what tonight?" she said slowly.

"Whatever we feel like doing. Dinner, a movie in Lafayette?"

"What about your son?"

"He can take care of himself. He's getting so he can cook almost as good as me."

"What time then?" She stuck the pencil behind her ear.

"How about six?"

"Good. That'll give me time to take a long, hot bath and a nap." She turned toward the kitchen to put in his order.

Lanclos stared at the front window and the traffic passing beyond without really seeing. He couldn't believe he'd just made a dinner date with Annie now of all times, when he was so close to cracking the case. The words had just flowed out of him without his even intending to tie up his evening like that. *You're going too fast with this,* he told himself. This was no time for getting involved with a woman. He needed time to ruminate and think about the case. He should be clearing his mind of anything but what he had been able to find out about Gerald's last night alive. He should maybe take a long walk on the headland around the fields with the dogs, sift through the possibilities, give insights room to take shape, not be socializing.

But despite this, he felt sparks of excitement at the very thought of being alone with her for the evening. Shaking his head, he gave up trying to figure it out. Human attraction was a great mystery. It had been for centuries and would forever remain so. There were too many variables; too many ingredients in the mix to sort it out. So why try? Better to just enjoy the feelings when they surface and leave the analysis for the psychologists. One thing was certain, he never thought he'd feel this way again. *That's what you get for thinking!* he chided himself, glancing at his watch.

She returned with his food. "I think you're really going to enjoy this," she said as she slid the plate before him with a sideways smile. He caught a whiff of a light floral scent that reminded him again of their night together.

"I'm sure I will," he assured her, as three new customers slid into the booth in front of him. She breezed away to take care of the newcomers.

Lanclos picked up the fork and began to eat, watching her take the order in the next booth. He loved looking at her. Her profile, her body, the jaunty way she always stood with one hip jutting out, her weight always on one leg. The easy, friendly way she had with each customer, whether she knew them or not.

She finished taking the order and turned suddenly, catching him looking at her.

He thought she winked at him as she hurried off to the swinging doors of the kitchen. He no longer regretted making a date
with her for that evening. He only regretted that he still had five
hours to go before he picked her up.

* * *

The Sheriff's sub-station was in a cement block building half
a block from St. Beatrice City Hall. Lanclos pulled open the front
glass door and nodded to the receptionist. "Good afternoon, Miss
Renee."

She patted her hair and smiled hopefully. "You have some messages on your desk," she said in a low voice as she answered the phone.

"Thank you," Lanclos slapped a hand in thanks on the reception counter and turned off down the hall toward his office.

The room was small and felt cramped to Lanclos, and one reason he was seldom there. The gray desk sat against a sheetrock
wall. On the wall hung two bulletin boards, a map of St. Beatrice
Parish, a map of Louisiana, and a map of the United States. On
his desk in a black metal two tiered in/out tray were the pink slip
messages Renee had left for him.

He sat in the drab gray upholstered office chair, snatching off
his visor cap and tossing it onto a stack of manila file folders on
the desk. Flipping through the messages, he stopped at one from
his cousin, Alton. Alton had used a lined page from a notebook to
write out a list of names from the *bourrée* game at Savoy's the previ-
ous Thursday night, the night Gerald had been killed.

Alton's handwriting was awkward, a mix of cursive and print-
ing. He expected to recognize each of the names on the list, however, when his eyes lighted on one of the names, he raised his
eyebrows. Crossing his legs, he jiggled one foot distractedly as he
stared at the paper in his hand.

The phone rang and broke his concentration. "Detective
Lanclos," he spoke gruffly.

"Mitch, this is Claudine." She waited.

"Yes, Claudine. What is it?"

"Roy told me something last night that he forgot to tell you when you spoke with him."

"Okay. When's he planning on telling me? Is he there?"

"No. He's out fishing today and so I said I'd call you myself."

"Okay. What did he forget to tell me?"

Claudine drew a deep breath. "See, the other night at the card game...that would be last Thursday night...the night Gerald was killed...Roy stopped by the Savoy on the way home from fishing, and he sat in on a couple of games. And somebody was telling Gerald how it was a shame he was kicking Miss Philomena out of her house. And Gerald said how he was headed over there that night to tell her she didn't have to leave after all." Claudine took another deep breath.

"Who was it that was talking to Gerald?"

"It was Maynard Ducette, but," she quickly added. "I'm not suggesting Maynard had anything to do with it. I've known Maynard all my life. No way would he ever hurt Gerald or anybody. He's one of the nicest people in town."

"Take it easy, Claudine. I'm not drawing any conclusions about Maynard. I know the man too."

"The point is...from what Roy says, anybody at that game could have known where Gerald was headed that night."

"I get the point, Claudine. Thank you for calling it in."

"Sure, Mitch. You sound nicer today, by the way," she said and clicked off.

Sure do, he thought. Picking up the list again, he resumed his study of it while rocking the office chair back and forth restlessly. After a few minutes of this, he suddenly stuffed the list into his pocket, quickly left the office and strode down the hallway to the reception room.

"I'm going to the Impound Yard," he called to Renee.

"All right, Detective. See you later," she trilled.

The Impound Yard was on the north side of St. Beatrice, along the highway across from Credeur's Slightly Used Cars. The glitter-decorated triangular banners of the car lot were sparkling and waving in the breeze. A tiny office sat in the middle of the lot and a short man hurried from it to talk to a portly customer standing by a cherry red Tundra.

Lanclos unlocked the giant padlock on the gate of the Impound yard and loosened the heavy chains that held the gate secure. He opened the gate, got back in his truck and drove into the eight-foot high fenced area. With barely a glance at Harlan Hoyt's Impala, he parked the truck in the middle of the lot and looked around for Gerald's truck, still not released to Celeste.

He started studying the truck as he approached it, then proceeded to slowly walk around and around it, examining every square inch of the exterior. At one point, he leaned over and stared at a place on the passenger side, then hunkered down and squinted at it for a long time, while he mulled something over in his mind. After he was satisfied, he stood and resumed his pacing around the vehicle. When he'd examined the truck for almost fifteen minutes, he looked at his watch, and with one last look at the truck, walked back to his pickup and drove out of the lot.

While he carefully repositioned the chain and relocked the padlock, Credeur got into the Tundra with the customer and sat in the shotgun seat so the man could take a test drive. Credeur leaned out the window as they passed. "Hey, Mitch! Long time, no see!"

Lanclos, preoccupied, barely acknowledged Credeur as he gave the man a distracted wave, popped the clutch, and drove off.

* * *

Lanclos was on time at 6:30 when he knocked on Annie's door. She opened it almost immediately. She wore a low-cut cotton dress that hugged her waist and buttoned all the way down the front. She was still in slippers. "You're on time, and I'm not quite ready," she said. "I fell asleep after my long hot soak in the tub." They stared at one another for a moment.

"Well, come on in," she said, not stepping back.

Lanclos hesitated a moment, waiting for her to step aside, finally passing over the threshold and putting his arms around her.

He turned her around so she faced the living room and kicked the door shut.

"I guess you don't care that I'm not ready, huh?" She looked up with a sly smile.

Lanclos placed both hands on the sides of her face and tilted her head to kiss her. She pressed against him, sliding her arms around his shoulders and returned his kiss with an energy that resonated within him. He pulled back from her, smoothing her hair, and watched her silently for a moment. Her eyes were luminous, and her hair, just washed, gave off a light citrus scent and fell in curls around her shoulders. His consciousness had shifted gears, and he found himself in a different place than he'd been only five minutes before. He felt removed from ordinary time and concerns as heat rose within him.

"If we're going to Lafayette, we'd better go now, or..." his voice rasped.

"Lafayette? Where's that?" she asked dreamily and slowly sliding her arms from around him, she took one of his hands, kicked off her slippers, and began leading him toward the bedroom.

The radio was playing *Light in Your Window* as he followed her into the dim bedroom. They fell side by side upon the vintage quilt covering the double bed, and he turned her so she was on her back and began to kiss her again.

She made a sound deep in her throat, like a cat's purr, as he began moving his hands over her dress. She guided his hand beneath the neckline, pressing against him. A floral scent rose from her skin as he kissed her throat.

She gently touched his face and arched her back, pushing hard against him. "I've wanted you again all day. I kept thinking about it. It was so hard to keep my mind on work."

Lanclos didn't answer. He slid his hand from beneath the fabric and began unbuttoning the dress, slowly and methodically.

WEDNESDAY

49

MOISE WAKES UP LANCLOS

L anclos dreamed he was lost in the woods, looking for a way out, not even sure in what direction he was headed. A light flickered through the trees as though someone were walking with a flashlight. The light bobbed up and down in a jerking manner. He walked carefully toward the light holding his arms out in front of him so he wouldn't get torn up by low branches and thorny vines. As he moved slowly along, coming closer to the light, he saw the source. It was a goat, with a flashlight clamped onto its head, a trick used by outlaw hunters attempting to throw Fish & Wildlife officers off their trail.

Lanclos' eyes blinked open, slowly becoming aware that the phone on the bedside table was ringing. He frowned and flopped an arm over toward the sound, grappling with the receiver in the dark. He brought it to his ear upside down, righted it and without raising his head from the pillow, spoke into it. "Yeah."

"Hey, man. Moise. I hate to wake you up at this hour, but there's something strange going on over here."

"Where are you?" Lanclos rasped.

"I'm over here by the side of the road near T'Bro's Auto Body."

"What's going on?" Lanclos looked at the luminous dial on the bedside table clock. It was one-thirty. He passed a hand over his face and blinked again.

"I was passing through here on my way to go home and I see Leon LeDoux driving his black Lincoln into T'Bro's. I'm thinking what's he doing going to a mechanic's in the middle of the night? So I pull up into Scooter's parking lot where he can't see me, but I can see over there through the bushes."

"You there now?"

"Yeah. I'm standing behind the bushes with my cell. Leon pulled around in back of the garage. He parked in the shadows in the back there and he's walking toward T'Bro's house. What in the hell could Leon LeDoux be doing at T'Bro's house in the dead of night? He's sure as hell no hunter. Neither one of them hunts, and I've never known either one of them to fish."

"I'm on my way. Stay right there in case he leaves before I get there, will you?"

"I'm staying put."

"And if Leon leaves, follow him. Can you do that?"

"Can I *do* that? Are you kidding? What do you think I do for a living?" Moise laughed. "Wait up. T'Bro's coming out of his house. He didn't put the porch light on so it's hard to make them out. He was waiting for Leon cause it only took him half a minute to open the door. Now they're walking toward a carport by the house."

"Can you make out any vehicles in there?"

"Naw. It's too dark."

"I'll get dressed, and I'm out of here."

Lanclos put the receiver back, rolled out of bed and shook his head to wake up. He headed for the highboy bureau on the opposite wall to grab some clothes to throw on, then carried them in a heap toward the bathroom down the hall.

* * *

Lanclos pulled off the road onto T'Bro's parking lot, and slowly drove toward the rear of the building. There was the black Lincoln just as Moise had reported it, and Lanclos could see the two men in deep shadow in the carport by the side of what looked like the same Avalon he'd seen there three days before. As soon as his car rounded the corner, he could see one of the men receding into the shadows.

He pulled up in front of the carport and turned off the ignition. Stepping out, he slowly closed the door behind him and moved forward. "T'Bro. Good evening. How you doing?"

T'Bro stepped out of the shadows.

"Hey, Detective. What's going on?" He flashed a wide smile.

"Somebody called in a burglary in your shop?"

"What? A burglary? That's news to me. Who called it in?"

"I don't know. They called me to check it out."

"Naw, naw. Somebody messed up. There's nothing wrong here."

"What you doing up so early, T'Bro?"

"I don't know. Couldn't sleep. It happens once in a while. I was just going to go mess around in the shop."

"Who you got with you?" Lanclos smiled and nodded toward the back of the carport.

"Oh, just a friend of mine. Came by to shoot the shit."

"Another one couldn't sleep, huh?"

"Something like that."

"Before I call them back we better check the shop…make sure nothing's going on in there."

"Yeah, okay. I'll meet you over there. Let me go get my keys from the house. Go on around to the front."

"All right then." Lanclos got back in his truck and started the engine, slowly driving it around the building. He parked in front of the garage and got out, nodding his head in the direction of the parking lot next door, where he knew Moise was watching.

He waited next to the garage door listening attentively to every sound. An owl hooted, and it sounded so authentic he didn't know if it was Moise doing his owl calls or a real owl in the vicinity. Finally, he heard a key in the lock and T'Bro opened the door. "I passed through the back door, looked in the garage, and came up here. There's nothing going on in here. It's a false alarm." T'Bro sounded disgusted.

"All right then. I'll call it in as a false alarm. I'll be going on home then."

"Thanks for checking it out."

"Good night, T'Bro."

"Same to you."

Lanclos turned from the doorway and slowly walked to his truck, his senses highly tuned. Once behind the wheel, he drove toward the road and turned left, back toward the country. He would select a wooded area, pull over and wait for LeDoux to leave, then he and Moise could follow at a distance. Pickups in the middle of the night on Louisiana country roads drew no attention. They shouldn't have too much of a wait before LeDoux took off. He pulled out his cell phone to discuss his plan with Moise.

50

TEXAS SWING

Coyotes howled from far down the road, their chorus initiating a response from dogs all along the farms that surrounded St. Beatrice. Owls hooted from a tree close by, and frogs increased the volume of their croaking from the bayou as if to drown out the rest of the night sounds. The full moon had activated and amplified the nightly chorus, and Lanclos thought even the crickets sounded louder under the influence of the cool, silvery moonlight.

Twenty minutes later, the Avalon pulled out of T'Bro's driveway, turning toward town. After the sedan had cruised down the road a half mile, Moise's pickup pulled out of the next door parking lot and headed in the same direction.

Lanclos drew a deep breath as he called Moise once again. "I'm going to stay back about a quarter mile. Something's going on, that's for sure." Lanclos started his engine, slowly drove onto Delcambre Road, and almost immediately had to swerve to avoid a pothole. "Tell you one thing, he can't lose you easily on these bad roads."

"Oh, don't worry. He's not going to lose me."

"Call me if you want me to move up," said Lanclos.

"Looks like he's passing up the turn-off to his house."

"That's good. If he thought he was being followed he'd go home. He'd make it look like nothing was going on."

"Leon LeDoux is slick. No telling what he's got in mind."

"You're right. Be careful." Lanclos clicked off and slid the cell into the leather holder attached to his belt just as Moise called back.

"He's turning off on Grange Road."

"Could be he's headed for the Interstate. Going to his office in Lafayette."

"Uh-oh. He sure isn't going to the office at this hour. Maybe we really got onto him at a good time."

"What do you mean?"

"I mean like what if he's hauling ass to Texas? Maybe we're in the middle of something real going down."

"I hear you." Lanclos felt elated at the very idea of catching Leon in the middle of something illegal. Something tangible a detective could really use. Something solid, not just the bits and pieces of rumors over the years that had filtered through the pipeline to him. Hell, maybe Leon really was on his way to Texas. They would be finding out within twenty minutes. That's when Leon might turn off to Westbound I-10. He readjusted his body in the seat, feeling restless. He pressed just enough on the accelerator to keep his pace. If he got any closer and tipped off LeDoux, they'd be missing out on the chance of a lifetime to nail the slippery bastard. He gripped the steering wheel in expectation, his headlights sweeping a freshly plowed wheat field as he followed along a curve in the road.

* * *

Leon felt free for the first time in weeks. He was on his way to Costa Rica. He had a million dollars stashed in the air bag. He was getting away from Georgette, Mona, the sad business of Gerald's death, the office, and his father. He'd told Georgette he had urgent business in Costa Rica. Real estate business. She was upset that he'd leave when she was grieving, but he insisted that he had no choice.

He sure did have business in Costa Rica. Brilliant business. He'd drive on down to Central America. He'd buy property on the Pacific through Ernesto Cavaldo. He'd do it all through a Panama

Bank he'd used in the past, and he'd be home free. He'd own property in Costa Rica fair and square. He'd have laundered a million dollars and be safe. It was beautiful. What a difference a day makes!

He felt his scalp tingling with his new freedom. He'd be gone two weeks. His new secretary would keep the office running, take his messages while he was out of town. And he could totally relax in his favorite hotel, the Barcelo, in San Jose.

He smiled as he watched the road passing in the headlights. He felt so relaxed he hoped he didn't get drowsy. He had a long way to go before he'd stop at any motels.

Gerald was dead. It was a tragedy, but *Leon* was alive. And he had a life to live to the fullest while he was alive. And he was on his way to new adventure. And the best part was, it would all be effortless. Ernesto expected him in a few days. He was ready to show him three Pacific properties. He'd quickly make up his mind; give the lawyer the cash and all would be accomplished with ease. End of story!

The deer sprang out in front of the Avalon. She panicked and leaped onto the hood of the car slamming into the windshield with a force that knocked Leon's head back so far his neck snapped. As the sedan veered off the road and into a utility pole, his head and torso plummeted forward smashing into the steering wheel.

The steering wheel breaking with the impact, ruptured the air bag and a windstorm of hundred dollar bills flew out, fluttering over Leon's body, the front seat and dashboard, covering all with a cloud of currency. Some of the bills flew over the smashed and collapsed windshield, dressing the dead deer, flattened onto four splayed legs, with hundreds of bills.

Moise braked in time, steering the truck to the side of the road. He slid from the pickup and raced to the smashed car. Leon's head lolled, twisted sideways, his mouth open, his tongue hanging out of the side of his mouth like a dead dog. One eye protruded, hanging precariously on the edge of the socket. Three one hundred dollar bills had fluttered onto his forehead and hair like a visor cap, casting a shadow over his face.

Moise called Lanclos' number again as he took a deep breath. "Here's a heads up, buddy. Slow down! We got a lot of dead meat to deal with here. And I'm not just talking about the venison."

* * *

Within thirty minutes, two crime scene technicians arrived from the Sheriff's Office in Gros Coulee, along with an ambulance, EMTs, Rusty Meaux, the Medical Examiner, two deputies and a truck from the St. Beatrice Volunteer Fire Department.

"Well, I'll be a son of a bitch," said Rusty to Lanclos.

"Yeah, it's a bitch, all right," said Lanclos, squinting at the wreck.

"How'd you get on it so fast?"

"Long story. Tell you later." Lanclos wiped his face with his sleeve, shaking his head.

"Get this money bagged and dust that air bag for prints," Lanclos ordered as soon as the technicians arrived.

"I want photos from every angle possible of this mess," said Rusty to his new assistant. "Get up and stand on the roof of the car if you have to."

"Who gets the deer?" asked one of the volunteers from the Fire Department.

"Not you, that's for sure, Cecil," said Moise shaking his head and trying not to laugh.

"Anybody heard any good lawyer jokes lately?" asked the younger of the two E.M.T.s.

"Yeah. Did you hear the one about the lawyer and the deer?" asked his partner.

"All right, all right," said Rusty. "Save it for later." He pointed to his assistant who was still staring at the accident, mesmerized. "We got to get good prints on that air bag. There's a lot riding on this. Be careful. Pretend you're dusting for the FBI. They've got to go right away into Metro Forensics. If we get lucky we can get a match through A.F.I.S. quick and we won't have to wait days for the Crime Lab in New Iberia. And you know how running them through A.F.I.S goes... the computer can't I.D. anything if the prints aren't good enough."

"Yes, sir." The tech blinked twice. "Don't worry. I'll take very special care with this. I'll take it slow and easy."

"And we've got to get that money bagged and to the Crime Lab in New Iberia. I want them to test it all for cocaine residue."

"Yes, sir."

Moise sniffed, speaking quietly to Lanclos. "Let's hope T'Bro doesn't watch the morning news. He might make a run for it."

"As soon as I get some prints from that air bag I'm going to take off for Lafayette with them. Will you be able to keep an eye on T'Bro's shop until I get back? I'll drop them off and when I get back I'll take him in for questioning."

"I'll do that."

"At least this didn't happen on a State Road or the troopers would take this investigation over and away from us," Lanclos said.

"Less of a headache for you that way," said Moise.

"Naw. I've been waiting to catch a break on LeDoux for a long time. This is one headache that's going to feel good."

"I hear you," said Moise.

51

JUDGE COMEAUX

Shortly after five, Lanclos and Moise huddled beside Moise's truck, the two concealed by trees and thick bushes dividing Scooter's parking lot from T'Bro's property. "We need to get T'Bro out of there and down to the station before he watches the news and finds out about Leon."

"You'll never get a warrant before about eleven o'clock," said Moise.

"Then we'll go over there, knock, and ask him to come down for questioning."

"What are you going to tell him it's for?"

"I'll think of something. Meanwhile, you go around by the back door and wait. He might try to sneak out. We've got to hurry though. He'll be opening his shop soon."

"If it was me, I'd call Judge Comeaux and get a verbal to go on in there. Don't even ask him to come in for questioning."

Lanclos clucked his tongue and ran a hand over the stubble already rough on his chin. "Yeah, you got a point. Why waste time talking him into coming with me? I'll just tell the son-of-a-bitch he *is* coming with me."

Lanclos pressed numbers on his cell phone. "I'm sure I can talk the judge into letting us go on into the house after what I've got to tell him."

"You do that, and I'm going around to the back in case anybody gets it in their head to run."

"Go." Lanclos motioned with his hand, then quickly turned his attention to the phone as the judge answered.

"Judge? Detective Lanclos. I'm over here with Officer Moise Angelle next door to Travis Desmoreaux's house and body shop. You know "T'Bro's?"

"I know where it is. What you got?" The judge stifled a yawn.

"About two hours ago there was a car accident on Grange Road. Leon LeDoux was killed when his Avalon struck a deer and the deer crashed through the windshield."

"Great God! Leon LeDoux is dead?"

"Yes, sir. His neck is broken. See, LeDoux had what looks like more than a million dollars stashed in the air bag. The steering wheel broke and the bag burst and money flew everywhere. It's a horror scene."

"What the hell? Wait a second," the judge called to his wife, "Doris, bring me some coffee, will you? I got some real trouble here." He spoke again into the phone. "Go on, Mitch. Tell me what you think is going on."

"Moise woke me up at one this morning. He thought something suspicious was going down at T'Bro's…I mean Desmoreaux's. I got over there as fast as I could to meet him. LeDoux was over there picking up a new Avalon that has been parked there for some days. T'Bro was behaving in a furtive manner. LeDoux kept himself hidden. Moise and I waited around next door until LeDoux left, then we followed him."

"I see. So you followed him and consequently witnessed the fatal accident? Is that right?" the judge asked. Thank you, Doris." Lanclos heard the clink of cup and saucer being set down.

"We did. And then we both started working the scene until the crime techs, EMT's, Rusty Meaux, and the patrol cars got there."

"No troopers?"

"One stopped to help, but had to leave almost immediately because an 18-wheeler jackknifed on the Interstate."

"If it was a State Road, he'd have taken the investigation away from you anyway."

"Yes."

"So you're telling me this when it's still dark, and I haven't even had my coffee yet, because you're afraid Desmoreaux is going to hear about the crash and run? And you want a search warrant? And you don't want to wait until you get the paperwork all lined up and signed?"

"Yes, sir. I believe LeDoux and Desmoreaux had been colluding in a money laundering conspiracy at the very least. We may get lucky and find some cocaine, but if not, we've at least got them on money laundering. T'Bro must have had the Avalon at his place so as to pack the cash into the air bag. His prints will be all over the money and car. Plus tampering with an air bag is a Federal crime, as I'm sure you know."

"Yes, yes, I do know that." The judge made a humming sound as he mulled the information over. Lanclos heard him take a sip of coffee. "And you're where now?"

"Next door to T'Bro's...Travis Desmoreaux's shop and house. The TV people were just starting to show up when we left the scene. Early morning news is going to come on in a little while. He probably watches it, and then he'll know about the crash and the money bursting out all over the place, and I figure him to run. I want us to be able to search any outbuildings, the house, and the shop. He's got a barn out back of the house, and a camper trailer where his brother, Ajax, lives."

"Okay, Detective. I'll give you your warrant. Go ahead in there and bring me the paperwork as soon as you can get your search accomplished and your man in custody."

"Thank you, Judge."

"Oh, you're welcome, Mitch. Leon LeDoux was in it up to his neck, wasn't he? No pun intended, Detective."

"No, sir, no pun taken. I'll see you in a couple of hours."

"Take your time. I'm going to have a big breakfast because I've got an unbelievably heavy day in court today. Just bring the warrant into my courtroom and on up to the bench and I'll sign it."

"Yes, sir."

"And tell Angelle he did good work spotting that mess going down."

"Yes, Judge, I will."

"Same goes for you, Mitch, by the way."

"Thank you."

The judge hung up, and Mitch pocketed the cell phone and started walking toward the house just as the lights clicked on in the north side of the house. T'Bro's wife was visible through ruffled cafe curtains. Her head was bowed, and she appeared to be doing something at the kitchen sink. She held up a glass coffee pot and eyed the level, then lowered it again to add more water.

As Lanclos passed that end of the house, another light went on toward the rear of the house. The glow from still another light from the back came on and showed between the few inches of sheers that separated the draperies in the living room. Lanclos took a deep breath, sighed, and rang the doorbell.

52

SEARCHING

Moise positioned himself by a stack of tires in T'Bro's back yard. A hundred feet beyond him a pole light by a metal building cast a cone of cool light that illuminated the rear of the property. Moise stayed close to the pyramid of used tires, remaining in its shadow, as he waited and surveyed the area, particularly the back door of the house.

A camper parked on the north side of the property was in darkness, and beyond that was the tree line that separated T'Bro's place from the business next door. Moise had perfected the art of patience over many years of waiting, watching and tracking in the woods and the swamp. He could remain in one position for hours without moving and with ease. Part of him was on full alert and part of him was resting in neutral, as he stood, weight distributed on both feet, ready to move instantly, yet relaxed as well.

He blended with the sounds of the night. An owl hooted from the direction of a stand of trees in back of the trailer. He kept his mind as still as his body, and the processing of the dramatic events of the night was put aside as he breathed slowly and deeply of the night air. The air was tainted with the smell of burned motor oil, stored in a fifty gallon black barrel a few yards from the tires.

A faint smell of bacon frying came from the house, and he felt a pang of hunger, but he quickly suppressed that, as he kept his focus and concentration on the back door.

A dog barked far away to the east, and then another responded from the south. A rooster crowed from down the road toward the farms, and then repeated his call every few minutes. The faintest light began to show beyond the trees to the east, and Moise inched closer to the hill of tires.

He heard the doorbells chime, and then a door slammed inside the house. Just as the wind began changing from southerly to southwest, the back door opened two feet and a woman came out of the doorway, a sack over her shoulder. He recognized Cecilia, T'Bro's wife, and thought she must be taking out the garbage, but then he saw that she toted a bulging striped pillowcase, and she was moving fast past the garbage cans by the door toward the barn to the rear of the property.

"Cecilia!" He spoke softly.

She jerked her head toward him and stopped short, gripping the pillowcase tighter to her shoulder.

"Who is it?" she cried, mouth wide open, as she started backing up.

"It's Moise Angelle. Where are you going with that?"

"I'm just taking some old rags out to the barn. What you doing here?" Her voice was shrill.

"Don't be afraid. We just want to ask you all some questions."

"What could you be wanting to ask and it's still dark out?"

"Why don't you go back in the house and talk with Detective Lanclos?"

"I'm just going to put these old rags in the barn. I'll be right back, Moise."

"Sorry, Cecilia. Please turn around and go back into the house."

She stared at him for a minute, mouth twitching. "I haven't done anything, so why are you ordering me around?"

"Cecilia. Go back into the house, please. Now." He stepped forward, leaving the shelter of the tire mound.

A light clicked on from the camper. T'Bro's brother stepped out of the door onto wooden steps. "What the hell's going on out here?" he called.

"Nothing, Ajax. Go back inside," Cecilia ordered, her voice rising in pitch. "Stay away!"

Ajax reached inside the door and retrieved a shotgun which he raised to his shoulder in a neat sweep. "I got the back of your head in my sights, mister." His voice was even and slow.

Moise swooped out, grabbed Cecilia, and pulled her with him as he hunkered down behind the mound of tires. "This is Officer Moise Angelle. Put the gun down or I'll shoot."

"What the hell? You got no business around this place."

"Ajax! Drop the gun and go back inside. Stay out of this!" Cecilia cried. She passed the back of her hand under her nose and sniffled.

"Son of a bitch! You all right, Cecilia?"

"I'm all right, damn it! Get the hell back inside your camper. Do it now before he shoots your ass! You're going to get us all killed."

Ajax lowered the shotgun. "You sure you're all right, Cecilia? Just say the word and I'll take care of this."

"I'm all right for the third damn time. Now go back inside and shut the hell up!"

"All right, all right, I'm going." Ajax turned and started to go back inside, the gun barrel slanted down as he held it in the crook of his elbow.

"Leave the gun on the steps!" called Moise. "Don't take that gun with you."

Ajax stopped short. "That's MY gun. I don't leave my gun anywhere."

"Place the gun on the steps. That's an order!" Moise stood, pistol held at arm's length.

Ajax began a slow turn back away from the door. As he turned, he opened his mouth as though to speak, then shut it again when he saw Moise aiming at him.

"Fuck it!" he said and slowly bending his knees, lowered the shotgun with great care to the top step and raised his hands like a Pentecostal in church. "Don't take my gun! I was just trying to protect my sister-in-law, damnit. I didn't know who you was."

"Leave the gun where it is and go back inside and stay there until you hear otherwise. You got that? Unless you want me to make the case that you were drawing down on a law officer."

"Yeah, yeah. Ten four. I got it." Ajax passed back into the camper and slammed the metal door so hard the twenty-foot camper rocked.

"Go on into your house, Cecilia. I'm going to retrieve the shotgun and I'll be right behind you."

By the time Moise and Cecilia entered the living room, Woody Blanchard and Farrell LeBlanc had arrived in two separate patrol cars to provide assistance and backup for Lanclos. Woody stood by a long burgundy couch where T'Bro sat, eyes narrowed, a frown deeply etched on his sloping forehead. Thick black eyebrows intensified the scowl, and his mouth dipped at the corners, accentuating the angry demeanor.

"Sit right there beside Travis," ordered Lanclos.

"This is my house," complained Cecilia.

"We know that. And we'll be careful during our search," Lanclos said slowly. "I've explained to Travis that we're looking for any evidence of money laundering today. And if we should happen to find something else while conducting the search, we can confiscate it, and that will be within the law as well. Understood?" He watched her, eyebrows raised, arms at his sides.

"It all sounds like fast talking horseshit to me," she countered.

"Whatever. But do you understand what I said?"

She gave a curt nod and looked away in disdain.

"You probably want to look at this first. Cecilia had this with her when she took off out the back door," said Moise, taking a few steps toward Lanclos and lowering it to the floor in front of him.

Lanclos slipped a pair of latex gloves from his pocket and worked his hands into them, while he eyed the couple on the couch. The smell of bacon and coffee drifted through the room from the kitchen. "Looks like we interrupted your breakfast. If you want to go ahead and eat, I'm sure Officer Blanchard won't mind going with you into the kitchen while you finish with that."

"We'll be staying right here watching the whole time," said T'Bro, his tone ugly and his words clipped.

"We surely will," said Cecilia. "We'll be watching everything you all do. You won't be planting any evidence on us…not while we're here."

"Doesn't look like you need to worry about anybody planting anything," smiled Lanclos, as he nodded toward the pillowcase. "We'll start with this," he said to Farrell LeBlanc. He hunkered down beside the pink and white striped bundle and untwisted the plastic ties that held the opening tightly wound. As he unfolded the fabric, he looked inside and whistled. "Whew! Looks like the auto shop is a real good business, T'Bro!"

"You're damn right it is! Because me and Ajax are out there every morning by seven-thirty on the job. For years now! Work, work, work. And there's the savings to prove it. I don't believe in banks. That right there is years of busting ass. You got a problem with that?"

"We're going to see if there's a problem with it. Just looking at all those fifties and hundred dollar bills there on the top, I'm thinking there's some real serious money in there. What do you think, Farrell?"

LeBlanc's eyes bulged as he peered at the stash. "Damn! I didn't think there was that much money in St. Beatrice." He pushed the visor of his black cap back and scratched his forehead.

"We'll be running some tests on these bills, T'Bro."

"You take our money out of here, you'll be counting it in front of us and giving us a receipt for it before you leave here."

"Call a lawyer, T. We're getting railroaded," Cecilia spit out the words, then set her lips in a line so tight, the outline of her mouth turned white.

"You arresting me?" asked T'Bro.

"Haven't yet. Like I said, we're looking for evidence of money laundering. And we're off to a good start." Still hunkered down, with both hands he gently parted some of the bills to look inside the mound of cash. "There's probably a couple of hundred thousand in here. And, look here, Farrell. You see that?" Lanclos held two stacks of bills apart to reveal a pistol cradled in the midst of the money.

"Put some gloves on and call that serial number in for me. And then we'll start on the bedroom." He spoke softly to LeBlanc as though they were alone in the room.

"Funny place to keep a gun, T'Bro," said Lanclos, directing his gaze toward the couch. "What good's a gun for home protection if you can't get to it?"

"What business is it of yours where I keep my gun?"

"I'm just saying it's unusual, that's all."

Lanclos turned his head toward Moise. "You ever hear of anybody burying a gun where they can't get to it?"

Moise laughed. "Not really."

"I mean you don't have any little kids running around here, do you?" Lanclos looked at T'Bro, then at Cecilia. Neither of them responded.

"I didn't think so," Lanclos said.

"Serial number is filed off," reported LeBlanc, holding the pistol by the butt close to his face as he peered at it.

"All right. Okay. That's an automatic confiscation. Say goodbye to your pistol, T'Bro. You'll be making a statement on it in my office later today."

"I found it. I don't know nothing about the damn thing."

"Like I said, T'Bro. Later. You can be thinking up your story while we're searching your house."

"There's no story," T'Bro said. "I told you I found the damn thing. Somebody must of tossed it from a car window. It was by the Interstate."

Lanclos shook his head. "T'Bro, give it a rest. You know as well as I do, you're not allowed to own any gun without a serial number. I don't care if you found it in church. You should have turned it in. What if it was a gun we were looking for? One we needed to complete an investigation. To prove a case? You may have let a killer off the hook. That is if you did find the gun by the Interstate, which I doubt."

Ajax banged in through the back door then, slamming it behind him. "I want to know what the hell is going on?" he yelled, face pinched, eyes slits and red-rimmed. His shoulders were hunched, making his chest concave.

"Calm down, A.J.," said T'Bro. "Go back and stay in your camper til I tell you."

"No. He looks out of control to me. I already had a run in with him when he pulled a gun on me. It was dark, and he didn't believe who I was, so I gave him a pass," Moise spoke to Lanclos. "This is the gun." He indicated the shotgun he still held in the crook of his arm.

"Sit down over there in that lounger, Ajax," ordered Lanclos. "And watch your mouth."

"I can say what I want in my brother's house," said Ajax, so angry that spittle flew from his lips.

"Shut up, A.J. You're going to get us in a world of trouble," said Cecilia. She pointed a warning finger at him.

"Shit!" said Ajax, crossing his arms. "This is bullshit."

"Ajax!" Cecilia leaped from the couch, long black hair swinging, crossed to the lounger and slapped him. "I told you to shut it, you damn, dumb coonass. You're going to make me snap here in a minute!" She blew out a whoosh of air, turned and returned to her seat, bouncing onto the cushion so hard, the springs squeaked. Ajax's cheek turned bright red.

Ajax rubbed where she'd slapped him, then wrinkled his nose as he sniffed the bacon. "Cecilia, lighten up, why don't you? I can go eat some of that breakfast you got going in there?"

"Stay right where you are, A.J. Forget the groceries," said Lanclos.

"Damn. I'm hungry," Ajax said, fumbling in his denim jacket pocket. He brought out a round container, opened it, and pinched out a bit of tobacco, tucking it quickly inside his bottom lip. He worked his mouth around, settling into the chew, and leaned back in the lounger.

"What you got there, A.J.?" asked Lanclos.

"What you think? Just my chew." Ajax began sliding the canister into his pocket.

"Let me see it."

"It ain't pot, Mr. Mitch," Ajax said wearily. "It's just my chew."

"Let me see it."

Ajax held out his hand flat, displaying the round Timberwolf container with the snarling wolf picture on it.

Lanclos nodded. "Okay. Put it away."

Ajax shook his head, slid the tobacco into his pocket. "Cops," he said looking at his brother for corroboration. "Always on your ass about nothin."

"Moise, lock Ajax's shotgun in the truck, then meet me in the bedroom," said Lanclos, heading for the hallway leading to the rear of the house.

Moise began crossing the living room for the front door, when Ajax shot out of the lounger yelling, "Where you going with my shotgun? You can't take my gun! You got no right to do that! Who in hell do you think you are?"

Cecilia, startled, jerked her head back as she watched her brother-in-law's outburst, then leaped from the couch, stabbing the air with a forefinger towards Moise. "You bring his gun back! You can't take his gun like that. He has rights just like anybody! Just cause he's brain-damaged, you people think you can run all over him." She rounded the coffee table and headed toward Moise, grabbing for the shotgun, as if she were going to wrestle it from him.

Moise fended her off with an arm block, backing up as he did so, which threw her off balance. She stumbled and half fell, then pulled upright, took a deep breath, and steadied herself. "Give it back!" she demanded. "We'll sue the St Beatrice Sheriff's Office. You can't do this!" Her breathing accelerated, and her chest rose and fell with such force that her robe fell open on one side, exposing a breast. She jerked the sash tighter, clutching the robe closed.

LeBlanc stepped forward with menace, hand held near his black leather holster. "Sit down, Cecilia. Do it now, or I'll do it for you!"

Moise watched her quietly for a moment as she composed herself. She pursed her lips, and clenched and unclenched her fists. "When you sit down, Cecilia, I'll explain to you why we can take A.J.'s gun." He spoke softly and slowly as though he were speaking to a patient in a locked psych unit. She blew a shank of hair from her eyes and turned for the couch, still breathing hard, fists clutching her robe tightly at the throat.

T'Bro grabbed her elbow and yanked her down. "What the hell are you doing, Ci-Ci? You can't fight with the cops, for God's sake. Have you gone crazy on me?"

Lanclos reentered the room and stood next to Moise. "What's all the noise in here?"

"We're fixing to hear how come you all think you can take my gun," said Ajax, face pinched and pale. "Let's hear it!"

"For starters, you should be in handcuffs right now for drawing down on a law officer," said Moise, still speaking as though he were communicating with psychiatric patients. "You can consider yourself lucky right there."

"And that's why I'm confiscating your gun. We're going to keep it for a while, and if you behave yourself, you'll only have to pay a fine," said Lanclos. "End of story. If you want it back, my advice to you is to stay quiet, keep your mouth shut, and don't give us any more trouble. That is, unless you would rather we take you in today for threatening an officer with a gun."

Ajax narrowed his eyes at the two men as he considered this, then lowered his gaze toward an Auto Shopper newspaper on the coffee table, his expression sullen.

Lanclos turned back toward the hallway to the bedrooms, and Moise resumed his walk toward the front door.

"Can we at least watch television while we're sitting here?" T'Bro called out.

"No," called Lanclos from the hallway.

T'Bro crossed his arms, heaved a sigh, and leaned back against the cushions of the couch, settling in for a long wait. Cecilia remained sitting rigidly, face still tight, jaw muscles working, her fingers fidgeting with the belt of her robe.

Once in the master bedroom, Lanclos pointed LeBlanc toward the closet, as he stood at the foot of the king-sized bed and gazed around the room. The unmade bed had a rumpled crimson comforter, black silky sheets, and a great assortment of pillows piled against the elaborate carved headboard. Matching gilt lamps with gold tasseled shades on each nightstand provided low light. The plastic case of a DVD titled, *A Very Private Club,* lay beneath one of the lamps, along with a stubby candle in a ceramic holder.

A black lace garment lay on the carpet beside the bed.

LeBlanc eyed the DVD on his way to the closet. "If I brought shit home like that, my old lady would beat me with a stick, and I'd be sleeping in the kennel with the Beagles."

As LeBlanc slid open the mirrored doors of the walk-in closet, Lanclos moved to a dark varnished wardrobe with brass fittings. "I'll start on the wardrobe, then the bureaus."

"Yeah, I'll be all day in here. They could rent this closet out."

"Take your time. We don't want to miss anything."

Lanclos began his search by pulling the wardrobe a foot away from the wall to examine the back of it. After a few minutes of shoving the heavy piece inch by inch, he felt all along the back of it, knocked on the wood, and felt underneath on all sides as far as his arm would stretch. When he was satisfied, he opened the break front doors and began to hunt inside. He began by parting the hangers to see behind the hanging clothes, then ran his hands down each of the garments. Dropping to his haunches, he felt along the bottom of the wardrobe, and searched through stacks of folded clothes.

When he moved on to the first bureau, he repeated the process on the outside, then removed each drawer and examined the back and bottom of all four. He riffled through sweaters, blouses, underwear, scarves, and coiled belts. Replacing the drawers, he turned to the second bureau, a highboy, and repeated the process on all six drawers.

Sifting through each item in the top drawer, he found a few battery-dead watches, a jailhouse Rosary, made of thick knotted blue string, a garnet class ring from St. Beatrice High School, a gold chain and cross in a red satin-lined gift box hidden inside a Remington ammo box, and a bone-handled sheathed knife.

Moise joined them, and stood in the center of the room looking around, "Where do you want me to look?"

Lanclos didn't look up. "Wherever you want. Nothing in the wardrobe or that bureau."

"I'll check the bedside tables then."

"They behaving out there?"

"Oh, yeah. T'Bro is pretending to sleep, and Cecilia looks like she's ready to catch a stroke."

"That porn flick they were looking at last night probably has her all stirred up."

Moise glanced at the DVD case and laughed. He opened the drawer of one nightstand and found some prescription bottles. He opened them one by one and carefully closed the plastic caps. There was an unopened package of condoms and a tube of Avon hand cream.

He pulled open the louvered door beneath the drawer and found a stash of DVDs. It was a mixed collection of thrillers, horror, and adult movies. He opened each case, checked inside, then closed them again. When he reached the bottom of the first stack, he saw a DVD case set on its side at the back of the compartment. He retrieved it, opened it, and discovered a clear envelope of white powder.

"Yo! Mitch! Farrell! Come see!" He sat back on his haunches and waited for the men to join him bedside.

"Check it out," said Lanclos.

Moise touched a finger to the powder and put it to the tip of his tongue, then nodded slowly.

Lanclos smiled. "That sly dog T'Bro. He's been siphoning off some of the commodities from Leon. And in a *Getaway* movie case too. He's just too smart for his own good, huh? Keep on looking. I bet we find some more surprises tucked around here before we're done." Lanclos laughed out loud. "This just warms my heart. How about you all?"

"Nothing like vindication to make my day," said Moise, as he carefully closed the case and took the plastic evidence bag Lanclos handed him.

53

THE BARN

L anclos was putting the last drawer back into the dresser when a shout came from the living room. LeBlanc, on his knees in the closet, dropped a shoebox, regaining his feet, and headed for the bedroom door. Lanclos, closing the drawer, immediately turned and rushed to follow him. "Don't leave that behind," he called to Moise who had placed the evidence bag with the DVD case on the bedside table.

"Not a chance!" Moise said as he followed the other two men out the door, sliding the bag into his jacket pocket.

"He took off!" Woody yelled, as they stampeded into the living room. "Ajax is gone! He said he couldn't stand sitting around any longer." He pointed toward the barn through the open back door.

"Go on after him then," said Lanclos, as the men gathered at the doorway. "That poor sap! All he had to do was sit there a while longer, and he'd have been all right. Go with Woody, Farrell." Woody opened the door and stepped out, with LeBlanc right behind him. Lanclos and Moise turned around from the back door to see T'Bro deadly still, and biting his lip, by himself on the couch.

Cecilia was backing up toward the front door, holding a .25 automatic straight-armed in front of her. "I've got something I have to do. Sorry about that, my baby," she said to her husband. "But I don't have the time to sit in any shithole with a bunch of screaming crack whores."

"Ci-Ci, come on, baby. You're gonna get yourself shot. Throw the gun down and come back here."

Ignoring him, she steadily waved the revolver thirty degrees from side to side as she backed to the door. "You should have checked my pockets, Detective," she chided, then laughed. "Go find A.J. out in the barn. Watch T'Bro. But don't bother chasing me. I'm just a housewife in her bathrobe checking out. I'm going to shoot through the door so don't be behind it." She turned and raced for the door, opening it and slamming it behind her. Moise and Lanclos waited a few moments for the shots that never came, then Lanclos told Moise to guard T'Bro, as he headed for the door.

"Don't shoot my old lady! She didn't do nothing. She's just scared out of her mind." T'Bro leaned forward, a pained expression on his face, as he called after Lanclos.

Lanclos opened the door wide and left it open as he ran outside, looking first to the left and then to the right. Cecilia had disappeared from view. He ran to the shop fifty feet from the house, and tried the back door. It was locked. He whirled, trying to catch a glimpse of her, but she was nowhere to be seen.

He walked back toward the house and circled the south side, heading toward the back yard. He saw Woody inside the center aisle of the barn, starting up the narrow steps to the loft. He headed toward the building, his head moving from side to side as he continued to scan for Cecilia. The only movement he saw was a stray floppy-eared black and tan hound, loping across the property.

He hurried to the barn, entered the wide center aisle, and after passing by a vintage Allis Chalmers tractor and three stalls, came to an open plank door. He passed over the threshold into a wide, shadowy, high ceilinged room, the only light coming from a single opening with a leaning shutter. A musty smell rose from two stacks of vintage wooden potato crates filled with dried corncobs and covered with cobwebs to the left of the doorway.

A canvas-covered car was parked in the center of the room. He stepped toward it and raised a corner of the blue cover a few feet to see what lay beneath. It was a 1967 highly waxed, cherry red Chevrolet with chrome rims. As he dropped the corner of the cover back down, there was a roar, from the other side of the building as a motorcycle fired up.

He ran back to the center aisle, just in time to see a dirt bike rumbling through one side of the rear double doors. The full-throated howl of the engine vibrated and echoed through the grand spaces of the huge barn. He ran to the door and looked out. Cecilia was tearing across the fields in back of the property, bathrobe fluttering around her, long hair streaming, as she raced the dirt bike between rows of charred sugar cane stubble. Lanclos kicked the barn door.

"Damnit all to hell. Four professionals at the house, and we let a five foot two woman get away!"

Boots sounded on the loft steps. "What's going on?" Woody asked as he led Ajax with a grip on his elbow, down to the dirt floor of the center aisle.

"Cecilia took off on a dirt bike through the fields." Lanclos walked back toward the two men. "There's no point going after her now. Can't cut through the fields like a dirt bike can. I'll have to call it in." He gazed at Ajax who was laughing.

"A.J.! What the hell were you thinking taking off like that?" He wiped a sticky, dusty cobweb from Ajax's cheek. "You gone crazy on us?"

"I told you I can't sit around like that too long. I just can't stand it." Ajax's brow was furrowed, and his brown eyes darted back and forth like he was still looking for an escape route.

"Take him back up there and sit him back down, and don't take your eyes off of him this time." Lanclos shook his head. "A.J. I told you before…I don't want to arrest you, dammit!"

Woody gripped his arm tighter. "Come on, A.J. We're going back in the house."

"Yeah, yeah. I'm going. I know when I'm fucked." Ajax twisted his mouth to the side like Popeye. "That was pretty good though… watching Cecilia take off like that. Makes you guys look bad, huh?" He laughed again. "I could watch that movie a few more times. How about you all?"

* * *

"Your wife has taken off, T'Bro," Lanclos said as they led Ajax back into the living room. "You got any idea where she might go?"

"Try the casino. She likes to play the slots. Or try the offtrack betting. She likes the ponies too." T'Bro sullenly stared at the floor. His cheeks had sunken since they'd arrived at his house, and he'd developed a nervous tic causing him to blink repeatedly.

"In her bathrobe? Quit jacking me around, T'Bro. You're in years of trouble just with the coke we found in the bedroom."

"You think I'm going to help you find my old lady?" T'Bro snarled, still not looking up. "That ain't going to happen. Give it up."

"Do you have a camp?" asked Lanclos.

"Yeah. But you can forget about that. She'd have to take a boat to it and the boat's on the trailer in the barn."

"I know where his camp is. He's right. You need a boat to get to it," said Moise.

"What about her mother? Would she go over there?"

"No. Her mother has a heart condition. She wouldn't bring trouble with the law over there. She just had open-heart surgery two months ago. Cecilia loves her mother."

"Where then? Come on, T'Bro. Give us something."

"I told you. I'm not helping you find her. She's probably out of the parish by now the way she rides that bike. She's a hardhead. *Tête dure!* She could be anywhere. Even if I wanted to help you find her, I couldn't. She's too smart for even me to figure it."

"They'll pick her up. I called it in," said LeBlanc.

"I want to call my lawyer," said T'Bro.

"Your lawyer's dead," said Lanclos.

T'Bro stared at him. "Who's dead?"

"Leon LeDoux. Isn't he your lawyer?" asked Lanclos.

T'Bro didn't answer for a moment as he, frowning, tried to assimilate the news. Finally he spoke. "He used to be. Now *I'm* my lawyer."

"That's dumb," advised Lanclos.

"I'm not paying some dickhead, scamming lawyer all my savings so he can give me the run around, charge me a hundred thousand or more, and take the house and shop away from Cecilia all for nothing, while I'm locked up and doing time anyway. Fuck a greedy bunch of lawyers. I'll defend myself for free. Cecilia had nothing to do with any of this."

"All right, I hear you. If you change your mind, let me know. Meanwhile, we'll finish with the house and then we'll start on the barn. You stay here with Ajax and T'Bro, Woody, and we'll keep searching."

"You can search my camper all you want. All you're going to find is a lot of old greasy work clothes and ashtrays full of cigarette butts. Yeah, and lots of Kit Kat bars," Ajax laughed, exposing one missing tooth and two chipped ones.

"Shut up, Ajax, He can't search your camper. He's only got a warrant for the house."

"We've got a warrant for the house and any outbuildings on the property. We'll be here for a while," said Lanclos.

T'Bro glared at him. "Since you'll be here for so long, can I at least eat my breakfast that you interrupted?"

Lanclos jerked a head toward the kitchen. "Let him eat his breakfast. He's going to need it when we take him in for questioning."

"You're not taking me in too?" barked Ajax, shaking the hair out of his eyes and shuffling his feet back and forth.

"No, not this time, A.J. Not unless we find something more than old clothes and cigarette butts in the camper."

"That's all you're going to find. So I'm not going anywhere then. That's just fine with me. I have a tune-up to do this morning, and a grease job." A fleck of chewing tobacco appeared on his bottom lip and he made a pffft sound as he flicked it away.

"If you'll settle down until we get done here, we're going to let you go to work. How'll that be?" Lanclos crossed his arms and watched Ajax squirm in the chair, trying to get comfortable.

"You're the boss," he said. "I'm not going to say another word. Just watch." He pressed his lips together.

"Shut up, A.J.," said T'Bro in a weary voice. "Please, for once, just shut the fuck up."

54

SWAMP

L ate that afternoon, after T'Bro had been arrested and taken to the Parish jail, and Ajax had been allowed to go to the shop to his work, Moise drove to Levee Town to his friend, Choo-Choo's fish house by the levee on the fringe of the swamp.

Choo-Choo was hosing down the cement floor of a metal building to the side of the fish house. Between the building and the fish house was a long dock stretching out into the waters of the Atchafalaya Basin. Two houseboats were anchored in the inlet beside the dock and three boats were tied to cletes on the dock. One of these was Moise's sixteen foot mud boat. Moise had four boats, but kept only one of them at Choo-Choo's.

Choo-Choo had gotten his name as a kid when he used to grab onto the cars of freight trains as they slowly passed his house on the outskirts of Levee Town, riding for a few minutes before he'd let go and tumble and roll off. The Sheriff had heard about it and talked to his father putting an end to the game, but the name stuck. Some years later a young girl and her brother adopted the practice until she was dragged under the train and killed. After that, Choo-Choo tried to get rid of his nickname, reminding people his real name was Wayne, but it was by then too much of a habit to everyone, and he finally gave up.

Choo-Choo cut off the hose to talk to Moise. He was wearing rubber waders and a rust stained tee shirt decorated with a large picture of a hooked bass. His hair was white stubble and his eight-inch long beard white with yellow streaks. His thin lips glistened from the lip balm he used daily, and his eyebrows were out of control with unruly black wiry hairs sticking out any which way. His face was chiseled with hard planes that had the rough edges of a hand-carved wooden Indian. His skin was the color of tobacco, and his hands were thick-fingered and callused.

"Moise, my good friend. You going out?"

"Yeah. I'm taking her out for an hour or two. You doing all right?"

"Oh, yeah. I got no complaints, me. It's all good. I sold all of Ernest's catch for him already today. Tourists. They pay me good. They rent those cabins over at the Hideaway and cook their own fresh fish every day. Every year they come down from Mississippi and do the same. They stay two weeks every time…the whole family. There's ten of them. And when they leave they always make me a big present."

"I remember those people. They're from Holly Springs."

"Naw, that's another family. These ones are from Meridian."

"I can't keep track of all your out-of-town customers, Choo-Choo. You got so many of them."

"It keeps the meat on the table, yeah."

"Look. I'll talk at you later. I got some business out there. I got to get going."

"Uh-oh. Somebody's in trouble. I know that look."

"We'll see about it," Moise said, clapping a hand on the old man's shoulder. He walked down to the dock and untied his boat, then jumped inside and turned the key in the ignition to start the Go-Devil motor. Standing at the hold bar, he backed the boat out and headed for the open water through the cypress graveyard of stumps left by the logging companies that had been steadily butchering their way through the swamp since the aftermath of the Civil War.

Interspersed among the great gray stumps were slender young trees with delicate fringes of needles. But a hundred year old cypress tree might only grow to a diameter of a few feet, and the loggers had stripped the swamp of the giant primordial cypresses.

He steered the boat toward Dago Island, where he knew T'Bro kept his camp. It had been named that in the last two decades because a drowned Italian from the Jersey Shore had been found washed up there twenty years before. Before that, it had been known as Cat Island because a fisherman claimed he'd seen two panthers there one night when the water was high and the cats had searched for high, dry land.

Within ten minutes, he spotted the island and slowed the boat so he could go in as quietly as possible. Moise cut his motor as he drew near, and spotted an aluminum john boat pulled up on the bank. He poled around the side into a cut among cypress stumps, orange-brown cypress knees, young slender cypresses and gum trees. He stepped out into a foot of water in his high rubber boots, and pulled the boat onto a muddy grass bank.

He hunkered down, listening, as he watched the plank cabin and waited. Harsh ripping sounds came from the interior of the camp, then grating, and a woman's voice screaming loud curses and then more ripping sounds. It sounded like Cecilia's voice, and it sounded like she had lost her mind and was tearing the house down in a fury.

He stood and began moving toward a cobwebbed murky window on his side of the house. One pane was broken and the cover of a motorcycle magazine was taped over it. He looked inside from a corner of the window and adjusting his eyes to the gloom of the interior, could see that Cecilia had ripped up some floorboards with a crowbar, and was now fighting with the crowbar, trying to tear off a sheet of wall paneling.

"Damn you, T'Bro! You have done it now! I told you what would happen, you bonehead!" she yelled. With each creak of the paneling as it threatened to give, she wrenched harder. She had changed from the bathrobe and was now wearing jeans and a black and gold Saints' tee shirt. The paneling gave way, and she finished the job of yanking it loose, nails and all. She looked inside and then hurled the crowbar in disgust onto the floor where it bounced up and hit her on the chin.

"Ow!" she yelped. "See! See what you've done now, you stupid bastard. I'm bleeding!" She bent over and looked at her leg, then wincing, snatched up the crowbar and began hammering at the paneling in out-of-control rage. "Stupid! Stupid retard!" She threw it again, this time against a black pot-bellied stove, leaving a dent in the side of it before it bounced against the wall and came to rest on the floor again.

She stopped then, chest heaving as she tried to catch her breath, and finally walked to a free-standing metal cabinet in the corner of the cabin by a cast iron sink. She flung open the door and grabbed a bottle from a shelf, unscrewed the lid, and took a deep swallow, then wiped her mouth with the back of her hand, looking back at the house-wrecking she'd just accomplished.

She took another swallow, then set the uncapped bottle on a thick chopping board on a counter by the sink and stared at the stove. She took a deep breath, then marched to the stove and threw open the little metal door and reaching in a hand began digging around inside the stove, so that a great cloud of ashes flew out and into the room. Coughing and sputtering, she continued fighting with something inside until she'd pulled out a grate before tossing it over her shoulder onto the floor. She felt around where the grate had been and pulled out a fire brick, and then another.

She stopped as she had such a fit of coughing she had to halt the search. She backed away from the stove, hacking and spitting, then returned to the counter and took another long pull from the bottle, and then another. Leaning against the counter, face dark with ash, eyes glistening with rage and coughing, she caught her breath as the ashes settled and swirls of dust drifted to the floor.

She put a hand to her forehead, bowed her head and began to weep. Shoulders curved inward, she wept from the depths of despair, her breath catching and rattling in her chest. Moise started to go in then. He backed away from the window, but then suddenly, her head came up, her eyes widened, and she stopped sobbing as quickly as she'd begun.

She grabbed a spindle-backed side chair and strode to the opposite side of the thirty-foot room with it held out in front of her. Moise moved to another window pane to see what she was doing. She shoved an iron bed a few feet from the back wall and positioned the chair in back of it. Then, climbing up on the chair, she stretched up to grab at a mounted wild boar head hung above where the bed had been. It teetered, sliding back and forth against the wall as she lunged at it again and again. Finally it toppled, falling onto the floor, four-inch tusks breaking and sliding along the floorboards.

Jumping from the chair, she set upon the boar head banging it against the floorboards. Then she ran for the crowbar and returning to it, began smashing it with the iron bar until it crumbled and fell apart. Within the ravaged hog head spilled out a plastic bag. She lunged upon it, laughing with glee. "You son of a bitch! You think you're so smart! But I got you now!" She ripped open the bag and bills spilled out in piles around the ruined head.

She pulled a pistol from the bag and set about gathering the money into an orderly stack. She stood looking around for something to put it in, spotted a khaki game bag on the wall and yanking it from its peg, returned to fill it with the money and the gun. Once the bag was secured, she stood and crossed back to the sink to wash, laying the bag on the counter next to the bottle.

Moise headed for the front door. As he opened the door, she had her head under the faucet, water splashing onto her hair draped into the iron sink. He stepped inside, slid the bag from the end of the counter and tossed it out onto the grass. She startled then as his shadow moved toward her and reared her head up, water streaming from her long hair. She pulled the hair from her face in two drenched sections and stared up at him, mouth open. "What the..." was all she managed to say.

Moise stood silently regarding her, still blocking the door.

"Oh, my God!" she said, bowing her head. Then using her arm like a whip, she snatched the bottle from the cutting board and flung it at him, the bourbon splashing into his eyes as he ducked from it. The bottle sailed over his head smashing against the door, and she was gone for the back door. It slammed behind her as she ran outside.

Moise wiping his eyes with his sleeve, squinting and blinking against the sting of the bourbon, headed back out the front door. He grabbed up the game bag he'd dropped and ran toward the john boat she'd pulled onto the bank in front of the cabin. At least he could stop her from leaving the island. He waited for five minutes, then heard a rush of birds fly up toward the back of the property. He removed the pin from the john boat motor and began walking toward the rear of the property. Making his way past the cabin and into the cypress and gum trees at the edge of the island, he stepped once again into mud and saw her poling away in an ancient, cypress dugout pirogue. He shook his head and began to laugh.

"That woman! She's a *pichou*, her." He shook his head, and still laughing, he headed back toward his own boat. She was such a wildcat, he almost wanted to just let her go and disappear into the swamp with the rest of her wild creature relatives. But Moise knew she wouldn't last the night, and the afternoon light was already growing dim.

He'd known seasoned fishermen and hunters who'd gotten lost in the Atchafalaya and couldn't find their way out because so much of the cypress and water looks the same. They thought they knew enough to not take a GPS with them, and he was certain she didn't have one with her.

When he got to the boat, he leaned over, cupped his hand, and splashed water on his face to wash off the last of the bourbon, then tossed the game bag into the locker, pushed the boat off, and jumped in.

* * *

Five minutes later Moise slowed beside Cecilia in the pirogue. "Stop, Cecilia. It's no use."

She looked at him over her shoulder and continued poling. "You're not taking me to any damn jail," she called, turning her head back around to see where she was heading.

"Cecilia! Stop!"

"No way!" she yelled back.

"I'm pulling my gun."

She threw him a fierce look. "Your sister taught me in first and second grade in Catholic school. You won't shoot me." She refocused on where she was going, ignoring him.

"I'll shoot a hole in the pirogue then."

"Endangering a woman in the Atchafalaya? No you won't." She poled with increased vigor.

Moise idled his motor, came alongside, reached out and grabbed the two-inch thick pirogue with both hands, bumping it against his own boat. "Cecilia! Put the pole down and give it up. You're not going anywhere."

"I'll jump in the water," she threatened.

"No, you won't. You're coming in the boat with me back to safety. It's already getting dark out here. Then what are you going to do?"

"I can survive out here. My daddy used to bring me out here all the time when I was a little girl. And I know my way out of here too."

Crosshanded, he worked the pirogue backwards as she tried to maneuver forward. Then with the same temper she'd thrown the crowbar down, she threw down the pole so that it clacked and clattered into the pirogue.

"All right, Moise. You win…. but I have to take the pirogue back to the island. It's almost a hundred years old. You can't just let it drift off for some swamp rat to steal."

"I'll pull it back with a line. Get in my boat."

She turned around and stepped carefully toward him, then crossed over into his boat with the grace of a dancer. She sat quietly on a seat and crossed her arms, tossing her wet hair. He tied a line around a primitive iron hook in the bow of the pirogue and secured it around a clete on his boat.

"Now we'll take it back to Dago Island and you can start telling me what's going on," he said, starting the engine. Defeated, she stared straight ahead, arms still crossed all the way back to the island.

When he'd delivered the pirogue back onto the bank where it had been hidden by a sheet of roofing tin, he coiled up his line and stowed it in the locker.

"Talk to me," he said, as he sat facing her.

"Do you have a cigarette?"

"I don't smoke."

"This whole nightmare is Gerald's fault. It all started with him. He and T'Bro go way back to when they were kids. They used to fight dogs together. They did lots of things together. Their parents are second cousins. Gerald was wild back then. He did things you'd never believe. And all this mess is because of him. I told T'Bro not to get messed up with anything, but he did it anyway. I told him he was going to ruin our lives, but he did it anyway. I begged him." She shook her head. "And it all started with Gerald."

"What did Gerald have to do with it?"

"It was Gerald who made the first run."

"What do you mean run?"

"He transported some dope for a couple of times. Then he met Celeste and fell all in love and got saved and then got married. That was the end of the wild days. He went altogether straight and would hardly have anything to do with T'Bro anymore. But not before he turned T'Bro onto the man he had made the hauls for."

"And who was that?"

"I don't even know. I don't know what ,who, or when or where. I didn't even know there was coke in the house or that sack of money until he told me to run out the back door with that pillowcase."

"What about the money you just found in the cabin? You must have known something about it or you wouldn't have worked so hard to find it."

"I know my husband. He's secretive. I figured if there was something hidden in the house, there was something hidden in the camp. And I needed money to get out of here."

It was rapidly growing darker. The swamp birds were clacking and rustling in the trees where they'd gone to roost. Mosquitoes began their nocturnal drone.

"All right. It's almost dark. I'm taking you back. If you can convince the prosecutor about your story, maybe you won't do much time. If you'd stayed put at the house, you might not have done any time. That is, if you convince the prosecutor, and if you cooperate with us instead of acting crazy like you've been doing."

"Living with T'Bro and A.J. would drive a saint crazy, and I'm no saint!" She hung her head and stared at her knees all the way back to Choo-Choo's dock in Levee Town.

THURSDAY

55

AJAX

L anclos found Ajax bent under the hood of a battered Dodge pickup, changing the spark plugs.

"Hey, Ajax. How're you doing?"

Ajax kept working and didn't raise his head. "I'm busy right now, Detective."

"Yes, I see that. How about taking a break from what you're doing and coming in your office with me for a minute or two. I just want to ask you a couple of questions, then you can go back to work."

Ajax kept working. "It's not enough you haul my brother off to jail. And you even got Cecilia down there in the lockup. Now you're after me too?"

"No, A.J. I'm not after you. I just want to ask you a couple of questions. Then I'm out of here."

Ajax raised his head and wiped his face with his sleeve. "All right. But I got to get this job done by twelve. That guy's on my ass about getting his truck back."

"Come on then. Let's get it over with."

Lanclos let Ajax lead the way through the garage and to the office. Once inside, the two men sat, Ajax behind the desk and Lanclos in a chair in front of it.

"Okay. I'm here. What you fishing for?'

"When's the last time you saw Gerald Theriot?"

Ajax, taken by surprise, jerked his head back. "Gerald? How did his name come up? I thought you was hitting T'Bro and Cecilia up for conspiracy to launder money and possession."

"Just T'Bro. Not Cecilia."

"Okay. Then how come you got Cecilia locked up to where she can't come home?"

"She may be home sooner than you think. It depends on what the prosecutor wants to do with her. I'm out of that."

"Yeah, right. You put her in there, but you're out of it." Ajax swiveled the chair and kicked his feet against the desk to push the chair back.

"She shouldn't have run away. She might have been left out of it if she'd cooperated."

"I don't blame her for running. You come busting in her place when she's just waked up. Woman hadn't even had her coffee yet. Who can think straight without their morning coffee?"

"You're forgetting she was running out the back door with a pillowcase full of money...and an illegal firearm."

"She told you already...she didn't know what was in it."

Lanclos held up a hand. "And don't forget Moise left you off the hook for aiming a shotgun at him. And you ran too. So you don't have much room to complain."

"Yeah, and you people still have daddy's shotgun. And I still don't know why."

"Yeah, yeah. Let's move on. Please answer the question. When did you last see Gerald Theriot?"

Ajax looked up and then around the room as he thought for a few minutes. He absently swiveled in the chair again and shifted the lump of tobacco in his mouth. He looked around for something, then settled on a gray metal wastebasket to spit brown tobacco juice.

"Must have been one day last week when I was buying a six-pack over at the grocery." He spit in the wastebasket again.

Lanclos took out his notebook. "You sure about that? Think back, A.J."

Ajax frowned, then rolled his eyes toward the ceiling, thinking again. "I used to see Gerald a lot around town...when he was still alive. I'm guessing it was at the grocery...I guess."

"You know what, A.J.? I think you better do some more think-ing about your answer because this is a murder investigation. I'll wait until you're sure." Lanclos settled back in his chair, crossing his arms, a bland look on his face.

"Well, maybe I'm wrong about the grocery. I don't know. How's that for an answer? And I get bad headaches when I worry about something too much." Ajax rubbed his forehead. 'I'm getting one now real bad."

"Let me help you think then. Turns out Gerald was at Savoy's playing *bourrée* the night he died. And so were you. Does that help jog your memory a little?" Lanclos said gently.

"Damn, son of a bitch! It's like somebody drilling holes in my head when I get these migraines. And I can't see right. See what you're doing to me?" Ajax placed his palms flat on his face, covering his eyes. "That light hurts my eyes," he said. "And you're getting me all mixed up. Is that what you're trying to do?"

"No, A.J. I'm not trying to confuse you," Lanclos said. "I'm just trying to remind you that you were at Savoy's at the same time Gerald was the night he died."

Ajax rolled the chair forward and laid his head on folded arms on the desk. "Damn, damn, damn! It hurts bad. If I take a pill, I can't go back to work. It'll make me too sleepy."

Lanclos watched and waited a few minutes before questioning him again. The air within the office was still. A cat meowed as it sauntered through the garage, finally peering through the open doorway to the office. Slow traffic passed on the road outside, an occasional horn beeping in the distance.

"Do you remember talking to Gerald that night at Savoy's?" Lanclos asked softly.

"Yeah. I guess I asked him how he was doing, or something like that."

"And did you see him leave Savoy's?"

"Yeah. He did good at cards and then he left." Ajax lifted his head and eyes half lidded, looked at Lanclos. "That's all I know about it, okay? Now will you leave me alone so I can get that tune-up done before Billy Fontenot chews me a new one?"

"I'm going as fast as I can. Now I have to tell you there's a witness says you followed Gerald out of Savoy's when he left with his winnings."

"What are you saying now? I tried to mug him?"

"No, no, nothing like that. But you were angry about something. My witness says you were chasing him to his truck looking angry. What were you so worked up about, A.J.?"

"Nothing. I wasn't mad about nothing. He's lying whoever he is."

"So you weren't angry with Gerald about anything?"

"No, I was not. In fact, I would have gone to his funeral but we had to keep the garage open."

"My witness said you were so angry you spit at him and then kicked his truck after he got in."

"Lying again," Ajax said, closing his eyes and replacing his hands over his face.

"Look, A.J. My witness has no reason to lie. My witness has no reason to try to get you into trouble. So why don't you tell me what happened?"

"I might have yelled at him a little. It wasn't nothing though. I was mad cause he's been bad-mouthing T'Bro, that's all. I was sticking up for T'Bro." Ajax grimaced. "Now will you leave me alone so I can go back out there?"

"Gerald was saying what bad things about T'Bro?"

"Making out like he was some kind of criminal. I stick up for my brother, me. Nobody says nothing about my brother to my face."

"T'Bro's been good to you all these years, huh, Ajax?"

"Oh, yeah, he has. And Cecilia too. All both of them."

"So you would never want T'Bro to get into trouble, would you?"

"No way."

"But see A.J., T'Bro's already in trouble. Big trouble. And I want you to help me figure out who killed Gerald so nobody thinks it was T'Bro. Understand me? Think about everything that happened that night. You wouldn't want T'Bro to get accused of killing Gerald on top of all his other problems with the law?"

"T'Bro didn't kill Gerald! Why would he do that?" Ajax took his hands away from his face and slapped them on the desk. "Don't be saying my brother is a killer. He didn't kill nobody!"

"A.J. Calm down! I didn't say T'Bro killed Gerald. I said we need to find out who did kill him so nobody thinks T'Bro did it."

"Why would anybody think that anyhow? You're talking crazy."

"Because you just said Gerald had been bad-mouthing him. Making him out to be a criminal."

Ajax sank his head onto folded arms again. "Leave me alone. You're getting me all mixed up I told you."

The cat meowed from the doorway. "A.J. Is that your cat?"

"No. It's Cecilia's."

"I think he's hungry. Did you feed him today?"

"Yes. He's always hungry."

"Okay, look. I'm going to leave here just as soon as you tell me what happened that night. After Gerald drove away from Savoy's."

"I got in my truck and followed him. Just messing with him that's all. I cut on my brights and messed with him all the way down the road."

"What road?"

"Delcambre Road. He was headed for Miss Philomena's. That's what he said anyhow back at Savoy's."

"Okay. You messed with him. Cut your brights on and off, is that all?"

"Kind of. I kept riding his bumper. I was still mad."

"How far did you go?"

"A couple miles. Then I quit and drove home. That's it. End of story." Ajax's voice was muffled as he talked into his folded arms.

"So you didn't run him off the road then?"

Ajax jerked his head up. "Run him off the road? Hell no! How I'm going to do that?"

"Simple. Just sideswipe him. He was already drunk. Wouldn't take much."

"No, I didn't mess with him that much."

"Somebody did. And left paint on his door which you and T'Bro buffed off before I got to the garage the next day. One of you should have rubbed some mud on it after cleaning it up so the shine wouldn't show."

"Bullcrap! I didn't run him off the road. Gerald had a gun in the truck. You think I want to go and get myself shot? No. I didn't do nothing worse than hit the brights off and on and ride his ass to aggravate him. Then I went home."

"I'm sure you wouldn't admit to sideswiping a man the night he was killed."

"I didn't sideswipe him. I went home. I ain't lying."

"All right, A.J. We'll let that ride. You went home, and then Gerald called T'Bro to give him a tow. Is that right?"

"Right! Nothing more than that. That's how it was."

"And so T'Bro went out there, dark as it was and raining, and pulled him out. Right?"

"That's it. Nothing more."

"And did you go with him?"

"Just to help him with the hookup is all. I usually go with him on night calls."

"Except T'Bro said he didn't go out that night. He didn't feel good. He said he waited until morning."

"Oh, yeah. Didn't I say that? It was already light out."

"A.J. Quit your lying. This is a murder investigation. I don't want to have to take you to jail too. Who's going to feed the cat? Keep the garage open?"

Ajax gave the cat a menacing look as though it was at fault for putting him into a tight spot. "Okay. I went with him when it was still nighttime. I don't even know what time it was. I don't wear a watch. All I know is it was raining off and on, and it was black out."

"So you went along in the tow truck?"

"Yeah."

"And then what?"

"We pulled his truck out. What you think?" Ajax looked at Lanclos with a puzzled expression.

"And then what?"

"That was it. We towed it back here."

"And where was Gerald?"

"Don't know."

"I think you do know. I think you and T'Bro and Gerald got into an argument, and I think it turned into a fight. If you don't tell me what happened, it may be that T'Bro goes down for killing Gerald. Or maybe *you* did it. Tell me what happened."

"T'Bro didn't kill Gerald. They threw a few licks is all. Is that so terrible? It goes on all the time around here when people get drunked up."

"So they threw a few punches. What kind of punches? Tell me about it."

"They were fighting over Gerald's big mouth. That Gerald had better keep his fat mouth shut about T'Bro being a drug-runner or whatever because Gerald was no angel, him. Then Gerald sucker punches T'Bro and he goes down, splat, into the mud. Then he's swinging at me. He gets me in the temple and I'm knocked down on my knees, me too. Now T'Bro is really mad because Gerald punched me, and I have this head injury and all. So all of a sudden T'Bro is back on his feet and he's clobbering Gerald with the butt of his pistol."

"His pistol? Why a pistol?"

"T'Bro always carries a pistol in his pocket when he makes night runs with the tow truck. You never know what you're getting into."

"So he hits Gerald where?"

"Somewhere in the head. I don't know. I'm seeing stars, me."

"So he hits Gerald with the pistol. Then what?"

"Gerald staggers like he's going down, but then he snatches up his rifle where he leaned it against the truck, and he looks at it like he's maybe going to use it, but then he shakes his head, cussing out T'Bro, and takes off toward the woods. And he's kind of running zig-zag off the road there cause he's half knocked out, I guess. And then he's kind of all hunched over and still running. And some kids over in the woods are headlighting rabbits, cause it's raining and that's when rabbits like to come out and run around playing."

"How do you know kids were over there? There was no moon to see who it was."

"I don't know. I could kind of tell they was just kids. Like maybe teenagers or whatever. Their headlights were bobbing up and down and they were acting crazy, not like grown hunters would.

And then they blasted Gerald. Must of thought he was a deer or something the way he was zig-zagging."

"So you're saying these kids headlighting rabbits shot Gerald?"

"That's right. They blasted him. I heard it. I saw it. And T'Bro had nothing to do with it just like I told you."

Lanclos watched Ajax for a few minutes without speaking as the cat continued to meow.

"Shut up, Minnie," Ajax barked at her. "I got a headache. Quit your damn meowing."

"So then how did Gerald get to Miss Philomena's?"

"We yelled at the kids. 'Hey, you idiots just shot a man!' They took off so fast we never did see where they went to. We heard a truck start up and take off from the woods. They didn't even cut on their headlights so we couldn't make out what kind of truck. We went running through the field into the woods and found him on the ground. We felt so bad about what happened that we picked him up, took him to the tow truck and carried him to his own property. To Miss Philomena's."

"If that's the way it was, why didn't you report it?"

"Are you kidding? We didn't want to get blamed for it. We'd just been in a fight with him. Who'd believe us? It was too dark to see who shot him. The law would've said we shot him cause we'd been fighting."

"All right, Ajax. If your story holds up after we get the tests back from your shotgun, you'll be cleared. Go back to work now. I'll write this report up, and you can sign it later. I don't want you to get chewed out by Billy Fontenot."

"Yeah. Okay. Just remember, T'Bro didn't kill Gerald." Ajax stood and stomped toward the door to the garage.

"And don't forget to feed the cat," said Lanclos as he followed him from the office. He clapped Ajax on the back. "Thanks, Ajax. You've been a big help. And I'm not going to forget it."

"Yeah, I wish I could," said Ajax as he trudged back to the Dodge pickup.

56

IN THE INTERVIEW ROOM

L anclos sat with T'Bro in the interview room of the St. Beatrice Parish jail. The stark look of the dull sand colored cement block walls was unmitigated by the metal table and chairs where the two men sat. T'Bro looked sallow and bedraggled after a night in jail, with dark shadows under his eyes. Lanclos was questioning him about the night of Gerald's death.

"I had to read you your rights again because this is a separate matter from your arrest, but you may be able to help us. Your assistance could help you with the mess you are in right now. I just need to run over the events of the night Gerald Theriot called you to tow his truck when he ran into the ditch. If you can help me figure out what happened to him, help me find his killer, it could be a good thing for you. Do you mind running that all by me again?"

"You mean how he called me in the middle of the night and woke me up?"

"Yeah, that's right."

T'Bro licked his dry, cracked lips. "Lemme see. He calls me to tow his truck. I'm half asleep on cold medicine and I ask him could it wait til morning. That what you mean?"

"That's what we're talking about here. Yeah. I'm still trying to figure out what happened to him. Do you remember anything else, anything else at all about that night? Something he might have said. Anything?"

"Naw. Like I told you. I rolled over and went back to sleep and drove over in the morning to tow his truck. Then you showed up at the garage and took over. That's about all I can tell you." T'Bro licked his lips again.

Lanclos sniffed, then rested his elbow on the table and supported his chin on the palm of his hand. The room was silent except for T'Bro scuffling his feet a few times.

Lanclos worked his jaw back and forth as he thought. "Now here's the thing, T'Bro. I have a witness says he saw you in the middle of the night on Delcambre Road arguing with Gerald. Says the two of you were in each other's face."

"Who said that?" T'Bro glowered and began tapping his foot.

"What do *you* say? I want to hear your side of the story."

"My side is….they're half blind or altogether blind or drunked up. I was home in bed zonked on Nyquil. Jesus, God! My nerves are shot staying in this damn noisy hellhole. I can't get any sleep with all the zoo animals yelling in there all night, and now you lay this on me."

"Now I understand T'Bro, if you're worried about coming clean about it knowing Gerald died that night…but if you're straight with me, it'll go a long way. Just because someone says they saw you there doesn't mean you killed Gerald."

"Of course I didn't kill Gerald! Why would I kill someone I've known all my life? Gerald was a good guy. Everybody knows that."

"Yeah, yeah, I know all that. It would be hard for anyone to believe that you killed Gerald, so why don't you just come clean and tell me if you were there after all, so I can figure out what happened to him? It might help because so far…" Lanclos held his hands out to indicate he was at a deadend.

"I'm not going to lie to you and say I was there!" T'Bro widened his eyes. "I told you I was sleeping like a log. Ask my wife."

Lanclos made a soothing gesture with his hand, patting the air. "Calm down, T'Bro. I know you've got a lot on your mind. I'm just filling in some details about that night, that's all."

T'Bro ran a hand through his hair. "So who's this witness?" he asked again.

"Your brother."

T'Bro gaped at Lanclos. "A.J.? You're shitting me! A.J.?" Lanclos nodded.

"What the hell?" T'Bro buried his face in his hands, shaking his head back and forth in despair. "Why? Why would he say something like that? He's not right in the head, you know that."

"He was trying to help clear things up, that's all," Lanclos said gently. "And that's all I'm trying to do...clear things up. If you're afraid of saying you got in a fight with him, I understand, but don't you see? Fights go on all the time. It's understandable if you lost your temper over an argument."

"A.J.'s not right in the head," T'Bro insisted, raising his head and jabbing a forefinger against his temple.

"Maybe so, but there are witnesses that he and Gerald left Savoy's after playing cards that night. I think he'll probably sign a statement about what happened."

T'Bro, reddening, looked wildly around the room in anger. "Damn! Damnit!"

"Look, man. If you'll just tell me what happened, I'll forget about the phony story you gave me and we'll start fresh. I just want to clear this investigation up. It'll be a lot easier on you if you tell me your side of it."

T'Bro threw up his hands in frustration. "It was just a stupid argument. That's all!" he cried out.

"Yes, and I understand that. We all lose our temper from time to time," Lanclos said, keeping his voice low.

T'Bro raised his head, squinting, eyes red-rimmed. "He sucker-punched me. I was flat on the ground seeing stars. I'm so pissed, I grab the pistol out of the back of my pants and come up swinging with it. I hit him with the butt of it, and he goes stumbling off. That's all I did. It was some hunters headlighting back in the woods that shot him. They must have thought he was a deer or a wild boar."

"I understand what you're saying. You were seeing stars, then you're seeing red, and you strike out in self defense, like a mad bull."

"That's all it was."

"So why did you make up that story about not going to tow the truck until morning, when it was just a simple fight?"

"Because some cars had gone by while we were arguing and fighting. I didn't know if somebody would of recognized me."

"I understand your fear. You were scared. So now take a deep breath. Do you feel any better getting it off your chest?"

T'Bro took a deep breath and wiped his hands over his face. "Maybe. Maybe I do. My nerves are so shot from staying in that animal cage two days, I couldn't tell you. I need some sleep more than anything. I can't even think straight with all those crack addict assholes yelling non-stop. And that noise in there all day and all night is like a hammer bouncing off the walls at you, hitting you in the head. Those morons never shut up. My head's killing me." T'Bro's forehead creased, and he rubbed the back of his neck.

"Yeah. I know what you mean, and I'm going to get you a hot cup of coffee in a minute. Maybe that'll help." Lanclos said. "But, first, can you tell me why you moved the body? Why didn't you just leave him where he was?"

"A.J. ran his mouth about that too?" T'Bro's jaw dropped, and he sank his face into his hands once more. "Son of a bitch."

"You and Gerald go back a long time. Maybe you were just trying to show him some respect putting him where you knew he was headed that night." Lanclos' tone remained gentle.

T'Bro raised his head nodding, eyes bloodshot. "That's it. We were all in shock, not thinking straight. I thought we should at least get him out of Delcambre's woods, and put him where he was trying to go on his own property. By the bayou where he loved to be."

"I can understand that, T'Bro," Lanclos said. "You're in shock. You're worried you were seen there, so you did what you thought was best at the time…even if it seems screwy in the light of day. Isn't that right?"

"Yeah. That's the way it was. I was just trying to respect him. Like you say, we go back a long ways. We grew up together. When you know somebody that long, they're sort of like family."

The two men sat completely still for a few minutes, with only the sound of T'Bro's rasping breathing breaking the silence.

Finally Lanclos spoke again. "Do you have any idea of who the hunters were?"

"Naw. It was black out. Drizzling. There was a mist coming up from the bayou. I have no clue who they were. They were teenagers, I'd bet though. They sounded like it anyhow. Grown men don't make noise when they're hunting."

"So you thought it was a hunting accident, and you didn't want to get linked to it. And that's why you made up the other story. To avoid being questioned about that night. Isn't that right?"

T'Bro nodded. "Yeah, I have enough to worry about with the shit I have to take care of at the garage and my crazy brother and all."

"I'm sure you do. And I appreciate you coming clean. Maybe one of the hunters will come forward one day so I can close this case."

"I wouldn't count on it." T'Bro closed his eyes and rubbed his forehead hard back and forth using his thumb and stiffened fingers.

"You never know. Somebody may get drunk and talk. I'm going to get you a hot cup of coffee before I send you back to the zoo. You look like you could use some." Lanclos slid his chair back and signaled to the guard outside the lone window.

"You got that right." T'Bro stretched out his legs and clasped his hands behind his head as he leaned back in his chair. "And could you make them turn the A/C down in the jail? You could hang meat in there, it stays so cold. All they give you is a thin blanket that's not worth a damn."

"I'll see what I can do for you," said Lanclos, looking toward the metal door as the guard opened it. "How about getting us some hot coffee? Could you do that for us, please?" he asked.

"With lots of sugar," said T'Bro, rapping his knuckles on the table.

"Black for me," said Lanclos.

The bulky guard nodded and closed the door again, as T'Bro fidgeted in his chair and cracked his knuckles.

"I'm going to ask you to sign a statement after I get it typed up. What we talked about in here. If your help leads us somehow to the shooter, it will help you. What goes around comes around."

"Yeah," said T'Bro, rubbing the back of his neck. "I can use all the help I can get right about now."

The door opened again, and the guard brought two Styrofoam cups of steaming coffee over to the table.

"I put four sugars in there, T'Bro. You think that'll do it?" asked the guard.

T'Bro took a wincing sip of the hot brew, his foot jiggling. "Whew! Tastes like Caro syrup. Just right!"

"Don't say I never gave you nothing," the guard laughed as he retreated, the door slamming behind him so that it echoed in the room.

FRIDAY

57

LANCLOS PHONES ANNIE

At last, Lanclos breathed deeply with relief. He'd showered, changed clothes, and pulled the tab on a beer to celebrate. His work was finished. T'Bro had signed a statement about the fight. The shooters were unknown. It would most likely go down as a manslaughter case, owing to the coroner's assessment of the damage from the pistol butt blow to Gerald's head. The case had the added complication of the hunting accident with an unknown shooter, all of which would end up in the hands of a jury. In the meantime, the case was turned over to the State's Attorney.

Lanclos was confident that in a few weeks T'Bro would be indicted on at least four counts: Conspiracy to money launder as his prints were all over the ruptured air bag and the bills; possession of two ounces of cocaine which was an automatic 'intent to distribute'; possession of the pistol with an obliterated serial number which became a felony when found along with narcotics; and homocide, owing to the pistol blow to Gerald's head, which Rusty Meaux was prepared to declare was what killed him.

T'Bro was going to be locked up in Angola for years, but Lanclos was a free man now. He basked in the pleasure of the closure, enjoying the relief of it, and took a long swallow of the icy cold beer. An investigation always hovered over his head like a five hundred pound weight bearing down on him. Now he could get back to his life. Since his philosophy was: Always just do the next thing - his brain automatically clicked to the next thing. And now the next thing was....call Annie.

He'd been too busy the last two days to get back with her, but he wanted to see her ASAP. He flipped open his phone, clicked on her number and thought about where he could take her in Lafayette to celebrate their new freedom.

"Hello," she said, her voice tentative.

"Any chance of you being able to go out tonight? I would like to take you out to dinner in Lafayette." He spoke slowly, low-keying it.

"I'm guessing this means you wrapped things up?" Her voice sounded dull, unlike her. A radio played in the background.

"The case is closed. We can actually spend some time together. Dinner? Maybe a movie?"

"Oh, yes. Okay. How are the dogs doing?"

The back of Lanclos' neck felt like someone had just pressed an ice bag on it. He waited a few beats, listening. He could hear a faint scraping noise near the telephone, along with the country twang from the radio. "The dogs are fine. I'm just going out to check on them now," he said, his voice gruff.

"Okay," she said. The scraping stopped. He thought he heard a cough, then a rustling sound like fabric being rubbed. He waited, pressing the phone to his ear to hear more, but she hung up. A wash of dread flooded his body, and he could feel the heartbeat at his temples.

Lanclos immediately called in for backup to meet him at Annie's apartment, then called out the back door for his son who was cleaning out the tool shed twenty feet from the house. "Paul. Got to go! Emergency! I'll catch up with you later."

Paul leaned out the door of the shed, a pitchfork in his hand. "I'm out here. You need me for something?"

"Hold the fort. I got to go!"

"What's the matter?"

"Later!"

He grabbed his gun from the kitchen counter and ran through the house slamming the front door behind him and raced to the pickup, still parked at the foot of the brick walkway. Jumping into the cab, he had the key in the ignition before he'd even slid fully onto the seat. He revved the engine and charged off down the drive toward the road, feeling his face grow hot as he headed for town.

Two farmers headed the other direction waved as they passed, but Lanclos didn't acknowledge them, just raced along the gravel road until he reached the St. Regis Highway, and then headed east toward St. Beatrice, tilting his visor cap back and wiping his forehead with the back of his hand.

"Damnit!" he yelled, clenching the steering wheel and jerking his head back and forth to relieve the steel grip of tension on the back of his neck.

A large hundred horsepower International tractor was getting ready to pull out from a freshly plowed field, the farmer watching from his air-conditioned cab as Lanclos leaned on the horn in warning as he sped by. The farmer's head swiveled as he watched Lanclos roar down the road.

His cell rang and he grabbed it from its leather holder, saw the number was a friend in Lafayette, so let it ring and placed it back into the holder. He was almost to town and passing the Savoy Roadhouse, the parking lot just beginning to fill up. He had less than five minutes before he'd be at Annie's apartment. He slowed when he saw the St. Beatrice town limit sign, and proceeded with more caution. He passed a used-car lot, a few houses, the high school, then City Hall. Just three more blocks to go.

Scanning as far as he could see in front of him, he saw no patrol cars yet, but knew he'd have company in a minute or two. He passed the Bayou Bed & Breakfast, then a few more historical houses, and he was at Viator Street.

As he turned the corner at Castille's Café, he surveyed the parking lot in back for Annie's Honda, but didn't see it. Parking at the curb, he slid out of the cab just as Farrell LeBlanc pulled alongside in his patrol car.

"What we got?" LeBlanc leaned out of the window.

"Somebody up there's got Annie. Come on," Lanclos jerked his head toward the back entrance to the building and pulled his gun.

LeBlanc parked in back of Lanclos' truck at the curb and followed him toward the rear metal doors to the building. One of the café's garbage cans had been knocked over and a bag of richly seasoned red crawfish shells had burst, releasing a sharp smell. A tiger cat was nosing its way into the mess with a scrawny kitten close behind.

Lanclos opened the metal door on the left that led to the upstairs apartment. He led the way into the entryway and started up the metal stairs. The men climbed the stairs in silence, hugging the wall, and when they reached the second floor, Lanclos nodded toward Annie's apartment door. They moved quietly forward, then Lanclos tried the door knob.

It opened easily. He opened it halfway and the two men, one on each side of the doorway, slowly stepped toward the threshold. A radio played softly from the kitchen counter. Lanclos leaned his head inside, eyes wide open as he peered around in the dim light from the kitchen windows. Two blouses lay folded over a chair. A sneaker lay on the carpet. Other than that, the room looked undisturbed.

His gun held at the ready, he stepped fully inside the apartment, LeBlanc in back of him with gun drawn and pointed toward the ceiling. They stepped through the living room and Lanclos nodded toward the bathroom, while he moved on into the bedroom. The bedroom appeared empty. He opened the closet door seeing only an empty shoebox, a purple scarf and plastic hangers lying on the floor. He kneeled down and looked under the bed. There was a pair of satin slippers and a piece of junk mail. LeBlanc opened the closet door in the bath that held only a water heater.

"Nothing," Lanclos called. "She's gone. He took her."

"Who took her?"

"That same asshole from Arkansas...the attempted kidnapping and assault from last week?" Lanclos spoke calmly, but was still conscious of the blood pumping at his temples.

"We ever hear anything more about him?" LeBlanc's eyes kept sweeping the apartment.

"Nothing. Annie said we wouldn't find him. He's a ridge-runner mountain man. What do you expect? He could probably stay gone for the rest of his life if he wanted."

"Except he decided to come back and try again to snatch Annie."

"Yeah, but what he doesn't know is, that ain't gonna happen." Lanclos slid his pistol back into its holster.

"Looks like it already did though, buddy," said LeBlanc, twisting his mouth back and forth, still looking around.

"For now. He's only got her for now."

Lanclos clapped a hand on LeBlanc's shoulder. "Thanks for the backup. We must have missed them by only five minutes."

"You gonna put out a BOLO on her car?"

"Yeah. Right now." Lanclos pulled out his cell as LeBlanc crossed to the refrigerator and opened it. The refrigerator was full of bowls of food, a carton of eggs, jars of condiments, bottles of juice, and a few cans of beer.

"You mind if I get a beer, Mitch?"

"Help yourself, brother. Looks like it's on the house."

58

THE CHASE

At the four-way, as he left St. Beatrice city limits, Lanclos chose Mouton Road headed north instead of the St. Regis Highway leading to State Road 70, because he felt certain Hoyt would travel the back roads on his way back to Arkansas. Not knowing yet that he had the law on his tail, he might be driving at the speed limit, trying to keep a low profile. Lanclos had to use all of his self control to keep his speed under ninety, because his rage was boiling over, and he finally had a clear understanding of the emotions that led up to people going over the edge.

His temper had flared, and he was in a dangerous state of mind. He was so angry he knew he shouldn't even be chasing Hoyt. It was unprofessional because he was personally involved, but he knew he couldn't stop and turn around, leaving the job for other personnel. He was driven to keep going, so full of adrenaline, that if Hoyt was within his reach, he could have torn him apart.

The road ran about a hundred feet from the bayou and as the bayou curved, the road did also, so that he slowed for what the locals called Cemetery Gate, which was a sharp bend in the road lined with white washed crosses and metal markers for the many who had lost their lives there. The crosses and markers, decorated with both fresh and plastic flowers, totaled eight, and didn't count the three teenagers who had died when their car had lost control on that curve and gone hurtling into the bayou on a foggy night three years before.

He made a wide pass around a young girl on a quarter horse, then resumed his speed on a long straight stretch of road that he hoped would give him the opportunity to catch up with Hoyt. He pushed the truck to ninety, and pressed on, feeling more and more confident he was going to overtake the Honda.

The portable radio crackled and Farrell LeBlanc came on, calling his number. "Hey. man. Where you at now?"

"Just passed the Guidry farm."

"I'm about ten miles out of town on St. Regis Highway. Keep in touch with me. Over and out."

Lanclos passed a light truck so loaded with round bales that its license plate and rear lights were obscured. Ordinarily he would have stopped the driver and ticketed him, but today the farmer got a free pass as Lanclos roared down the road with only one thing on his mind.

The road was fairly free of traffic and he was able to drive another fifteen miles, past farms, an occasional country store with two or three gasoline pumps, and woods. He came to a village, slowed to the thirty-mile speed limit, then immediately accelerated again once he'd left it behind. The road ahead began to curve toward the Interstate, leaving the bayou, and he passed one more village, this one not much more than an intersection with half a dozen frame buildings and a brick hardware store.

Farrell called in again on the portable radio. "You got anything yet?"

"No. I just passed Gautraux."

Within five minutes of that call, Lanclos spotted a speeding red car up ahead. It was in trouble because it was fast approaching a slow moving hay wagon, and it couldn't pass because of an oncoming car. As he came closer, he saw it was the Honda, and its tires left black tire tracks on the road as its brakes screeched, trying to avoid hitting the wagon.

Suddenly, the Honda jerked to the right, careened toward the ditch, flipped once and settled on its roof, tires spinning. Lanclos slowed his truck, coming up to the scene as he called the accident in on the radio.

He was able to brake safely on the side of the road, twenty feet from the Honda, the smell of burning rubber filling the air. The hay wagon continued slowly down the road, the driver apparently oblivious to the accident. He stepped out of the truck, gun out, cautiously approaching the overturned car.

The driver's side opened and Hoyt unfolded himself from the vehicle, hoisting himself out of the car and holding his hands in the air. "She's in there. I didn't hurt her. Put that gun away. I didn't force her to come with me. She wanted me to take her home. Just ask her."

Lanclos stepped closer, not lowering the gun. Hoyt stepped away from the car. "You can't shoot me. She wanted to go home!" Hoyt stepped backwards, hands still in the air.

Lanclos began lowering the gun, and then in a flash, Hoyt spun on his heels and took off running. He yelled as he ran, "I'll be back for you, Annie. Keep watching! I'm coming back for you!" He disappeared into a thicket of high grass, surrounded by wide spreading oaks, as large black crows flew from the branches, their loud caws drowning out his cries.

Lanclos holstered his gun while leaning into the car. Annie was struggling to climb out the driver's side. "You all right, Annie?"

"I'm fine now. Just help me get the hell out of here, will you?"

He reached out his arms, and she hauled herself along the seat until she was sitting up behind the steering wheel. She easily slid from the seat then and standing, leaned into his arms.

Lanclos pulled her close to him and held her for long moments, as they rocked to and fro silently. She pressed her face against his chest and eyes closed, relaxed as he smoothed her hair and rubbed the back of her neck.

"Thank God you called me when you did," she finally said.

"Yes," he said.

"I'd of been locked in some cabin in those mountains somewhere in back of beyond by nightfall. Nobody would of ever found me."

"I would have," said Lanclos. "I'd have found you."

SATURDAY

59

THE CATFISH FESTIVAL

ntoinette's new band was singing *The Opelousas Waltz*
by the time Lanclos and Annie finished parking in the
church lot and buying tickets at the entrance to the
church grounds. The property, five grassy acres in back of the
church, was surrounded by spreading two-hundred year old oak
trees. Each of the trees had branches that stretched as much as
thirty feet, covered with curling resurrection fern. Food and drink
stands were set up in a long row on one side of the property. The
bandstand was a wooden stage built for the festival on the opposite
side. A large crowd of people milled about, mostly congregating
toward the music. Loudspeakers were stacked on both sides of the
stage, a red and white cloth banner advertising the festival strung
overhead.

Paul, in front of the bandstand, waved to them through the
crowd. A broad smile on his face, he tilted his head proudly toward
Antoinette, who was standing between the washtub bass and the
guitar player, forehead creased as she concentrated hard on her
fiddling. Lanclos and Annie worked their way toward Paul and
finally reached his side in the front row of the crowd.

"Look at her, Dad. Isn't she great on that fiddle?" Paul's
eyes were shining with delight as he danced in place, watching
Antoinette play.

"She is. She sure is!" Lanclos said, startled at the resemblance
between Antoinette and her mother. She was dressed in a scoop

necked cotton print dress that buttoned all the way down the front
to her knees. She wore red leather roper boots, and her long hair
was loose, draping around her shoulders. Although her complexion was dark like her father's, her face, hair and figure reminded
him powerfully of Claudine when she was that age. The young
woman's talent for the violin, however, soon took over in importance. She played the traditional song with a fervor and expertise
that could only have come from years of practice.

"How long's she been at this?" he asked Paul, leaning toward
his ear.

"Since she was like nine or ten," Paul called above the music.
"She's nervous today though. First time playing in public."

"She's wonderful," said Annie to Paul, smiling and nodding to
him. Paul looked at her curiously.

"Have you met Annie?" Lanclos asked, leaning toward him
again.

"Hello," Paul nodded to her, the happy smile never leaving his
face, then returned his full attention to Antoinette.

When they finished the song, the crowd cheered and
applauded with great energy, and Antoinette stepped closer to the
microphone to thank them and announce their next song: *Allons
a Lafayette,* drawing another wave of applause and cheering. She
smiled at Paul and stepped back, positioning her fiddle and bow.

"Wait'll you hear this," Paul said, pushing even closer to the
bandstand.

The band took off into the lively song, and then Antoinette
began singing and Paul nudged his father with his elbow, shaking
his head in admiration. "What'd I tell you?" he called out in glee.

Lanclos took a moment to survey the crowd. He was good at
estimating crowds, and he figured there were about three hundred
people at the festival, which meant a good take for the church.
Most were dressed in visor caps, jeans and tee shirts with a few
wearing dresses. People had formed a haphazard circle for about
twenty dancing couples. Food and drink booths lined the perimeter of the festival grounds, along with booths selling a variety of
hats, tee shirts, condiments, and homemade items such as alligator
tooth necklaces, rosaries, and cypress picture frames and benches.

He spotted Moise and Dixie in front of a stand that sold catfish sandwiches. They were starting toward one of the picnic tables placed near the food and drink stands. He saw Claudine and Roy sitting on low folding chairs toward the side of the crowd, drinking from plastic beer cups, heads tilted toward each other as they critiqued their daughter's first public appearance.

"Her dress is cut too low," complained Roy.

"It is not! You're being over-protective. She's using her God given talent, and that's what everybody's supposed to do," chided Claudine. "They are terrific!"

"Yep!" beamed Roy, "They sure are!"

Groups of teenagers were scattered through the crowd, and one young man caught Lanclos' eye, nodded, and looked away quickly. He had seen the boy around town in the past, and knew his father. "Dad!" Paul nudged him again. "Look!"

Antoinette finished the song and to great applause and encouraging cheers, she stepped closer to the microphone again. "Thank you! Thank you so much! We are The Lost Bayou Band, and this is our very first public appearance. We are so glad to be here with you all today. And we're so glad you all came out for the twelfth annual St. Joseph Catholic Church catfish festival. Don't forget to eat lots of catfish today and buy raffle tickets so you can maybe win that John Deere lawn tractor over there." She waved toward a grasshopper green tractor resting on pallets under a striped canvas tent.

"And now for our last song, we're going to play *Les Veuves de la Coulee* for you."

The crowd started up again with waves of yelling, whistling, and clapping that followed her as she stepped back and raised the fiddle again, bow poised to begin.

Paul turned to Lanclos and Annie. "Isn't she something? Have you ever seen anything like her?"

Lanclos shook his head as he lied, "No, son. I've never seen anything like her."

When the band finished the song, the crowd cheered and yelled for more, so the band conferred, then began playing the perennial favorite, *La Porte Dans Arriere*. Dancers immediately began swirling, stomping, and fast stepping as some of the crowd watched them and clapped in time with the music, while others continued to face the stage and watch the band. When the song was over, the band bowed and waved at the crowd as they basked in the applause, and began gathering up their instruments and clearing the stage for the next scheduled performers.

Paul turned toward his father and Annie. "Gotta go, Dad. I'm going to go help her pack up. See you later, okay?" He held out his hand to Annie. "Nice to meet you, Miss Annie."

"You never met Annie in Castille's?" asked Lanclos.

"Not really. I hardly ever have time to go in there anymore," Paul said as he shook Annie's hand. "I've seen you a couple of times though."

"Me too," Annie said. "I didn't realize you were Mitch's son."

"Can't you see the resemblance now though?" asked Paul, looking at his father's profile. He touched his nose. "Same nose, same chin."

Annie looked from one to the other. "Yes, I can see it."

"Well, gotta go. See you later," Paul said as left them and headed for the side of the stage. "Oh, wait a minute." He turned back around and stepped toward his father. "I forgot to tell you something." He looked at Annie. "Excuse me just a minute, please."

Annie nodded. "Okay, I'll be over there at that catfish booth." She started walking away through the crowd already breaking up to go to the booths for beer and catfish while the next band was setting up.

"One of the guys I went to school with wants to talk to you. Derek Doucet." Paul lowered his voice. "Something about what Father Jules told him to do. I don't know. He just asked me if I'd run it by you first. He's pretty nervous about something." He raised his hands. "But I swear that's all I know. So if he did something he's worried about, I don't know anything about it. Okay?"

"See over there, son? Those boys looking at the tractor? The one with the blue tee shirt? That him?"

"Yep. That's the one. How'd you know?"

"Lucky guess, that's all. You go ahead and help Antoinette. I'll take it from here."

"You know what it's about, huh, Dad?"

"Maybe. I'll talk to him later. Tell Antoinette she sounded terrific, okay?"

Paul flashed another proud smile. "That's exactly what I'm going to do, Pop. See ya!" He headed back toward the far end of the stage, just as Antoinette was rounding the corner, carrying a worn and scuffed violin case under her arm and looking for him.

Lanclos started toward one of the catfish booths to join Annie who was pointing to an overhead menu sign and ordering for them. By the time he reached her side, one of the women working the booth was handing her two grilled catfish sandwiches wrapped in wax paper.

"Let's take those over there and sit with my friends, Moise and Dixie, okay?" asked Lanclos, steering her toward the picnic table where Moise and Dixie were still sitting.

"I've seen him around town. Who is he?" Annie asked as she handed him his sandwich.

"An old friend, Moise Angelle. Just don't ever let him catch you without a fishing or a hunting license."

"Oh, I got you. Fish & Wildlife, huh?"

"That's it. One of the best. Comes from a long line of people you could blindfold and drop off in the middle of the Atchafalaya and they'd be right at home."

"Sounds like a good friend to have."

"Oh, he is. And you'll like Dixie too. She's another one."

"What do you mean another one?"

"She's another one like you. Adventurous."

"Oh, is that what I am?" she asked as they drew near to the picnic table. "I'm not so sure. Not after what I've just been through."

"Don't worry. That's all over now," he said as Moise and Dixie waved them over. "It's history."

"I wish I knew that was true," she said as they slid their sandwiches onto the plank table and Lanclos began the introductions.

Later, as Lanclos and Annie were walking toward the parking area, the young man, Derek, who had been looking at him from time to time during the afternoon, broke away from his friends and loped toward them. He stopped beside a paneled truck and waited, half-heartedly raising a hand to motion to Lanclos.

Lanclos handed the keys to Annie. "Do you mind going on by yourself for a few minutes? Just go ahead and get in the truck and wait for me. I'll be along as soon as I can."

"Sure. Take your time," she said, swinging the keys. "I'll be fine." She walked toward the pickup and Lanclos turned to approach Derek, who had shoved his hands into his jeans pockets, and was standing half turned away, head tilted back, staring at the branches of an overhanging crepe myrtle.

"You need to talk to me?" asked Lanclos as he drew near.

Derek lowered his head and faced Lanclos. His forehead was damp, and he pushed back his visor cap, wiping his face with the back of his hand. His fingers were trembling and as Lanclos stepped up to him, he stepped back a foot. He smelled of tobacco, and there were dark sweat stains on his tee shirt.

"Yes, sir," Derek said, and then his lips began trembling as well.

"Something wrong?" Lanclos asked gently.

"Yes, sir. I got something to tell you." He rubbed the tip of his nose and then the back of his neck, as he scuffled his feet in the dirt.

"I'm listening. What you got?" Lanclos squinted in the bright light.

"Father Jules told me to tell you this. It ain't easy."

"Go ahead. Spit it out, son."

Derek ran a tongue over his teeth and drew a deep breath. "See. Me and my partners were hunting the other night. Rabbits. And..." He stopped, looking around, then found Lanclos' eyes again.

"And?"

He dropped his gaze and shoved hands back into his pockets once more. "We got kind of lost in the woods, I guess." His voice dropped off.

"Speak up, son."

He raised his head. "See. We couldn't see that good. It was kind of raining off and on, and well, while we were shooting, uh, I shot at what I thought was a wild hog running around out there, and well, it wasn't no hog." He took a hand out of his pocket and rubbed his cheek so hard a red splotch appeared.

"When was this?"

"Last week. The night Gerald Theriot died." Derek looked back at the ground, lost his balance for a moment, then righted himself.

"You're trying to tell me you were shooting in the woods the night Gerald Theriot died?"

Derek looked up. "Yes, sir."

"What woods?"

"I guess we were kind of trespassing over there by the bayou. It must have been old man Delcambre's woods where we were at," Derek mumbled. He spotted a candy bar wrapper in the grass at the edge of the parking area and kicked at it.

"So you're telling me you all were shooting out there in the woods, and you shot at what you thought was a wild pig?" Lanclos watched him closely.

Derek took his hands out of his pockets and gestured wildly with his long arms.

"I guess," he finished lamely. "Something like that."

"Are you trying to tell me you think you shot at Gerald Theriot? A hunting accident?"

There was a long pause as Derek twisted his face in pain. "Maybe. I don't know really what happened. It was black out. We heard somebody yelling, and we took off running. But Father Jules says I have to tell you about it, or else I'll make myself go crazy or something." A new band started playing and a traditional waltz tune filled the air.

"Son," Lanclos placed a hand on the boy's shoulder. "I'm off duty here today. Tell you what." He looked around them, but no one was nearby. "I can see you're upset about this because maybe you think you killed Gerald. Is that it?"

"I don't know what I think anymore," Derek said, eyes filling with tears. He pressed his knuckles into his eyes and rubbed them hard, as though to stop the tears. He swallowed and dropped his hands. His eyes had rapidly grown swollen and red, and his chest began to heave as his breathing accelerated.

"Look, Derek. I don't believe you killed Gerald, all right? I can't say anything more than that right now. But I'm fairly certain a gunshot didn't kill him. This isn't a good place to talk about this. Now, here's what I want you to do."

Derek looked up at him with hound dog eyes. "What you want me to do, Detective?"

"I want you to come into my office tomorrow where we can sit down and go over this. I'll meet you first thing in the morning. Will you do that?"

The boy nodded, eyes closed tightly, his lips moving, but no sound coming out.

"You did the right thing coming to me. And if it's a hunting accident, they're going to go easy on you. It happens. But it wasn't a shotgun that killed Gerald. You got that?" Lanclos watched the boy's breathing, fearful he'd hyperventilate. "What you need to do now is get home and take it easy until tomorrow. We'll get it all sorted out then." He spoke soothingly. "Your family still live over there on Meche Street?"

Derek nodded, sniffling.

"Why don't you leave your friends here and go home? You can walk it. It's only six blocks. The walk will do you good."

"They're waiting for me." Derek jerked his head toward the festival.

"Do they know what you told me?"

"I guess. They probably figured it out by now. They know I been worrying."

"They were shooting too?"

Derek nodded.

"So you couldn't swear that it was just you shot at something in the woods that maybe was Gerald Theriot."

"No. I couldn't swear to anything right now. I don't know for sure what happened."

Lanclos saw that Derek's breathing was slowing. "All right then. Do you feel better for having told me what you did?"

"Yes, sir."

"Will you come see me first thing in the morning so we can get this report straight?"

"Yes, sir."

"If you don't come down to my office, I'm going to have to find you. You know that, right?"

Derek gave a quick nod. "I know I got to come in. I'll be there."

"All right then. You did the right thing. It's going to be all right. You believe me?" Lanclos tried to continue the conversation to make sure the boy had regained his emotional balance.

"If you can, bring your father along. I've known your father for twenty years and counting."

"He's working."

"Bring your mother then."

"She's not doing good. She caught a stroke last month."

"All right then, Derek. Bring yourself. We'll get it worked out."

"See you tomorrow." Derek turned and began walking back toward the festival as applause rose at the end of the waltz and a fast shuffle began.

Lanclos watched him until he cleared the trees that bordered the parking area, then he turned and headed for the pickup.

"What did that poor fellow want?" asked Annie, as he slid into the truck. "He looked so upset."

"Just some unfinished business," he said as he leaned over and kissed her lightly on the cheek.

"Is he okay? I thought he was going to fall over there for a minute."

"He had a lot on his mind, but we're going to work it out at the office tomorrow," he said as he started the engine. "How about we go back to the farm and relax. You like that idea, *chère?*"

"Like it? That's the best idea you've had all day!" she said, sliding close enough for him to smell her perfume.

Music from the loudspeakers followed them as Lanclos slowly drove the ten blocks to the turnoff for St. Regis Highway. As he turned onto the blacktop, the faint sounds of another waltz could still be heard as he took her hand and headed off toward the farm.

Made in the USA
Charleston, SC
16 October 2013